Praise for #1 *New York Times* bestselling author

NORA ROBERTS

"You can't bottle wish fulfillment, but Nora Roberts
certainly knows how to put it on the page."
—*New York Times*

"Roberts' style has a fresh, contemporary snap."
—*Kirkus Reviews*

"America's favorite writer."
—*The New Yorker*

"When Roberts puts her expert fingers on the pulse of
romance, legions of fans feel the heartbeat."
—*Publishers Weekly*

"Nora Roberts is among the best."
—*The Washington Post*

"Roberts' bestselling novels are some of the best in the
romance genre."
—*USA TODAY*

NORA ROBERTS

ONLY YOU

Published by Silhouette Books

America's Publisher of Contemporary Romance

 SILHOUETTE BOOKS

Recycling programs for this product may not exist in your area.

Only You

ISBN-13: 978-1-335-09046-1

Copyright © 2018 by Harlequin Books S.A.

The publisher acknowledges the copyright holder of the individual works as follows:

Boundary Lines
Copyright © 1985 by Nora Roberts

The Right Path
Copyright © 1985 by Nora Roberts

Visit Silhouette Books at www.Harlequin.com

Printed in U.S.A.

CONTENTS

BOUNDARY LINES

For Ruth Langan, for all the years.

Chapter 1

The wind whipped against her cheeks. It flowed through her hair, smelling faintly of spring and growing things. Jillian lifted her face to it, as much in challenge as in appreciation. Beneath her, the sleek mare strained for more speed. They'd ride, two free spirits, as long as the sun stayed high.

Short, tough grass was crushed under hooves, along with stray wildflowers. Jillian gave no thought to the buttercups as she crossed to the path. Here the soil was hard, chestnut in color and bordered by the silver-gray sage.

There were no trees along this rough, open plain, but Jillian wasn't looking for shade. She galloped by a field of wheat bleaching in the sun with hardly a stray breeze to rustle it. Farther on there was hay, acres of it, nearly ready for the first harvesting. She heard and recognized the call of a meadowlark. But she wasn't a farmer. If

someone had termed her one, Jillian would have laughed
or bristled, depending on her mood.

The crops were grown because they were needed, in
the same way the vegetable patch was sown and tended.
Growing your own feed made you self-reliant. There was
nothing more important than that in Jillian's estimation.
In a good year there were enough crops left over to bring
in a few extra dollars. The few extra dollars would buy
more cattle. It was always the cattle.

She was a rancher—like her grandfather had been,
and his father before him.

The land stretched as far as she could see. Her land.
It was rolling and rich. Acre after acre of grain sprouted
up, and beyond it were the plains and pastures where
the cattle and horses grazed. But she wasn't riding fence
today, counting head or poring over the books in her
grandfather's leather-and-oak office. Today she wanted
freedom, and was taking it.

Jillian hadn't been raised on the rugged, spacious
plains of Montana. She hadn't been born in the saddle.
She'd grown up in Chicago because her father had chosen medicine over ranching, and east over west. Jillian
hadn't blamed him as her grandfather had—it was a
matter of choice. Everyone was entitled to the life they
chose. That was why she'd come here, back to her heri-
tage, five years before when she'd turned twenty.

At the top of the hill Jillian stopped the mare. From
here she could see over the planted fields to the pastures,
fenced in with wire that could hardly be seen from that
distance. It gave the illusion of open range where the cattle could roam at will. Once, it would've been like that,
she mused as she tossed her hair back over her shoulder.
If she narrowed her eyes, she could almost see it—open,

free—the way it had been when her ancestors had first come to settle. The gold rush had brought them, but the land had kept them. It kept her.

Gold, she thought with a shake of her head. Who needed gold when there was priceless wealth in space alone? She preferred the spread of land with its isolated mountains and valleys. If her people had gone farther west, into the higher mountains, her great-great-grandparents might have toiled in the streams and the mines. They might have staked their claim there, plucking out nuggets and digging out gold dust, but they would never have found anything richer than this. Jillian had understood the land's worth and its allure the first moment she'd seen it.

She'd been ten. At her grandfather's invitation—command, Jillian corrected with a smirk—both she and her brother, Marc, had made the trip west, to Utopia. Marc had been there before, of course. He'd been sixteen and quietly capable in the way of their father. And no more interested in ranching than his father had been.

Her first glimpse of the ranch hadn't surprised her, though it wasn't what many children might've expected after years of exposure to Western cinema. It was vast, and somehow tidy. Paddocks, stables, barns and the sturdy charm of the ranch house itself. Even at ten, even after one look, Jillian had known she hadn't been meant for the streets and sidewalks of Chicago, but for this open sky and endless land. At ten, she'd had her first experience with love at first sight.

But it wasn't love at first sight with her grandfather. He'd been a tough, weathered, opinionated old man. The ranch and his herd had been his life. He hadn't the least idea what to do with a spindly girl who happened to be his son's daughter. They'd circled each other warily for days, until he'd made the mistake of letting out some caustic remark about her father and his choice of pills and needles. Quick tempered, Jillian had flown to her father's defense. They'd ended up shouting at each other, Jillian red-faced and dry-eyed even after being threatened with a razor strap.

They'd parted at the end of that visit with a combination of mutual respect and dislike. Then he'd sent her a custom-made, buff-colored Stetson for her birthday. And it began...

Perhaps they'd grown to love one another so deeply because they'd taken their time about it. Those sporadic weeks during her adolescence he'd taught her everything, hardly seeming to teach at all: how to gauge the weather by the smell of the air, the look of the sky; how to deliver a breech calf; how to ride fence and herd a steer. She'd called him Clay because they'd been friends. And when she'd tried her first and only plug of tobacco, he'd held her head when she'd been sick. He hadn't lectured.

When his eyes had grown weak, Jillian had taken over the books. They'd never discussed it—just as they'd never discussed that her move there in the summer of her twentieth year would be permanent. When his illness had begun to take over, she'd gradually assumed the responsibilities of the ranch, though no words had passed between them to make it official.

When he died, the ranch was hers. Jillian hadn't needed to hear the will read to know it. Clay had known she would stay. She'd left the east behind—and if there were memories from there that still twisted inside her, she buried them. More easily than she'd buried her grandfather.

It was herself she grieved for, and knowing it made her impatient. Clay had lived long and hard, doing as he chose the way he chose. His illness had wasted him, and would have brought him pain and humiliation had it continued. He would have hated that, would have railed at her if he could have seen how she'd wept over him.

God Almighty, girl! What're you wasting time here for? Don't you know there's a ranch to run? Get some hands out to check the fence in the west forty before we've got cattle roaming all over Montana.

Yes, she thought with a half smile. He'd have said something like that—cursed her a bit, then would've turned away with a grunt. Of course, she'd have cursed right back at him.

"You mangy old bear," she muttered. "I'm going to turn Utopia into the best ranch in Montana just to spite you." Laughing, she threw her face up to the sky. "See if I don't!"

Sensing her change of mood, the mare began to dance impatiently, tossing her head. "All right, Delilah." Jillian leaned over to pat her creamy neck. "We've got all afternoon." In a deft move she turned the mare around and started off at an easy lope.

There weren't many free hours like this, so they were prized. As it was, Jillian knew she'd stolen them. That made it all the sweeter. If she had to work eighteen hours tomorrow to make up for it, she'd do it without complaint. Even the bookwork, she thought with a sigh. Though there was that sick heifer that needed watching, and the damn Jeep that'd broken down for the third time this month. And the fence along the boundary line. The Murdock boundary line, she thought with a grimace.

The feud between the Barons and the Murdocks

stretched back to the early 1900s when Noah Baron, her great-grandfather, came to southeast Montana. He'd meant to go on, to the mountains and the gold, but had stayed to homestead. The Murdocks had already been there, with their vast, rich ranch. The Barons had been peasants to them, intruders doomed to fail—or to be driven out. Jillian gritted her teeth as she remembered the stories her grandfather had told her: cut fences, stolen cattle, ruined crops.

But the Barons had stayed, survived, and succeeded. No, they didn't have the amount of land the Murdocks did, or the money, but they knew how to make the best use of what they did have. If her grandfather had struck oil as the Murdocks had, Jillian thought with a smirk, they could have afforded to specialize in purebred beef, as well. That had been a matter of chance, not skill.

She told herself she didn't care about the purebred part of it. Let the Murdock clan wave their blue ribbons and shout about improving the line. She'd raise her Herefords and shorthorns and get the best price for them at the Exchange. Baron beef was prime, and everyone knew it.

When was the last time one of the high-and-mighty Murdocks rode the miles of fence, sweating under the sun while checking for a break? When was the last time one of them had eaten dust on a drive? Jillian knew for a fact that Paul J. Murdock, her grandfather's contemporary, hadn't bothered to ride fence or flank cattle in more than a year.

She let out a short, derisive laugh. All they knew about was the figures in the account books and politicking. By the time she was finished, Utopia would make the Double M look like a dude ranch.

The idea put her in a better mood, so that the line between her brows vanished. She wouldn't think of the Murdocks today, or of the back-breaking work that promised to begin before the sun came up tomorrow. She would think only of the sweetness of these stolen hours, of the rich smell of spring…and the endless hard blue of the sky.

Jillian knew this path well. It ran along the western-most tip of her land. Too tough for the plow, too stubborn for grazing, it was left alone. It was here she always came when she wanted both a sense of solitude and excitement. No one else came here, from her own ranch or from the Murdock spread that ran parallel to it. Even the fence that had once formed the boundary had fallen years before, and had been forgotten. No one cared about this little slice of useless land but her, which made her care all the more.

Now there were a few trees, the cottonwood and aspen just beginning to green. Over the sound of the mare's hooves she heard a warbler begin to sing. There might be coyotes, too, and certainly rattlesnakes. Jillian wasn't so enchanted she didn't remember that. There was a rifle, oiled and loaded, strapped to the back of her saddle.

The mare scented the water from the pond, and Jillian let her have her head. The thought of stripping off her sweaty clothes and diving in appealed immensely. Five minutes in that clear, icy water would be exhilarating, and Delilah could rest and drink before they began the long trip back. Spotting the glistening water, Jillian let the reins drop, relaxing. Her grandfather would have cursed her for her lack of attention, but she was already thinking about the luxury of sliding naked into the cold water, then drying in the sun.

But the mare scented something else. Abruptly she reared, plunging so that Jillian's first thought was rattler. While she struggled to control Delilah with one hand, she reached behind for the rifle. Before she could draw a breath, she was hurtling through space. Jillian only had time for one muttered oath before she landed bottom first in the pond. But she'd seen that the rattlesnake had legs.

Sputtering and furious, she struggled to her feet, wiping her wet hair out of her eyes so that she could glare at the man astride a buckskin stallion. Delilah danced nervously while he held the glistening stallion still.

He didn't need to have his feet on the ground for her to see that he was tall. His hair was dark, waving thick and long beneath a black Stetson that shadowed a rawboned, weathered face. His nose was straight and aristocratic, his mouth well shaped and solemn. Jillian didn't take the time to admire the way he sat the stallion—with a casual sort of control that exuded confidence and power. What she did see was that his eyes were nearly as black as his hair. And laughing.

Narrowing her own, she spat at him, "What the hell are you doing on my land?"

He looked at her in silence, the only movement a very slow lifting of his left brow. Unlike Jillian, he was taking the time to admire. Her fiery hair was darkened almost to copper with the water and clung wetly to accent the elegance of bone and skin—fine boned, honey-toned skin. He could see the flash of green that was her eyes, dark as jade and dangerous as a cat's. Her mouth, clamped together in fury, had a luxuriously full, promising lower lip that contrasted with the firm stubborn chin.

Casually he let his gaze slide down. She was a long

one, he thought, with hardly more curves than a boy. But just now, with the shirt wet and snug as a second skin… Slowly his gaze climbed back to hers. She didn't blush at the survey, though she recognized it. There wasn't apprehension or fear in her eyes. Instead, she shot him a hard look that might have withered another man.

"I said," Jillian began in a low, clipped voice, "what the hell are you doing on my land?"

Instead of answering he swung out of the saddle—the move smooth and economic enough to tell her he'd been in and out of one most of his life. He walked toward her with a loose, easy stride that still carried the air of command. Then he smiled. In one quick flash his face changed from dangerously sexy to dangerously charming. It was a smile that said, you can trust me…for the moment. He held out a hand.

"Ma'am."

Jillian drew in one deep breath and let it out again. Ignoring the offered hand, she climbed out of the water by herself. Dripping, cold, but far from cooled off, Jillian stuck her hands on her hips. "You haven't answered my question."

Nerve, he thought, still studying her. She's got plenty of that. Temper and—he noticed the way her chin was thrown up in challenge—arrogance. He liked the combination. Hooking his thumbs in his pockets, he shifted his weight, thinking it was a shame she'd dry off quickly in the full sun.

"This isn't your land," he said smoothly, with only a hint of a Western drawl. "Miss…"

"Baron," Jillian snapped. "And who the hell are you to tell me this isn't my land?"

He tipped his hat with more insolence than respect.

"Aaron Murdock." His lips twitched at her hiss of breath. "Boundary runs straight up through here." He looked down at the toes of his boots inches away from the toes of hers as if he could see the line drawn there. "Cuts about clean down the middle of the pond." He brought his gaze back to hers—mouth solemn, eyes laughing. "I think you landed on my side."

Aaron Murdock, son and heir. Wasn't he supposed to be out in Billings playing in their damn oil fields? Frowning, Jillian decided he didn't look like the smooth college boy her grandfather had described to her. That was something she'd think about later. Right now, it was imperative she make her stand, and make it stick.

"*If* I landed on your side," she said scathingly, "it was because you were lurking around with that." She jerked her thumb at his horse. Gorgeous animal, she thought with an admiration she had to fight to conceal.

"Your hands were slack on the reins," he pointed out mildly.

The truth of it only added fuel to the fire. "His scent spooked Delilah."

"Delilah." A flicker of amusement ran over his face as he pushed back his hat and studied the smooth clean lines of Jillian's mare. "Must've been fate," he murmured. "Samson." At the sound of his name the stallion walked over to nuzzle Aaron's shoulder.

Jillian choked back a chuckle, but not in time to conceal the play of a small dimple at the side of her mouth. "Just remember what Samson's fate was," she retorted. "And keep him away from my mare."

"A mighty pretty filly," Aaron said easily. While he stroked his horse's head his eyes remained on Jillian.

"A bit high strung," he continued, "but well built. She'd breed well."

Jillian's eyes narrowed again. Aaron found he liked the way they glinted through the thick, luxurious lashes. "I'll worry about her breeding, Murdock." She planted her feet in the ground that soaked up the water still dripping from her. "What're you doing up here?" she demanded. "You won't find any oil."

Aaron tilted his head. "I wasn't looking for any. I wasn't looking for a woman either." Casually he reached over and lifted a strand of her heavy hair. "But I found one."

Jillian felt that quick, breathless pressure in her chest and recognized it. Oh, no, she'd let that happen to her once before. She let her gaze drop down to where his long brown fingers toyed with the ends of her hair, then lifted it to his face again. "You wouldn't want to lose that hand," she said softly.

For a moment, his fingers tightened, as if he considered picking up the challenge she'd thrown down. Then, as casually as he'd captured her hair, he released it. "Testy, aren't you?" Aaron said mildly. "But then, you Barons've always been quick to draw."

"To defend," Jillian corrected, standing her ground.

They measured each other a moment, both surprised to find the opposition so attractive. Tread carefully. The command went through each of their minds, though it was an order both habitually had trouble carrying out.

"I'm sorry about the old man," Aaron said at length. "He'd have been your—grandfather?"

Jillian's chin stayed up, but Aaron saw the shadow that briefly clouded her eyes. "Yes."

She'd loved him, Aaron thought with some surprise.

From his few run-ins with Clay Baron, he'd found a singularly unlovable man. He let his memory play back with the snatches of information he'd gleaned since his return to the Double M. "You'd be the little girl who spent some summers here years back," he commented, trying to remember if he'd ever caught sight of her before. "From back east." His hand came back to stroke his chin, a bit rough from the lack of razor that morning. "Jill, isn't it?"

"Jillian," she corrected coldly.

"Jillian." The swift smile transformed his face again. "It suits you better."

"Miss Baron suits me best," she told him, damning his smile.

Aaron didn't bother to acknowledge her deliberate unfriendliness, instead giving in to the urge to let his gaze slip briefly to her mouth again. No, he didn't believe he'd seen her before. That wasn't a mouth a man forgot. "If Gil Haley's running things at Utopia, you should do well enough."

She bristled. He could almost see her spine snap straight. "I run things at Utopia," she said evenly.

His mouth tilted at one corner. "You?"

"That's right, Murdock, me. I haven't been pushing papers in Billings for the last five years." Something flashed in his eyes, but she ignored it and plunged ahead. "Utopia's mine, every inch of ground, every blade of grass. The difference is I work it instead of strutting around the State Fair waving my blue ribbons."

Intrigued, he took her hands, ignoring her protest as he turned them over to study the palms. They were slender, but hard and capable. Running his thumb over a line of callus, Aaron felt a ripple of admiration—and desire.

He'd grown very weary of pampered helpless hands in Billings. "Well, well," he murmured, keeping her hands in his as he looked back into her eyes.

She was furious—that his hands were so strong, that they held hers so effortlessly. That her heartbeat was roaring in her ears. The warbler had begun to sing again and she could hear the gentle swish of the horses' tails as they stood.

He smelled pleasantly of leather and sweat. Too pleasantly. There was a rim of amber around the outside of his irises that only accented the depth of brown. A scar, very thin and white, rode along the edge of his jaw. You wouldn't notice it unless you looked very closely. Just as you might not notice how strong and lean his hands were unless yours were caught in them.

Jillian snapped back quickly. It didn't pay to notice things like that. It didn't pay to listen to that roaring in your head. She'd done that once before and where had it gotten her? Dewy-eyed, submissive and soft-headed. She was a lot smarter than she'd been five years before. The most important thing was to remember who he was—a Murdock. And who she was—a Baron.

"I warned you about your hands before," she said quietly.

"So you did," Aaron agreed, watching her face. "Why?"

"I don't like to be touched."

"No?" His brow lifted again, but he didn't yet release her hands. "Most living things do—if they're touched properly." His eyes locked on hers abruptly, very direct, very intuitive. "Someone touch you wrong once, Jillian?"

Her gaze didn't falter. "You're trespassing, Murdock."

Again, that faint inclination of the head. "Maybe. We could always string the fence again."

She knew he hadn't misunderstood her. This time, when she tugged on her hands, he released them. "Just stay on your side," she suggested.

He adjusted his hat so that the shadow fell over his face again. "And if I don't?"

Her chin came up. "Then I'll have to deal with you." Turning her back, she walked to Delilah and gathered the reins. It took an effort not to pass her hand over the buckskin stallion, but she resisted. Without looking at Aaron, Jillian swung easily into the saddle, then fit her own damp, flat-brimmed hat back on her head. Now she had the satisfaction of being able to look down at him.

In a better humor, Jillian leaned on the saddle horn. Leather creaked easily beneath her as Delilah shifted her weight. Her shirt was drying warm on her back. "You have a nice vacation, Murdock," she told him with a faint smile. "Don't wear yourself out while you're here."

He reached up to stroke Delilah's neck. "Now, I'm going to try real hard to take your advice on that, Jillian."

She leaned down a bit closer. "Miss Baron."

Aaron surprised her by tugging the brim of her hat down to her nose. "I like Jillian." He grabbed the string tie of the hat before she could straighten, then gave her a long, odd look. "I swear," he murmured, "you smell like something a man could just close his eyes and wallow in."

She was amused. Jillian told herself she was amused while she pretended not to feel the quick trip of her pulse. She removed his hand from the string of her hat, straightened and smiled. "You disappoint me. I'd've thought a man who'd spent so much time in college and the big city would have a snappier line and a smoother delivery."

He slipped his hands into his back pockets as he looked up at her. It was fascinating to watch the way the sun shot into her eyes without drawing out the smallest fleck of gold or gray in that cool, deep green. The eyes were too stubborn to allow for any interference; they suited the woman. "I'll practice," Aaron told her with the hint of a smile. "I'll do better next time."

She gave a snort of laughter and started to turn her horse. "There won't be a next time."

His hand was firm on the bridle before she could trot off. The look he gave her was calm, and only slightly amused. "You look smarter than that, Jillian. We'll have a number of next times before we're through."

She didn't know how she'd lost the advantage so quickly, only that she had. Her chin angled. "You seem determined to lose that hand, Murdock."

He gave her an easy smile, patted Delilah's neck, then turned toward his own horse. "I'll see you soon, Jillian."

She waited, seething, until he'd swung into the saddle. Delilah sidestepped skittishly until the horses were nearly nose to nose. "Stay on your own side," Jillian ordered, then pressed in her heels. The straining mare lunged forward.

Samson tossed his head and pranced as they both watched Jillian race off on Delilah. "Not this time," Aaron murmured to himself, soothing his horse. "But soon." He gave a quick laugh, then pointed his horse in the opposite direction. "Damn soon."

Jillian could get rid of a lot of anger and frustration with the speed and the wind. She rode as the mare wanted—fast. Perhaps Delilah needed to outrace her blood, as well, Jillian thought wryly. Both male animals had been compelling. If the stallion had belonged to anyone but a Murdock, she would've found a way to have Delilah bred with him—no matter what the stud fee. If she had any hope of increasing and improving Utopia's line of horses, the bulk of the burden rested with her own mare. And there wasn't a stallion on her ranch that could compare with Murdock's Samson.

It was a pity Aaron Murdock hadn't been the smooth, fastidious, boring businessman she'd envisioned him. That type would never have made her blood heat. A woman in her position couldn't afford to acknowledge that kind of attraction, especially with a rival. It would put her at an immediate disadvantage when she needed every edge she could get.

So much depended on the next six months if she was going to have the chance to expand. Oh, the ranch could go on, making its cozy little profit, but she wanted more. The fire of her grandfather's ambition hadn't dimmed so much with age as it had been transferred to her. With her youth and energy, and with that fickle lady called luck, she could turn Utopia into the empire her ancestors had dreamed about.

She had the land and the knowledge. She had the skill and the determination. Already, Jillian had poured the cash portion of her inheritance back into the ranch. She'd put a down payment on the small plane her grandfather had been too stubborn to buy. With a plane, the ranch could be patrolled in hours, stray cattle spotted, broken fences reported. Though she still believed in the necessity of a skilled puncher and cow pony, Jillian understood the beauty of mixing new techniques with the old.

Pickups and Jeeps roamed the range as well as horses.

CBs could be used to communicate over long distances, while the lariat was still carried by every hand—in the saddle or behind the wheel. The cattle would be driven to feed lots when necessary and the calves herded into the corral for branding, though the iron would be heated by a butane torch rather than an open fire. Times had changed, but the spirit and the code remained.

Above all, the rancher, like any other country person, depended on two things: the sky and the earth. Because the first was always fickle and the second often unyielding, the rancher had no choice but to rely, ultimately, on himself. That was Jillian's philosophy.

With that in mind, she changed directions without changing her pace. She'd ride along the Murdock boundary and check the fences after all.

She trotted along an open pasture while broadrumped, white-faced Herefords barely glanced up from their grazing. The spring grass was growing thick and full. Hearing the rumble of an engine, she stopped. In almost the same manner as her mount, Jillian scented the air. Gasoline. It was a shame to spoil the scent of grass and cattle with it. Philosophically she turned Delilah in the direction of the sound and rode.

It was easy to spot the battered pickup in the rolling terrain. Jillian lifted her hand in half salute and rode toward it. Her mood had lifted again, though her jeans were still damp and her boots soggy. She considered Gil Haley one of the few dyed-in-the-wool cowboys left on her ranch or any other. A hundred years before, he'd have been happy riding the range with his saddle, bedroll and plug of tobacco. If he had the chance, she mused, he'd be just as happy that way today.

"Gil." Jillian stopped Delilah by the driver's window and grinned at him.

"You disappeared this morning." His greeting was brusque in a voice that sounded perpetually peppery. He didn't expect an explanation, nor would she have given one.

Jillian nodded to the two men with him, another breed of cowhand, distinguished by their heavy work shoes. Gil might give in to the pickup because he could patrol fifty thousand acres quicker and more thoroughly than on horseback, but he'd never give up his boots. "Any problem?"

"Dumb cow tangled in the wire a ways back." He shifted his tobacco plug while looking up at her with his perpetual squint. "Got her out before she did any damage. Looks like we've got to clear out some of that damn tumbleweed again. Knocked down some line."

Jillian accepted this with a nod. "Anyone check the fence along the west section today?"

There was no change in the squint as he eyed her. "Nope."

"I'll see to it now, then." Jillian hesitated. If there was anyone who knew the gossip, it would be Gil. "I happened to run into Aaron Murdock about an hour ago," she put in casually. "I thought he was in Billings."

"Nope."

Jillian gave him a mild look. "I realize that, Gil. What's he doing around here?"

"Got himself a ranch."

Gamely Jillian hung on to her temper. "I realize that, too. He's also got himself an oil field—or his father does."

"Kid sister married herself an oil man," Gil told her.

"The old man did some shifting around and got the boy back where he wants him."

"You mean…" Jillian narrowed her eyes. "Aaron Murdock's staying on the Double M?"

"Managing it," Gil stated, then spit expertly. "Guess things've simmered down after the blowup a few years back. Murdock's getting on, you know, close on to seventy or more. Maybe he wants to sit back and relax now."

"Managing it," Jillian muttered. So she was going to be plagued with a Murdock after all. At least she and the old man had managed to stay out of each other's way. Aaron had already invaded what she considered her private haven—even if he did own half of it. "How long's he been back?"

Gil took his time answering, tugging absently at the grizzled gray mustache that hung over his lip—a habit Jillian usually found amusing. "Couple weeks."

And she'd already plowed into him. Well, she'd had five years of peace, Jillian reminded herself. In country with this much space, she should be able to avoid one man without too much trouble. There were other questions she wanted to ask, but they'd wait until she and Gil were alone.

"I'll check the fence," she said briefly, then turned the mare and rode west.

Gil watched her with a twinkle. He might squint, but his eyesight was sharp enough to have noticed her damp clothes. And the fire in her eyes. Ran into Aaron Murdock, did she? With a wheeze and a chuckle, he started the pickup. It gave a man something to speculate on.

"Keep your eyes front, son," he grumbled to the young hand who was craning his neck to get a last look of Jillian as she galloped over the pasture.

Chapter 2

The day began before sunrise. There was stock to be fed, eggs to be gathered, cows to be milked. Even with machines, capable hands were needed. Jillian had grown so accustomed to helping with the early morning chores, it never occurred to her to stop now that she was the owner. Ranch life was a routine that varied only in the number of animals to be tended and the weather in which you tended them.

It was pleasantly cool when Jillian made the trip from the ranch house to the stables, but she'd crossed the same ground when the air had been so hot and thick it seemed to stick to her skin, or when the snow had been past her boot tops. There was only a faint lessening in the dark, a hint of color in the eastern sky, but the ranch yard already held signs of life. She caught the scent of grilled meat and coffee as the ranch cook started breakfast.

Men and women went about their chores quietly, with an occasional oath, or a quick laugh. Because all of them had just been through a Montana winter, this sweet spring morning was prized. Spring gave way to summer heat, and summer drought too quickly.

Jillian crossed the concrete passageway and opened Delilah's stall. As always, she would tend her first before going on to the other horses, then the dairy cows. A few of the men were there before her, measuring out grain, filling troughs. There was the click of boot heels on concrete, the jingle of spurs.

Some of them owned their own horses, but the bulk of them used Utopia's line. All of them owned their own saddles. Her grandfather's hard-and-fast rule.

The stables smelled comfortably of horses and hay and sweet grain. By the time the stock had been fed and led out to the corrals, it was nearly light. Automatically, Jillian headed for the vast white barn where cows waited to be milked.

"Jillian."

She stopped, waiting for Joe Carlson, her herdsman, to cross the ranch yard. He didn't walk like a cowboy, or dress like one, simply because he wasn't one. He had a smooth, even gait that suited his rather cocky good looks. The early sun teased out the gold in his curling hair. He rode a Jeep rather than a horse and preferred a dry wine to beer, but he knew cattle. Jillian needed him if she was to make a real success out of what was now just dabbling in the purebred industry. She'd hired him six months before over her grandfather's grumbles, and didn't regret it.

"Morning, Joe."

"Jillian." He shook his head when he reached her,

then pushed back the powder-gray hat he kept meticulously clean. "When are you going to stop working a fifteen-hour day?"

She laughed and started toward the dairy barn again, matching her longer, looser stride with his. "In August, when I have to start working an eighteen-hour day."

"Jillian." He put a hand on her shoulder, stopping her at the entrance of the barn. His hand was neat and well shaped, tanned but not callused. For some reason it reminded her of a stronger hand, a harder one. She frowned at the horizon. "You know it's not necessary for you to tie yourself down to every aspect of this ranch. You've got enough hands working for you. If you'd hire a manager..."

It was an old routine and Jillian answered it in the usual way. "I am the manager," she said simply. "I don't consider the ranch a toy or a tax break, Joe. Before I hire someone to take over for me, I'll sell out."

"You work too damn hard."

"You worry too much," she countered, but smiled. "I appreciate it. How's the bull?"

Joe's teeth flashed, straight, even, and white. "Mean as ever, but he's bred with every cow we've let within ten feet of him. He's a beauty."

"I hope so," Jillian murmured, remembering just what the purebred Hereford bull had cost her. Still, if he was everything Joe had claimed, he was her start in improving the quality of Utopia's beef.

"Just wait till the calves start dropping," Joe advised, giving her shoulder a quick squeeze. "You want to come take a look at him?"

"Mmmm, maybe later." She took a step inside the barn, then shot a look over her shoulder. "I'd like to see that bull take the blue ribbon over the Murdock entry in July." She grinned, quick and insolent. "Damned if I wouldn't."

By the time the stock had been fed and Jillian had bolted down her own breakfast, it was full light. The long hours and demands should have kept her mind occupied. They always had. Between her concerns over feed and wages and fence, there shouldn't have been room for thoughts of Aaron Murdock. But there was. Jillian decided that once she had the answers to her questions she'd be able to put him out of her mind. So she'd better see about getting them. She hailed Gil before he could climb into his pickup.

"I'm going with you today," she told him as she hopped into the passenger's seat.

He shrugged and spit tobacco out the window. "Suit yourself."

Jillian grinned at the greeting and pushed her hat back on her head. A few heavy red curls dipped over her brow. "Why is it you've never gotten married, Gil? You're such a charmer."

Beneath his grizzled mustache his lips quivered. "Always was a smart aleck." He started the engine and aimed his squint at her. "What about you? You might be skinny, but you ain't ugly."

She propped a booted foot on his dash. "I'd rather run my own life," she said easily. "Men want to tell you what to do and how to do it."

"Woman ain't got no business out here on her own," Gil said stubbornly as he drove out of the ranch yard.

"And men do?" Jillian countered, lazily examining the toe of her boot.

"Men's different."

"Better?"

He shifted, knowing he was already getting out of his depth. "Different," he said again and clamped his lips.

Jillian laughed and settled back. "You old coot," she said fondly. "Tell me about this blowup at the Murdocks'."

"Had a few of them. They're a hardheaded bunch."

"So I've heard. The one that happened before Aaron Murdock went to Billings."

"Kid had lots of ideas when he come back from college." He snorted at education in the way of a man who considered the best learning came from doing. "Maybe some of them were right enough," he conceded. "Always was smart, and knew how to sit a horse."

"Isn't that why he went to college?" Jillian probed. "To get ideas?"

Gil grunted. "Seems the old man felt the boy was taking over too quick. Rumor is the boy agreed to work for his father for three years, then he was supposed to take over. Manage the place like."

Gil stopped at a gate and Jillian climbed out to open it, waiting until he'd driven through before closing and locking it behind her. Another dry day, she thought with a glance at the sky. They'd need some rain soon. A pheasant shot out of the field to her right and wheeled with a flash of color into the sky. She could smell sweet clover.

"So?" she said when she hopped into the truck again.

"So when the three years was up, the old man balked. Wouldn't give the boy the authority they'd agreed on. Well, they got tempers, those Murdocks." He grinned, showing off his dentures. "The boy up and quit, said he'd start his own spread."

"That's what I'd've done," Jillian muttered. "Murdock had no right to go back on his word."

"Maybe not. But he talked the boy into going to Billings 'cause there was some trouble there with the books and such. Nobody could much figure why he did it, unless the old man made it worth his while."

Jillian sneered. Money, she thought derisively. If Aaron had had any guts, he'd've thumbed his nose at his father and started his own place. Probably couldn't handle the idea of starting from the ground up. But she remembered his face, the hard, strong feel of his hand. Something, she thought, puzzled, didn't fit.

"What do you think of him, Gil—personally?"

"Who?"

"Aaron Murdock," she snapped.

"Can't say much," Gil began slowly, rubbing a hand over his face to conceal another grin. "Was a bright kid and full of sass, like one or two others I've known." He gave a hoot when Jillian narrowed her eyes at him. "Wasn't afraid of work neither. By the time he'd grown whiskers, he had the ladies sighing over him, too." Gil put a hand to his heart and gave an exaggerated sigh of his own. Jillian punched him enthusiastically in the arm.

"I'm not interested in his love life, Gil," she began and then immediately changed gears. "He's never married?"

"Guess he figured a woman might want to tell him what to do and how to do it," Gil returned blandly.

Jillian started to swear at him, then laughed instead. "You're a clever old devil, Gil Haley. Look here!" She put a hand on his arm. "We've got calves."

They got out to walk the pasture together, taking a head count and enjoying one of the first true pleasures of spring: new life.

"These'd be from the new bull." Jillian watched a calf nurse frantically while its mother half dozed in the sun.

"Yep." Gil's squint narrowed further while he skimmed over the grazing herd and the new offspring. "I reckon Joe knows what he's about," he murmured and rubbed his chin. "How many younguns you count?"

"Ten and looks like twenty more cows nearly ready to drop." She frowned over the numbers a moment. "Wasn't there—" Jillian broke off as a new sound came over the bored mooing and rustling. "Over there," she said even as Gil started forward.

They found him collapsed and frightened beside his dying mother. A day old, no more than two, Jillian estimated as she gathered up the calf, crooning to him. The cow lay bleeding, barely breathing. The birth had gone wrong. Jillian didn't need Gil to tell her that. The cow had survived the breech, then had crawled off to die.

If the plane had been up... Jillian thought grimly as Gil walked silently back to the pickup. If the plane had been up, someone would've spotted her from the air, and... She shook her head and nuzzled the calf. This was the price of it, she reminded herself. You couldn't mourn over every cow or horse you lost in the course of a year. But when she saw Gil returning with his rifle, she gave him a look of helpless grief. Then she turned and walked away.

One shudder rippled through her at the sound of the shot, then she forced herself to push the weakness away. Still carrying the calf, she went back to Gil.

"Going to have to call for some men on the CB," he told her. "It's going to take more than you and me to load her up." He cupped the calf's head in his hand and studied him. "Hope this one's got some fight in him or he ain't going to make it."

"He'll make it," Jillian said simply. "I'm going to see to it." She went back to the truck, murmuring to soothe the newborn in her arms.

By nine o'clock that evening she was exhausted. Antelope had raced through a hay field and damaged half an acre's crop. One of her men fractured his arm when his horse was spooked by a snake. They'd found three breaks in the wire along the Murdock boundary and some of her cows had strayed. It had taken the better part of the day to round them up again and repair the fence.

Every spare minute Jillian had been able to scrape together had been dedicated to the orphaned calf. She'd given him a warm, dry stall in the cattle barn and had taken charge of his feeding herself. She ended her day there, with one low light burning and the scent and sound of animals around her.

"Here, now." She sat cross-legged on the fresh hay and stroked the calf's small white face. "You're feeling better." He let out a high, shaky sound that made her laugh. "Yes, Baby, I'm your momma now."

To her relief he took the nipple easily. Twice before, she'd had to force feed him. This time, she had to take a firm hold on the bottle to prevent him from tugging it right out of her hand. He's catching on, she thought, stroking him as he sucked. It's a tough life, but the only one we've got.

"Pretty Baby," she murmured, then laughed when he wobbled and sat down hard, back legs spread, without releasing the nipple. "Go ahead and be greedy." Jillian tilted the bottle higher. "You're entitled." His eyes clung to hers as he pulled in his feed. "In a few months you'll be out in the pasture with the rest of them, eating grass and raising hell. I've got a feeling about you, Baby," she said thoughtfully as she scratched his ears. "You might just be a real success with the ladies."

When he started to suck air, Jillian pulled the nipple away. The calf immediately began to nibble at her jeans. "Idiot, you're not a goat." Jillian gave him a gentle shove so that he rolled over and lay, content to have her stroke him.

"Making a pet out of him?"

She whipped her head around quickly and stared up at Aaron Murdock. While he watched, the laughter died out of her eyes. "What are you doing here?"

"One of your favorite questions," he commented as he stepped inside the stall. "Nice-looking calf." He crouched beside her.

Sandalwood and leather. Jillian caught just a whiff of it on him and automatically shifted away. She wanted no scent to creep up and remind her of him when he was gone. "Did you take a wrong turn, Murdock?" she asked dryly. "This is my ranch."

Slowly, he turned his head until their eyes met. Aaron wasn't certain just how long he'd stood watching her—he hadn't intended to watch at all. Maybe it had been the way she'd laughed, that low, smoky sound that had a way of rippling along a man's skin. Maybe it had been the way her hair had glistened—firelike in the low light. Or maybe it had just been that softness he'd seen in her eyes when she'd murmured to the calf. There'd been something about that look that had had tiny aches rushing to the surface. A man needed a woman to look at him like that—first thing in the morning, last thing at night.

There was no softness in her eyes now, but a challenge, a defiance. That stirred something in him, as well, something he recognized with more ease. Desire was so simple to label. He smiled.

"I didn't take a wrong turn, Jillian. I wanted to talk to you."

She wouldn't allow herself the luxury of shifting away from him again, or him the pleasure of knowing how badly she wanted to. She sat where she was and tilted her chin. "About what?"

His gaze skimmed over her face. He was beginning to wish he hadn't stayed in Billings quite so long. "Horse breeding—for a start."

Excitement flickered into her eyes and gave her away even though she schooled her voice to casual disinterest. "Horse breeding?"

"Your Delilah." Casually he wound her hair around his finger. What kind of secret female trick did she use to make it so soft? he wondered. "My Samson. I'm too romantic to let a coincidence like that pass."

"Romantic, my foot." Jillian brushed his hand aside only to find her fingers caught in his.

"You'd be surprised," Aaron said softly. So softly only a well-tuned ear would have heard the steel in it. "I also know a—" his gaze skimmed insolently over her face again "—prime filly when I see one." He laughed when her eyes flashed at him. "Are you always so ready to wrestle, Jillian?"

"I'm always ready to talk business, Murdock," she countered. *Don't be too anxious.* Jillian remembered her grandfather's schooling well. *Always play your cards close to your chest.* "I might be interested in breeding Delilah with your stallion, but I'll need another look at him first."

"Fair enough. Come by tomorrow—nine."

She wanted to jump at it. Five years in Montana and she'd never seen the Murdock spread. And that stallion… Still, she'd been taught too well. "If I can manage it. Middle of the morning's a busy time." Then she was laughing because the calf, weary of being ignored, was butting against her knee. "Spoiled already." Obligingly she tickled his belly.

"Acts more like a puppy than a cow," Aaron stated, but reached over to scratch the calf's ears. It surprised her how gentle his fingers could be. "How'd he lose his mother?"

"Birthing went wrong." She grinned when the calf licked the back of Aaron's hand. "He likes you. Too young to know better."

Amused, Aaron lifted a brow. "Like I said, it's a matter of touching the right way." He slid one lean hand over the calf's head and massaged its neck. "There's one technique for soothing babies, another for breaking horses and another for gentling a woman."

"Gentling a woman?" Jillian sent him an arch look that held humor rather than annoyance. "That's a remarkable phrase."

"An apt one, in certain cases."

She watched as the calf, satisfied, his belly full, curled up on the hay to sleep. "A typical male animal," Jillian remarked, still smiling, "Apparently, you're another."

There wasn't any heat in the comment, but an acceptance. "Could be," he agreed, "though I wouldn't say you were typical."

Unconsciously relaxed, Jillian studied him. "I don't *think* you meant that as a compliment."

"No, it was an observation. You'd spit a compliment back in my face."

Delighted, Jillian threw back her head and laughed. "Whatever else you are, Murdock, you're not stupid." Still chuckling, she leaned back against the wall of the stall, bringing up one knee and circling it with her hands. At the moment she didn't want to question why she was pleased to have his company.

"I have a first name." A trick of the angle had the light slanting over her eyes, highlighting them and casting her face in shadow. He felt the stir again. "Ever thought of using it?"

"Not really." But that was a lie, she realized. She already thought of him as Aaron. The real trouble was that she thought of him at all. Yet she smiled again, too comfortable to make an issue of it. "Baby's asleep," she murmured.

Aaron glanced over, grinning. Would she still call him Baby when he was a bull weighing several hundred pounds? Probably. "It's been a long day."

"Mmmm." She stretched her arms to the ceiling, feeling her muscles loosen. The exhaustion she dragged into the barn with her had become a rather pleasant fatigue. "They're never long enough. If I had just ten hours more in a week, I'd catch up."

With what? he wondered. Herself? "Ever heard of overachievement, Jillian?"

"Ambition," she corrected. Her eyes met his again and held. "I'm not the one who's willing to settle for what's handed to her."

Temper surged into him so quickly he clenched at the hay under him. It was clear she was referring to his father's ranch and his own position there. His expression remained completely passive as he battled back the need to strike out where he was struck. "Each of us does what he has to do," Aaron said mildly and let the hay sift through his hands.

It annoyed her that he didn't defend himself. She wanted him to give her his excuses, his reasons. It shouldn't matter, Jillian reminded herself. He shouldn't matter. He didn't, she assured herself with something perilously close to panic. Of course he didn't. Rising, she dusted off her jeans.

"I've got paperwork to see to before I turn in."

He rose, too, more slowly, so that it was too late when she realized she was backed into the corner of the stall. "Not even going to offer me a cup of coffee, Jillian?"

There was a band of tension at the back of her neck, a thudding at her ribs. She recognized the temper in his eyes, and though she wondered that she hadn't noticed it before, it wasn't his temper that worried her. It was her own shaky pulse. "No," she said evenly. "I'm not."

He hooked his thumbs through his belt loops and studied her lazily. "You've got a problem with manners."

Her chin came up. "Manners don't concern me."

"No?" He smiled then, in a way that made her brace herself. "Then we'll drop them."

In a move too quick for her to evade, he gathered her shirtfront in one hand and yanked her against him. The first shock came from the feel of that long, hard body against hers. "Damn you, Murdock—" The second shock came when his mouth closed over hers.

Oh, no... It was that sweet, weak thought that drifted through her mind even as she fought back like a tiger. Oh, no. He shouldn't feel so good, taste so wonderful. She shouldn't want it to go on and on and on.

Jillian shoved against him and found herself caught closer so that she couldn't shove again. She squirmed and only succeeded in driving herself mad at the feel of her body rubbing against his. Stop it! her mind shouted as the fire began to flicker inside her. She couldn't—wouldn't—let it happen. She knew how to outwit desire. For five years she'd done so with hardly an effort. But now…now something was sprinting inside her too fast, twisting and turning so that she couldn't grab on and stop it from getting further and further out of her reach.

Her blood began to swim, her hands began to clutch. And her mouth began to answer.

He'd expected her temper. Because his own had peaked, he'd wanted it. He'd known she'd be furious, that she'd fight against him for outmaneuvering her and taking something without her permission. His anger demanded that she fight, just as his desire demanded that he take.

He'd expected her mouth to be soft. Why else would he have wanted to taste it so badly that he'd spent two days thinking of little else? He'd known her body would be firm with only hints of the subtle dips and curves of woman. It fit unerringly to his as though it had been fashioned to do so. She strained away from him, shifting, making his skin tingle at the friction her movements caused.

Then, abruptly, her arms were clasped around him. Her lips parted, not in surrender but with an urgency that rocked him. If her passion had been simmering, she'd concealed it well. It seemed to explode in one blinding white flash of heat that came from nowhere. Shaken, Aaron drew back, trying to judge his own reaction, fighting to keep his own needs in perspective.

Jillian stared up at him, her breath coming in jerks. Her hair streamed behind her back, catching the light while her eyes glinted in the dark. Her mind was reeling and she shook her head as if to clear it. Just as she began to draw her first coherent thought, he swore and crushed his mouth to hers again.

There was no hint of struggle this time, nor any hint of surrender. Passion for passion she met him, matching his need with hers, degree by degree. Sandalwood and leather. Now she drew it in, absorbed the aroma as she absorbed the hard, relentless texture of his lips. She let her tongue toy with his while she drank up all those hot, heady male tastes. There was something unapologetically primitive in the way he held her, kissed her. Jillian reveled in it. If she was to take a man, she neither needed nor wanted any polish or gloss that clouded or chipped away so easily.

She let her body take control. How long had she yearned for this? To have someone hold her, spin her away so that she couldn't think, couldn't worry? There were no responsibilities here, and the only demands were of the flesh. Here, with a warm, moist mouth on hers, with a hard body against her, she was finally and ultimately only a woman. Selfishly a woman. She'd forgotten just how glorious it could feel, or perhaps she'd never fully known the sensation before.

What was she doing to him? Aaron tried to pull himself back and found his hands were trapped in the thick softness of her hair. He tried to think and found his senses swimming with the scent of her. And the taste… A low sound started in his throat as he ravaged her mouth. How could he have known she'd taste like this? Seductive, pungent, alluring. Her flavor held all the lushness her body lacked, and the combination was devastating. He wondered how he'd ever lived without it. With that thought came the knowledge that he was getting in much too deep much too fast.

Aaron drew away carefully because the hands on her shoulders weren't as steady as he'd have liked.

Jillian started to sway and caught herself. Good God, what was she doing? What had she done? As the breath rushed swiftly and unevenly through her lips, she stared up at him. Those dark, wicked looks and clever mouth… She'd forgotten. She'd forgotten who she was, and who he was. Forgotten everything but that heady feeling of freedom and heat. He'd use that against her, she thought grimly. If she let him. But something had happened when—

Don't think now! she ordered herself. *Just get him out of here before you make a complete fool of yourself.* Very carefully, Jillian brushed Aaron's hands from her shoulders. Tilting her chin, she prayed her voice would be steady.

"Well, Murdock, you've had your fun. Now clear out."

Fun? he thought, staring at her. Whatever had happened it didn't have anything to do with fun. The room was tilting a bit, like it had when he'd downed his first six-pack of beer a hundred years before. That hadn't been much fun either, but it'd been a hell of an experience. And he'd paid for it the next day. He supposed he'd pay for this one, as well.

He wouldn't apologize, he told himself as he forced himself to relax. Damned if he would, but he would back off while he still could. Casually he bent down to pick up the hat that had fallen off when her fingers had combed through his hair. He took his time putting it on.

"You're right, Jillian," he said mildly—when he could. "A man would have a hard time resisting a woman like you." He grinned at her and tipped his hat. "But I'll do my best."

"See that you do, Murdock!" she called out after him, then hugged herself because she'd begun to tremble.

Even after his footsteps died away, she waited five full minutes before leaving the barn. When Jillian stepped outside, the ranch yard was dark and quiet. She thought she could just hear the murmur of a television or radio from the bunkhouse. There were a few lights farther down the road where her grandfather had built quarters for the married hands. She stopped and listened, but couldn't hear the engine of whatever vehicle Aaron had used to drive from his ranch to hers.

Long gone, she thought, and turned on her heel to stride to the house. It was a two-story stone-and-wood structure. All native Montana material. The rambling building had been constructed on the site of the original homestead. Her grandfather had been fond of bragging that he'd been born in a house that would have fit into the kitchen of this one. Jillian entered by the front door, which was still never locked.

She'd always loved the space, and the clever use of wood and tile and stone that made up the living area. You could roast one of Utopia's steers in the fireplace. Her grandmother's ivory lace curtains still hung at the windows. Jillian often wished she'd known her. All she knew was that she'd been an Irishwoman with dainty looks and a strong back. Jillian had inherited her coloring and, from her grandfather's accounting, her temper. And perhaps, Jillian thought wryly as she climbed the stairs, her back.

God, she wished she had a woman to talk to. Halfway up the stairs she paused and pressed her fingers to her temple. Where did that come from? she wondered. As far back as she could remember, she'd never sought out the company of women. So few of them were interested in the same things she was. And, when there was no niggling sexual problem to overcome, she found men easier to deal with.

But now, with the house so empty around her, with her blood still churning, she wished for a woman who might understand the war going on inside her. Her mother? With a quiet laugh, Jillian pushed open the door to her bedroom. If she called her mother and said she was burning up with desire and had no place to put it, the gentle doctor's wife would blush crimson and stammer out a recommendation for a good book on the subjcct.

No, as fond as she was of her mother, she wasn't a woman who would understand—well, cravings, Jillian admitted, stripping out of her work shirt. If she was going to be honest, that's what she'd felt in Aaron's arms. Perhaps it was all she was capable of feeling. Frowning, she dropped her jeans into a heap on top of her work shirt and walked naked to the bath.

She should probably be grateful she'd felt that. With a jerk of the wrist, she turned the hot water on full, then added a trickle of cold. She'd felt nothing at all for any man in years. Five years, Jillian admitted and dumped in bath salts with a lavish hand. With an expert twist and a couple of pins, she secured her hair to the top of her head.

It was a good thing she remembered Kevin and that very brief, very unhappy affair. Did one night in bed equal an affair? she wondered ruefully, then lowered herself into the steaming water. Whatever you called it, it had been a fiasco. That's what she had to remember. She'd been so young. Jillian could almost—almost—think of it with amusement now.

The young, dewy-eyed virgin, the smooth, charming intern with eyes as clear as a lake. He hadn't talked her into bed, hadn't pressured her. No, Jillian had to admit that she'd wanted to go with him. And he'd been gentle and sweet with her. It had simply been that the words *I love you* had meant two different things to each of them. To Jillian, they'd been a pledge. To him, they'd been a phrase.

She'd learned the hard way that making love didn't equal love or commitment or marriage. He'd laughed at her, perhaps not unkindly, when she'd naively talked of their future together. He hadn't wanted a wife, or even a partner, but a companion willing to share his bed from time to time. His casualness had devastated her.

She'd been willing to mold herself into whatever he'd wanted—a tidy, socially wise doctor's wife like her mother; a clever, dedicated housewife; an organized marriage partner who could juggle career and family. It had taken her months before she'd realized that she'd made a fool of herself over him, taking every compliment or sweet word literally, because that's what she'd wanted to hear. It had taken more time and several thousand miles of distance before she'd been able to admit that he'd done her a favor.

Not only had he saved her from trying to force her personality into a mold that would never have fit, but he'd given her a solid view of the male species. They weren't to be trusted on a personal level. Once you gave them your love, the power to hurt you, you were lost, ready to do anything to please them even at the loss of self.

When she was young, she'd tried to please her father that way and had failed because she was too like her grandfather. The only man she'd ever loved who'd accepted her for what she was had been Clay Baron. And he was gone.

Jillian lay back, closed her eyes and let the hot water steam away her fatigue. Aaron Murdock wasn't looking for a partner and neither was she. What had happened between them in the barn was a mistake that wouldn't be repeated. He might be looking for a lover, but she wasn't.

Jillian Baron was on her own, and that's the way she liked it.

Chapter 3

He wondered if she would come. Aaron drove back from a line camp on a road that had once been fit only for horses or mules. It wasn't in much better shape now. The Jeep bucked along much like a bad-tempered bronc might, dipping into ruts, bounding over rocks. He rather liked it. Just as he'd enjoyed the early morning visit with five of his men at the line camp. If he could spare the time, he would appreciate a few days at one of the camps in unabashedly male company. Hard, sweaty work during the day, a few beers and a poker game at night. Riding herd far enough from the ranch so that you could forget there was civilization anywhere. Yes, he'd enjoy that, but...

He appreciated the conservative, traditional ways of his father—particularly when they were mixed with his own experimental ideas. The men would still rope and flank cattle in the open pasture, but two tractors dragging a cable would clear off more brush in a day than axmen could in a month. And a plane…

With a wry smile Aaron remembered how he'd fought six years before for the plane his father had considered a foolish luxury. He'd ended up paying for it himself and flying it himself. His father had never admitted that the plane had become indispensable. That didn't matter to Aaron, as long as it was used. He had no desire to push the cowboy out of existence, just to make him sweat a little less.

Downshifting for the decline, he let the Jeep bump its way down the hill. The differences with his father that had come to a head five years before had eased, but not vanished. Aaron knew he'd have to fight for every change, every improvement, every deviation. And he'd win. Paul Murdock might be stubborn, but he wasn't stupid. And he was sick. In six months…

Aaron rammed the Jeep back into Fourth. He didn't like to dwell on the battle his father was losing. A battle Aaron could do nothing about. Helplessness was something Aaron wasn't accustomed to. He was too much like his father. Perhaps that's why they spent most of their time arguing.

He pushed his father and mortality out of his mind and thought of Jillian. There was life, and youth, and vitality.

Would she come? Grinning, Aaron sped past a pasture covered with mesquite grass. Damn right she would. She'd come if for no other reason than to prove to him that she couldn't be intimidated. She'd throw her chin up and give him one of those cool go-to-hell looks. No wonder he wanted her so badly it caused an ache in the pit of his belly. The ache had burned like fire when he'd kissed her.

There hadn't been a female who'd made him come so close to stammering since Emma Lou Swanson had initiated him into life's pleasures in the hayloft. It was one thing for a teenager to lose the power of speech and reason with soft arms around him, and quite another for it to happen to a grown man who'd made a study of the delights and frustrations of women. Aaron couldn't quite account for it, but he knew he was going to have to have more. Soon.

She was a typical Baron, he decided. Hotheaded, stubborn, opinionated. Aaron grinned again. He figured the main reason the Barons and Murdocks had never gotten on was that they'd been too much alike. She wasn't going to have an easy time taking over the ranch, but he didn't doubt she'd do it. He didn't doubt he was going to enjoy watching her. Almost as much as he was going to enjoy bedding her.

Whistling between his teeth, Aaron braked in front of the ranch house. Over near the cattle barn a dog was barking halfheartedly. Someone was playing a radio by the feed lot—a slow, twangy country lament. There were asters popping up in the flower bed and not a weed in sight. As he climbed out of the Jeep he heard the porch door open and glanced over. His mother walked out, lips curved, eyes weary.

She was so beautiful—he'd never gotten used to it. Very small, very slender, Karen Murdock walked with the gliding step of a runway model. She was twenty-two years younger than her husband, and neither the cold winters nor the bright sun of Montana had dimmed the luster of her skin. His sister had those looks, Aaron mused, the classic blond beauty that went on and on with the years. Karen wore slimming slacks, a rose-colored blouse, with her hair loosely coiled at the neck. She could've walked into the Beverly Wilshire without changing a stitch. If the need had arisen, she could've saddled up a horse and ridden out to string wire.

"Everything all right?" she asked him, holding out a hand.

"Fine. They've rounded up the strays we were losing through the south fence." Studying her face, Aaron took her hand. "You look tired."

"No." She squeezed his fingers as much for support as reassurance. "Your father didn't sleep well last night. You didn't come by to see him."

"That wouldn't've made him sleep any better."

"Arguing with you is about all the entertainment he has these days."

Aaron grinned because she wanted him to. "I'll come in later and tell him about the five hundred acres of mesquite I want to clear."

Karen laughed and put her hands on her son's shoulders. With her standing on the porch and him on the ground, their eyes were level. "You're good for him, Aaron. No, don't raise your brow at me," she told him mildly.

"When I saw him yesterday morning, he told me to go to the devil."

"Exactly." Her fingers kneaded absently at his shoulders. "I tend to pamper him, even though I shouldn't. He needs you around to make him angry enough to live a bit longer. He knows you're right—that you've been right all along. He's proud of you."

"You don't have to explain him to me." The steel had

crept into his voice before he could prevent it. "I know him well enough."

"Almost well enough," Karen murmured, laying her cheek against Aaron's.

When Jillian drove into the ranch yard, she saw Aaron with his arms around a slim, elegant blonde. The surge of jealousy stunned, then infuriated her. He was a man after all, she reminded herself, gripping the steering wheel tightly for a moment. It was so easy for a man to enjoy quick passion in a horse stall one evening, then a sweet embrace in the sunshine the next day. True emotion never entered into it. Why should it? she thought, setting her teeth. She braked sharply beside Aaron's Jeep.

He turned, and while she had the disadvantage of the sun in her eyes, she met his amused look with ice. Not for a moment would she give him the satisfaction of knowing she'd spent a restless, dream-disturbed night. Jillian stepped out of her aging compact and managed not to slam the door.

"Murdock," she said curtly.

"Good morning, Jillian." He gave her a bland smile with something sharper hovering in his eyes.

She walked to him, since he didn't seem inclined to drop the blonde's hand and come to her. "I've come to see your stud."

"We talked about manners last night, didn't we?" His grin only widened when she glared at him. "I don't think you two have met."

"No, indeed." Karen came down the porch steps, amused by the gleam in her son's eye, and the fire in the woman's. "You must be Jillian Baron. I'm Karen Murdock, Aaron's mother."

As her mouth fell open Jillian turned to look at Mrs.

Murdock. Soft, elegant, beautiful. "Mother?" she repeated before she could stop herself.

Karen laughed, and rested a hand on Aaron's shoulder. "I think I've just been given a wonderful compliment."

He grinned down at her. "Or I have."

Laughing again, she turned back to Jillian. Karen filed away her quick assessment. "I'll leave you two to go about your business. Please, stop in for coffee before you go if you've time, Jillian. I have so little opportunity these days to talk with another woman."

"Yes, ah—thank you." With her brows drawn together, Jillian watched her go back through the porch door.

"I don't think you're often at a loss for words," Aaron commented.

"No." With a little shake of her head she looked up at him. "Your mother's beautiful."

"Surprised?"

"No. That is, I'd heard she was lovely, but…" Jillian shrugged and wished he'd stop looking down at her with that infernal smile on his face. "You don't look a thing like her."

Aaron swung his arm around her shoulders as they turned away from the house. "You're trying to charm me again, Jillian."

She had to bite down on her lip to keep the chuckle back. "I've better uses for my time." Though the weight felt good, she plucked his arm away.

"You smell of jasmine," he said lazily. "Did you wear it for me?"

Rather than dignify the question with an answer, Jillian stopped, tilted her chin and gave him one long icy look that only wavered when he began to laugh. With a careless flick he knocked the hat from her head, pulled her against him and gave her a hard, thorough kiss. She felt her legs dissolve from the knees down.

Though he released her before she'd even thought to demand it, Jillian gathered her wits quickly enough. "What the hell do you think—"

"Sorry." His eyes were laughing, but he held his hands up, palms out in a gesture of peace. "Lost my head. Something comes over me when you look at me as though you'd like to cut me into small pieces. *Very* small pieces," he added as he took the hat from where it hung at her back and placed it back on her head.

"Next time I won't just look," she said precisely, wheeling away toward the corral.

Aaron fell into step beside her. "How's the calf?"

"He's doing well. Vet's coming by to check him over this afternoon, but he took the bottle again this morning."

"Was he sired by that new bull of yours?" When Jillian sent him a sharp look, Aaron smiled blandly. "Word gets around. As it happens, you snatched him up from under my nose. I was making arrangements to go to England to check him out for myself when I heard you'd bought him."

"Really?" It was news—and news she couldn't help but be pleased to hear.

"Thought that might make your day," Aaron said mildly.

"Nasty of me," Jillian admitted as they came to the corral fence. Resting a foot on the lower rail, she smiled at him. "I'm not a nice person, Murdock."

He gave her an odd look and nodded. "Then we'll

deal well enough together. What's the nickname your hands have dubbed that bull?"

Her smile warmed so that the dimple flickered. He was going to have to find out what it felt like to put his lips just there. "The Terror's the cleanest in polite company."

He chuckled. "I don't think that was the one I heard. How many calves so far?"

"Fifty. It's early yet."

"Mmm. Are you using artificial insemination?"

Her eyes narrowed. "Why?"

"Just curious. We are in the same business, Jillian."

"That's not something I'll forget," she said evenly.

Annoyance tightened his mouth. "Which doesn't mean we have to be opponents."

"Doesn't it?" Jillian shifted her hat lower on her forehead. "I came to look at your stud, Murdock."

He stood watching her a moment, long enough, directly enough, to make Jillian want to squirm. "So you did," Aaron said quietly. Plucking a halter from the fence post, he swung lithely over the corral fence.

Rude, Jillian condemned herself. It was one thing to be cautious, even unfriendly, but another to be pointedly rude. It wasn't like her. Frowning, Jillian leaned on the fence and rested her chin in her open hand. Yet she'd been rude to Aaron almost continually since their first encounter. Her frown cleared as she watched him approach the stallion.

Both males were strong and well built, and each was inclined to want his own way. At the moment the stallion wasn't in the mood for the halter. He pranced away from Aaron to lap disinterestedly at his water trough.

Aaron murmured something that had Samson shaking his head and trotting off again.

"You devil," she heard Aaron say, but there was a laugh in his voice. Aaron crossed to him again, and again the stallion danced off in the opposite direction.

Laughing, Jillian climbed the fence and sat on the top rung. "Round 'em up, cowboy," she drawled.

Aaron flashed her a grin, then shrugged as though he'd given up and turned his back on the stallion. By the time he'd crossed the center of the corral, Samson had come up behind him to nudge his head into Aaron's back.

"Now you wanna make up," he murmured, turning to ruffle the horse's mane before he slipped on the halter. "After you've made me look like a greenhorn in front of the lady."

Greenhorn, hell, Jillian thought, watching the way he handled the skittish stallion. If he cared about impressing anyone, he'd have made the difficult look difficult instead of making it look easy. With a sigh, she felt her respect for him go up another notch.

Automatically she reached out to stroke the stallion's neck as Aaron led him to her. He had a coat like silk, and eyes that were wary but not mean. "Aaron..." She glanced down in time to see his brow lift at her voluntary use of his name. "I'm sorry," she said simply.

Something flickered in his eyes, but they were so dark it was difficult to read it. "All right," he said just as simply and held out a hand. She took it and hopped down.

"He's beautiful." Jillian ran her hands along Samson's wide chest and sleek flank. "Have you bred him before?"

"Twice in Billings," he said, watching her.

"How long have you had him?" She went to Samson's head, then passed under him to the other side.

"Since he was a foal. It took me five days to catch his father." Jillian looked up and caught the light in his eyes. "There must've been a hundred and fifty mustangs in his herd. He was a cagey devil, damn near killed me the first time I got a rope around him. Then he busted down the stall and nearly got away again. You should've seen him, blood spurting out of his leg, fire in his eyes. It took six of us to control him when we bred him to the mare."

"What did you do with him?" Jillian swallowed, thinking how easy it would be to breed the wild stallion again and again, then geld him. Break his spirit.

Aaron's eyes met hers over Samson's withers. "I let him go. Some things you don't fence."

She smiled. Before she realized it, she reached over Samson for Aaron's hand. "I'm glad."

With his eyes on hers, Aaron stroked a thumb over her knuckles. The palm of his hand was rough, the back of hers smooth. "You're an interesting woman, Jillian, with a few rather appealing soft spots."

Disturbed, she tried to slip her hand from his. "Very few."

"Which is why they're appealing. You were beautiful last night, sitting in the hay, crooning to the calf, with the light in your hair."

She knew about clever words. Why were these making her pulse jerky? "I'm not beautiful," she said flatly. "I don't want to be."

He tilted his head when he realized she was perfectly serious. "Well, we can't have everything we want, can we?"

"Don't start again, Murdock," she ordered, sharply

enough that the stallion moved restlessly under their joined hands.

"Start what?"

"You know, I wondered why I always end up being rude to you," she began. "I realize it's simply because you don't understand anything else. Let go of my hand."

His eyes narrowed at her tone. "No." Tightening his hold, he gave the stallion a quick pat that sent him trotting off, leaving nothing between himself and Jillian. "I wondered why I always end up wanting to toss you over my knee—or my shoulder," he added thoughtfully. "Must be for the same reason."

"Your reasons don't interest me, Murdock."

His lips curved slowly, but his eyes held something entirely different from humor. "Now, I might've believed that, Jillian, if it hadn't been for last night." He took a step closer. "Maybe I kissed you first, but, lady, you kissed me right back. I had a whole long night to think about that. And about just what I was going to do about it."

Maybe it was because he'd spoken the truth when she didn't care to hear it. Maybe it had something to do with the wicked gleam in his eyes or the insolence of his smile. It might have been a combination of all three that loosened Jillian's temper. Before she had a chance to think about it, or Aaron a chance to react, she'd drawn back her fist and plunged it hard into his stomach.

"That's what *I* intend to do about it!" she declared as he grunted. She had only a fleeting glimpse of the astonishment on his face before she spun on her heel and strode away. She didn't get far.

Jillian's breath was knocked out of her as he brought her down in a tackle. She found herself flat on her back, pinned under him with a face filled with fury rather than astonishment looming over hers. It only took her a second to fight back, and little more to realize she was outmatched.

"You hellion," Aaron grunted as he held her down. "You've been asking for a thrashing since the first time I laid eyes on you."

"It'll take a better man than you, Murdock." She nearly succeeded in bringing her knee up and scoring a very important point. Instead he shifted until her position was only more vulnerable. Heat that had nothing to do with temper surged into her stomach.

"By God, you tempt me to prove you wrong." She squirmed again and stirred something dangerous in him. "Woman, if you want to fight dirty, you've come to the right place." He closed his mouth over hers before she could swear at him. At the instant of contact he felt the pulse in her wrist bound under his hands. Then he felt nothing but the hot give of her mouth.

If she was still struggling beneath him, he wasn't aware of it. Aaron felt himself sinking, and sinking much deeper than he'd expected. The sun was warm on his back, she was soft under him, yet he felt only that moist, silky texture that was her lips. He thought he could make do with that sensation alone for the rest of his life. It scared him to death.

Pulling himself back, he stared down at her. She'd stolen the breath from him much more successfully this time than she had with the quick jab to the gut. "I ought to beat you," he said softly.

Somehow in her prone position she managed to thrust her chin out. "I'd prefer it." It wasn't the first lie she'd told, but it might have been the biggest.

She told herself a woman didn't want to be kissed by a man who tossed her on the ground. Yet her conscience played back that she'd deserved that at the least. She wasn't a fragile doll and didn't want to be treated like one. But she shouldn't want him to kiss her again...want it so badly she could already taste it. "Will you get off me?" she said between her teeth. "You're not as skinny as you look."

"It's safer talking to you this way."

"I don't want to talk to you."

The gleam shot back in his eyes. "Then we won't talk."

Before Jillian could protest, or Aaron could do what he'd intended, Samson lowered his head between their faces.

"Get your own filly," Aaron muttered, shoving him aside.

"He's got a smoother technique than you," Jillian began, then choked on a laugh as the horse bent down again. "Oh, for God's sake, Aaron, let me up. This is ridiculous."

Instead of obliging he looked back down at her. Her eyes were bright with laughter now, her dimple flashing. Her hair spread like fire in the dust. "I'm beginning to like it. You don't do that enough."

She blew the hair out of her eyes. "What?"

"Smile at me."

She laughed again and he felt the arms under his hands relax. "Why should I?"

"Because I like it."

She tried to give a long-winded sigh, but it ended on a chuckle. "If I apologize for hitting you, will you let me up?"

"Don't spoil it—besides, you won't catch me off guard again."

No, she didn't imagine she would. "Well, in any case you deserved it—and you paid me back. Now get up, Murdock. This ground's hard."

"Is it? You're not." He lifted a brow as he shifted into a more comfortable position. He wondered if her legs would look as nice as they felt. "Anyway, we still have to discuss that remark about my technique."

"The best I can say about it," Jillian began as Aaron pushed absently at Samson's head again, "is that it needs some polishing. If you'll excuse me, I really have to get back. Some of us work for a living."

"Polishing," he murmured, ignoring the rest. "You'd like something a little—smoother." His voice dropped intimately as he brushed his lips over her cheek, light as a whisper. He heard the quick, involuntary sound she made as he moved lazily toward her mouth.

"Don't." Her voice trembled on the word so that he looked down at her again. Vulnerability. It was in her eyes. That, and a touch of panic. He hadn't expected to see either.

"An Achilles' heel," he murmured, moved, aroused. "You've given me an advantage, Jillian." Lifting a hand, he traced her mouth with a fingertip and felt it tremble. "It's only fair to warn you that I'll use it."

"Your only advantage at the moment is your weight."

He grinned, but before he could speak a shadow fell over them.

"Boy, what're you doing with that little lady on the ground?"

Jillian turned her head and saw an old man with sharp, well-defined features and dark eyes. Though he was pale and had an air of fragility, she saw the resemblance. Astonished, she stared at him. Could this bent old man who leaned heavily on a cane, who was so painfully thin, be the much feared and respected Paul Murdock? His eyes, dark and intense as Aaron's, skimmed over her. The hand on the cane had the faintest of tremors.

Aaron looked up at his father and grinned. "I'm not sure yet," he said easily. "It's a choice between beating her or making love."

Murdock gave a wheezing laugh and curled one hand around the rail of the fence. "It's a stupid man who wouldn't know which choice to make, but you'll do neither here. Let the filly up so I can have a look at her."

Aaron obliged, taking Jillian by the arm and hauling her unceremoniously to her feet. She slanted him a killing glare before she looked back at his father. What nasty twist of fate had decided that she would meet Paul J. Murdock for the first time with corral dust clinging to her and her body still warm from his son's? she wondered as she silently cursed Aaron. Then she tossed back her hair and lifted her chin.

Murdock's face remained calm and unexpressive. "So, you're Clay Baron's granddaughter."

She met his steady hawklike gaze levelly. "Yes, I am."

"You look like your grandmother."

Her chin lifted a fraction higher. "So I've been told."

"She was a fire-eater." A ghost of a smile touched his eyes. "Hasn't been a Baron on my land since she marched over here to pay her respects to Karen after the wedding. If some young buck had tried to wrestle with her, she'd have blackened his eye."

Aaron leaned on the fence, running a hand over his

stomach. "She hit me first," he drawled, grinning at Jillian. "Hard."

Jillian slipped her hat from her back and meticulously began to dust it off and straighten it. "Better tighten up those muscles, Murdock," she suggested as she set the hat back on her head. "I can hit a lot harder." She glanced over as Paul Murdock began to laugh.

"I always thought I should've thrashed him a sight more. What's your name, girl?"

She eyed him uncertainly. "Jillian."

"You're a pretty thing," he said with a nod. "And it doesn't appear you lack for sense. My wife would be glad for some company."

For a minute she could only stare at him. This was the fierce Murdock—her grandfather's archrival—inviting her into his home? "Thank you, Mr. Murdock."

"Come in for coffee, then," he said briskly, then shot a look at Aaron. "You and I have some business to clear up."

Jillian felt something pass between the two men that wasn't entirely pleasant before Murdock turned to walk back toward the house. "You'll come in," Aaron said as he unlatched the gate. It wasn't an invitation but a statement. Curious, Jillian let it pass.

"For a little while. I've got to get back."

They walked through the gate together and relatched it. Though they moved slowly, they caught up with Murdock as he reached the porch steps. Seeing his struggle to negotiate them with the cane, Jillian automatically started to reach out for his arm. Aaron grabbed her wrist. He shook his head, then waited until his father had painstakingly gained the porch.

"Karen!" It might have been a bellow if it hadn't been

so breathless. "You've got company." Murdock swung open the front door and gestured Jillian in.

It was more palatial than Utopia's main building, but had the same Western feel that had first charmed a little girl from Chicago. All the wood was highly polished— the floor, the beams in the ceilings, the woodwork—all satiny oak. But here was something Utopia lacked. That subtle woman's touch.

There were fresh flowers arranged in a pottery bowl, and softer colors. Though Jillian's grandfather had kept the ivory lace curtains at the windows, his ranch house had reverted to a man's dwelling over the years. Until she walked into the Murdock home and felt Karen's presence, Jillian hadn't realized it.

There was a huge Indian rug spread over the floor in the living area and glossy brass urns beside the fireplace that held tall dried flowers. A seat was fashioned into a bow window and piled with hand-worked pillows. The room had a sense of order and welcome.

"Aren't either of you men going to offer Jillian a chair?" Karen asked mildly as she wheeled in a coffee cart.

"She seems to be Aaron's filly," Murdock commented as he lowered himself into a wing-backed chair and hooked his cane over the arm.

Jillian's automatic retort was stifled as Aaron nudged her onto the sofa. Gritting her teeth, she turned to Karen. "You have a lovely home, Mrs. Murdock."

Karen didn't attempt to disguise her amusement. "Thank you. I believe I saw you at the rodeo last year," she continued as she began to pour coffee. "I remember thinking you looked like Maggie—your grandmother. Do you plan to compete again this year?"

"Yes." Jillian accepted the cup, declining cream or sugar. "Even though my foreman squawked quite a bit when I beat his time in the calf roping."

Aaron reached over to toy with her hair. "That tempts me to enter myself."

"It'd be a pretty sorry day when a son of mine couldn't rope a calf quicker than a female," Murdock muttered.

Aaron sent him a bland look. "That would depend on the female."

"You might be out of practice," Jillian said coolly as she sipped her coffee. "After five years behind a desk." As soon as she'd said it, Jillian felt the tension between father and son, a bit more strained, a bit more unpleasant than she'd felt once before.

"I suppose things like that are in the blood," Karen said smoothly. "You've taken to ranch life, but you were raised back east, weren't you?"

"Chicago," Jillian admitted, wondering what she'd stirred up. "I never fit in." It was out before she realized it. A frown flickered briefly in her eyes before she controlled it. "I suppose ranching just skipped a generation in my family," she said easily.

"You have a brother, don't you?" Karen stirred the slightest bit of cream into her own coffee.

"Yes, he's a doctor. He and my father share a practice now."

"I remember the boy—your father," Murdock told her, then chugged down half a cup of coffee. "Quiet, serious fellow who never said three words if two would do."

Jillian had to smile. "You remember him well."

"Easy to understand why Baron left the ranch to you instead." Murdock held out his cup for more coffee, but Jillian noticed that Karen only filled it halfway. "Guess you can't do much better than Gil Haley for running things."

Her dimple flickered. It was, she supposed, a compliment of sorts. "Gil's the best foreman I could ask for," Jillian said mildly. "But I run Utopia."

Murdock's brows drew together. "Women don't run ranches, girl."

Her chin angled. "This one does."

"Nothing but trouble when you start having cowboys in skirts," he said with a snort.

"I don't wear them when I'm hazing cattle."

He set down his cup and leaned forward. "Whatever I felt about your grandfather, it wouldn't sit well with me to see what he worked for blown away because of some female."

"Paul," Karen began, but Jillian was already rolling.

"Clay wasn't so narrow-minded," Jillian shot back. "If a person was capable, it didn't matter what sex they were. I run Utopia, and before I'm done you'll be watching your back door." She rose, unconsciously regal. "I've got work to do. Thank you for the coffee, Mrs. Murdock." She shot a look at Aaron, who was still lounging back on the sofa. "We still have to discuss your stud."

"What's this?" Murdock demanded, banging his cane.

"I'm breeding Samson to one of Jillian's mares," Aaron said easily.

Color surged into Murdock's pale face. "A Murdock doesn't do business with a Baron."

Aaron unfolded himself slowly and stood. "I do business as I please," Jillian heard him say as she started for the door. She was already at her car when Aaron caught up with her.

"What's your fee?" she said between her teeth.

He leaned against the car. If he was angry, she couldn't see it. "You spark easily, Jillian. I'm usually the only one who can put my father in a rage these days."

"Your father," she said precisely, "is a bigot."

With his thumbs hooked idly in his pockets, Aaron studied the house. "Yeah. But he knows his cows."

She let out a long breath because she wanted to chuckle. "About the stud fee, Murdock."

"Come to dinner tonight, we'll talk about it."

"I haven't time for socializing," she said flatly.

"You've been around long enough to know the advantages of a business dinner."

She frowned at the house. An evening with the Murdocks? No, she didn't think she could get through one without throwing something. "Look, Aaron, I'd like to breed Delilah with Samson—if the terms are right. I'm not interested in anything more to do with you or your family."

"Why?"

"There's been bad blood between the Barons and Murdocks for almost a century."

He gave her a lazy look under lowered lids. "Now who's a bigot?"

Bull's-eye, she thought and sighed. Putting her hands on her hips, she tried to bring her temper to order. Murdock was an old man, and from the looks of him, a sick one. He was also, though she'd choke rather than admit it, a great deal like her grandfather. She'd be a pretty poor individual if she couldn't drum up some understanding. "All right, I'll come to dinner." She turned back to him. "But I won't be responsible if it ends up with a lot of shouting."

"I think we might avoid that. I'll pick you up at seven."

"I know the way," she countered and started to push him aside to open her door. His hand curled over her forearm.

"I'll pick you up, Jillian." The steel was back, in his eyes, his voice.

She shrugged. "Suit yourself."

He cupped the back of her head and kissed her before she could prevent it. "I intend to," he told her easily, then left her to walk back into the house.

Chapter 4

Jillian was still smarting when she returned to Utopia.
Murdock's comments, and Aaron's arrogance, had set
her back up. She wasn't the sort of woman who made a
habit of calming down gracefully. She told herself the
only reason she was going back to the Double M to deal
with the Murdocks again was because she was interested
in a breeding contract. She wanted to believe it.

Dust flew out from her wheels as she drove up the
hard-packed road to the ranch yard. It was nearly deserted now at mid-morning, with most of the men out
on the range, others busy in the outbuildings. But even
an audience wouldn't have prevented her from springing out of her car and slamming the door with a vicious
swing. She'd never been a woman who believed in letting her temper simmer if it could boil.

The sound of the door slam echoed like a pistol shot.

Fleetingly she thought of the paperwork waiting for her in the office, then brushed it aside. She couldn't deal with ledgers and numbers at the moment. She needed something physical to drain off the anger before she tackled the dry practicality of checks and balances. Spinning on her heel, she headed for the stables. There'd be stalls to muck out and tack to clean.

"Anybody in particular you'd like to mow down?"

With her eyes still sparkling with anger, Jillian whipped her head around. Joe Carlson walked toward her, his neat hat shading his eyes, a faint, friendly smile on his lips.

"Murdocks."

He nodded after the short explosion of the word. "Figured it was something along those lines. Couldn't come to an agreement on the stud fee?"

"We haven't started negotiating yet." Her jaw clenched. "I'm going back this evening."

Joe scanned her face, wondering that a woman who played poker so craftily should be so utterly readable when riled. "Oh?" he said simply and earned a glare.

"That's right." She bit off each word. "If Murdock didn't have such a damn beautiful horse, I'd tell him to go to the devil and to take his father with him."

This time Joe grinned. "You met Paul Murdock, then."

"He gave me his opinion on cowboys in skirts." Her teeth shut with an audible click.

"Really?"

The dry tone was irresistible. Jillian grinned back at him. "Yes, really." Then she sighed, remembering how difficult it had been for Paul Murdock to climb the four steps to his own porch. "Oh, hell," she murmured, cooling off as quickly as she'd flared. "I shouldn't have let him get under my skin. He's an old man and—"

She broke off, stopping herself before she added *ill*. For some indefinable reason she found it necessary to allow Murdock whatever illusions he had left. Instead she shrugged and glanced toward the corral. "I suppose I'm just used to the way Clay was. If you could ride and drive cattle, he didn't care if you were male or female."

Joe gave her one sharp glance. It wasn't what she'd started to say, but he'd get nothing out of her by probing. One thing he'd learned in the past six months was that Jillian Baron was a woman who did things her way. If a man got too close, one freezing look reminded him how much distance was expected.

"Maybe you'd like to take another look at the bull now, if you've got a few minutes."

"Hmm?" Abstracted, she looked back at him.

"The bull," Joe repeated.

"Oh, yeah." Hooking her thumbs in her pockets, she began to walk with him. "Gil told you about the calves we counted yesterday?"

"Took a look in the south section today. You've got some more."

"How many?"

"Oh, thirty or so. In another week all the calves should be dropped."

"You know, when we were checking the pasture yesterday, I thought the numbers were a little light." Frowning, she went over the numbers in her head again. "I'm going to need someone to go out there and see that some of the bred cows haven't strayed."

"I'll take care of it. How's the orphan?"

With a grin Jillian glanced back toward the cattle

barn. "He's going to be fine." Attachments were a mistake, she knew. But it was already too late between her and Baby. "I'd swear he's grown since yesterday."

"And here's Poppa," Joe announced as they came to the bull's paddock.

After angling the hat farther over her eyes, Jillian leaned on the fence. Beautiful, she thought. Absolutely beautiful.

The bull eyed them balefully and snorted air. He didn't have the bulk or girth of an Angus but was built, Jillian thought, like a sleek tank. His red hide glistened as he stood in the full sun. She didn't see boredom in his expression as she'd seen in so many of the steers or cows, but arrogance. His horns curved around the wide white face and gave him a sense of dangerous royalty. It occurred to her that the little orphan she had sheltered in the cattle barn would look essentially the same in a year's time. The bull snorted again and pawed the ground as if daring them to come inside and try their luck.

"His personality's grim at best," Joe commented.

"I don't need him to be polite," Jillian murmured. "I just need him to produce."

"Well, you don't have any problem there." His gaze skimmed over the bull. "From the looks of the calves in this first batch, he's already done a good job for us. Since we're using artificial insemination now, he should be able to service every Hereford cow on the ranch this spring. Your shorthorn bull's a fine piece of beef, Jillian, but he doesn't come up to this one."

"No." Smiling, she rested her elbows on the rail. "As a matter of fact, I found out today that Aaron Murdock was interested in our, ah, Casanova. I can't help but pat myself on the back when I remember how I sent off to England for him on a hunch. Damned expensive hunch," she added, thinking of the hefty dent in the books. "Aaron told me today that he was planning on going over to England to take a look at the bull himself when he learned we'd bought him."

"That was a year ago," Joe commented with a frown. "He was still in Billings."

Jillian shrugged. "I guess he was keeping his finger in the pie. In any case, we've got him." She pushed away from the rail. "I meant what I said about the fair in July, Joe. I can't say I cared much about competition and ribbons before. This year I want to win."

Joe brought his attention from the bull and studied her. "Personal?"

"Yeah." She gave him a grim smile. "You could say it's personal. In the meantime, I'm counting on this guy to give me the best line of beef cattle in Montana. I need a good price in Miles City if I'm going to keep the books in the black. And next year when some of his calves are ready..." She trailed off with a last look at the bull. "Well, we'll just take it a bit at a time. Get back to me on those numbers, Joe. I want to take a look at Baby before I go into the office."

"I'll take care of it," he said again and watched her walk away.

By five Jillian had brought the books up to date and was, if not elated with the figures, at least satisfied. True, the expenses had taken a sharp increase over the past year, but by roundup time, she anticipated a tidy profit from the Livestock Auction Saleyard in Miles City. The expenses had been a gamble, but a necessary one. The plane would be in use within the week and the bull had already proved himself.

Tipping back in her grandfather's worn leather chair, she studied the ceiling. If she could find the time, she'd like to learn how to fly the plane herself. As owner she felt it imperative that she have at least a working knowledge of every aspect of the ranch. In a pinch she could shoe a horse or stitch up a rent hide. She'd learned to operate a hay baler and a bulldozer during a summer visit when she'd still been a teenager—the same year she'd wielded her first and last knife to turn a calf into a steer.

When and if she could afford the luxury, she thought, she'd hire someone to take over the books. Grimacing, she closed the ledger. She had more energy left after ten hours on horseback than she did after four behind a desk.

For now it couldn't be helped. She could justify adding another puncher to the payroll, but not a paper pusher. Next year... She laughed at herself and rested her feet on the desk.

Trouble was, she was counting too heavily on next year and too many things could happen. A drought could mean the loss of crops, a blizzard the loss of cattle. And that was just nature. If feed prices continued to rise, she was going to have to seriously consider selling off a larger portion of the calves as baby beef. Then there was the repair bill for the Jeep, the vet bill, the food bill for the hands. The bill for fuel that would rise once the plane was in use. Yes, she was going to need top dollar in Miles City and a blue ribbon or two wouldn't hurt.

In the meantime she was going to keep an eye on her spring calves. And Aaron Murdock. With a half smile, Jillian thought of him. He was an arrogant son of a bitch, she mused with something very close to admiration, and sharp as they came. It was a pity she didn't trust him enough to discuss ranch business with him and kick around ideas. She'd missed that luxury since her grandfather died. The men were friendly enough, but you didn't talk about your business with a hand who might be working for someone else next year. And Gil was... Gil was Gil, she thought with a grin. He was fond of her, even respected her abilities, though he wouldn't come out and say so. But he was too steeped in his own ways to talk about ideas and changes. So that left—no one, Jillian admitted.

There had been times in Chicago when she could have screamed for privacy, for solitude. Now there were times she ached just to have someone to share an hour's conversation with. With a shake of her head she rose. She was getting foolish. She had dozens of people to talk to. All she had to do was go down to the barn or the stables. Wherever this sudden discontent had come from it would fade again quickly enough. She didn't have time for it.

Her boots clicked lightly on the floor as she walked through the house and up the stairs. From outside she could hear the ring of the triangle, those quick three notes that ran faster and faster until it was one high sound. Her hands would be sitting down to their meal. She'd better get ready for her own.

Jillian toyed with the idea of just slipping into clean jeans and a shirt. The deliberate casualness of such an outfit would be pointedly rude. She was still annoyed enough at both Aaron and his father to do it, but she thought of Karen Murdock. With a sigh, Jillian rejected the idea and hunted through her closet.

It was a matter of her own choice that she had few dresses. They were relegated to one side of her closet, and she rooted them out on the occasions when she entertained other ranchers or businessmen. She stuck with simple styles, having found it to her advantage not to call her femininity to attention. Standing in a brief teddy, she skimmed over her options.

The oversized white cotton shirt wasn't precisely masculine in cut, but it was still casual. Matched with a full white wrap skirt with yards of sash, it made an outfit she thought not only suitable but understated. She made a small concession with a touch of makeup, hesitated over jewelry, then, shrugging, clipped small swirls of gold at her ears. Her mother, Jillian thought, would have badgered her to do something more sophisticated with her hair. Instead she ran a brush through it and left it down. She didn't need elegant styles to discuss breeding contracts.

When she heard the sound of a car drive up outside, she stopped herself from going to the window to peer out. Deliberately she took her time going back downstairs.

Aaron wasn't wearing a hat. Without it Jillian realized he still looked like what he was—a rugged outdoorsman with touches of the aristocracy. He didn't need the uniform to show it.

Looking at him, she wondered how he had found the patience to sit in Billings behind a desk. Trim black slacks and a thin black sweater fit him as truly as his work clothes, yet they seemed to accent the wickedness of his dark looks. She felt an involuntary stir and met his eyes coolly.

"You're prompt," she commented and let the door swing shut behind her. It might not be wise to be alone with him any longer than necessary.

"So are you." He let his gaze move over her slowly, appreciating the simplicity of her outfit—the way the sash accented her small waist and narrow hips, the way the unrelieved white made her skin glow and her hair spark like fire. "And beautiful," he added, taking her hand. "Whether you like it or not."

Because her pulse reacted immediately, Jillian knew she had to tread carefully. "You keep risking that hand of yours, Murdock." When she tried to slip hers from it, he merely tightened his fingers.

"One thing I've learned is that nothing's worth having if you don't have trouble getting it." Very deliberately he brought her hand to his lips, watching her steadily.

It wasn't a gesture she expected from him. Perhaps that was why she did nothing but stare at him as the sun dipped lower in the sky. She should've jerked her hand away—she wanted to spread her fingers so that she could touch that high curve of cheekbone, that lean line of jaw. She did nothing—until he smiled.

"Maybe I should warn you," Jillian said evenly, "that the next time I hit you, I'm going to aim a bit lower."

He grinned, then kissed her hand again before he released it. "I believe it."

Because she couldn't stop her own smile, she gave up. "Are you going to feed me, Murdock, or not?" Without waiting for an answer, she walked down the steps in front of him.

His car was more in tune with the oil man she'd first envisioned. A low, sleek Maserati. She admired anything well built and fast and settled into her seat with a little sigh. "Nice toy," she commented with a hint of the smile still playing around her mouth.

"I like it," Aaron said easily when he started the engine. It roared into life, then settled down to a purr. "A man doesn't always like to take a woman out in a Jeep or pickup."

"This isn't a date," she reminded him but skimmed her fingers over the smooth leather of the upholstery.

"I admire your practical streak—most of the time."

Jillian turned in her seat to watch the way he handled the car. As well as he handles a horse, she decided. As well as she was certain he handled a woman. The smile curved her lips again. He was going to discover that she wasn't a woman who took to being handled. She settled back to enjoy the ride.

"How does your father feel about me coming to dinner?" she asked idly. Those last slanting rays of the sun were tipping the grass with gold. She heard a cow moo lazily.

"How should he feel about it?" Aaron countered.

"He was amiable enough when I was simply Clay Baron's granddaughter," Jillian pointed out. "But once he found out I was *the* Baron, so to speak, he changed his tune. You're fraternizing with the enemy, aren't you?"

Aaron took his eyes off the road long enough to meet her amused look with one of his own. "So to speak. Aren't you?"

"I suppose I prefer to look at it as making a mutually advantageous bargain. Aaron…" She hesitated, picking her way carefully over what she knew was none of her business. "Your father's very ill, isn't he?"

She could see his expression draw inward, though it barely changed at all. "Yes."

"I'm sorry." Jillian turned to look out the side window. "It's hard," she murmured, thinking of her grandfather. "It's so hard for them."

"He's dying," Aaron said flatly.

"Oh, but—"

"He's dying," he repeated. "Five years ago they told him he had a year, two at most. He outfoxed them. But now..." His fingers contracted briefly on the wheel, then relaxed again. "He might make it to the first snow, but he won't make it to the last."

He sounded so matter-of-fact. Perhaps she'd imagined that quick tension in his fingers. "There hasn't even been a rumor of his illness."

"No, we intend to keep it that way."

She frowned at his profile. "Then why did you tell me?"

"Because you understand about pride and you don't play games."

Jillian studied him another moment, then turned away. No soft words or whispered compliments could have moved her more than that brisk, emotionless statement. "It must be difficult for your mother."

"She's tougher than she looks."

"Yes." Jillian smiled again. "She'd have to be to put up with him."

They drove under the high-arched *Double M* at the entrance to the ranch. The day was hovering at dusk when the light grew lazy and the air soft. Cattle stood slack-hipped in the pasture to the right. She saw a mother licking patiently to clean her baby's hide while other calves were busy at their evening feeding. In another few months they'd be heifers and steers, the maternal bond forgotten, but for now they were just babies with awkward legs and demanding stomachs.

"I like this time of day," she murmured, half to herself. "When work's over and it isn't time to think about tomorrow yet."

He glanced down at her hand that lay relaxed against the seat. Competent, unpampered, with narrow bones and slender fingers. "Did you ever consider that you work too hard?"

Jillian turned and met his gaze calmly. "No."

"I didn't think you did."

"Cowboys in skirts again, Murdock?"

"No." But he'd made a few discreet inquiries. Jillian Baron had a reputation for working a twelve-hour day— on a horse, in a pickup, on her feet. If she wasn't riding fence or hazing cattle, she was feeding her stock, overseeing repairs or poring over the books. "What do you do to relax?" he asked abruptly. Her blank look gave him the answer before she did.

"I don't have a lot of time for that right now. When I do there are books or the toy Clay bought a couple years ago."

"Toy?"

"Videotape machine," she said with a grin. "He loved the movies."

"Solitary entertainments," Aaron mused.

"It's a solitary way of life," Jillian countered, then glanced over curiously when he stopped in front of a simple white frame house. "What's this?"

"It's where I live," Aaron told her easily before he stepped from the car.

She sat where she was, frowning at the house. She'd taken it for granted that he lived in the sprawling main house another quarter mile or so up the road. Just as she'd taken it for granted that they were having dinner there, with his parents. Jillian turned her head as he opened her door and sent him an uncompromising look. "What are you up to, Murdock?"

"Dinner." Taking her hand, he pulled her from the car. "Isn't that what we'd agreed on?"

"I was under the impression we were having it up there." She gestured in the general direction of the ranch house.

Aaron followed the movement of her hand. When he turned back to her, his mouth was solemn, his eyes amused. "Wrong impression."

"You didn't do anything to correct it."

"Or to promote it," he countered. "My parents don't have anything to do with what's between us, Jillian."

"Nothing is."

Now his lips smiled, as well. "There's a matter of the horses—yours and mine." When she continued to frown, he stepped closer, his body just brushing hers. "Afraid to be alone with me, Jillian?"

Her chin came up. "You overestimate yourself, Murdock."

He saw from the look in her eyes that she wouldn't back down no matter what he did. The temptation was too great. Lowering his head, he nipped at her bottom lip. "Maybe," he said softly. "Maybe not. We can always ride on up to the main house if you're—nervous."

Her heart had already risen to the base of her throat to pound. But she knew what it was to deal with a stray wildcat. "You don't worry me," she said mildly, then turned to walk to the house.

Oh, yes, I do, Aaron thought, and admired her all the more because she was determined to face him down. He decided, as he moved to open the front door, that it promised to be an interesting evening.

She couldn't fault his taste. Jillian glanced around his living quarters, wondering just how much she could learn about him from his choice of furnishings. Apparently, he had his mother's flair for style and color, though there were no subtle feminine touches here. Buffs and creams were offset by a stunning wall hanging slashed with vivid blues and greens. He favored antiques and clean lines. Though the room was small, there was no sense of clutter. Curious, she wandered to a curved mahogany shelf and studied his collection of pewter.

The mustang at full gallop caught her attention, though all the animals in the miniature menagerie were finely crafted. For a moment she wished he wasn't a man who appreciated what appealed to her quite so much. Then, remembering the stand she had to take, she turned around. "This is very nice. Though it is a bit simple for a man who grew up the way you did."

His brow lifted. "I'll take the compliment. How do you like your steak?"

Jillian dipped her hands in the wide pockets of her skirt. "Medium rare."

"Keep me company while I fix them." He curled a hand around her arm and moved through the house with her.

"So, I get Murdock beef prepared by a Murdock." She shot him a look. "I suppose I should be complimented."

"We might consider it a peace offering."

"We might," Jillian said cautiously, then smiled. "Providing you know how to cook. I haven't eaten since breakfast."

"Why not?"

He gave her such a disapproving look that she laughed. "I got bogged down in paperwork. I can't work up much of an appetite sitting at a desk. Well, well," she added, glancing around his kitchen. Its simplicity suited the house, with its hardwood floor and plain counters. There wasn't a crumb out of place. "You're a tidy one, aren't you?"

"I lived in the bunkhouse for a while." Aaron uncorked a bottle of wine that stood on the counter next to two glasses. "It either corrupts or reforms you."

"Why the bunkhouse when—" She cut herself off, annoyed that she'd begun to pry again.

"My father and I deal together better when there's some distance." He poured wine into both glasses. "You'd have heard by now that we don't always agree."

"I heard you'd had a falling-out a few years ago, before you went to Billings."

"And you wondered why I—buckled under instead of telling him to go to hell and starting my own place."

Jillian accepted the wine he handed her. "All right, yes, I wondered. It's none of my business."

He looked into his glass a moment, as if studying the dark red color of the wine. "No." Aaron glanced back up and sipped. "It's not."

Without another word he turned to take two hefty steaks out of the refrigerator. Jillian sipped her wine and remained quiet, watching him as he began preparation of the meal with the deft, economical moves that were characteristic of him. Five years ago they'd given his father a year, perhaps two, to live. Aaron had told her that without even a hint of emotion in his voice. And he'd gone to Billings five years before.

To wait his father out? she wondered and winced at the thought. No, she couldn't believe that of him—a man cool and calculating enough to wait for his father to die? Even if his feelings for his father didn't run deep, it was too cold, too heartless. With a shudder, Jillian took a deep swallow of her wine, then set it down. She wouldn't believe it of him.

"Anything I can do?"

Aaron glanced over his shoulder to see her calmly watching him. He knew what direction her thoughts had taken—the logical direction. Now he saw she'd decided in his favor. He told himself he didn't give a damn one way or the other. It wasn't just astonishing to find out he did, it was enervating. He could feel the emotion stir, and drain him. To give himself a moment to settle, he slipped the steaks under the broiler and turned it on.

"Yeah, there's something you can do." Crossing to her, Aaron framed her face in his hands, seeing her eyes widen in surprise just before his mouth closed over hers. He meant to keep it hard and brief. A gesture—a gesture only to rid him of whatever emotion had suddenly sprung up in him. But as his lips moved over hers the emotion swelled, threatening to take over as the kiss lingered.

She stiffened, and lifted her hands to his chest in automatic defense. Aaron found he didn't want the struggle that usually appealed to him, but the softness he knew she'd give to very few. "Jillian, don't." His fingers tangled in her hair. His voice had roughened with feelings—mysterious, unnamed—he didn't pause to question. "Don't fight me—just this once."

Something in his voice, that quiet hint of need, had her hands relaxing against him before the thought to do so had registered. So she yielded, and in yielding brought herself a moment of sweet, mindless pleasure.

His mouth gentled on hers even as he took her deeper. Her hands crept up to his shoulders, her head tilted back so that he might take what he needed and bring her more of that soft, soft delight she hadn't been aware existed. With a sigh that came from discovery, she gave.

He hadn't known he was capable of tenderness. There'd never been a woman who'd drawn it from him before. He hadn't been aware that desire could ever be calm and easy. Yet while the need built inside him, he felt a quiet wave of contentment. Aaron basked in it until it made him light-headed. Shaken, he eased her away, studying her face like a man who had seen something he didn't quite understand. And wasn't sure he wanted to.

Jillian took a step back, regaining her balance by placing her palm down on the scrubbed wooden table. She found sweetness in the last place she expected to. There was nothing she was more determined to fight. "I came here for dinner," she began, eyeing him just as warily as he was eyeing her. "And to talk business. Don't do that again."

"You've got a point," he murmured before he turned back to the stove to tend the steaks. "Drink your wine, Jillian. We'll both be safer."

She did as he suggested only because she wanted something to calm her nerves. "I'll set the table," she offered.

"Dishes're up there." Aaron pointed to a cabinet without looking up. The steaks sizzled when he flipped them. "There's salad in the refrigerator."

They finished up the cooking and preparation in silence, with only the sound of sizzling meat and frying potatoes. Jillian finished off her first glass of wine and looked at the food with real enthusiasm.

"Either you know what you're doing, or I'm starved."

"Both." Aaron passed her some ranch dressing. "Eat. When you're skinny you can't afford to miss meals."

Unoffended, she shrugged. "Metabolism," she told him as she speared into the salad. "It doesn't matter how much I eat, nothing sticks."

"Some people call it nervous energy."

She glanced up as he tilted more wine into her glass. "I call it metabolism. I'm never nervous."

"Not often, in any case," he acknowledged. "Why did you leave Chicago?" Aaron asked before she could formulate a response.

"I didn't belong there."

"You could have, if you'd chosen to."

Jillian gave him a long neutral look, then nodded. "I didn't choose to, then. I felt at home here the first summer I visited."

"What about your family?"

She laughed. "They didn't."

"I mean, how do they feel about you living here, running Utopia?"

"How should they feel?" Jillian countered. She frowned into her wine a moment, then shrugged again. "I suppose you could say my father feels about Chicago the way I feel about Montana. It's where he belongs. You'd think he'd been born and raised there. And of course, my mother was, so… We just never worked out as a family."

"How?"

Jillian dashed some salt on her steak and cut into it. "I hated my piano lessons," she said simply.

"As easy as that?"

"As basic as that. Marc—my brother—he just melded right in. I suppose it helped that he developed an interest in medicine early, and he loves opera. My mother's quite a fan," she said with a smile. "Anyway, I still cringe a bit when I have to use a needle on a cow, and I've never been able to appreciate *La Traviata*."

"Is that what it takes to suit as a family?" Aaron wondered.

"It was important in mine. When I came here the first time, things started to change. Clay understood me. He yelled and swore instead of lecturing."

Aaron grinned, offering her more steak fries. "You like being yelled at?"

"Patient lecturing is the worst form of punishment."

"I guess I've never had to deal with it. We had a wood shed." He liked the way she laughed, low, appreciative. "Why didn't you come out to stay sooner?"

She moved her shoulders restlessly as she continued to eat. "I was in college. Both my parents thought a degree was vital, and I felt it was important to try to please them in that if nothing else. Then I got involved with—" She stopped herself, stunned that she'd almost told him of her relationship with that long-ago intern. Meticulously she cut a piece of steak. "It just didn't work out," she concluded, "so I came out here."

The someone who touched her wrong, Aaron decided. The astonishment in her eyes had been brief, her cover-up swift and smooth, but not smooth enough. He wouldn't probe there, not on a spot that was obviously tender. But he wondered who it had been who had touched her, and hurt her while she'd still been too young to build defenses.

"I think my mother was right," he commented. "Some things are just in the blood. You belong here."

There was something in the tone that made her look up carefully. She wasn't certain at that moment whether he referred to the ranch or to himself. His eyes reminded her just how ruthless he could be when he wanted something. "I belong at Utopia," she said precisely. "And I intend to stay. Your father said something today, too," she reminded him. "That a Murdock doesn't do business with a Baron."

"My father doesn't run my life, personally or professionally."

"Are you going to breed your stallion with Delilah to spite him?"

"I don't waste time with spite." It was said very simply, with that undercurrent of steel that made her think if he wanted revenge, he'd choose a very direct route. "I want the mare—" his dark eyes met hers and held "—for reasons of my own."

"Which are?"

Lifting his wine, he drank. "My own."

Jillian opened her mouth to speak, then shut it again. His reasons didn't matter. Business was business. "All right, what fee are you asking?"

Aaron took his time, calmly watching her face. "You seem to be finished."

Distracted, Jillian looked down to see that she'd eaten every bite on her plate. "Apparently," she said with a half laugh. "Well, I almost hate to admit it, Murdock, but it was good—almost as good as Utopia beef."

He answered her grin as he rose to clear off the table. "Why don't we take the wine in the other room, unless you'd like some coffee."

"No." She got up to help him stack the dishes. "I drank a full pot when I was fooling with the damn books."

"Don't care for paperwork?" Aaron picked up the half-full bottle of wine as they walked out of the kitchen.

"Putting it mildly," she murmured. "But someone has to do it."

"You could get a bookkeeper."

"The thought's crossed my mind. Maybe next year," she said with a move of her shoulders. "I've gotten used to keeping my finger on the pulse, let's say."

"Rumor is you rope a steer with the best of them."

Jillian sat on the couch, the full white skirt billowing around her. "Rumor's fact, Murdock," she said with a cocky smile. "Anytime you want to put some money on it, we'll go head to head."

He sat down beside her and toyed with the end of her sash. "I'll keep that in mind. But I have to admit, it isn't a hardship to look at you in a skirt."

Over the rim of her glass she watched him. "We were talking stud fees. What'd you have in mind for Samson?"

Idly he twisted a lock of her hair around his finger. "The first foal."

Chapter 5

For a moment there was complete silence in the room as they measured each other. She'd thought she had him pegged. It infuriated her to realize he was still a step ahead of her. "The first—" Jillian set down her glass of wine with a snap. "You're out of your mind."

"I'm not interested in cash. Two guaranteed breedings. I take the first foal, colt or filly. You take the second. I like the looks of your mare."

"You expect me to breed Delilah, cover all the expenses while she's carrying a foal, lose the use of her for three to four months, deal with the vet fees, then turn the result over to you?"

Relaxed, Aaron leaned back. He'd almost forgotten how good it was to haggle. "You'd have the second for nothing. I'd be willing to negotiate on the expenses."

"A flat fee," Jillian said, rising. "We're not talking about dogs, where you can take the pick of the litter."

"I don't need cash," Aaron repeated, lounging back on the couch. "I want a foal, take it or leave it."

Oh, she'd like to leave it. She'd like to have tossed it back in his face. Simmering, she stalked over to the window and stared out. It surprised her that she didn't. Until that moment Jillian hadn't realized just how much she wanted to breed those two horses. Another hunch, she thought, remembering the bull. She could feel that something special would come out of it. Clay had often told her she had a feel. More than once she'd singled out an animal for no other reason than a feeling. Now she had to weigh that with the absurdity of Aaron's suggestion.

She stared hard out of the window into the full night, full dark. Behind her, Aaron remained silent, waiting, watching her with a faint smile. He wondered if she knew just how lovely she was when she was annoyed. It was tempting to keep her that way.

"I get the first foal," she said suddenly. "You get the second. It's my mare who's taking the risk in pregnancy, who won't be any use for working when she's at term and nursing. I'm the one bearing the brunt of the expense."

Aaron considered a moment. She was playing it precisely as he'd have done himself if the situation was reversed. He found it pleased him. "We breed her back as soon as she's weaned the foal."

"Agreed. You pay half the vet bills—on both foalings."

His brows raised. Whatever she knew about cattle, she wasn't a fool when it came to horse trading. "Half," he agreed. "We breed them as soon as she comes in season."

With a nod, Jillian offered her hand on it. "Do you want to draw up the papers or shall I?"

Standing, Aaron took her hand. "I'm not particular. A handshake's binding enough for me."

"Agreed," she said again. "But it never hurts to have words written down."

He grinned, skimming his thumb over her knuckles. "Don't you trust me, Jillian?"

"Not an inch," she said easily, then laughed because he seemed more pleased than offended. "No, not an inch. And you'd be disappointed if I did."

"You have a way of cutting through to the heart of things. It's a pity I've been away for five years." He inclined his head. "But I have a feeling we'll be making up for lost time."

"I haven't lost any time," Jillian countered. "Now that we've concluded our business successfully, Murdock, I have a long day tomorrow."

He tightened his fingers on hers before she could turn away. "Not all our business."

"All I came for." Her voice was cool, even when he stepped closer. "I don't want to make a habit out of hitting you."

"You won't connect this time." He took her other hand and held both lightly, though not so lightly she could draw away. "I'm going to have you, Jillian."

She didn't try to pull her hands away. She didn't back up. Her eyes stayed level with his and her voice just as matter-of-fact. "The hell you are."

"And when I do," he went on as if she hadn't spoken, "it's not going to be something either one of us is going to forget. You stirred something in me—" he yanked her closer so that the unrelieved white of her skirt flowed against the stark black of his slacks "—from the first minute I saw you. It hasn't settled yet."

"Your problem." She angled her chin, but her voice was breathless. "You don't interest me, Murdock."

"Tell me that again," he challenged, "in just a minute."

He brought his mouth down on hers, harder, rougher than he'd intended. His emotions seemed to have no middle ground with her. It was either all soft tenderness or raw passion. Her arms strained against his hold, her body jerked as if to reject him. Then he felt it—the instant she became as consumed as he. In seconds his arms were around her, and hers around him.

It felt just as she'd wanted it to. Heady, overpowering. She could forget everything but that delicious churning within her own body. The rich flavor of wine that lingered on his tongue would make her drunk, but it didn't matter. Her head could whirl and spin, but she could only be grateful for the giddiness. With unapologetic passion, she met his demand with demand.

When his mouth left hers, she would have protested, but the sound became a moan as his lips raced down her throat. Instinctively she tilted her head back to give him more freedom, and the sharp scent of soap drifted over her, laced with a hint of sandalwood. Then his mouth was at her ear, his teeth tugging and nipping before he whispered something she didn't understand. The words didn't matter, the sound alone made her tremble. With a murmur of desperation, she dragged his lips back to hers.

Jillian was demanding he take more. Aaron could feel the strain of her body against his and knew she was aching to be touched. But his hands were still tangled in her hair as they tumbled onto the couch. Then his hands were everywhere, and he couldn't touch enough fast enough. Her body was so slender under all those yards of thin white cotton. So responsive. Her breast was almost lost under the span of his hand, yet it was so firm. And her heartbeat pounded like thunder beneath it.

His legs tangled with hers before he slipped between them. When she sank into the cushions, he nearly lost himself in the simple give of her body. His mouth ravaged hers—he couldn't prevent it, she didn't protest. She only answered and demanded until he was half mad again. Her scent, part subtle, part sultry, enveloped him so that he knew he'd be able to smell her when she was miles from him. He could hear her breath rush from between her lips into his mouth, where it whispered warm and sweet and promising.

Her body was responding of its own accord while her mind raced off in a dozen directions. His weight, that hard, firm press of his body, felt so good, so natural against hers. Those rough, ruthless kisses gave her everything she needed long before she knew she needed. He threatened her with words of passion that were only whispered madness in a world of color without form.

His cheek grazed hers as his lips raced over her face. No one had ever wanted her like this. But more, she'd never wanted this wildly. Her only taste of lovemaking had been so mild, so quiet. Nothing had prepared her for a violence of need that came from within herself. She wanted to fly with it. Too much.

His hand skimmed up her leg, seeking, and everything that was inside her built to a fever pitch. If it exploded, she'd be lost. Pieces of herself might scatter so that she'd never be strong enough to stand on her own again.

In a panic, she began to struggle while part of her fought to yield. And to take.

"No." Moaning, she pushed against him.

"Jillian, for God's sake." Her name came out in a gasp as he felt himself drowning.

"No!" With the strength of fear, she managed to shove him aside and scramble up. Before either of them could think, she was dashing outside, running away from something that followed much too closely. Aaron was cursing steadily when he caught her.

"What the hell's wrong with you?" he demanded as he whipped her back around.

"Let me go! I won't be pawed that way."

"Pawed?" He didn't even hear her gasp as his fingers tightened. "Damn you," he said under his breath. "You were doing some pawing of your own, if that's what you want to call it."

"Just let me go," she said unsteadily. "I told you I don't like to be touched."

"Oh, you like to be touched," he grated, then caught the glint of fear in her eyes. There was pride there, as well, a kind of terrorized pride laced with passion. It reminded him sharply of the eyes of a stallion he'd once tied in a stall. Then he realized his fingers were digging into the flesh of very slender arms.

No, he wasn't a gentle man, but she was the first and only woman who'd caused him to lose control to the point where he'd mark her skin. Carefully he loosened his hold without releasing her. Even as his fingers relaxed, he knew he could drag her back inside and have her willing to give herself to him within moments. But some things you didn't fence.

"Jillian." His voice was still rough, only slightly calmer. "You can postpone what's going to happen between us, but you can't stop it." She opened her mouth, but he shook his head in warning. "No, you'd be much better off not to say anything just now. I want you, and at the moment it's a damned uncomfortable feeling. I'm

going to take you home while I've got myself convinced
I play by the rules. It wouldn't take me long to remember I've never followed any."

He pulled open the passenger door, then strode around
to the driver's seat without another word. They drove
away in a silence that remained thick for miles. Because
her body was still throbbing, Jillian sat very straight. She
cursed Aaron, then when she began to calm, she cursed
herself. She'd wanted him, and every time he touched
her, her initial restraint vanished within moments.

The hands in her lap balled into fists. There was a
name for a woman who was willing and eager one moment and hurling accusations the next. It wasn't pleasant.
She'd never played that kind of game and had nothing
but disdain for anyone who did.

He had a right to be furious, Jillian admitted, but
then, so did she. He was the one who'd come barging
into her life, stirring things up she wanted left alone. She
didn't want to feel all those hungers, all those aches that
raged through her when he held her.

She couldn't give in to them. Once she did, she'd start
depending. If that happened, she'd start chipping away
at her own self-reliance until he had more of who and
what she was than she did. It had happened before and
the need had been nothing like this. She'd gotten a hint,
during that strangely gentle kiss in his kitchen, just how
easily she could lose herself to him. And yet... Yet when
it was all said and done, Jillian was forced to admit, she'd
acted like an idiot. The one thing she detested more than
anything else was finding herself in the wrong.

A deer bounded over the fence to the left, pausing
in the road, as it was trapped in the headlights. Even as
Aaron braked, it was sprinting off, slender legs lifting

as it took the next fence and disappeared into the darkness. The sight warmed Jillian as it always did. With a soft laugh, she turned back to see the smile in Aaron's eyes. The flood of emotion swamped her.

"I'm sorry." The words came quickly, before she realized she would say them. "I overreacted."

He gave her a long look. He'd wanted to stay angry. Somehow it was easier—now it was impossible. "Maybe we both did. We have a tendency to spark something off each other."

She couldn't deny that, but neither did she want to think about it too carefully just then. "Since we're going to have to deal with each other from time to time, maybe we should come to some kind of understanding."

A smile began to tug at his mouth. "That sounds reasonable. What kind of understanding did you have in mind?"

"We're business associates," she said very dryly because of the amusement in his question.

"Uh-huh." Aaron rested his arm on the back of the seat as he began to enjoy himself.

"Do you practice being an idiot, Murdock, or does it come naturally?"

"Oh, no, no insults, Jillian. We're coming to an understanding."

Jillian fought against a grin and lost. "You have a strange sense of humor."

"A keen sense of the ridiculous," he countered. "So we're business associates. You forgot neighbors."

"And neighbors," she agreed with a nod. "Colleagues, if you want to belabor a point."

"Belabor it," Aaron suggested. "But can I ask you a question?"

"Yes." She drew out the word cautiously.

"What *is* the point?"

"Damn it, Aaron," she said with a laugh. "I'm trying to put things in order so I don't end up apologizing again. I hate apologizing."

"I like the way you do it, very simple and sincere right before you lose your temper again."

"I'm not going to lose my temper again."

"I'll give you five to one."

"Damn it, Aaron." Her laugh rippled, low and smooth. "If I took that bet, you'd go out of your way to make me mad."

"You see, we understand each other already. But you were telling me your point." He pulled into the darkened ranch yard. The light from Jillian's front porch spilled into the car and cast his face in shadows.

"We could have a successful business association *if* we both put a lot of effort into it."

"Agreed." He turned and in the small confines of the car was already touching her. Just the skim of his fingers over her shoulder, the brush of leg against leg.

"We'll continue to be neighbors because neither of us is moving. As long as we remember those things, we should be able to deal with each other without too much fighting."

"You forgot something."

"Did I?"

"You've said what we are to each other, not what we're going to be." He watched her eyes narrow.

"Which is?"

"Lovers." He ran his finger casually down the side of her neck. "I still mean to have you."

Jillian let out a long breath and worked on keeping

her temper in check. "It's obvious you can't carry on a reasonable conversation."

"A lot of things are obvious." He put his hand over hers as she reached for the handle. With their faces close, he let his gaze linger on her mouth just long enough for the ache to spread. "I'm not a patient man," Aaron murmured. "But there are some things I can wait for."

"You'll have a long wait."

"Maybe longer than I'd like," he agreed. "But shorter than you think." His hand was still over hers as he pressed down the handle to release the door. "Sleep well, Jillian."

She swung out of the car, then gave him a smoldering look. "Don't cross the line until you're invited, Murdock." Slamming the door, she sprinted up the steps, cursing the low, easy laughter that followed her.

In the days that followed, Jillian tried not to think about Aaron. When she couldn't stop him from creeping into her mind, she did her best to think of him with scorn. Occasionally she was successful enough to dismiss him as a spoiled, willful man who was used to getting what he wanted by demanding it. If she were successful, she could forget that he made her laugh, made her want.

Her days were long and full and demanding enough that she had little time to dwell on him or her feelings. But though the nights were growing shorter, she swore against the hours she spent alone and unoccupied. It was then she remembered exactly how it felt to be held against him. It was then she remembered how his eyes could laugh while the rest of his face remained serious and solemn. And how firm and strong his mouth could be against hers.

She began to rise earlier, to work later. She exhausted herself on the range or in the outbuildings until she could tumble boneless into bed. But still there were dreams.

Jillian was out in the pasture as soon as it was light. The sky was still tipped with the colors of sunrise so that gold and rose tinted the hazy blue. Like most of her men, she wore a light work jacket and chaps as they began the job of rounding up the first hundred calves and cows for corral branding. This part of the job would be slow and easy. It was too common to run twenty-five pounds off a cow with a lot of racing and roping. A good deal of the work could be done on foot, the rest with experienced horses or four wheels. If they hazed the mothers along gently, the babies would follow.

Jillian turned Delilah, keeping her at a walk as she urged a cow and calf away from a group of heifers. She looked forward to a long hard morning and the satisfaction of a job well done. When she saw Joe slowly prodding cows along on foot, she tipped her hat to him.

"I always thought branding was a kind of stag party," he commented as he came alongside of her.

Looking down, she laughed. "Not on Utopia." She looked around as punchers nudged cows along with soft calls and footwork. "When we brand again in a couple of days, the plane should be in. God knows it'll be easier to spot the strays."

"You've been working too hard. No, don't give me that look," he insisted. "You know you have. What's up?"

Aaron sneaked past her defenses, but now she just shook her head. "Nothing. It's a busy time of year. We'll be haying soon, first crop should come in right after the spring branding. Then there's the rodeo." She glanced down again as Delilah shifted under her. "I'm counting on those blue ribbons, Joe."

"You've been working from first light to last for a week," he pointed out. "You're entitled to a couple days off."

"The boss is the last one entitled to a couple days off." Satisfied that her cows had joined the slowly moving group headed for the pasture, she wheeled Delilah around. She spotted a calf racing west, spooked by the number of men, horses and trucks. Sending Delilah into an easy lope, Jillian went after him.

Her first amusement at the frantic pace the dogie was setting faded as she saw he was heading directly for the wire. With a soft oath, she nudged more speed out of her mare and reached for her rope. With an expert movement of arm and wrist, she swung it over her head, then shot it out to loop over the maverick's neck. Jillian pulled him up a foot from the wire where he cried and struggled until his mother caught up.

"Dumb cow," she muttered as she dismounted to release him. "Fat lot of good you'd've done yourself if you'd tangled in that." She cast a glance at the sharp points of wire before she slipped the rope from around his head. The mother eyed her with annoyance as she began to recoil the rope. "Yeah, you're welcome," Jillian told her with a grin. Glancing over, she saw Gil crossing to her on foot. "Still think you can beat my time in July?" she demanded.

"You put too much fancy work on the spin."

Though his words were said in his usual rough-and-ready style, something in his eyes alerted her. "What is it?"

"Something you oughta see down here a ways."

Without a word, she gathered Delilah's reins in her hand and began to walk beside him. There was no use asking, so she didn't bother. Part of her mind still registered the sights and sounds around her—the irritated mooing, the high sound of puzzled calves, the ponderous majestic movements of their mothers, the swish of men and animals through grass. They'd start branding by mid-morning.

"Look here."

Jillian saw the small section of broken fence and swore. "Damn it, we just took care of this line a week ago. I rode this section myself." Jillian scowled into the opposite pasture wondering how many of her cattle had strayed. That would account for the fact that though the numbers reported to her were right, her eye had told her differently that morning. "I'll need a few hands to round up the strays."

"Yeah." Reaching over, he caught a strand of wire in his fingers. "Take a look."

Distracted, she glanced down. Almost immediately, Jillian stiffened and took the wire in her own fingers. The break was much too sharp, much too clean. "It's been cut," she said quietly, then looked up and over into the next pasture. Murdock land.

She expected to feel rage and was stunned when she felt hurt instead. Was he capable? Jillian thought he could be ruthless, even lawless if it suited him. But to deliberately cut wire… Could he have found his own way to pay her back for their personal differences and professional enmity? She let the wire fall.

"Send three of the men over to check for strays," she said flatly. "I'd like you to see to this wire yourself."

She met Gil's eyes coolly and on level. "And keep it to yourself."

He squinted at her, then spit. "You're the boss."

"If I'm not back by the time the cattle are ready in the corral, get started. We don't have any time to waste getting brands on the calves."

"Maybe we waited a few days too long already."

Jillian swung into the saddle. "We'll see about that." She led Delilah carefully through the break in the wire, then dug in her heels.

It didn't take her long to come across her first group of men. Delilah pulled up at the Jeep and Jillian stared down her nose. "Where's Murdock?" she demanded. "Aaron Murdock."

The man tipped his hat, recognizing an outraged female when he saw one. "In the north section, ma'am, rounding up calves."

"There's a break in the fence," she said briefly. "Some of my men are coming over to look for strays. You might want to do the same."

"Yes, ma'am." But he said it to her back as she galloped away.

The Murdock crew worked essentially the same way her own did. She saw them fanned out, moving slowly, steadily, with the cows plodding along in front of them. A few were farther afield, outflanking the mavericks and driving them back to the herd.

Jillian saw him well out to the right, twisting and turning Samson around a reluctant calf. Ignoring the curious glances of his men, Jillian picked her way through them. She heard them laugh, then shout something short and rude at the calf before he saw her.

The brim of his hat shaded his face from the early

morning sun. She couldn't see his expression, only that he watched her come toward him. Delilah pricked up her ears as she scented the stallion and sidestepped skittishly.

Aaron waited until they were side by side. "Jillian." Because he could already see that something was wrong, he didn't bother with any more words.

"I want to talk to you, Murdock."

"So talk." He nudged the calf, but Jillian reached over to grip his saddle horn. His eyes flicked down to rest on her restraining hand.

"Alone."

His expression remained placid—but she still couldn't see his eyes. Signaling to one of his men to take charge of the maverick, Aaron turned his horse and walked farther north. "You'll have to keep it short, I haven't got time to socialize right now."

"This isn't a social call," she bit off, controlling Delilah as the mare eyed the stallion cautiously.

"So I gathered. What's the problem?"

When she was certain they were out of earshot, Jillian pulled up her mount. "There's a break in the west boundary line."

He looked over her head to watch his men. "You want one of my hands to fix it?"

"I want to know who cut it."

His eyes came back to hers quickly. She could see only that they were dark. The single sign of his mood was the sudden nervous shift of his stallion. Aaron controlled him without taking his eyes off Jillian. "Cut it?"

"That's right." Her voice was even now, with rage bubbling just beneath. "Gil found it, and I saw it myself."

Very slowly he tipped back his hat. For the first time

she saw his face unshadowed. She'd seen that expression once before—when it had loomed over her as he pinned her to the ground in Samson's corral. "What are you accusing me of?"

"I'm telling you what I know." Her eyes caught the slant of the morning sun and glittered with it. "You can take it from there."

In what seemed to be a very calm, very deliberate motion, he reached over and gathered the front of her jacket in his hand. "I don't cut fence."

She didn't jerk away from him and her gaze remained steady. A single stray breeze stirred the flame-colored curls that flowed from her hat. "Maybe you don't, but you've got a lot of men working your place. Three of my men are in your pasture now, rounding up my strays. I'm missing some cows."

"I'll send some men to check your herd for any of mine."

"I already suggested that to one of your hands in the border pasture."

He nodded, but his eyes remained very intense and very angry. "A wire can be cut from either side, Jillian."

Dumbfounded, she stared at him. Rage boiled out as she knocked his hand away from her jacket. "That's ridiculous. I wouldn't be telling you about the damn wire if I'd cut it."

Aaron watched her settle her moody mare before he gave her a grim smile. "You have a lot of men working your place," he repeated.

As she continued to stare her angry color drained. Hurt and anger hadn't allowed her to think through the logic of it. Some of her men she'd known and trusted for years. Others—they came and they went, earning a stake, then drifting to another ranch, another county. You rarely knew their names, only their faces. But it was her count that was short, she reminded herself.

"You missing any cattle?" she demanded.

"I'll let you know."

"I'll be doing a thorough count in the west section." She turned away to stare at the rising sun. It could've been one of her men just as easily as it could've been one of his. And she was responsible for everyone who was on Utopia's payroll. She had to face that. "I've no use for your beef, Aaron," she said quietly.

"Any more than I do for yours."

"It wouldn't be the first time." When she looked back at him, her chin stayed up. "The Murdocks made a habit out of cutting Baron wire."

"You want to go back eighty years?" he demanded. "There's two sides to a story, Jillian, just like there's two sides to a line. You and I weren't even alive then, what the hell difference does it make to us?"

"I don't know, but it happened—it could happen again. Clay may be gone, but your father still has some bad feelings."

Temper sprang back into his eyes. "Maybe he dragged himself out here and cut the wire so he could cause you trouble."

"I'm not a fool," she retorted.

"No?" Furious, he wheeled his horse so that they were face-to-face. "You do a damn good imitation. I'll check the west line myself and get back to you."

Before she could throw any of her fury back at him, he galloped away. Teeth gritted, Jillian headed south, back to Utopia.

Chapter 6

By the time Jillian galloped into the ranch yard the cattle were already penned. A glance at the sun told her it was only shortly after eight. Cows and calves were milling and mooing in the largest board pen and the workmen had already begun to separate them. No easy task. Listening to the sounds of men and cattle, Jillian dismounted and unsaddled her mare. There wasn't time to brood over the cut wire when branding was under way.

Some of the men remained on horseback, keeping the cows moving as they worked to chase the frantic mothers into a wire pen while the calves were herded into another board corral. The air was already peppered with curses that were more imaginative than profane.

With blows and shouts, a cow and her calf were driven out of the big corral. Men on foot were strung out in a line too tight to allow the cow to follow as the calf slipped through. Relying mostly on arm waving, shrieks, and whistles, the men propelled the cow into the wire pen. Then the process repeated itself. She watched Gil spinning his wiry little body and cheering with an energy that promised to see him through the day despite his years. With a half laugh, Jillian settled her hat firmly on her head and went to join them, lariat in hand.

Calves streaked like terriers back into the cow pen. Dust flew. Cows bullied their way through the line for a reunion with their offspring. Men ran them back with shouts, brute force, or ropes. Men might be outnumbered and outweighed, but the cattle were no match for Western ingenuity.

Gil singled a calf out in the cow pen, roped it, and dragged it to him, cursing all the way. With a swat on the flank, he sent it into the calf corral, then squinted at Jillian.

"Fence repaired?" she asked briefly.

"Yep."

"I'll see to the rest myself." She paused, then swung her lariat. "I'm going to want to talk to you later, Gil."

He removed his hat, swiped the sweat off his brow with the arm of his dusty shirt, then perched it on his head again. "When you're ready." He glanced around as Jillian pulled in a calf. "Just about done—time to gang up on 'em."

So saying, he joined the line of men who closed in on the unruly cows to drive the last of them into their proper place. Inside the smaller corral calves bawled and crowded together.

"It isn't pleasant," Jillian muttered to them. "But it'll be quick."

The gate creaked as it was swung across to hold them in. The rest wasn't a business she cared for, though she never would've admitted it to anyone but herself. Knife and needle and iron were used with precision, with a rhythm that started off uneven, then gained fluidity and speed. Calves came through the chute one at a time, dreaming of liberation, only to be hoisted onto the calf table.

She watched the next calf roll his big eyes in astonishment as the table tilted, leaving him helpless on his side, as high as a man's waist. Then he was dealt with as any calf is at a roundup.

It was hot, dirty work. There was a smell of sweat, blood, smoking hide and medicine. Throughout the steady action reminiscences could be heard—stories no one would believe and everyone tried to top. Cows surged in the wire pen; their babies squealed at the bite of needle or knife. The language grew as steamy as the air in the pen.

It wasn't Jillian's first branding, and yet each one— for all the sweat and blood—made her remember why she was here instead of on one of the wide busy streets back east. It was hard work, but honest. It took a special brand of person to do it. The cattle milling and calling in the corral were hers. Just as the land was. She relieved a man at the table and began her turn at the vaccinations.

The sun rose higher, heading toward afternoon before the last calf was released. When it was done, the men were hungry, the calves exhausted and bawling pitifully for their mothers.

Hot and hungry herself, Jillian sat on a handy crate and wiped the grime from her face. Her shirt stuck to her with patches of wet cutting through the dirt. That was only the first hundred, she thought as she arched her back. They wouldn't finish with the spring brandings until the end of that week or into the next. She waited until nearly all the men had made their way toward the cookhouse before she signaled to Gil. He plucked two beers out of a cooler and went to join her.

"Thanks." Jillian twisted off the cap, then let the cold, yeasty taste wash away some of the dust. "Murdock's going to check the rest of the line himself," she began without preamble. "Tell me straight—" she held the bottle to her brow a moment, enjoying the chill "—is he the kind of man who'd play this sort of game?"

"What do you think?" he countered.

What could she think? Jillian asked herself. No matter how hard she tried, her feelings kept getting in the way. Feelings she'd yet to understand because she didn't dare. "I'm asking you."

"Kid's got class," Gil said briefly. "Now, the old man…" He grinned a bit, then squinted into the sun. "Well, he might've done something of the sort years back, just for devilment. Give your grandpaw something to swear about. But the kid—don't strike me like his devilment runs that way. Another thing…" He spit tobacco and shifted his weight. "I did a head count in the pasture this morning. Might be a few off, seeing as they were spread out and scattered during roundup."

Jillian took another swig from the bottle, then set it aside. "But?"

"Looked to me like we were light an easy hundred."

"A hundred?" she repeated in a whisper of shock. "That many cattle aren't going to stray through a break in the fence, not on their own."

"Boys got back midway through the branding. Only rounded up a dozen on Murdock land."

"I see." She let out a long breath. "Then it doesn't look like the wire was cut for mischief, does it?"

"Nope."

"I want an accurate head count in the morning, down to the last calf. Start with the west pasture." She looked down at her hands. They were filthy. Her fingers ached. It was as innate in her to work for what was hers as it was to fight for it. "Gil, the chances are pretty good that someone on the Murdock payroll's rustling our cattle, maybe for the Double M, but more likely for themselves."

He tugged on his ear. "Maybe."

"Or, it's one of our own."

He met her eyes calmly. He'd wondered if that would occur to her. "Just as likely," he said simply. "Murdock might find his numbers light, too."

"I want that head count by sundown tomorrow." She rose to face him. "Pick men you're sure of, no one that's been here less than a season. Men who know how to keep their thoughts to themselves."

He nodded, understanding the need for discretion. Rustling wasn't any less deadly a foe than it had been a century before. "You gonna work with Murdock on this?"

"If I have to." She remembered the fury on his face—something she recognized as angry pride. She had plenty of that herself. The sigh came before she could prevent it and spoke of weariness. "Go get something to eat."

"You coming?"

"No." She walked back to Delilah and hefted the saddle. Mechanically she began to hook cinches and tighten them. In the corral the cattle were beginning to calm.

When she'd finished, Gil tapped her on the shoulder.

Turning her head, she saw him hold out a thick biscuit crammed with meat.

"You eat this, damn it," he said gruffly. "You're going to blow away in a high wind if you keep it up."

Accepting the biscuit, she took a huge bite. "You mangy old dog," she muttered with her mouth full. Then, because no one was around to see and razz him, she kissed both his cheeks. Though it pleased him, he cursed her for it and made her laugh as she vaulted into the saddle.

Jillian trotted the mare out of the ranch yard, then, turning toward solitude, rode her hard.

To satisfy her own curiosity, she headed for the west pasture first. Riding slowly now, she checked the repaired fence, then began to count the cattle still grazing. It didn't take long for her to conclude that Gil's estimate had been very close to the mark. A hundred head. Closing her eyes, she tried to think calmly.

The winter had only cost her twenty—that was something every rancher had to deal with. But it hadn't been nature who'd taken these cows from her. She had to find out who, and quickly, before the losses continued. Jillian glanced over the boundary line. On both sides cattle grazed placidly, at peace now that man had left them to their own pursuits. As far as she could see there was nothing but rolling grass and the cattle growing sleek on it. A hundred head, she thought again. Enough to put a small but appreciable dent in her herd—and her profit. She wasn't going to sit still for it.

Grimly she sent Delilah into a gallop. She couldn't afford the luxury of panicking. She'd have to take it step by step, ascertaining a firm and accurate account of her losses before she went to the authorities. But for now she was tired, dirty and discouraged. The best thing to do was to take care of that before she went back to the ranch.

It had been only a week since she'd last ridden out to the pond, but even in that short time the aspen and cottonwood were greener. She could see hints of bitterroot and of the wild roses that were lovely and so destructive when they sprang up in the pastures. The sun was beginning its gradual decline westward. Jillian judged it to be somewhere between one and two. She'd give herself an hour here to recharge before she went back to begin the painstaking job of checking and rechecking the number of cattle in her books, and their locations. Dismounting, she tethered her mare to a branch of an aspen and let her graze.

Carelessly Jillian tossed her hat aside, then sat on a rock to pull off her boots. As her jeans and shirt followed she listened to the sound of a warbler singing importantly of spring and sunshine. Black-eyed Susans were springing up at the edge of the grass.

The water was deliciously cool. When she lowered herself into it, she could forget about the aches in her muscles, the faint, dull pain in her lower back, and the sense of despair that had followed her out of the west pasture. As owner and boss of Utopia, she'd deal with what needed to be dealt with. For now, she needed to be only Jillian. It was spring, the sun was warm. If the breeze was right, she could smell the young roses. Dipping her head back, she let the water flow over her face and hair.

Aaron didn't ask himself how he'd known she'd be there. He didn't ask himself why knowing it, he'd come. Both he and the stallion remained still as he watched her.

She didn't splash around but simply drifted quietly so that the water made soft lapping sounds that didn't disturb the birdsong. He thought he could see the fatigue drain from her. It was the first time he'd seen her completely relaxed without the light of adventure or temper or even laughter in her eyes. This was something she did for herself, and though he knew he intruded, he stayed where he was.

Her skin was milky pale where the sun hadn't touched it. Beneath the rippling water, he could see the slender curves of her body. Her hair clung to her head and shoulders and burned like fire. So did the need that started low in his stomach and spread through his blood.

Did she know how exquisite she was with that long, limber body and creamy skin? Did she know how seductive she looked with that mass of chestnut hair sleek around a face that held both delicacy and strength? No, he thought as she sank beneath the surface, she wouldn't know—wouldn't allow herself to know. Perhaps it was time he showed her. With the slightest of signals, he walked Samson to a tree on his side of the boundary.

Jillian surfaced and found herself looking directly up into Aaron's eyes. Her first shock gave way to annoyance and annoyance to outrage when she remembered her disadvantage. Aaron saw all three emotions. His lips twitched.

"What're you doing here?" she demanded. She knew she could do nothing about modesty and didn't attempt to. Instead she relied on bravado.

"How's the water?" Aaron asked easily. Another woman, he mused, would've made some frantic and useless attempt to conceal herself. Not Jillian. She just tossed up her chin.

"It's cold. Now, why don't you go back to wherever you came from so I can finish what I'm doing."

"It was a long, dusty morning." He sat on a rock near the edge of the pool and smiled companionably. Like Jillian's, his clothes and skin were streaked with grime and sweat. The signs of hard work and effort suited him. Aaron tilted back his hat. "Looks inviting."

"I was here first," she said between her teeth. "If you had any sense of decency, you'd go away."

"Yep." He bent over and pulled off his boots.

Jillian watched first one then the other hit the grass. "What the hell do you think you're doing?"

"Thought I'd take a dip." He gave her an engaging grin as he tossed his hat aside.

"Think again."

He rose, and his brow lifted slowly as he unbuttoned his shirt. "I'm on my own land," he pointed out. He tossed the shirt aside so that Jillian had an unwanted and fascinating view of a hard, lean torso with brown skin stretched tight over the rib cage and a dark vee of hair that trailed down to the low-slung waist of his jeans.

"Damn you, Murdock," she muttered, and judged the distance to her own clothes. Too far to be any use.

"Relax," he suggested, enjoying himself. "We can pretend there's wire strung clean down the middle." With this he unhooked his belt.

His eyes stayed on hers. Jillian's first instinct to look away was overruled by the amusement she saw there. Coolly she watched him strip. If she had to swallow, she did it quietly.

Damn, did he have to be so beautiful? she asked herself and kept well to her own side as he slid into the water. The ripples his body made spread out to tease her own skin. Shivering, she sank a little deeper.

"You're really getting a kick out of this, aren't you?"

Aaron gave a long sigh as the water rinsed away dust and cooled his blood. "Have to admit I am. View from in here's no different from the one I had out there," he reminded her easily. "And I'd already given some thought to what you'd look like without your clothes. Most redheads have freckles."

"I'm just lucky, I guess." Her dimple flickered briefly. At least they were on equal ground again. "You're built like most cowboys," she told him in a drawl. "Lots of leg, no hips." She let her arms float lazily. "I've seen better," she lied. Laughing, she tilted her head and let her legs come up, unable to resist the urge to tease him.

He had only to reach out to grab her ankle and drag her to him. Aaron rubbed his itchy palm on his thigh and relaxed. "You make a habit of skinny-dipping up here?"

"No one comes here." Tossing the hair out of her eyes, she shot him a look. "Or no one did. If you're going to start using the pond regularly, we'll have to work out some kind of schedule."

"I don't mind the company." He drifted closer so that his body brushed the imaginary line.

"Keep to your own side, Murdock," she warned softly, but smiled. "Trespassers still get shot these days." To show her lack of concern, she closed her eyes and floated. "I like to come here on Sunday afternoons, when the men are in the ranch yard, pitching horseshoes and swapping lies."

Aaron studied her face. No, he'd never seen her this relaxed. He wondered if she realized just how little space she gave herself. "Don't you like to swap lies?"

"Men tend to remember I'm a woman on Sunday afternoons. Having me around puts a censor on the—ah, kind of lies."

"They only remember on Sunday afternoons?"

"It's easy to forget the way a person's built when you're out on the range or shoveling out stalls."

He let his eyes skim down the length of her, covered by only a few inches of water. "You say so," he murmured.

"And they need time to complain." With another laugh, she let her legs sink. "About the food, the pay, the work. Hard to do all that when the boss is there." She spun her hand just under the surface and sent the water waving all the way to the edge. He thought it was the first purely frivolous gesture he'd ever seen her make. "Your men complain, Murdock?"

"You should've heard them when my sister decided to fix up the bunkhouse six or seven years back." The memory made him grin. "Seems she thought the place needed some pretty paint and curtains—gingham curtains, baby-blue paint."

"Oh, my God." Jillian tried to imagine what her crew's reaction would be if they were faced with gingham. Throwing back her head, she laughed until her sides ached. "What did they do?"

"They refused to wash anything, sweep anything, or throw anything away. In two weeks' time the place looked like the county dump—smelled like it, too."

"Why'd your father let her do it?" Jillian asked, wiping her eyes.

"She looks like my mother," Aaron said simply.

Nodding, she sighed from the effort of laughing. "But they got rid of the curtains."

"I—let's say they disappeared one night," he amended.

Jillian gave him a swift appraising look. "You took them down and burned them."

"If I haven't admitted that in seven years, I'm not going to admit it now. It took damned near a week to get that place cleared out," he remembered. She was smiling at him in such an easy, friendly way it took all his willpower not to reach over and pull her to his side. "Did you do the orphan today?"

"Earmarked, vaccinated and branded," Jillian returned, trailing her hands through the water again.

"Is that all?"

She grinned, knowing his meaning. "In a couple of years Baby's going to be giving his poppa some competition." She shrugged, so that her body shifted and the water lapped close at the curve of her breast. The less she seemed concerned about her body, the more he became fascinated by it. "I have a feeling about him," she continued. "No use making a steer out of a potential breeder." A cloud of worry came into her eyes. "I rode the west fence before I came up here. I didn't see any more breaks."

"There weren't any more." He'd known they had to discuss it, but it annoyed him to have the few moments of simple camaraderie interrupted. He couldn't remember sharing that sort of simplicity with a woman before. "My men rounded up six cows that had strayed to your side. Seemed like you had about twice that many on mine."

She hesitated a moment, worrying her bottom lip. "Then your count balances?"

He heard the tension in her voice and narrowed his eyes. "Seems to. Why?"

She kept her eyes level and expressionless. "I'm a good hundred head short."

"Hundred?" He'd grabbed her arm before he realized it. "A hundred head? Are you sure?"

"As sure as I can be until we count again and go over the books. But we're short, I'm sure of that."

He stared at her as his thoughts ran along the same path hers had. That many cows didn't stray on their own. "I'll do a count of my own herd in the morning, but I can tell you, I'd know if I had that much extra cattle in my pasture."

"I'm sure you would. I don't think that's where they are."

Aaron reached up to touch her cheek. "I'd like to help you—if you need some extra hands. We can take the plane up. Maybe they wandered in the other direction."

She felt something soften inside her that shouldn't have. A simple offer of help when she needed it—and his hand was gentle on her face. "I appreciate it," Jillian began unsteadily. "But I don't think the cattle wandered any more than you do."

"No." He combed the hair away from her face. "I'll go with you to the sheriff."

Unused to unselfish support, she stared at him. Neither was aware that they were both drifting to the line, and each other. "No—I...it isn't necessary, I can deal with it."

"You don't have to deal with it alone." How was it he'd never noticed how fragile she was? he wondered. Her eyes were so young, so vulnerable. The curve of her cheek was so delicate. He ran his thumb over it and felt her tremble. Somehow his hand was at her lower back, bringing her closer. "Jillian…" But he didn't have the words, only the needs. His mouth came to hers gently.

Her hands ran up his back, skimming up wet, cool skin. Her lips parted softly under his. The tip of his tongue ran lazily around the inside of her mouth, stopping to tease hers. Jillian relaxed against him, content for the long, moist kiss to go on and on. She couldn't remember ever feeling so pliant, so much in tune with another's movements and wishes. His lips grew warmer and heated hers. Against her own, she could feel his heartbeat—quick and steady. His mouth left hers only long enough to change the angle before he began to slowly deepen the kiss.

It happened so gradually she had no defense. It was an emptiness that started in her stomach like a hunger, then spread until it was an ache to be loved. Her body yearned for it. Her heart began to tell her he was the one she could share herself with, not without risk, not without pain, but with something she'd almost forgotten to ask for: hope.

But when her mind started to cloud, she struggled to clear it. It wasn't sharing, she told herself even as his lips slanted over hers to persuade her. It was giving, and if she gave she could lose. Only a fool would forget the boundary line that stood between them.

She pulled out of his hold and stared at him. Was she mad? Making love to a Murdock when her fence had been cut and a hundred of her cows were missing? Was she so weak that a gentle touch, a tender kiss, made her forget her responsibilities and obligations?

"I told you to stay on your own side," she said unsteadily. "I meant it." Turning away, she cut through the water and scrambled up the bank.

Breathing fast, Aaron watched her. She'd been so soft, so giving in his arms. He'd never wanted a woman more—never felt just that way. It came like a blow that she was the first who'd really mattered, and the first to throw his own emotion back in his face. Grimly he swam back to his own side.

"You're one tough lady, aren't you?"

Jillian heard the water lap as he pulled himself from it. Without bothering to shake it out, she dragged on her dusty shirt. "That's right. God knows why I was fool enough to think I could trust you." Why did she want so badly to weep when she never wept? she wondered and buttoned her shirt with shaky fingers. "All that talk about helping me, just so you could get what you wanted." Keeping her back to him, she pulled up her brief panties.

Aaron's hands paused on the snap of his jeans. Rage and frustration tumbled through him so quickly he didn't think he'd be able to control it. "Be careful, Jillian."

She whirled around, eyes brilliant, breasts heaving. "Don't you tell me what to do. You've been clear right from the beginning about what you wanted."

Muscles tense, he laid a hand on the saddle of his stallion. "That's right."

The calm answer only filled her with more fury. "I might've respected your honesty if it wasn't for the fact that I've got a cut fence and missing cattle. Things like that didn't happen when you were in Billings waiting for your father to—" She cut herself off, appalled at what she'd been about to say. Whatever apology she might have made was swallowed at the murderous look he sent her.

"Waiting for him to what?" Aaron said softly—too softly.

The ripple of fear made her lift her chin. "That's for you to answer."

He knew he didn't dare go near her. If he did she might not come out whole. His fingers tightened on the rope that hung on his saddle. "Then you'd better keep your thoughts to yourself."

She'd have given half her spread to have been able to take those hateful, spiteful words back. But they'd been said. "And you keep your hands to yourself," she said evenly. "I want you to stay away from me and mine. I don't need soft words, Murdock. I don't want them from you or anyone. You're a damn sight easier to take without the pretense." She stalked away to grab at her jeans.

He acted swiftly. He didn't think. His mind was still reeling from her words—words that had stung because he'd never felt or shown that kind of tenderness to another woman. What had flowed through him in the pond had been much more than a physical need and complex enough to allow him to be hurt for the first time by a woman.

Jillian gave out a gasp of astonishment as the circle of rope slipped around her, snapping snugly just about her waist and pinning her arms above the elbows. Whirling on her heel, she grabbed at the line. "What the hell do you think you're doing?"

With a jerk, Aaron brought her stumbling forward. "What I should've done a week ago." His eyes were nearly black with fury as she fell helplessly against him. "You won't get any more soft words out of me."

She struggled impotently against the rope, but her

eyes were defiant and fearless. "You're going to pay for this, Murdock."

He didn't doubt it, but at that moment he didn't give a damn. Gathering her wet hair in one hand, he dragged her closer. "By God," he muttered. "I think it'll be worth it. You make a man ache, Jillian, in the middle of the night when he should have some peace. One minute you're so damn soft, and the next you're snarling. Since you can't make up your mind, I'll do it for you."

His mouth came down on hers so that she could taste enraged desire. She fought against it even as it found some answering chord in her. His chest was still naked, still wet, so that her shirt soaked up the moisture. The air rippled against her bare legs as he scooped them out from under her. With her mouth still imprisoned by his, she found herself lying on the sun-warmed grass beneath him. Her fury didn't leave room for panic.

She squirmed under him, kicking and straining against the rope, cursing him when he released her mouth to savage her neck. But an oath ended on a moan when his mouth came back to hers. He nipped into her full bottom lip as if to draw out passion. Her movements beneath him altered in tone from protest to demand, but neither of them noticed. Jillian only knew her body was on fire, and that this time she'd submit to it no matter what the cost.

He was drowning in her. He'd forgotten about the rope, forgotten his anger and his hurt. All he knew was that she was warm and slender beneath him and that her mouth was enough to drive a man over the line of reason. Nothing about her was calm. Her lips were avid and seeking; her fingers dug into his waist. He could feel the thunder of her heart race to match his. When she caught his lip between her teeth and drew it into her mouth, he groaned and let her have her way.

Jillian flew with the sensations. The grass rubbed against her legs as she shifted them to allow him more intimacy. His hair smelled of the water that ran from it onto her skin. She tasted it, and the light flavor of salt and flesh when she pressed her lips to his throat. Her name shivered in a desperate whisper against her ear. No soft words. There was nothing soft, nothing gentle about what they brought to each other now. This was a raw, primitive passion that she understood even as it was tapped for the first time. She felt his fingers skim down her shirt, releasing buttons so that he could find her. But it was his mouth not his hand that closed over the taut peak, hot and greedy. The need erupted and shattered her.

Lips, teeth and tongue were busy on her flesh as she lay dazed from the first swift, unexpected crest. While she fought to catch her breath, Aaron tugged on her shirt to remove it, cursing when it remained tight at her waist. In an urgent move his hand swept down. His fingers touched rope. He froze, his breath heaving in his lungs.

Good God, what was he doing? Squeezing his eyes tight, he fought for reason. His face was nuzzled in the slender valley between her breasts so that he could feel as well as hear the frantic beat of her heart.

He was about to force himself on a helpless woman. No matter what the provocation, there could be no absolution for what he was on the edge of doing. Cursing himself, Aaron tugged on the rope, then yanked it over her head. After he'd tossed it aside, he looked down at her.

Her mouth was swollen from his. Her eyes were nearly closed and so clouded he couldn't read them. She lay so still he could feel each separate tremor from her body. He wanted her badly enough to beg. "You can make me pay now," he said softly and rolled from her onto his back.

She didn't move, but looked up into the calm blue sky while needs churned inside her. The warbler was still singing, the roses still blooming.

Yes, she could make him pay—she'd recognized the look of self-disgust in his eyes. She had only to get up and walk away to do it. She'd never considered herself a fool. Deliberately she rolled over on top of him. Aaron automatically put his hands on her arms to steady her. Their eyes met so that desire stared into desire.

"You'll pay—if you don't finish what you've started." Diving her hands into his hair, she brought her mouth down on his.

Her shirt fluttered open so that her naked skin slid over his. Jillian felt his groan of pleasure every bit as clearly as she heard it. Then it was all speed and fire, so fast, so hot, there wasn't time for thought. Tasting, feeling was enough as they raced over each other in a frenzy of demand. Her shirt fell away just before she pulled at the snap of his jeans.

She tugged them down, then lost herself in the long lean line of his hips. Her fingers found a narrow raised scar that ran six inches down the bone. She felt a ripple of pain as if her own skin had been rent. Then he was struggling out of his jeans and the feel of him, hot and ready against her, drove everything else out of her mind. But when she reached for him, he shifted so she was beneath him again.

"Aaron…" What she would have demanded ended in a helpless moan as he slid a finger under the elastic riding high on her thigh. With a clever, thorough touch of fingertips he brought her to a racking climax.

She was pulsing all over, inside and out. No longer was she aware that she clung to him, her hands bringing him as much torturous pleasure as his brought her. She only knew that her need built and was met time and time again while he held off that last, that ultimate fulfillment. With eyes dazed with passion, she watched his mouth come toward hers again. Their lips met—he plunged into her, swallowing her gasps.

For a long time she lay spent. The sky overhead was still calm. With her hands on Aaron's shoulders, she could feel each labored breath. There seemed to be no peace for them even in the aftermath of passion. Was this the way it was supposed to be? she wondered. She'd known nothing like this before. Needs that hurt and remained unsettled even after they'd been satisfied. She still wanted him—that moment when her body was hot and trembling from their merging.

After all the years she'd been so careful to distance herself from any chance of an involvement, she found herself needing a man she hardly knew. A man she'd been schooled to distrust. Yet she did trust him…that's what frightened her most of all. She had no reason to— no logical reason. He'd made her forget her ambitions, her work, her responsibilities, and reminded her that beneath it all, she was first a woman. More, he'd made her glory in it.

Aaron raised his head slowly, for the first time in his memory unsure of himself. She'd gotten to a place inside him no one had ever touched. He realized he didn't want her to walk away and leave it empty again—and that he'd never be able to hold her unless she was willing. "Jillian..." He brushed her damp, tangled hair from her cheek. "This was supposed to be easy. Why isn't it?"

"I don't know." She held onto the weakness another moment, bringing his cheek down to hers so that she could draw in his scent and remember. "I need to think."

"About what?"

She closed her eyes a moment and shook her head. "I don't know. Let me go now, Aaron."

His fingers tightened in her hair. "For how long?"

"I don't know that either. I need some time."

It would be easy to keep her—for the moment. He had only to lower his mouth to hers again. He remembered the wild mustang—the hell he'd gone through to catch it, the hell he'd gone through to set it free. Saying nothing, he released her.

They dressed in silence—both of them too battered by feelings they'd never tried to put into words. When Jillian reached for her hat, Aaron took her arm.

"If I told you this meant something to me, more than I'd expected, maybe more than I'd wanted, would you believe me?"

Jillian moistened her lips. "I do now. I have to be sure I do tomorrow."

Aaron picked up his own hat and shaded his face with it. "I'll wait—but I won't wait long." Lifting a hand, he cupped her chin. "If you don't come to me, I'll come after you."

She ignored the little thrill of excitement that rushed up her spine. "If I don't come to you, you won't be able to come after me." Turning away, she untied her mare and vaulted into the saddle. Aaron slipped his hand under the bridle and gave her one long look.

"Don't bet on it," he said quietly. He walked back over the boundary line to his own mount.

Chapter 7

If you don't come to me, I'll come after you.

They weren't words Jillian would forget. She hadn't yet decided what to do about them—any more than she'd decided what to do about what had happened between her and Aaron. There'd been more than passion in that fiery afternoon at the pond, more than pleasure, however intense. Perhaps she could have faced the passion and the pleasure, but it was the something more that kept her awake at nights.

If she went to him, what would she be going to? A man she'd yet to scratch the surface of—an affair that promised to have more hills and valleys than she knew how to negotiate. The risk—she was beginning to understand the risk too well. If she relaxed her hands on the reins this time, she'd tumble into love before she could regain control. That was difficult for her to admit, and impossible for her to understand.

She'd always believed that people fell in love because they wanted to, because they were looking for, or were ready for, romance. Certainly she'd been ready for it once before, open for all those soft feelings and heightened emotions. Yet now, when she believed she was on the border of love again, she was neither ready for it, nor was she experiencing any soft feelings. Aaron Murdock didn't ask for them—and in not asking, he demanded so much more.

If she went to him…could she balance her responsibilities, her ambitions, with the needs he drew out of her? When she was in his arms she didn't think of the ranch, or her position there that she had to struggle every day to maintain.

If she fell in love with him…could she deal with the imbalance of feelings between them and cope when the time came for him to go his own way? She never doubted he would. Other than Clay, there'd never been a man who'd remained constant to her.

Indecision tore at her, as it would in a woman accustomed to following her own route in her own way.

And while her personal life was in turmoil, her professional one fared no better. Five hundred of her cattle were missing. There was no longer any doubt that her herd had been systematically and successfully rustled.

Jillian hung up the phone, rubbing at the headache that drummed behind her temples.

"Well?" Hat in lap, Joe Carlson sat on the other side of her desk.

"They can't deliver the plane until the end of the week." Grimly she set her jaw as she looked over at him.

"It hardly matters now. Unless they're fools, they've got the cattle well away by this time. Probably transported them over the border into Wyoming."

He studied the brim of his neat Stetson. "Maybe not, that would make it federal."

"It's what I'd do," she murmured. "You can't hide five hundred head of prime beef." Rising, she dragged her hands through her hair. *Five hundred.* The words continued to flash in her mind—a sign of failure, impotence, vulnerability. "Well, the sheriff's doing what he can, but they've got the jump on us, Joe. There's nothing I can do." On a sound of frustration, she balled her fists. "I hate being helpless."

"Jillian…" Joe ran the brim of his hat through his hands, frowning down at it another moment. During his silence she could hear the old clock on her grandfather's desk tick the time away. "I wouldn't feel right if I didn't bring it up," he said at length and looked back at her. "It wouldn't be too difficult to hide five hundred head if they were scattered through a few thousand."

Her eyes chilled. "Why don't you speak plainly, Joe?"

He rose. After more than six months on Utopia, he still looked more businessman than outdoorsman. And she understood it was the businessman who spoke now. "Jillian, you can't just ignore the fact that the west boundary line was cut. That pasture leads directly onto Murdock land."

"I know where it leads," she said coolly. "Just as I know I need more than a cut line to accuse anyone, particularly the Murdocks, of rustling."

Joe opened his mouth to speak again, met her uncompromising look, then shut it. "Okay."

The simplicity of his answer only fanned her temper.

And her doubts. "Aaron told me he was going to take a thorough head count. He'd know if there were fifty extra head on his spread, much less five hundred."

It was her tone much more than her words that told him where the land lay now. "I know."

Jillian stared at him. His eyes were steady and compassionate. "Damn it, he doesn't need to steal cattle from me."

"Jillian, you lose five hundred head now and your profit dwindles down to nothing. Lose that much again, half that much again, and…you might have to start thinking about selling off some of your pasture. There're other reasons than the price per head for rustling."

She spun around, shutting her eyes tight. She'd thought of that—and hated herself for it. "He would've asked me if he wanted to buy my land."

"Maybe, but your answer would've been no. Rumor is he was going to start his own place a few years back. He didn't—but that doesn't mean he's content to make do with what his father has."

She couldn't contradict him, not on anything he'd said. But she couldn't live with it either. "Leave the investigating to the sheriff, Joe. That's his job."

He drew very straight and very stiff at the clipped tone of her voice. "All right. I guess I better get back to mine."

On a wave of frustration and guilt, she turned before he reached the door. "Joe—I'm sorry. I know you're only thinking about Utopia."

"I'm thinking about you, too."

"I appreciate it, I really do." She picked up her worn leather work glove from the desk and ran it through her hands. "I have to handle this my own way, and I need a little more time to decide just what that is."

"Okay." He put his hat on and lowered the brim with his finger. "Just so you know you've got support if you need it."

"I won't forget it."

When he'd gone, Jillian stopped in the center of the office. God, she wanted so badly to panic. Just to throw up her hands and tell whoever'd listen that she couldn't deal with it. There had to be someone else, somewhere, who could take over and see her through until everything was back in order. But she wasn't allowed to panic, or to turn over her responsibilities even for a minute. The land was hers, and all that went with it.

Jillian picked up her hat and her other glove. There was work to be done. If they cleaned her out down to the last hundred head, there would still be work to be done, and a way to build things back up again. She had the land, and her grandfather's legacy of determination.

Even as she opened the front door to go out, she saw Karen Murdock drive up in front of the house. Surprised, Jillian hesitated, then went out on the porch to meet her.

"Hello, I hope you don't mind that I just dropped by."

"No, of course not." Jillian smiled, marveling for the second time at the soft, elegant looks of Aaron's mother. "It's nice to see you again, Mrs. Murdock."

"I've caught you at a bad time," she said, glancing down at the work gloves in Jillian's hand.

"No." Jillian stuck the gloves in her back pocket. "Would you like some coffee?"

"I'd love it."

Karen followed Jillian into the house, glancing around idly as they walked toward the kitchen. "Lord, it's been years since I've been in here. I used to visit your grandmother," she said with a rueful smile. "Of course your grandfather and Paul both knew, but we were all very careful not to mention it. How do you feel about old feuds, Jillian?"

There was a laugh in her voice that might have set Jillian's back up at one time. Now it simply nudged a smile from her. "Not precisely the same way I felt a few weeks ago."

"I'm glad to hear it." Karen took a seat at the kitchen table while Jillian began to brew a fresh pot of coffee. "I realize Paul said some things the other day that were bound to rub you the wrong way. I have to confess he does some of it on purpose. Your reaction was the high point of his day."

Jillian smiled a little as she looked over her shoulder. "Maybe he's more like Clay than I'd imagined."

"They were out of the same mold. There aren't many of them," she murmured. "Jillian—we've heard about your missing cattle. I can't tell you how badly I feel. I realize the words *if there's anything I can do* sound empty, but I mean them."

Turning back to the coffeepot, Jillian managed to shrug. She wasn't sure she could deal easily with sympathy right then. "It's a risk we all take. The sheriff's doing what he can."

"A risk we all take," Karen agreed. "When it happens to one of us, all of us feel it." She hesitated a moment, knowing the ground was delicate. "Jillian, Aaron mentioned the cut line to me, though he's kept it from his father."

"I'm not worried about the cut line," Jillian told her

quietly. "I know Aaron didn't have any part in it—I'm not a fool."

No, Karen thought, studying the clean-lined profile. *A fool you're not.* "He's very concerned about you."

"He needn't be." She swung open a cupboard door for cups. "It's my problem, I have to deal with it."

Karen watched calmly as Jillian poured. "No support accepted?"

With a sigh, Jillian turned around. "I don't mean to be rude, Mrs. Murdock. Running a ranch is a difficult, chancy business. When you're a woman you double those stakes." Bringing the coffee to the table, she sat across from her. "I have to be twice as good as a man would be in my place because this is still a man's world. I can't afford to cave in."

"I understand that." Karen sipped and glanced around the room. "There's no one here you have to prove anything to."

Jillian looked up from her own cup and saw the compassion, and the unique bond one woman can have with another. As she did, the tight band of control loosened. "I'm so scared," she whispered. "Most of the time I don't dare admit it to myself because there's so much riding on this year. I've taken a lot of gambles—if they pay off... Five hundred head." She let out a long breath as the numbers pounded in her mind. "It won't put me under, I can't let it put me under, but it's going to take a long time to recover."

Reaching out, Karen covered her hand with her own. "They could be found."

"You know the chances of that now." For a moment she sat still, accepting the comfort of the touch before she put her hand back on her cup. "Whichever way it goes, I'm still boss at Utopia. I have a responsibility to make what was passed on to me work. Clay trusted me with what was his. I'm going to make it work."

Karen gave her a long, thorough look very much like one of her son's. "For Clay or for yourself?"

"For both of us," Jillian told her. "I owe him for the land, and for what he taught me."

"You can put too much of yourself into this land," Karen said abruptly. "Paul would swear I'd taken leave of my senses if he heard me say so, but it's true. Aaron—" She smiled, indulgent, proud. "He's a great deal like his father, but he doesn't have Paul's rigidity. Perhaps he hasn't needed it. You can't let the land swallow you, Jillian."

"It's all I have."

"You don't mean that. Oh, you think you do," she murmured when Jillian said nothing. "But if you lost every acre of this land tomorrow, you'd make something else. You've the guts for it. I recognize it in you just as I've always seen it in Aaron."

"He had other options." Agitated, Jillian rose to pour coffee she no longer wanted.

"You're thinking of the oil." For a moment Karen said nothing as she weighed the pros and cons of what she was going to say. "He did that for me—and for his father," she said at length. "I hope I don't ever have to ask anything like that of him again."

Jillian came back to the table but didn't sit. "I don't understand."

"Paul was wrong. He's a good man and his mistakes have always been made with the same force and vigor as he does everything." A smile flickered on her lips, but her eyes were serious. "He'd promised something to

Aaron, something that had been understood since Aaron
was a boy. The Double M would be his, if he'd earned
it. By God, he did," she whispered. "I think you understand what I mean."

"Yes." Jillian looked down at her cup, then set it
down. "Yes, I do."

"When Aaron came back from college, Paul wasn't
ready to let go. That's when Aaron agreed to work it
his father's way for three years. He was to take over as
manager after that—with full authority."

"I've heard," Jillian began, then changed her tack. "It
can't be easy for a man to give up what he's worked for,
even to his own son."

"It was time for Paul to give," Karen told her, but she
held her head high. "Perhaps he would have if…" She
gestured with her hands as though she were slowing
herself down. "When he refused to stick to the bargain,
Aaron was furious. They had a terrible argument—the
kind that's inevitable between two strong, self-willed
men. Aaron was determined to go down to Wyoming,
buy some land for himself, and start from scratch. As
much as he loved the ranch, I think it was something
he'd been itching to do in any case."

"But he didn't."

"No." Karen's eyes were very clear. "Because I asked
him not to. The doctors had just diagnosed Paul as ter-
minal. They'd given him two years at the outside. He
was infuriated that age had caught up with him, that his
body was betraying him. He's a very proud man, Jillian. He'd beaten everything he'd ever gone up against."

She remembered the hawklike gaze and trembling
hands. "I'm sorry."

"He didn't want anyone to know, not even Aaron. I

can count the times I've gone against Paul on one hand." She glanced down at her own palms. Something in her expression told Jillian very clearly that if the woman had acquiesced over the years, it had been because of strength and not weakness. "I knew if Aaron went away like that, Paul would stop fighting for whatever time he had left. And then Aaron, once he knew, would never be able to live with it. So I told him." She let out a long sigh and turned her hands over. "I asked him to give up what he wanted. He went to Billings, and though I'm sure he's always thought he did it for me, I know he did it for his father. I don't imagine the doctors would agree, but Aaron gave his father five years."

Jillian turned away as her throat began to ache. "I've said some horrible things to him."

"You wouldn't be the first, I'm sure. Aaron knew what it would look like. He's never given a damn what people think of him. What most people think," she corrected softly.

"I can't apologize," Jillian said as she fought to control herself. "He'd be furious if I told him I knew."

"You know him well."

"I don't," Jillian returned with sudden passion. "I don't know him, I don't understand him, and—" She cut herself off, amazed that she was about to bare her soul to Aaron's mother.

"I'm his mother," Karen said, interpreting the look. "But I'm still a woman. And one who understands very well what it is to have feelings for a man that promise to lead to difficulties." This time she didn't weigh her words but spoke freely. "I was barely twenty when I met Paul, he was past forty. His friends thought he was mad and that I wanted his money." She laughed, then sat back with a little sigh. "I can promise you, I didn't see the humor in it thirty years ago. I'm not here to offer advice on whatever's between you and Aaron, but to offer support if you'll take it."

Jillian looked at her—the enduring beauty, the strength that showed in her eyes, the kindness. "I'm not sure I know how."

Rising, Karen placed her hands on Jillian's shoulders. So young, she thought wistfully. So dead set. "Do you know how to accept friendship?"

Jillian smiled and touched Karen's hands, still resting on her shoulders. "Yes."

"That'll do. You're busy," she said briskly, giving Jillian a quick squeeze before she released her. "But if you need a woman, as we sometimes do, call me."

"I will. Thank you."

Karen shook her head. "No, it's not all unselfish. I've lived over thirty years in this man's world." Briefly she touched Jillian's cheek. "I miss my daughter."

Aaron stood on the porch and watched the moon rise. The night was so still he heard the whisk of a hawk's wings over his head before it dove after its night prey. In one hand he held a can of iced beer that he sipped occasionally, though he wasn't registering the taste. It was one of those warm spring nights when you could taste the scent of the flowers and smell the hint of summer, which was creeping closer.

He'd be damned if he'd wait much longer.

It had been a week since he'd touched her. Every night after the long, dusty day was over, he found himself aching to have her with him, to fill that emptiness inside him he'd become so suddenly aware of. It was difficult enough to have discovered he didn't want Jillian in the same way he'd wanted any other woman, but to have discovered his own vulnerabilities...

She could hurt him—had hurt him. That was a first, Aaron thought grimly and lifted his beer. He hadn't yet worked out how to prevent it from happening again. But that didn't stop him from wanting her.

She didn't trust him. Though he'd once agreed that he didn't want her to, Aaron had learned that was a lie. He wanted her to give him her trust—to believe in him enough to share her problems with him. She must be going through hell now, he thought as his fingers tightened on the can. But she wouldn't come to him, wouldn't let him help. Maybe it was about time he did something about that—whether she liked it or not.

Abruptly impatient, angry, he started toward the steps. The sound of an approaching car reached him before the headlights did. Glancing toward the sound, he watched the twin beams cut through the darkness. His initial disinterest became a tension he felt in his shoulder and stomach muscles.

Aaron set the half-empty beer on the porch rail as Jillian pulled up in front of his house. Whatever his needs were, he still had enough sense of self-preservation to prevent himself from just rushing down the stairs and grabbing her. He waited.

She'd been so sure her nerves would calm during the drive over. It was difficult for her, as a woman who simply didn't permit herself to be nervous, to deal with a jumpy stomach and dry throat. Not once since his mother had left her that morning had Aaron been out of her thoughts. Yet Jillian had gone through an agony of doubt before she'd made the final decision to come.

In coming, she was giving him something she'd never intended to—a portion of her private self.

With the moon at her back she stood by her car a moment, looking up at him. Perhaps because her legs weren't as strong as they should've been, she kept her chin high as she walked up the porch steps.

"This is a mistake," she told him.

Aaron remained where he was, one shoulder leaning against the rail post. "Is it?"

"It's going to complicate things at a time when my life's complicated enough."

His stomach had twisted into a mass of knots that were only tugging tighter as he looked at her. She was pale, but there wasn't a hint of a tremor in her voice. "You took your sweet time coming here," he said mildly, but he folded his fingers into his palm to keep from touching her.

"I wouldn't have come at all if I could've stopped myself."

"That so?" It was more of an admission than he'd expected. The first muscles began to relax. "Well, since you're here, why don't you come a little closer?"

He wasn't going to make it easy for her, Jillian realized. And she'd have detested herself if she'd let him. With her eyes on his, she stepped forward until their bodies brushed. "Is this close enough?"

His eyes skimmed her face, then he smiled. "No."

Jillian hooked her hands behind his head and pressed her lips to his. "Now?"

"Closer." He allowed himself to touch her—one hand at the small of her back rode slowly up to grip her hair. His eyes glittered in the moonlight, touched with triumph, amusement, and passion. "A damn sight closer, Jillian."

Her eyes stayed open as she fit her body more intimately to his. She felt the answering response of his muscles against her own, the echoing thud of his heart. "If we get much closer out here on the porch," she murmured with her mouth a whisper from his, "we're going to be illegal."

"Yeah." He traced her bottom lip, moistening it, and felt her little jerk of breath on his tongue. "I'll post bond if you're worried."

Her lips throbbed from the expert flick of his tongue. "Shut up, Murdock," she muttered and crushed her mouth to his. Jillian let all the passions, all the emotions that had been chasing her around for days, have their way. Even as they sprang out of her, they consumed her. Mindlessly she pressed against him so that he was caught between her body and the post.

The thrill of pleasure was so intense it almost sliced through his skin. Aaron's arm came around her so that he could cup the back of her head and keep that wildly aggressive mouth on his own. Then, swiftly, his arm scooped under her knees and lifted her off her feet.

"Aaron—" Her protest was smothered by another ruthless kiss before he walked across the porch to the door. Though she admired the way he could swing the screen open, and slam the heavy door with his arms full, she laughed. "Aaron, put me down. I can walk."

"Don't see how when I'm carrying you," he pointed out as he started up the narrow steps to the second floor.

"Is this the sort of thing you do to express male dominance?"

She was rewarded with a narrow-eyed glare and smiled sweetly.

"No," Aaron said in mild tones. "This is the sort of thing I do to express romance. Now, when I want to express male dominance…" As he drew near the top of the steps he shifted her quickly so that she hung over his shoulder.

After the initial shock Jillian had to acknowledge a hit. "Had that one coming," she admitted, blowing the hair out of her face. "I think my point was that I wasn't looking for romance or dominance."

Aaron's brow lifted as he walked into the bedroom. The words had been light enough, but he'd caught the sincerity of tone. Slowly he drew her down so that before her feet had touched the floor every angle of her body had rubbed against his. Weakened by the maneuver, she stared up at him with eyes already stormy with desire. "Don't you like romance, Jillian?"

"That's not what I'm asking for," she managed, reaching for him.

He grabbed her wrists, holding her off. "That's too bad, then." Very lightly he nipped at her ear. "You'll just have to put up with it. Do you reckon straight passion's safer?"

"As anything could be with you." She caught her breath as his tongue traced down the side of her throat.

Aaron laughed, then began lazily, determinedly, to seduce her with his mouth alone. "This right here," he murmured, nibbling at a point just above her collar. "So soft, so delicate. A man could almost forget there're places like this on you until he finds them for himself. You throw up that damn-the-devil chin and it's tempting to give it one good clip, but then—" he tilted his head to a new angle and his lips skimmed along her skin "—right under it's just like silk."

He tugged with his teeth at the cord of her neck and felt her arms go boneless. That's what he wanted, he thought with rising excitement. To have her melting and pliant and out of control, if only for a few minutes. Hot blood and fire were rewards in themselves, but this time, perhaps only this time, he wanted the satisfaction of knowing he could make her as weak as she could make him.

He slanted his mouth over hers, teasing her tongue with the tip of his until her breath was short and shallow. Her pulse pounded into his palms. He was going to take his time undressing her, he thought. A long, leisurely time that would drive them both crazy.

Without hurry Aaron backed her toward the bed, then eased her down until she sat on the edge. In the moonlight he could see that her eyes had already misted with need, her skin softly flushed with it. Watching her, he ran a long finger down her throat to the first button on her shirt. His eyes remained steady as he undid it, then the second—then the third. He stopped there to move his hands down her, lightly over her breasts, the nipped waist, and narrow hips to the long, slender thighs. She was very still but for the quiver of her flesh.

Turning, he tucked her leg between his and began pulling off her boot. The first hit the floor, but when he took the other and tugged, Jillian gave him some assistance with a well-placed foot.

Surprised, he glanced back to see her shoot him a cocky smile. She recovered quickly, he thought. It would be all the more exciting to turn her to putty again. "You might do the same for me," Aaron suggested, then dropped on the bed, leaned back on his elbows, and held out a booted foot.

Jillian rose to oblige him and straddled his leg. This— the wicked grin, the reckless eyes—she knew how to deal with. It might light a fire in her, but it didn't bring on that uncontrollable softness. When she'd finally made her decision to come, she'd made it to come on equal terms, with no quiet promises or tender phrases that meant no more than the breath it took to make them. She'd told herself she wouldn't fall in love with him as long as she listened to her body and blocked off her heart.

The minute his second boot hit the floor, Aaron grabbed her around the waist and swung her back so that she fell onto the bed, laughing. "You're a tough guy, Murdock." Jillian hooked her arms around his neck and grinned up at him. "Always tossing women around."

"Bad habit of mine." Lowering his head, he nibbled idly at her lips, resisting her attempt to deepen the kiss. "I like your mouth," he murmured. "It's another of those soft, surprising places." Gently he sucked on her lower lip until he felt the hands at his neck grow lax.

The mists were closing in again and she forgot the ways and means to hold them off. This wasn't what she wanted…was it? Yet it seemed to be everything she wanted. Her mind was floating, out of her body, so that she could almost see herself lying languorous and pliant under Aaron. She could see the tension and anxieties of the past days drain out of her own face until it was soft and relaxed under the lazy touch of his mouth and tongue. She could feel her heartbeat drop to a light pace that wasn't quite steady but not yet frantic. Perhaps this was what it felt like to be pampered, to be prized. She wasn't sure, but knew she couldn't bear to lose the sensation. Her sigh came slowly with the release of doubts.

When he bent to whisper something foolish in her ear, she could smell his evening shower on him. His face was rough with the stubble of a long day, but she rubbed her cheek against it, enjoying the scrape. Then his lips grazed across the skin that was alive and tingling until they found their way back to hers.

She felt the brush of strong, clever fingers as they trailed down to release the last buttons of her shirt. Then they skimmed over her rib cage, lightly, effortlessly drawing her deeper into the realm of sensation. He barely touched her. The kisses remained soft, his hands gentle. All coherent thought spun away.

"My shirt's in the way," he murmured against her ear. "I want to feel you against me."

She lifted her hands, and though her fingers didn't fumble, she couldn't make them move quickly. It seemed like hours before she felt the press of his flesh against hers. With a sigh, she slid her hands up to his shoulders and back until she'd drawn the shirt away. The ridge of muscle was so hard. As she rubbed her palms over him, Jillian realized she'd only had flashes of impressions the first time they'd made love. Everything had been so fast and wild she hadn't been able to appreciate just how well he was formed.

Tight sinew, taut flesh. Aaron was a man used to using his back and his hands to do a day's work. She didn't stop to reason why that in itself was a pleasure to her. Then she could reason nothing because his mouth had begun to roam.

He hadn't known he could gain such complete satisfaction in thinking of another's pleasure. He wanted her—wanted her quick and fast and furious, and yet it was a heady feeling to know he had the power to make her weak with a touch.

The underside of her breast was so soft…and he lingered. The skin above the waistband of her jeans was white and smooth…and his hand was content to move just there. He felt her first trembles; they rippled under his lips and hands until his senses swam. Denim strained against denim until he pulled the jeans down over her hips to find her.

Jillian wasn't certain when the languor had become hunger. She arched against him, demanding, but he continued to move without haste. She couldn't understand his fascination with her body when she'd always considered it too straight, too slim and practical. Yet now he seemed anxious to touch, to taste every inch. And the murmurs that reached her whispered approval. His hand cupped her knee so that his fingers trailed over the sensitive back. Years of riding, walking, working, had made her legs strong, and very susceptible.

When his teeth scraped down her thigh, she cried out, stunned to be catapulted to the taut edge of the first peak. But he didn't allow her to go over. Not yet. His warm breath teased her, then the light play of his tongue. She felt the threat of explosion building, growing in power and depth. Yet somehow he knew the instant before it shattered her, and retreated. Again and again he took her to the verge and brought her back until she was weak and desperate.

Jillian shifted beneath Aaron, willing him to take anything, all that he wanted—not even aware that he'd removed the last barrier of clothing until he was once more lying full length on her. She felt each warm, unsteady breath on her face just before his lips raced over it.

"This time…" Aaron pulled air into his lungs so that he could speak. "This time you tell me—you tell me that you want me."

"Yes." She locked herself around him, shuddering with need. "Yes, I want you. Now."

Something flashed in his eyes. "Not just now," he said roughly and drove into her.

Jillian slid over the first edge and was blinded. But there was more, so much more.

Chapter 8

It was the scent of her hair that slowly brought him back to reason. His face was buried in it. The fragrance reminded him of the wildflowers his mother would sometimes gather and place in a little porcelain vase on a window ledge. It was tangled in his hands, and so soft against his skin he knew he'd be content to stay just as he was through the night.

She lay still beneath him, her breathing so quiet and even she might have been asleep. But when he turned his head to press his lips to her neck, her arms tightened around him. Lifting his head, he looked down at her.

Her eyes were nearly closed, heavy. He'd seen the shadows beneath them when she'd first walked toward him on the porch. With a small frown, Aaron traced his thumb over them. "You haven't been sleeping well."

Surprised by the statement, and his tone, she lifted

her brows. After where they'd just gone together, she might've expected him to say something foolish or arousing. Instead his brows had drawn together and his tone was disapproving. She wasn't sure why it made her want to laugh, but it did.

"I'm fine," she said with a smile.

"No." He cut her off and cupped her chin in his hand. "You're not."

She stared up, realizing how easy it would be to just pour out her thoughts and feelings. The worries, the fears, the problems that seemed to build up faster than she could cope with them—how reassuring it would be to say it all out loud, to him.

She'd done too much of that with his mother, but somehow Jillian could justify that. It was one thing to confess fears and doubts to another woman, and another to give a man an insight on your weaknesses. At dawn they'd both be ranchers again, with a boundary line between them that had stood for nearly a century.

"Aaron, I didn't come here to—"

"I know why you came," he interrupted. His voice was much milder than his eyes. "Because you couldn't stay away. I understand that. Now you're just going to have to accept what comes with it."

It was difficult to drum up a great deal of dignity when she was naked and warm beneath him, but she came close to succeeding. "Which is?"

The annoyance in his eyes lightened to amusement. "I like the way you say that—just like my third grade teacher."

Her lips quivered. "It's one of the few things I managed to pick up from my mother. But you haven't answered the question, Murdock."

"I'm crazy about you," he said suddenly and the mouth that had curved into a smile fell open. She wasn't ready to hear that one, Aaron mused. He wasn't sure he was ready for the consequences of it himself, and decided to play it light. "Of course, I've always been partial to nasty-tempered females. I mean to help you, Jillian." His eyes were abruptly sober. "If I have to climb over your back to do it."

"There isn't anything you can do even if I wanted you to."

He didn't comment immediately but shifted, pulling the pillows up against the headboard, then leaning back before he drew her against him. Jillian didn't stiffen as much as go still. There was something quietly possessive about the move, and irresistibly sweet. Before she could stop it, she'd relaxed against him.

Aaron felt the hesitation but didn't comment. When you went after trust, you did it slowly. "Tell me what's been done."

"Aaron, I don't want to bring you into this."

"I am in it, if for no other reason than that cut line."

She could accept that, and let her eyes close. "We did a full head count and came up five hundred short. As a precaution, we branded what calves were left right away. I estimate we lost fifty or sixty of them. The sheriff's been out."

"What'd he find?"

She moved her shoulders. "Can't tell where they took them out. If they'd cut any more wire, they'd fixed it. Very neat and tidy," she murmured, knowing something died inside her each time she thought of it. "It seems as though they didn't take them all at once, but skimmed a few head here and there."

"Seems odd they left the one line down."

"Maybe they didn't have time to fix it."

"Or maybe they wanted to throw your attention my way until they'd finished."

"Maybe." She turned her face into his shoulder—only slightly, only for an instant—but for Jillian it was a large step toward sharing. "Aaron, I didn't mean the things I said about you and your father."

"Forget it."

She tilted her head back and looked at him. "I can't."

He kissed her roughly. "Try harder," he suggested. "I heard you were getting a plane."

"Yes." She dropped her head on his shoulder and tried to order her thoughts. "It doesn't look like it's going to be ready until next week."

"Then we'll go up in mine tomorrow."

"But why—"

"Nothing against the sheriff," he said easily. "But you know your land better."

Jillian pressed her lips together. "Aaron, I don't want to be obligated to you. I don't know how to explain it, but—"

"Then don't." Taking hold of her hair, he jerked it until her face came up to his. "You're going to find I'm not the kind who'll always give a damn about what you want. You can fight me, sometimes you might even win. But you won't stop me."

Her eyes kindled. "Why do you gear me up for a fight when I'm trying to be grateful?"

In one swift move he shifted so that they lay crosswise across the bed. "Maybe I like you better that way. You're a hell of a lot more dangerous when you soften up."

She threw up her chin. "That's not something that's going to happen very often around you."

"Good," he said and crushed his mouth onto hers. "You'll stay with me tonight."

"I'm not—" Then he silenced her with a savage kiss that left no room for thought, much less words.

"Tonight," he said with a laugh that held more challenge than humor, "you stay with me."

And he took her in a fury that whispered of desperation.

The birds woke her. There was a short stretch of time during the summer when the sun rose early enough that the birds were up before her. With a sigh, Jillian snuggled into the pillow. She could always fool her system into thinking she'd been lazy when she woke to daylight and birdsong.

Groggily she went over the day's workload. She'd have to check Baby before she went in to the horses. He liked to have his bottle right off. With one luxurious stretch, she rolled over, then stared blankly around the room. Aaron's room. He'd won that battle.

Lying back for a moment, she thought about the night with a mixture of pleasure and discomfort. He'd said once before that it wasn't as easy as it should've been. But could he have any idea what it had done to her to lie beside him through the night? She'd never known the simple pleasure of sleeping with someone else, sharing warmth and quiet and darkness. What had made her believe that she could have an affair and remain practical about it?

But she wasn't in love with him. Jillian reached over to touch the side of the bed where he'd slept. She still had too much sense to let that happen. Her fingers dug into the sheet as she closed her eyes. Oh, God, she hoped she did.

The birdcalls distracted her so that she looked over at the window. The sun poured through. But it wasn't summer, Jillian remembered abruptly. What was she still doing in bed when the sun was up? Furious with herself, she sat up just as the door opened. Aaron walked in, carrying a mug of coffee.

"Too bad," he commented as he crossed to her. "I was looking forward to waking you up."

"I've got to get back," she said, tossing her hair from her eyes. "I should've been up hours ago."

Aaron held her in place effortlessly with a hand on her shoulder. "What you should do is sleep till noon," he corrected as he studied her face. "But you look better."

"I've got a ranch to run."

"And there isn't a ranch in the country that can't do without one person for one day." He sat down beside her and pushed the cup into her hand. "Drink your coffee."

She might've been annoyed by his peremptory order, but the scent of coffee was more persuasive. "What time is it?" she asked between sips.

"A bit after nine."

"Nine!" Her eyes grew comically wide. "Good God, I've got to get back."

Again Aaron held her in bed without effort. "You've got to drink your coffee," he corrected. "Then you've got to have some breakfast."

After a quick, abortive struggle, Jillian shot him an exasperated look. "Will you stop treating me as though I were eight years old?"

He glanced down to where she held the sheet absently at her breasts. "It's tempting," he agreed.

"Eyes front, Murdock," she ordered when her mouth twitched. "Look, I appreciate the service," Jillian continued, gesturing with her cup, "but I can't sit around until midday."

"When's the last time you had eight hours' sleep?" He watched the annoyance flicker into her eyes as she lifted the coffee again, sipping rather than answering. "You'd have had more than that last night if you hadn't—distracted me."

She lifted her brows. "Is that what I did?"

"Several times, as I recall." Something in her expression, a question, a hint of doubt, made him study her a bit more carefully. Was it possible a woman like her would need reassurance after the night they'd spent together? What a strange mixture of tough and vulnerable she was. Aaron bent over and brushed his lips over her brow, knowing what would happen if he allowed himself just one taste of her mouth. "Apparently, you don't have to try very hard," he murmured. His lips trailed down to her temple before he could prevent them. "If you'd like to take advantage of me..."

Jillian let out an unsteady breath. "I think—I'd better have pity on you this morning, Murdock."

"Well..." He hooked a finger under the sheet and began to draw it down. "Can't say I've ever cared much for pity."

"Aaron." Jillian tightened her hold on the sheet. "It's nine o'clock in the morning."

"Probably a bit past that by now."

When he started to lean closer, she lifted the mug and held it against his chest. "I've got stock to check and fences to ride," she reminded him. "And so do you."

He had a woman to protect, he thought, surprising

himself. But he had enough sense not to mention it to the woman. "Sometimes," he began, then gave her a friendly kiss, "you're just no fun, Jillian."

Laughing, she drained the coffee. "Why don't you get out of here so I can have a shower and get dressed?"

"See what I mean." But he rose. "I'll fix your breakfast," he told her, then continued before she could say it wasn't necessary. "And neither of us is riding fence today. We're going up in the plane."

"Aaron, you don't have to take the time away from your own ranch to do this."

He hooked his hands in his pockets and studied her for so long her brows drew together. "For a sharp woman, you can be amazingly slow. If it's easier for you, just remember that rustling is every rancher's business."

She could see he was annoyed; she could hear it in the sudden coolness of tone. "I don't understand you."

"No." He inclined his head in a gesture that might've been resignation or acceptance. "I can see that." He started for the door, and Jillian watched him, baffled.

"I..." What the devil did she want to say? "I have to drive over and let Gil know what I'm doing."

"I sent a man over earlier." Aaron paused at the door and turned back to her. "He knows you're with me."

"He knows—you sent—" She broke off, her fingers tightening on the handle of the mug. "You sent a man over to tell him I was here, this morning?"

"That's right."

She dragged a hand through her hair and sunlight shimmered gold at the ends. "Do you realize what that looks like?"

His eyes became very cool and remote. "It looks like

what it is. Sorry, I didn't realize you wanted an assignation."

"Aaron—" But he was already closing the door behind him. Jillian brought the mug back in a full swing and barely prevented herself from following through. With a sound of disgust, she set it down and pulled herself from bed. That had been clumsy of her, she berated herself. How was he to understand that it wasn't shame, but insecurity? Perhaps it was better if he didn't understand.

Aaron could cheerfully have strangled her. In the kitchen, he slapped a slice of ham into the skillet. His own fault, he thought as it began to sizzle. Damn it, it was his own fault. He'd had no business letting things get beyond what they were meant to. If he stretched things, he could say that she had a wary sort of affection for him. It was unlikely it would ever go beyond that. If his feelings had, he had only himself to blame, and himself to deal with.

Since when did he want fences around him? Aaron thought savagely as he plunged a kitchen fork into the grilling meat. Since when did he want more from a woman, any woman, than companionship, intelligence, and a warm bed? Maybe his feelings had slipped a bit past that, but he wasn't out of control yet.

Pouring coffee, he drank it hot and black. He'd been around too long to lose his head over a firebrand who didn't want anything more than a practical, uncomplicated affair. After all, he hadn't been looking for any more than that himself. He'd just let himself get caught up because of the problems she was facing, and the unwavering manner with which she faced them.

The coffee calmed him. Reassured, he pulled a carton of eggs out of the refrigerator. He'd help her as much as he could over the rustling, take her to bed as often as possible, and that would be that.

When she came into the room, he glanced over casually. Her hair was still wet, her face naked and glowing with health and a good night's sleep.

Oh, God, he was in love with her. And what the hell was he going to do?

The easy comment she'd been about to make about the smell of food vanished. Why was he staring at her as if he'd never seen her before? Uncharacteristically self-conscious, she shifted her weight. He looked as though someone had just knocked the wind from him. "Is something wrong?"

"What?"

His answer was so dazed she smiled. What in the world had he been thinking about when she'd interrupted him? she wondered. "I said, is something wrong? You look like you've just taken a quick fall from a tall horse."

He cursed himself and turned away. "Nothing. How do you want your eggs?"

"Over easy, thanks." She took a step toward him, then hesitated. It wasn't a simple matter for her to make an outward show of affection. She'd met with too many lukewarm receptions in her life. Drawing up her courage, she crossed the room and touched his shoulder. He stiffened. She withdrew. "Aaron…" How calm her voice was, she mused. But then, she'd grown very adept very early at concealing hurt. "I'm not very good at accepting support."

"I've noticed." He cracked an egg and let it slide into the pan.

She blinked because her eyes had filled. Stupid! she

railed at herself. *Never put your weaknesses on display.* Swallowing pride came hard to her, but there were times it was necessary. "What I'd like to say is that I appreciate what you're doing. I appreciate it very much."

Emotions were clawing him. He smacked another egg on the side of the pan. "Don't mention it."

She backed away. *What else did you expect?* she asked herself. *You've never been the kind of person who inspires tender feelings. You don't want to be.* "Fine," she said carelessly. "I won't." Moving to the coffeepot, she filled her mug again. "Aren't you eating?"

"I ate before." Aaron flipped the eggs, then reached for a plate.

She eyed his back with dislike. "I realize I'm keeping you from a lot of pressing matters. Why don't you just send me up with one of your men?"

"I said I'd take you." He piled her plate with food, then dropped it unceremoniously on the table.

Chin lifted, Jillian took her seat. "Suit yourself, Murdock."

He turned to see her hack a slice from the ham. "I always do." On impulse he grabbed the back of her head and covered her mouth in a long, ruthlessly thorough kiss that left them both simmering with anger and need.

When it was done, Jillian put all her concentration into keeping her hands steady. "A man should be more cautious," she said mildly as she cut another slice, "when a woman's holding a knife."

With a short laugh, he dropped into the chair across from her. "Caution doesn't seem to be something I hold on to well around you." Sipping his coffee, Aaron watched her as she worked her way systematically through the meal. Maybe it was too late to realize that intimacy between them had been a mistake, but if he could keep their relationship on its old footing otherwise, he might get his feelings back in line.

"You know, you should've bought a plane for Utopia years ago," he commented, perfectly aware that it would annoy her.

Her gaze lifted from her plate, slow and deliberate. "Is that so?"

"Only an idiot argues with progress."

Jillian tapped her fork against her empty plate. "What a fascinating statement," she said sweetly. "Do you have any other suggestions on how I might improve the running of Utopia?"

"As a matter of fact—" Aaron drained his coffee "—I could come up with several."

"Really." She set down the fork before she stabbed him with it. "Would you like me to tell you what you can do with each and every one of them?"

"Maybe later." He rose. "Let's get going. The day's half gone already."

Grinding her teeth, Jillian followed him out the back door. She thought it was a pity she'd wasted even a moment on gratitude.

The small two-seater plane gave her a bad moment. She eyed the propellers while Aaron checked the gauges before takeoff. She trusted things with four legs or four wheels. There, she felt, you had some control—a control she'd be relinquishing the moment Aaron took the plane off the ground. With a show of indifference, she hooked her seat belt while he started the engine.

"Ever been up in one of these?" he asked idly. He slipped on sunglasses before he started down the narrow paved runway.

"Of course I went up in the one I bought." She didn't mention the jitters that one ride had given her. As much as she hated to agree with him, a plane was a necessary part of ranch life in the late twentieth century.

The engine roared and the ground tilted away. She'd just have to get used to it, she reminded herself, since she was going to learn to fly herself. She let her hands lie loosely on her knees and ignored the rolling pitch of her stomach.

"Are you the only one who flies this?" *This tuna can with propellers,* she thought dismally.

"No, two of our men are licensed pilots. It isn't smart to have only one person who can handle a specific job."

She nodded. "Yes. I've had a man on the payroll for over a month who can fly, but I'm going to have to get a license myself."

He glanced over. "I could teach you." Aaron noticed that her fingers were moving back and forth rhythmically over her knees. Nerves, he realized with some surprise. She hid them very well. "These little jobs're small," he said idly. "But the beauty is maneuverability. You can set them down in a pasture if you have to and hardly disturb the cattle."

"They're very small," Jillian muttered.

"Look down," he suggested. "It's very big."

She did so because she wouldn't, for a moment, have let him know how badly she wanted to be safe on the ground. Oddly her stomach stopped jumping when she did. Her fingers relaxed.

The landscape rolled under them, green and fresh, with strips of brown and amber so neat and tidy they seemed laid out with a ruler. She saw the stream that ran through her property and his, winding blue. Cattle were clumps of black and brown and red. Two young foals frolicked in a pasture while adult horses sunned themselves and grazed. She saw men riding below. Now and again one would take off his hat and wave it in a salute. Aaron dipped his wings in answer. Laughing, Jillian looked farther, to the plains and isolated mountains.

"It's fabulous. God, sometimes I look at it and I can't believe it belongs to me."

"I know." He skimmed the border line and banked the plane over her land. "You can't get tired of looking at it, smelling it."

She rested her head against the window. He loves it as much as I do, she thought. Those five years in Billings must have eaten at him. Every time she thought of it, of the five years he'd given up, her admiration for him grew.

"Don't laugh," she told him and watched him glance over curiously. No, he wouldn't laugh, she realized. "When I was little—the first time I came out—I got a box and dug up a couple handfuls of pasture to take home with me. It didn't stay sweet for long, but it didn't matter."

Good God, sometimes she was so totally disarming it took his breath away. "How long did you keep it?"

"Until my mother found it and threw it away."

He had to bite back an angry remark on insensitivity and ignorance. "She didn't understand you," Aaron said instead.

"No, of course not." She gave a quick laugh at the idea. Who could've expected her to? "Look, that's Gil's truck." The idea of waving down to him distracted her so that she missed Aaron's smoldering look. He'd had some rocky times with his own father, some painful times, but he'd always been understood.

"Tell me about your family."

Jillian turned her head to look at him, not quite trusting the fact that she couldn't see his eyes through his tinted sunglasses. "No, not now." She looked back out the window. "I wish I knew what I was looking for," she murmured.

So do I, he thought grimly and banked down his frustration. It wasn't going to work, he decided. He wasn't going to be able to talk himself out of needing her, all of her, any time soon. "Maybe you'll know when you see it. Could you figure if they took more cattle from any specific section?"

"It seems the north section was the hardest hit. I can't figure out how it got by me. Five hundred head, right under my nose."

"You wouldn't be the first," he reminded her. "Or the last. If you were going to drive cattle out of your north section, where would you go with them?"

"If they weren't mine," she said dryly, "I suppose I'd load them up and get them over the border."

"Maybe." He wondered if his own idea would be any harder for her to take. "Packaged beef's a lot easier to transport than it is on the hoof."

Slowly she turned back to him. She'd thought of it herself—more than once. But every time she'd pushed it aside. The last fragile hope of recovering what was hers would be lost. "I know that." Her voice was calm, her eyes steady. "If that's what was done, there's still the matter of catching who did it. They're not going to get away with it."

Aaron grinned in pure admiration. "Okay. Then let's

think about it from this angle a minute. You've got the cattle—the cows are worth a lot more than the calves at this point, so maybe you're going to ship them off to greener pastures for a while. Unless we're dealing with a bunch of idiots, they're not going to slaughter a registered cow for the few hundred the calf would bring."

"A bunch of idiots couldn't have rustled my cattle," she said precisely.

"No." He nodded in simple agreement. "The steers, now…it might be a smart choice to pick out a quiet spot and butcher them. The meat would bring in some quick cash while you worked out the deal for the rest." He made a slight adjustment in course and headed north.

"If you were smarter still, you'd have already set up a deal for the cows and the yearlings," Jillian pointed out. "That accounts for nearly half of what I lost. If I were using a trailer, and slipping them out a few head at a time, I'd make use of one of the canyons in the mountains."

"Yeah. Thought we'd take a look."

Her euphoria was gone, though the landscape below was a rambling map of color and texture. The ground grew more uneven, with the asphalt two-lane road cutting through the twists and angles. The barren clump of mountain wasn't majestic like its brothers farther west, but sat alone, inhabited by coyotes and wildcats who preferred to keep man at a distance.

Aaron took the plane higher and circled. Jillian looked down at jagged peaks and flat-bottomed canyons. Yes, if she had butchering in mind, no place made better sense. Then she saw the vultures, and her heart sank down to her stomach.

"I'm going to set her down," Aaron said simply.

Jillian said nothing but began to check off her options if they found what she thought they would. There were a few economies she could and would have to make before winter, even after the livestock auction at the end of the summer. The old Jeep would simply have to be repaired again instead of being replaced. There were two foals she could sell and keep her books in the black. Checks and balances, she thought as the plane bumped on the ground. Nothing personal.

Aaron shut off the engine. "Why don't you wait here while I take a look?"

"My cattle," she said simply and climbed out of the plane.

The ground was hard and dusty from the lack of rain. She could smell its faintly metallic odor, so unlike the scent of grass and animals that permeated her own land. With no trees for shade, the sun beat down hard and bright. She heard the flap of a vulture's wings as one circled in and settled on a ridge.

It wasn't difficult going over the low rocky ground through the break in the mountain. No problem at all for a four-wheel drive, she thought and angled the brim of her hat to compensate for the glare of sunlight.

The canyon wasn't large and was cupped between three walls of rock, worn gray with some stubborn sage clinging here and there. Their boots made echoing hollow sounds. From somewhere, surprisingly, she heard a faint tinkling of water. The spring must be small, she mused, or she'd smell it. All she smelled here was...

She stopped and let out a long breath. "Oh, God."

Aaron recognized the odor, sickeningly hot and sweet, even as she did. "Jillian—"

She shook her head. There was no longer room for comfort or hope. "Damn. I wonder how many."

They walked on and saw, behind a rock, the bones a coyote had dug up and picked clean.

Aaron swore in a low soft stream that was all the more pungent in its control. "There's a shovel in the plane," he began. "We can see what's here, or go back for the sheriff."

"It's my business." Jillian wiped her damp hands on her jeans. "I'd rather know now."

He knew better than to suggest she wait at the plane again. In her place, he'd have done precisely what she was ready to do. Without another word, he left her alone.

When she heard his footsteps die away, she squeezed her eyes tight, doubled her hands into fists. She wanted to scream out the useless, impotent rage. What was hers had been stolen, slaughtered, and sold. There could be no restitution now, no bringing back this part of what she'd worked for. Slowly, painfully, she brought herself under tight control. No restitution, but she'd have justice. Sometimes it was just a cleaner word for revenge.

When Aaron returned with the shovel, he saw the anger glittering in her eyes. He preferred it to that brief glimpse of despair he'd seen. "Let's just make sure. After we know, we go into town for the sheriff."

She agreed with a nod. If they found one hide, it would be one too many. The shovel bit into the ground with a thud.

Aaron didn't have to dig long. He glanced up at Jillian to see her face perfectly composed, then uncovered the first stack of hides. Though the stench was vile, she crouched down and made out the *U* of her brand.

"Well, this should be proof enough," she murmured

and stayed where she was because she wanted to drop her head to her knees and weep. "How many—"

"Let the sheriff deal with it," Aaron bit off, as infuriated by their find as he would have been if the hide had borne his own brand. With an oath, he scraped the shovel across the loosened dirt and dislodged something.

Jillian reached down and picked it up. The glove was filthy, but the leather was quality—the kind any cowhand would need for working with the wire. A bubble of excitement rose in her. "One of them must've lost it when they were burying these." She sprang to her feet, holding the glove in both hands. "Oh, they're going to pay for it," she said savagely. "This is one mistake they're going to pay for. Most of my hands score their initials on the inside." Ignoring the grime, she turned the bottom of the glove over and found them.

Aaron watched her color drain as she stared at the inside flap of the glove. Her fingers whitened against the leather before she lifted her eyes to his. Without a word, she handed it to him. Watching her, he took the soiled leather in his hand, then glanced down. There were initials inside. His own.

His face was expressionless when he looked back at her. "Well," he said coolly, "it looks like we're back to square one, doesn't it?" He passed the glove back to her. "You'll need this for the sheriff."

She sent him a look of smoldering anger that cut straight through him. "Do you think I'm stupid enough to believe you had anything to do with this?" Spinning around, she stalked away before he had a chance to understand, much less react. Then he stood where he was for another instant as it struck him, forcibly.

He caught her before she had clambered over the last

rocks leading out of the canyon. His hands weren't gentle as he whirled her around, his breath wasn't steady.

"Maybe I do." She jerked away only to have him grab her again. "Maybe I want you to tell me why you don't."

"I might believe a lot of things of you, I might not like everything I believe. But not this." Her voice broke and she fought to even it. "Integrity—integrity isn't something that has to be polite. You wouldn't cut my lines and you wouldn't butcher my cattle."

Her words alone would've shaken him, but he saw her eyes were swimming with tears. What he knew about comforting a woman could be said in one sentence: get out of the way. Aaron held on to her and lifted a hand to her cheek. "Jillian…"

"No! For God's sake, don't be kind now." She tried to turn away, only to find herself held close, her face buried against his shoulder. His body was like a solid wall of support and understanding. If she leaned against it now, what would she do when he removed it? "Aaron, don't do this." But her hands clutched at him as he held on.

"I've got to do something," he murmured, stroking her hair. "Lean on me for a minute. It won't hurt you."

But it did. She'd always found tears a painful experience. There was no stopping them, so she wept with the passion they both understood while he held her near the barren mountain under the strong light of the sun.

Chapter 9

Jillian didn't have time to grieve over her losses. Over two hundred hides had been unearthed from the canyon floor, all bearing the Utopia brand. She'd had interviews with the sheriff, talked to the Cattlemen's Association and dealt with the visits and calls from neighboring ranchers. After her single bout of weeping, her despair had iced over to a frigid rage she found much more useful. It carried her through each day, pushing her to work just that much harder, helping her not to break down when she was faced with sympathetic words.

For two weeks she knew there was little talk of anything else, on her ranch or for miles around. There hadn't been a rustling of this size in thirty years. It became easier for her when the talk began to die down, though it became equally more difficult to go on believing that the investigation would yield fruit. She had accepted the loss of her cattle because she had no choice, but she couldn't accept the total victory of the thieves.

They were clever—she had to admit it. They'd pulled off a rustling as smooth as anything the old-timers in the area claimed to remember. The cut wire, Aaron's glove; deliberate and subtle "mistakes" that were designed to turn her attention toward Murdock land. Perhaps the first of them had worked well enough to give the rustlers just enough extra time to cover their tracks. Jillian's only comfort was that she hadn't fallen for the second.

Aaron had given her no choice but to accept his support. She'd balked, particularly after recovering from her lapse in the canyon, but he'd proven to be every bit as obstinate as she. He'd taken her to the sheriff himself, stood by her with the Cattlemen's Association, and one evening had come by to drag her forty miles to a movie. Through it all he wasn't gentle with her, didn't pamper. For that more than anything else, Jillian felt she owed him. Kindness left her no defense and edged her back toward despair.

As the days passed, Jillian forced herself to take each one of them separately. She could fill the hours with dozens of tasks and worries and responsibilities. Then there wouldn't be time to mourn. For now, her first concern was the breeding of her mare with Aaron's stallion.

He'd brought two of his own men with him. With Gil and another of Jillian's hands, they would hold the restraining ropes on the stallion. Once he caught the scent of Jillian's mare in heat, he'd be as wild as his father had been, and as dangerous.

When Jillian brought Delilah into the paddock, she cast a look at the stallion surrounded by men. A gorgeous creature, she thought, wholly male—not quite tamed. Her gaze flicked over to Aaron, who stood at the horse's head.

His dark hair sprang from under his hat to curl carelessly over his neck and ears. His body was erect and lean. One might look at him and think he was perfectly relaxed. But Jillian saw more—the coiled tension beneath, the power that was always there and came out unexpectedly. Eyes nearly as dark as his hair were half hidden by the brim of his hat as he both soothed and controlled his stallion.

No mount could've suited him more. Her lover, she realized with the peculiar little jolt that always accompanied the thought. Would her nerves ever stop skidding along whenever she remembered what it was like to be with him—or imagined what it would be like to be with him again? He'd opened up so many places inside of her. When she was alone, it came close to frightening her; when she saw him, her feelings had nothing to do with fear.

Maybe it was the thick, heavy air that threatened rain or the half-nervous, half-impatient quiverings of her mare, but Jillian's heart was already pounding. The horses caught each other's scent.

Samson plunged and began to fight against the ropes. With his head thrown back, his mane flowing, he called the mare. One of the men cursed in reflex. Jillian tightened her grip on Delilah's bridle as the mare began to struggle—against the restraint or against the inevitable, Jillian would never be sure. She soothed her with words that weren't even heard. Samson gave a long, passionate whinny that was answered. Delilah reared, nearly ripping the bridle from Jillian's hand. Watching the struggle and flying hooves, Aaron felt his heart leap into his throat.

"Help her hold the mare," he ordered.

"No." Jillian fought for new purchase and got it. "She doesn't trust anyone but me. Let's get it done." A long line of sweat held her shirt to her back.

The stallion was wild, plunging and straining, his coat glossy with sweat, his eyes fierce. With five men surrounding him, he reared back, hanging poised and magnificent for a heartbeat before he mounted the mare.

The horses were beyond any thought, any fear, any respect for the humans now. Instinct drove them, primitive and consuming. Jillian forgot her aching arms and the rivulets of sweat that poured down her sides. Her feet were planted, her leg muscles taut as she pitted all her strength toward keeping the mare from bolting or rearing and injuring herself.

She was caught up in the fire and desperation of the horses, and the elemental beauty. The air was ripe with the scent of sweat and animal passion. She couldn't breathe but that she drew it in. Since she'd been a child she'd seen animals breed, helped with the matings whenever necessary, but now, for the first time, she understood the consuming force that drove them. The need of a woman for a man could be equally unrestrained, equally primitive.

Then it began to rain, slowly, heavily, coolly over her skin. With her face lifted to the mare's, Jillian let it flow over her cheeks. Another of the men swore as the ropes grew wet and slippery.

When her eyes met Aaron's, she found her heart was still in her throat, the beat as lurching and uneven as the mare's would be. She felt the flash of need that was both shocking and basic. He saw and recognized. As the rain poured over him, he smiled. Her thigh muscles went lax so quickly she had to fight to strengthen them again and maintain her control of the mare. But she didn't look away. Excitement was nearly painful, knowledge enervating. As if his hands were on her, she felt the need pulse from him.

Gradually a softer feeling drifted in. There was a strange sensation of being safe even though the safety was circled with dangers. This time she didn't question it or fight against it. They were helping to create new life. Now there was a bond between them.

The horses' sides were heaving when they drew them apart. The rain continued to sluice down. She heard Gil give a cackle of laughter over something one of the men said under his breath. Jillian forgot them, giving her full attention to the mare. Soothing and murmuring, she walked her back into the stables.

The light was dim, the air heavy with the scent of dry hay and oiled leather. After removing the bridle, Jillian began to groom the mare with long slow strokes until the quivering stopped.

"There now, love." Jillian nuzzled her face into Delilah's neck. "There's not much any of us can do about their bodies."

"Is that how you look at it?"

Jillian turned her head to see Aaron standing at the entrance to the stall. He was drenched and apparently unconcerned about it. She saw his eyes make a short but very thorough scan of her face—a habit he'd developed since their discovery in the canyon. She knew he looked for signs of strain and somewhere along the line had stopped resenting it.

"I'm not a horse," she returned easily and patted Delilah's neck.

Aaron came into the stall and ran his hands over the mare himself. She was dry and still. "She all right?"

"Mmmm. We were right not to field breed them," she added. "Both of them are spirited enough to have done damage." Laughing, she turned to him. "The foal's going to be a champion. I can feel it. There was something special out there just now, something important." On impulse, she threw her arms around Aaron's neck and kissed him ardently.

Surprise held him very still. His hands came to her waist more in instinct than response. It was the first time she'd given him any spontaneous show of affection or offered him any part of herself without reluctance. The ache of need wove through him, throbbing with what he now understood was connected to passion but not exclusive of it.

She was still smiling when she drew away, but he wasn't. Before the puzzlement over what was in his eyes had fully registered with her, Aaron drew her back against him and just held on. Jillian found the unexpected sweetness disconcerting and wonderful.

"Hadn't you better see to Samson?" she murmured.

"My men have already taken him back."

She rubbed her cheek against his wet shirt. They'd steal some time, she thought. An hour, a moment—just some time. "I'll fix you some coffee."

"Yeah." He slipped an arm around her shoulders as they went back into the rain. "Heard anything from the sheriff?"

"Nothing new."

They crossed the ranch yard together, both too accustomed to the elements to heed the rain as anything but necessary.

"It's got the whole county in an uproar."

"I know." They paused at the kitchen door to rid themselves of muddy boots. Jillian ran a careless hand through her hair and scattered rain. "It might do more good than anything else. Every rancher I know or've heard of in this part of Montana's got his eyes open. And any number over the border, from what I'm told. I'm toying with offering a reward."

"Not a bad idea." Aaron sat down at the table and stretched out long legs as Jillian brewed coffee. The rain was a constant soothing sound against the roof and windows. He found an odd comfort there in the gloomy light, in the warm kitchen. It might be like this if it were their ranch they were in rather than hers, or his. It might be like this if he could ever make her a permanent part of his life.

It took only a second for the thoughts to go through his head, and another for him to be jolted by them. Marriage. He was thinking marriage. He sat for a moment while the idea settled over him, not uncomfortably but inevitably. *I'll be damned,* he thought and nearly laughed before he brought himself back to what she'd been saying.

"Let me do it," he said briskly. She turned, words of refusal on the tip of her tongue. "Wait," Aaron ordered. "Hear me out. My father got wind of the cut wire." He watched her subside before she turned away for mugs. "Obviously it didn't set well with him. These old stories between the Murdocks and Barons don't need much fanning to come to life again. Some people are going to think, even if they don't say, that he's eating your beef."

Jillian poured the coffee, then turned with a mug in each hand. "I don't think it."

"I know." He gave her an odd look, holding out a hand. She placed a mug in it, but Aaron set it down on the table and lightly took her fingers. "That means a great deal to me." Because she didn't know how to respond to that tone, she didn't respond at all but only continued to look down at him. "Jillian, this has set him back some. A few years ago the idea of people thinking he'd done something unethical or illegal would probably have pleased him. He's not as strong as he was. Your grandfather was a rival, but he was also a contemporary, someone he understood, even respected. It would help if he could do something. I don't like to ask for favors any more than you like to accept them."

She looked down at their joined hands, both tanned, both lean and strong, yet hers was so easily swallowed up by his. "You love him very much."

"Yes." It was said very simply, in the same emotionless tone he'd used to tell her his father was dying. This time Jillian understood him better.

"I'd appreciate it if you'd stake the reward."

He laced his fingers with hers. "Good."

"Want some more coffee?"

"No." That wicked light of humor shot into his eyes. "But I was thinking I should help you out of those wet clothes."

With a laugh, Jillian sat down. "You know I'm still planning on beating out the Double M on July Fourth."

"I was hoping you were planning on it," Aaron returned easily. "But about doing it…"

"You a gambling man, Murdock?"

He lifted his brow. "It's been said."

"I've got fifty that says my Hereford bull will take the blue ribbon over anything you have to put against him."

Aaron contemplated the dregs of his coffee as if considering. If everything he'd heard about Jillian's bull was true, he was tolerably sure he was throwing money away. "Fifty," he agreed and smiled. "And another fifty that says I beat your time in the calf roping."

"My pleasure." Jillian held out a hand to seal it.

"Are you competing in anything else?"

"I don't think so." She stretched her back, thinking what a luxury it was to sit stone still in the middle of the afternoon. "The barrel racing doesn't much interest me and I know better than to try bronc riding."

"Know better?"

"Two reasons. First the men would do a lot of muttering and complaining if I did. And second—" she grinned and shrugged "—I'd probably break my neck."

It occurred to him that she wouldn't have admitted the second to him even a week before. Laughing, he leaned over and kissed her. But the friendly kiss stirred something, and cupping the back of her neck, he kissed her again, lingeringly. "It's your mouth," he murmured while his fingertips toyed with her skin. "Once I get started on it, I can't find a single reason to stop."

Her breath fluttered unevenly through her lips, through his. "It's the middle of the day."

He smiled, then teased her tongue with the tip of his. "Yeah. Are you going to take me to bed?"

The eyes that were nearly closed opened again. In them he saw desire and confusion, a combination he found very much to his liking. "I have to check the—" His teeth nipped persuasively into her bottom lip.

"The what?" he whispered as her words ended on a little shiver.

"The, uh…" His lips were skimming over hers in something much more provocative than a kiss. The lazy caress of his tongue kept them moist. His fingers were very light on the back of her neck. Their knees were brushing. Somehow she could already feel the press of his body against hers and the issuing warmth the pressure always brought. "I can't think," she murmured.

It was what he wanted. Or he wanted her to think of him and only him. For himself, he needed to know that she put him first this time, or at least her need for him. Over her ranch, her men, her cattle, her ambitions. If he could draw her feelings out to match his once, he might be able to do so again and again until she was as rashly in love with him as he was with her. "Why do you have to?" he asked and, rising, drew her to her feet. "You can feel."

Yes, with her arms around him and her head cradled against his chest, she could feel. Emotions nudging at her, urging her to acknowledge them—needs, pressing and searingly urgent, demanding that she fulfill them. They were all connected to him, the hungers, the tiny fears, the wishes. She couldn't deny them all. Perhaps, just this once, she didn't need to.

"I want to make love with you." She sighed with the words and nuzzled closer. "I can't seem to stop wanting to."

He tilted her head back so that he could see her face, then, half smiling, skimmed his thumb over her jaw. "In the middle of the day?"

She tossed the hair out of her eyes and settled her

linked hands comfortably behind his neck. "I'm going to have you now, Murdock. Right now."

He glanced at the tidy kitchen table and his grin was wicked. "Right now?"

"Your mind takes some unusual turns," she commented. "I think I can give you time enough to get upstairs." Releasing him, she walked over and flicked off the coffeepot. "If you hurry." Even as he grinned, she crossed back to him. Putting her hands on his shoulders, she leaped up, locking her legs around his waist, her arms around his neck. "You know where the stairs are?"

"I can find them."

She pressed her lips to his throat. "Top of the stairs, second door on the right," she told him as she began to please herself with his taste.

As Aaron wound through the house Jillian wondered what he would think or say if he knew she'd never done anything quite like this before. She'd come to realize that the man from her youth hadn't been a lover, but an incident. It took more than one night to make a lover. She'd feel much too foolish telling Aaron he was the first— much too inadequate. How could she tell him that the first rush of passion had loosened the locks she'd put on parts of herself? How could she trust her own feelings when they were so muddled and new?

She rested her head on his shoulder a moment and closed her eyes. For once in her life she was going to enjoy without worrying about the consequences. Shifting, she leaned back so that she could smile at him. "You're out of shape, Murdock. One flight of stairs and your heart's pounding."

"So's yours," he pointed out. "And you had a ride up."

"Must be the rain," she said loftily.

"Your clothes're still damp." He moved into the room she'd directed him to and glanced around briefly.

It was consistent with her style—understated femininity, practicality. It was a room without frills or pastels, but he'd have known it for a woman's. It had none of the feminine disorder of his sister's old room at the ranch, nor the subtle elegance of his mother's. Like the woman he still held, Aaron found the room unique.

Plain walls, plain floors, easy colors, no clutter. No, Jillian wasn't a woman to clutter her life. She wouldn't give herself the time. Perhaps it was the few indulgences she'd allowed herself that gave him the most insight.

A stoneware vase with fluted edges held pussy willow—soft brown nubs that wouldn't quite be considered a flower. There was a small carved box on her dresser he was certain would play some soft tune when the top was lifted. She might lift it sometimes when she was alone, or lonely. On the wall was a watercolor with all the bleeding passion of sunset. How carefully, how painstakingly, he thought, she'd controlled whatever romanticism she was prone to. How surprised she'd be to know that because she did, it only shouted out louder.

Recognizing his survey, Jillian cocked her head. "There's not a lot to see in here."

"You'd be surprised," he murmured.

The enigmatic answer made her glance around herself. "I don't spend a lot of time in here," she began, realizing it was rather sparse even compared to his room in the white frame house.

"You misunderstood me." Aaron let his hands run up her sides as she slid down. "I'd've known this was your room. It even smells like you."

She laughed, pleased without knowing why. "Are you being poetic?"

"Maybe."

Lifting a hand, she toyed with the top button of his shirt. "Want me to help you out of those wet clothes?"

"Absolutely."

She began to oblige him, then shot him an amused look as she slid the shirt over his shoulders. "If you expect me to seduce you, you're going to be disappointed."

His stomach muscles were already knotted with need. "I am?"

"I don't know any tricks." Before he could comment, she launched herself at him, overbalancing him so that they tumbled back onto the bed. "No wiles," she continued. "No subtlety."

"You're a pushy lady, all right." He could feel the heat of her body through her damp shirt.

"I like the way you look, Murdock." She trailed her fingers through his thick dark hair as she studied his face. "It used to annoy the hell out of me, but now it's kind of nice."

"The way I look?"

"That I like the way you look. It's ruthless," she decided, skimming a finger down his jawline. "And when you smile it can be very charming—the kind of charm a smart woman recognizes as highly dangerous."

He grinned, cupping her hips in his hands. "Did you?"

"I'm a smart woman." With a little laugh, she rubbed her nose against his. "I know a rattlesnake when I see one."

"But not enough to keep your distance."

"Apparently not—then I don't always look for a long, safe ride."

But a short, rocky one, he thought as her lips came down to his. He'd be happy to give her the wisps of danger and trouble, he decided, drawing her closer. But she was going to find out he intended it to last.

He started to shift her, but then her lips were racing over his face. Soft, light, but with a heat that seeped right into him. Her long, limber body seemed almost weightless over his, yet he could feel every line and curve. Moisture still clung to her hair and reminded him of the first time, when he'd dragged her to the ground, consumed with need and fury. Now he was helpless against her rapid assault on his senses. No, she had no wiles, nor he the patience for them.

He could hear the rain patter rhythmically against the window. He could smell it on her. When his lips brushed through her hair, he could taste it. It was almost as though they were alone in a quiet field, with the scent of wet grass and the rain slipping over their skin. The light was gray and indistinct; her mouth was vivid wherever it touched him.

She hadn't known it could be so exciting to weaken a man with herself. Feeling the strength drain from him made her almost light-headed with power. She'd met him on equal terms, and from time to time to her disadvantage, but never when she'd been so certain she could dominate. Her laugh was low and confident as it whispered along his skin, warm and sultry as it brushed over his lips.

He seemed content to lie still while she learned of him. She thought the air grew thicker. Perhaps that alone weighed him down and kept him from challenging her control. Her hands were eager, rushing here then there to linger over some small fascination: tight cords of muscle that ran down his upper arms to bunch and gather at her touch; smooth, taut skin that was surprisingly soft over his rib cage; the narrow, raised scar along his hipbone.

"Where'd you get this?" she murmured, outlining it with a fingertip.

"Brahma," he managed as she tugged his jeans down infinitesimally lower. "Jillian—" But her lips drifted over his again and silenced him.

"A bull?"

"Rodeo, when I had more guts than brains."

She heard the sound of pleasure in his throat as her mouth journeyed down. His body was a treasure of delight to her. In the soft rainy light she could see it, brown and hard against the plain, serviceable bedspread. Rangy and loose limbed, it was made for riding well and long, toughened by physical work, burnished by the elements. Tiny jumping thrills coursed through her as she thought that it was hers to touch and taste, to look at as long as she liked.

She took a wandering route down him, feeling his skin heat and pulse as she stripped him. The room was filled with the sound of rain and quickening breathing. It was all she heard. The sweet scent of passion enveloped her—a fragrance mixed of the essence of both of them. Intimate. She could taste desire on his skin, a heady flavor that made her greedy when she felt the thud of his heart under her tongue. Even when her excitement grew until her blood was racing, she could have luxuriated in him for hours. The sharp urgency she'd once felt had mellowed into a glowing contentment. She pleasured him. It was more than she'd believed she could do for anyone.

There were flames in his stomach, spreading. God,

she was like a drug and he was lost, half dreaming while his flesh was burning up. Her fingers were so cool as they tortured him, her mouth so hot. He'd never explored his own vulnerabilities; it had always been more important to work around them or ignore them altogether. Now he had no choice and he found the sensation incredible.

She aroused, teased and withdrew only to arouse again. Her enervating, openmouthed kisses ranged over him while her hands stroked and explored lazily, finding point after sensitive point until he trembled. No woman had ever made him tremble. Even as this thought ran through his ravaged mind, she caused him to do so again. Then he knew she was driving him mad.

The wind kicked up, hurling rain against the window, then retreating with a distant howl. Something crazed sprang into him. Roughly he grabbed her, rolling over and pinning her, her arms above her head. His breathing was labored as he looked down.

Her chin was up, her hair spread out, her eyes glowing. There was no fear on her face, and nothing of submission. Though her own breathing came quickly, there was challenge in the look she gave him. A dare. He could take her, take her anyway he chose. And when he did so, he'd be taken, as well.

So be it, he thought with a muffled oath. His mouth devoured hers.

She matched his urgency, aroused simply by knowing she had taken him to the edge. He wanted her. Her. In some ways he knew her better than anyone ever had, and still he wanted her. She'd waited so long for that, not even knowing that she'd waited at all. She couldn't think of this, or what the effects might be when his long desperate kisses were rousing her, when she could see small, silvery explosions going on behind her closed lids.

She felt him tug at the buttons of her shirt, heard him swear. When she felt the material rip away she knew only that at last she could feel his flesh against hers. As it was meant to be. His hands wouldn't be still and drove her as she had driven him. He pulled clothes from her in a frenzy as his mouth greedily searched. Somewhere in her hazy brain she felt wonder that she could bring him to this just by being.

Their bodies pressed, their limbs entwined. Their mouths joined. He thought the mixing of their tastes the most intimate thing he'd ever known. Under him she arched, more a demand than an offer. He raised himself over her, wanting to see her, wanting her to see him when he made her his.

Her eyes were dark, misted with need. Need for him. He knew he had what he'd wanted: she thought of nothing and no one else. "I wanted you from the first minute," he murmured as he slipped inside her.

He saw the change in her face as he moved slowly, the flicker of pleasure, the softening that came just before delirium. Pushing back the rushing need in his blood, he drew out the sensations with a control so exquisite it burned in his muscles. Lowering his head, he nibbled at her lips.

She couldn't bear it. She couldn't stop it. When she thought she finally understood what passion was, he showed her there was more. Sensation after sensation slammed into her, leaving her weak and gasping. Even as the pressure built inside her, drumming under her skin and threatening to implode, she wanted it to go on. She could have wept from the joy of it, moaned from the ache. Unwittingly it was she who changed things simply by breathing his name as if she knew no other.

The instant his control snapped, she felt it. There was time only for a tingle of nervous excitement before he was catapulting her with him into a dark, frantic sky where it was all thunder and no air.

Chapter 10

The lengthy, dusty drive into town and the soaring temperatures couldn't dull the spirit. It was the Fourth of July, and the long, raucous holiday had barely begun.

By early morning the fairgrounds were crowded—ranchers, punchers, wives and sweethearts, and those looking for a sweetheart to share the celebration with. Prized animals were on display to be discussed, bragged about and studied. Quilts and pies and preserves waited to be judged. As always, there was a pervasive air of expectancy.

Cowboys wore their best uniform—crisp shirts and pressed jeans, with the boots and hats that were saved and cherished for special occasions. Belt buckles gleamed. Children sported their finest, which promised to be dirt streaked and grass stained by the end of the long day.

For Jillian, it was the first carefree day in the season, and one she was all the more determined to enjoy because of her recent problems. For twenty-four hours she was going to forget her worries, the numbers in her account books and the title of boss she worked day after day to earn. On this one sun-filled, heat-soaked day, she was going to simply enjoy the fact that she was part of a unique group of men and women who both lived and played off the land.

There was an excited babble of voices near the paddock and stable areas. The pungent aroma of animals permeated the air. From somewhere in the distance she could already hear fiddle music. There'd be more music after sundown, and dancing. Before then, there'd be games for young and old, the judgings, and enough food to feed the entire county twice over. She could smell the spicy aroma of an apple pie, still warm, as someone passed her with a laden basket. Her mouth watered.

First things first, she reminded herself as she wandered over to check out her bull's competition.

There were six entries altogether, all well muscled and fierce to look at. Horns gleamed, sharp and dangerous. Hides were sleek and well tended. Objectively Jillian studied each one, noting their high points and their weaknesses. There wasn't any doubt that her stiffest competitor would be the Double M's entry. He'd taken the blue ribbon three years running.

Not this year, she told him silently as her gaze skimmed over him. Pound for pound, he probably had her bull beat, but she thought hers had a bit more breadth in the shoulders. And there was no mistaking that her Hereford's coloring and markings were perfect, the shape of his head superior.

Time for you to move over and make room for new blood, she told the reigning champion. Rather pleased with herself, she hooked her thumbs in her back pockets. First place and that little swatch of blue ribbon would go a long way to making up for everything that'd gone wrong in the past few weeks.

"Know a winner when you see one?"

Jillian turned at the thready voice that still held a hint of steel. Paul Murdock was dressed to perfection, but his hawklike face had little color under his Stetson. His cane was elegant and tipped with gold, but he leaned on it heavily. As they met hers, however, his eyes were very much alive and challenging.

"I know a winner when I see one," she agreed, then let her gaze skim over to her own bull.

He gave a snort of laughter and shifted his weight. "Been hearing a lot about your new boy." He studied the bull with a faint frown and couldn't prevent a twinge of envy. He, too, knew a winner when he saw one.

He felt the sun warm on his back and for a moment, for just a moment, wished desperately for his youth again. Years ate at strength. If he were fifty again and owned that bull... But he wasn't a man to sigh. "Got possibilities," he said shortly.

She recognized something of the envy and smiled. Nothing could've pleased her more. "Nothing wrong with second place," she said lightly.

Murdock glanced over sharply, pinned her eyes with his, then laughed when she didn't falter. "Damn, you're quite a woman, aren't you, Jillian Baron? The old man taught you well enough."

Her smile held more challenge than humor. "Well enough to run Utopia."

"Could be," he acknowledged. "Times change." There wasn't any mistaking the resentment in the statement, but she understood it. Sympathized with it. "This rustling…" He glanced over to see her face, impassive and still. Murdock had a quick desire to sit across a poker table from her with a large, juicy pot in between. "It's a damn abomination," he said with a savagery that made him momentarily breathless. "There was a time a man'd have his neck stretched for stealing another man's beef."

"Hanging them won't get my cattle back," Jillian said calmly.

"Aaron told me about what you found in the canyon." Murdock stared at the well-muscled bulls. These were the life's blood of their ranches—the profit and the status. "A hard thing for you—for all of us," he added, shifting his eyes to hers again. "I want you to understand that your grandfather and I had our problems. He was a stubborn, stiff-necked bastard."

"Yes," Jillian agreed easily, so easily Murdock laughed. "You'd understand a man like that," she added.

Murdock stopped laughing to fix her with a glittering look. She returned it. "I understand a man like that," he acknowledged. "And I want you to know that if this had happened to him, I'd've been behind him, just as I'd've expected him to be behind me. Personal feelings don't come into it. We're ranchers."

It was said with a sting of pride that made her own chin lift. "I do know it."

"It'd be easy to say the cattle could've been driven over to my land."

"Easy to say," Jillian said with a nod. "If you knew me better, Mr. Murdock, you'd know I'm not a fool. If I believed you'd had my beef on your table, you'd already be paying for it."

His lips curved in a rock-hard, admiring smile.

"Baron did well by you," he said after a moment. "Though I still think a woman needs a man beside her if she's going to run a ranch."

"Be careful, Mr. Murdock, I was just beginning to think I could tolerate you."

He laughed again, so obviously pleased that Jillian grinned. "Can't change an old dog, girl." His eyes narrowed fractionally as she'd seen his son's do. It occurred to her that in forty years Aaron would look like this— that honed-down strength that was just a little bit mean. It was the kind of strength you'd want behind you when there was trouble. "I've heard my boy's had his eye on you—can't say I fault his taste."

"Have you?" she returned mildly. "Do you believe everything you hear?"

"If he hasn't had his eye on you," Murdock countered, "he's not as smart as I give him credit for. Man needs a woman to settle him down."

"Really?" Jillian said very dryly.

"Don't get fired up, girl," Murdock ordered. "There'd've been a time when I'd have had his hide for looking twice at a Baron. Times change," he repeated with obvious reluctance. "Our land has run side by side for most of this century, whether we like it or not."

Jillian took a moment to brush off her sleeve. "I'm not looking to settle anyone, Mr. Murdock. And I'm not looking for a merger."

"Sometimes we wind up getting things we're not looking for." He smiled as she stared at him. "You take my Karen—never figured to hitch myself with a beauty who always made me feel like I should wipe my feet whether I'd been in the pastures or not."

Despite herself Jillian laughed, then surprised them

both by hooking her arm through his as they began to walk. "I get the feeling you're trying to bury the hatchet." When he stiffened, she muffled a chuckle and continued. "Don't *you* get fired up," she said easily. "I'm willing to try a truce. Aaron and I have...we understand each other," she decided. "I like your wife, and I can just about tolerate you."

"You're your grandmother all over again," Murdock muttered.

"Thanks." As they walked Jillian noted the few speculative glances tossed their way. Baron and Murdock arm in arm; times had indeed changed. She wondered how Clay would feel and decided, in his grudging way, he would've approved. Especially if it caused talk.

When Aaron saw them walking slowly toward the arena area, he broke off the conversation he'd been having with a puncher. Jillian tossed back her hair, tilted her head slightly toward his father's and murmured something that made the old man hoot with laughter. If he hadn't already, Aaron would've fallen in love with her at that moment.

"Hey, isn't that Jillian Baron with your paw?"

"Hmmm? Yeah." Aaron didn't waste time glancing back at the puncher when he could look at Jillian.

"She sure is easy on the eyes," the puncher concluded a bit wistfully. "Heard you and her—" He broke off, chilled by the cool, neutral look Aaron aimed at him. The cowboy coughed into his hand. "Just meant people wonder about it, seeing as the Murdocks and Barons never had much dealings with each other."

"Do they?" Aaron relieved the cowboy by grinning before he walked off. Murdocks, the puncher thought with a shake of his head. You could never be too sure of them.

"Life's full of surprises," Aaron commented as he walked toward them. "No blood spilled?"

"Your father and I've reached a limited understanding." Jillian smiled at him, and though they touched in no way, Murdock was now certain the rumors he'd heard about Jillian and his son were true. Intimacy was something people often foolishly believed they could conceal, and rarely did.

"Your mother's got me judging the mincemeat," Murdock grumbled. This time he didn't feel that twinge of regret for what he'd lost, but an odd contentment at seeing his slice of immortality in his son. "We'll be in the stands later to watch you." He gave Jillian an arch look. "Both of you."

He walked off slowly. Jillian had to stuff her hands in her pockets to keep from helping him. That, she knew, would be met with cold annoyance. "He came over to the pens," Jillian told Aaron when Murdock was out of earshot. "I think he did it on purpose so that he could talk to me. He was very kind."

"Not many people see him as kind."

"Not many people had a grandfather like Clay Baron." She turned to Aaron and smiled.

"How are you?" He couldn't have resisted the urge to touch her if he'd wanted to. His fingertips skimmed along her jaw.

"How do I look?"

"You don't like me to tell you you're beautiful."

She laughed, and the under-the-lashes look she sent him was the first flirtatious move he'd ever seen from her. "It's a holiday."

"Spend it with me?" He held out a hand, knowing if she put hers in it, in public, where there were curious eyes and tongues that appreciated a nice bit of gossip, it would be a commitment of sorts.

Her fingers laced with his. "I thought you'd never ask."

They spent the morning doing what couples had done at county fairs for decades. There was lemonade to be drunk, contests to be watched. It was easy to laugh when the sky was clear and the sun promised a dry, golden day.

Children raced by with balloons held by sticky fingers. Teenagers flirted with the nonchalance peculiar to their age. Old-timers chewed tobacco and out-lied each other. The air was touched with the scent of food and animals, and the starch in bandbox shirts had not yet wilted with sweat.

With Aaron's arm around her, Jillian crowded to the fence to watch the greased pig contest. The ground had been flooded and churned up so that the state of the mud was perfection. The pig was slick with lard and quick, so that he eluded the five men who lunged after him. The crowd called out suggestions and hooted with laughter. The pig squealed and shot, like a bullet, out of capturing arms. Men fell on their faces and swore good-naturedly.

Jillian shot him a look, then inclined her head toward the pen where the activity was still wild and loud. "Don't you like games, Murdock?"

"I like to make up my own." He swung her around. "Now, there's this real quiet hayloft I know of."

With a laugh, she eluded him. He'd never known her to be deliberately provocative and found himself not quite certain how to deal with it. The glitter in her eyes made him decide. In one smooth move, Aaron gathered her close and kissed her soundly. There was an approving whoop from a group of cowboys behind them. When Jillian managed to untangle herself, she glanced over to see two of her own men grinning at her.

"It's a holiday," Aaron reminded her when she let out a huff of breath.

She brought her head back slowly and took his measure. Oh, he was damn proud of himself, she decided. And two could play. Her smile had him wondering just what she had up her sleeve.

"You want fireworks?" she asked, then threw her arms around him and silenced him before he could agree or deny.

While his kiss had been firm yet still friendly, hers whispered of secrets only the two of them knew. Aaron never heard the second cheer go up, but he wouldn't have been surprised to feel the ground move.

"I missed you last night, Murdock," she whispered, then went from her toes to her flat feet so that their lips parted. She took a step back before she offered her hand, and the smile on those fascinating lips was cocky.

Carefully Aaron drew air into his lungs and released it. "You're going to finish that one later, Jillian."

She only laughed again. "I certainly hope so. Let's go see if Gil can win the pie-eating contest again this year."

He went wherever she wanted and felt foolishly, and appealingly, like a kid on his first date. It was the sudden carefree aura around her. Jillian had dropped everything, all worries and responsibilities, and had given herself a day for fun. Perhaps because she felt a slight twinge of guilt, like a kid playing hooky, the day was all the sweeter.

She would have sworn the sun had never been brighter,

the sky so blue. In all of her life, she couldn't remember ever laughing so easily. A slice of cherry pie was ambrosia. If she could have concentrated the day down, section by section, she would have put it into a box where she could have taken out an hour at a time when she was alone and tired. Because she was too practical to believe that possible, Jillian chose to live each moment to the fullest.

By the time the rodeo officially opened, Jillian was nearly drunk on freedom. As the Fourth of July Queen and her court rode sedately around the arena, she still clutched her bull's blue ribbon in her hand. "That's fifty you owe me," she told Aaron with a grin.

He sat on the ground exchanging dress boots for worn, patched riding favorites. "Why don't we wait and see how the second bet comes out?"

"Okay." She perched on a barrel and listened to the crowd cheer from the stands. She was riding high and knew it. Her luck had turned—there wasn't a problem she could be hit with that she couldn't handle.

A lot of cowboys and potential competitors had already collected behind the chutes. Though it all seemed very casual—the lounging, the rigging bags set carelessly against the chain link fence—there was an air of suppressed excitement. There was the scent of tobacco from the little cans invariably carried in the right rear pocket of jeans, and mink oil on leather. Already she heard the jingle of spurs and harnesses as equipment was checked. The bareback riding was first. When she heard the announcement, Jillian rose and wandered to the fence to watch.

"I'm surprised you didn't give this one a try," Aaron commented.

She tilted her head so that it brushed his arm—one of the rare signs of affection that made him weak. "Too much energy," she said with a laugh. "I'm dedicating the day to laziness. I noticed you were signed up for the bronc riding." Jillian nudged her hat back as she looked up at him. "Still more guts than brains?"

He grinned and shrugged. "Worried about me?"

Jillian gave a snort of laughter. "I've got some good liniment—it'll take the soreness out of the bruises you're going to get."

He ran a fingertip down her spine. "The idea tempts me to make sure I get a few. You know—" he turned her into his arms in a move both smooth and possessive "—it wouldn't take much for me to forget all about this little competition." Lowering his head, he nibbled at her lips, oblivious of whoever might be milling around them. "It's not such a long drive back to the ranch. Not a soul there. Pretty day like this—I start thinking about taking a swim."

"Do you?" She drew her head back so their eyes met.

"Mmmm. Water'd be cool, and quiet."

Chuckling, she pressed her lips to his. "After the calf roping," she said and drew away.

Jillian preferred the chutes to the stands. There she could listen to the men talk of other rodeos, other rides, while she checked over her own equipment. She watched a young girl in a stunning buckskin suit rev up her nerves before the barrel racing. An old hand worked rosin into the palm of a glove with tireless patience. The little breeze carried the scent of grilled meat from the concessions.

No, she thought, her family could never understand the appeal of this. The earthy smells, the earthy talk.

They'd be just as much out of their element here as she'd always been at her mother's box at the opera. It was times like these, when she was accepted for simply being what she was, that she stopped remembering the little twinges of panic that had plagued her while she grew up. No, there was nothing lacking in her as she'd often thought. She was simply different.

She watched the bull riding, thrilling to the danger and daring as men pitted themselves against a ton of beef. There were spills and close calls and clowns who made the terrifying seem amusing. Half dreaming, she leaned on the fence as a riderless bull charged and snorted around the arena, poking bad temperedly at a clown in a barrel. The crowd was loud, but she could hear Aaron in an easy conversation with Gil from somewhere behind her. She caught snatches about the little sorrel mare Aaron had drawn in the bronc riding. A fire-eater. Out of the chute, then a lunge to the right. Liked to spin. Relaxed, Jillian thought she'd enjoy watching Aaron pit himself against the little fire-eater. After she'd won another fifty from him.

She thought the day had simply been set aside for her, warm and sunny and without demands. Perhaps she'd been this relaxed before, this happy, but it was difficult to remember when she'd shared the two sensations so clearly. She savored them.

Then everything happened so quickly she didn't have time to think, only to act.

She heard the childish laughter as she stretched her back muscles. She saw the quick flash of red zip through the fence and bounce on the dirt without fully registering it. But she saw the child skim through the rungs of the fence and into the arena. He was so close his jeans brushed hers as he scrambled through after his ball. Jillian was over the fence and running before his mother screamed. Part of her registered Aaron's voice, either furious or terrified, as he called her name.

Out of the corner of her eye Jillian saw the bull turn. His eyes, already wild from the ride, met hers, though she never paused. Her blood went cold.

She didn't hear the chaos as the crowd leaped to their feet or the mass confusion from behind the chutes as she sprinted after the boy. She did feel the ground tremble as the bull began its charge. There wasn't time to waste her breath on shouting. Running on instinct, she lunged, letting the momentum carry her forward. She went down hard, full length on the boy, and knocked the breath out of both of them. As the bull skimmed by them, she felt the hot rush of air.

Don't move, she told herself, mercilessly pinning the boy beneath her when he started to squirm. *Don't even breathe.* She could hear shouting, very close by now, but didn't dare move her head to look. She wasn't gored. Jillian swallowed on the thought. No, she'd know it if he'd caught her with his horns. And he hadn't trampled her. Yet.

Someone was cursing furiously. Jillian closed her eyes and wondered if she'd ever be able to stand up again. The boy was beginning to cry lustily. She tried to smother the sound with her body.

When hands came under her arms, she jolted and started to struggle. "You *idiot*!" Recognizing the voice, Jillian relaxed and allowed herself to be hauled to her feet. She might have swayed if she hadn't been held so tightly. "What kind of a stunt was that?" She stared up at Aaron's deathly white face while he shook her. "Are you hurt?" he demanded. "Are you hurt anywhere?"

"What?"

He shook her again because his hands were trembling. "Damn it, Jillian!"

Her head was spinning a bit like it had when she'd had that first plug of tobacco. It took her a moment to realize someone was gripping her hand. Bemused, she listened to the tearful gratitude of the mother while the boy wept loudly with his face buried in his father's shirt. The Simmons boy, she thought dazedly. The little Simmons boy, who played in the yard while his mother hung out the wash and his father worked on her own land.

"He's all right, Joleen," she managed, though her mouth didn't want to follow the order of her brain. "I might've put some bruises on him, though."

Aaron cut her off, barely suppressing the urge to suggest someone introduce the boy to a razor strap before he dragged Jillian away. She had a misty impression of a sea of faces and Aaron's simmering rage.

"...get you over to first aid."

"What?" she said again as his voice drifted in and out of her mind.

"I said I'm going to get you over to first aid." He bit off the words as he came to the fence.

"No, I'm fine." The light went gray for a moment and she shook her head.

"As soon as I'm sure of that, I'm going to strangle you."

She pulled her hand from his and straightened her shoulders. "I said I'm fine," she repeated. Then the ground tilted and rushed up at her.

The first thing she felt was the tickle of grass under her palm. Then there was a cool cloth, more wet than damp, on her face. Jillian moaned in annoyance as water trickled down to her collar. Opening her eyes, she saw a blur of light and shadow. She closed them again, then concentrated on focusing.

She saw Aaron first, grim and pale as he hitched her up to a half-sitting position and held a glass to her lips. Then Gil, shifting his weight from foot to foot while he ran his hat through his hands. "She ain't hurt none," he told Aaron in a voice raised to convince everyone, including himself. "Just had herself a spell, that's all. Women do."

"A lot you know," she muttered, then discovered what Aaron held to her lips wasn't a glass but a flask of neat brandy. It burned very effectively through the mists. "I didn't faint," Jillian said in disgust.

"You did a damn good imitation, then," Aaron snapped at her.

"Let the child breathe." Karen Murdock's calm, elegant voice had the magic effect of moving the crowd back. She slipped through and knelt at Jillian's side. Clucking her tongue, she took the dripping cloth from Jillian's brow and wrung it out. "Men'll always try to overcompensate. Well, Jillian, you caused quite a sensation."

Grimacing, Jillian sat up. "Did I?" She pressed her forehead to her knees a minute until she was certain the world wasn't going to do any more spinning. "I can't believe I fainted," she mumbled.

Aaron swore and took a healthy swig from the flask himself. "She almost gets herself killed and she's worried about what fainting's going to do to her image."

Jillian's head snapped up. "Look, Murdock—"

"I wouldn't push it if I were you," he warned and

meticulously capped the flask. "If you can stand, I'll take you home."

"Of course I can stand," she retorted. "And I'm not going home."

"I'm sure you're fine," Karen began and shot her son a telling look. For a smart man, Karen mused, Aaron was showing a remarkable lack of sense. Then again, when love was around, sense customarily went out the window. "Trouble is, you're a seven-day wonder," she told Jillian with a brief glance at the gathering crowd. "You're going to be congratulated to death if you stay around here." She smiled as she saw her words sink in.

Grumbling, Jillian rose. "All right." The bruises were beginning to be felt. Rather than admit it, she brushed at the dust on her jeans. "There's no need for you to go," she told Aaron stiffly. "I'm perfectly capable of—"

His fingers were wrapped tight around her arm as he dragged her away. "I don't know what your problem is, Murdock," she said through her teeth. "But I don't have to take this."

"I'd keep a lid on it for a while if I were you." The crowd fell back as he strode through. If anyone considered speaking to Jillian, Aaron's challenging look changed their minds.

After wrenching open the door of his truck, Aaron gave her a none-too-gentle boost inside. Jillian pulled her hat from her back and, taking the brim in both hands, slammed it down on her head. Folding her arms, she prepared to endure the next hour's drive in absolute silence. As Aaron pulled out it occurred to her that she had missed not only the calf roping, but also her sacred right to gloat over her bull's victory at the evening barbecue. The injustice of it made her smolder.

And just what's he so worked up about? Jillian asked herself righteously. He hadn't scared himself blind, wrenched his knee, or humiliated himself by fainting in public. Gingerly she touched her elbow where she'd scraped most of the skin away. After all, if you wanted to be technical, she'd probably saved that kid's life. Jillian's chin angled as her arm began to ache with real enthusiasm. So why was he acting as though she'd committed some crime?

"One of these days you're going to put your chin out like that and someone's going to take you up on it."

Slowly she turned her head to glare at him. "You want to give it a shot, Murdock?"

"Don't tempt me." He punched on the gas until the speedometer hovered at seventy.

"Look, I don't know what your problem is," she said tightly. "But since you've got one, why don't you just spill it? I'm not in the mood for your nasty little comments."

He swung the truck over to the side of the road so abruptly she crashed into the door. By the time she'd recovered, he was out of his side and striding across the tough wild grass of a narrow field. Rubbing her sore arm, Jillian pushed out of the truck and went after him.

"What the hell is all this about?" Anger made her breathless as she caught at his shirtsleeve. "If you want to drive like a maniac, I'll hitch a ride back to the ranch."

"Just shut up." He jerked away from her. Distance, he told himself. He just needed some distance until he pulled himself together. He was still seeing those lowered horns sweeping past Jillian's tumbling body. His rope might've missed the mark, and then— He couldn't afford to think of any *and thens*. As it was, it had taken three well-placed ropes and several strong arms before they'd been able to drag the bull away from those two prone bodies. He'd nearly lost her. In one split second he'd nearly lost her.

"Don't you tell me to shut up." Spinning in front of him, Jillian gripped his shirtfront. Her hat tumbled down her back as she tossed her head and rage poured out of her. "I've had all I'm going to take from you. God knows why I've let you get away with this much, but no more. Now you can just hop back in your truck and head it in whatever direction you like. To hell would suit me just fine."

She whirled away, but before she could storm off she was spun back and crushed in his arms. Spitting mad, she struggled only to have his grip tighten. It wasn't until she stopped to marshal her forces that she realized he was trembling and that his breathing came fast and uneven. Emotion ruled him, yes, but it wasn't anger. Subsiding, she waited. Not certain what she was offering comfort for, she stroked his back. "Aaron?"

He shook his head and buried his face in her hair. It was the closest he could remember to just falling apart. It hadn't been distance he'd needed, he discovered, but this. To feel her warm and safe and solid in his arms.

"Oh, God, Jillian, do you know what you did to me?"

Baffled, she let her cheek rest against his drumming heart and continued to stroke his back. "I'm sorry," she offered, hoping it would be enough for whatever she'd done.

"It was so close. Inches—just inches more. I wasn't sure at first that he hadn't gotten you."

The bull, Jillian realized. It hadn't been anger, but fear. Something warm and sweet moved through her. "Don't," she murmured. "I wasn't hurt. It wasn't nearly as bad as it must've looked."

"The hell it wasn't." His hands came to her face and jerked it back. "I was only a few yards back when I got the first rope around him. He was more'n half crazy by then. Another couple of seconds and he'd've scooped you right up off that ground."

Jillian stared up at him and finally managed to swallow. "I—I didn't know."

He watched as the color her temper had given her fled from her cheeks. And I just had to tell you, he thought furiously. Taking both her hands, he brought them to his lips, burying his mouth in one palm, then the other. The gesture alone was enough to distract her. "It's done," Aaron said with more control. "I guess I overreacted. It's not easy to watch something like that." Because she needed it, he smiled at her. "I wouldn't have cared for it if you'd picked up any holes."

Relaxing a bit, she answered the smile. "Neither would I. As it is, I picked up a few bruises I'm not too fond of."

Still holding her hands, he bent over and kissed her with such exquisite gentleness that she felt the ground tilt for the second time. There was something different here, she realized dimly. Something... But she couldn't hold on to it.

Aaron drew away, knowing the time was coming when he'd have to tell her what he felt, whether she was ready to hear it or not. As he led her back to the truck he decided that since he was only going to bare his heart to one woman in his life, he was going to do it right.

"You're going to take a hot bath," he told her as he lifted her into the truck. "Then I'm going to fix you dinner."

Jillian settled back against the seat. "Maybe fainting isn't such a bad thing after all."

Chapter 11

By the time they drove into the ranch yard, Jillian had decided she'd probably enjoy a few hours of pampering. As far as she could remember, no one had ever fussed over her before. As a child, she'd been strong and healthy. Whenever she'd been ill, she'd been treated with competent practicality by her doctor father. She'd learned early that the fewer complaints you made the less likelihood there was for a hypodermic to come out of that little black bag. Clay had always treated bumps and blood as a routine part of the life. Wash up and get back to work.

Now she thought it might be a rather interesting experience to have someone murmur over her scrapes and bruises. Especially if he kissed her like he had on the side of the road...in that soft, gentle way that made the top of her head threaten to spin off.

Perhaps they wouldn't have the noise and lights and

music of the fairgrounds, but they could make their own fireworks, alone, on Utopia.

All the buildings were quiet, bunkhouse, barns, stables. Instead of the noise and action that would accompany any late afternoon, there was simple, absolute peace over acres of land. Whatever animals hadn't been taken to the fair had been left to graze for the day. It would be hours before anyone returned to Utopia.

"I don't think I've ever been here alone before," Jillian murmured when Aaron stopped the truck. She sat for a moment and absorbed the quiet and the stillness. It occurred to her that she could cup her hands and shout if she liked—no one would even hear the echo.

"It's funny, it even feels different. You always know there're people around." She stepped out of the truck, then listened to the echo of the slam. "Somebody in the bunkhouse or the cookhouse or one of the outbuildings. Some of the wives or children hanging out clothes or working in the gardens. You hardly think about it, but it's like a little town."

"Self-sufficient, independent." He took her hand, thinking that the words described her just as accurately as they described the ranch. They were two of the reasons he'd been drawn to her.

"It has to be, doesn't it? It's so easy to get cut off— one bad storm. Besides, it's what makes it all so special." Though she didn't understand the smile he sent her, she answered it. "I'm glad I've got so many married hands who've settled," she added. "It's harder to depend on the drifters." Jillian scanned the ranch yard, not quite understanding her own reluctance to go inside. It was as if she were missing something. With a shrug, she put it down to the oddity of being alone, but she caught herself searching the area again.

Aaron glanced down and saw the lowered-brow look of concentration. "Something wrong?"

"I don't know... It seems like there is." With another shrug, she turned to him. "I must be getting jumpy." Reaching up, she tipped back the brim of his hat. She liked the way it shadowed his face, accenting the angle of bone, adding just one more shade of darkness to his eyes. "You didn't mention anything about scrubbing my back when I took that hot bath, did you?"

"No, but I could probably be persuaded."

Agreeably she went into his arms. She thought she could catch just a trace of rosin on him, perhaps a hint of saddle soap. "Did I mention how sore I am?"

"No, you didn't."

"I don't like to complain..." She snuggled against him.

"But?" he prompted with a grin.

"Well, now that you mention it—there are one or two places that sting, just a bit."

"Want me to kiss them and make them better?"

She sighed as he nuzzled her ear. "If it wouldn't be too much trouble."

"I'm a humanitarian," he told her, then began to nudge her slowly toward the porch steps. It was then Jillian remembered. With a gasp, she broke out of his arms and raced across the yard. "Jillian—" Swearing, Aaron followed her.

Oh, God, how could she've missed it! Jillian raced to the paddock fence and leaned breathlessly against it. Empty. *Empty.* She balled her hands into fists as she looked at the bottle she'd left hanging at an angle in the shade. The trough of water glimmered in the sun. The few scoops of grain she'd left were barely touched.

"What's going on?"

"Baby," she muttered, tapping her hand rhythmically against the fence. "They've taken Baby." Her tone started out calm, then became more and more agitated. "They walked right into my backyard, right into my backyard, and stole from me."

"Maybe one of your hands put him back in the barn."

She only shook her head and continued to tap her hand on the fence. "The five hundred weren't enough," she murmured. "They had to come here and steal within a stone's throw of my house. I should've left Joe—he offered to stay. I should've stayed myself."

"Come on, we'll check the barn."

She looked at him, and her eyes were flat and dark. "He's not in the barn."

He'd rather have had her rage, weep, than look so—resigned. "Maybe not, but we'll be sure. Then we'll see if anything else was taken before we call the sheriff."

"The sheriff." Jillian laughed under her breath and stared blindly into the empty paddock. "The sheriff."

"Jillian—" Aaron slipped his arms around her, but she drew away immediately.

"No, I'm not going to fall apart this time." Her voice trembled slightly, but her eyes were clear. "They won't do that to me again."

It might be better if she did, Aaron thought. Her face was pale, but he knew that expression by now. There'd be no backing down. "You check the barn," he suggested. "I'll look in the stables."

Jillian followed the routine, though she knew it was hopeless. Baby's stall was empty. She watched the little motes of hay and dust as they floated in the slant of sunlight. Someone had taken her yearling. Someone. Her hands balled into fists. Somehow, some way, she was going to get a name. Spinning on her heel, she strode back out. Though she itched with impatience, she waited until Aaron crossed the yard to her. There wasn't any need for words. Together, they went into the house.

She's not going to take this one lying down, he decided, with as much admiration as concern. Yes, she was still pale, but her voice was strong and clear as she spoke to the sheriff's office. Resigned—yes, she was still resigned that it had been done. But she didn't consider it over.

He remembered the way she'd nuzzled the calf when it'd been newborn—the way her eyes had softened when she spoke of it. It was always a mistake to make a pet out of one of your stock, but there were times it happened. She was paying for it now.

Thoughtfully he began to brew coffee. Aaron considered it a foolish move for anyone to have stolen Utopia's prize yearling. For butchering? It hardly seemed worth the risk or effort. Yet what rancher in the area would buy a young Hereford so easily identified? Someone had gotten greedy, or stupid. Either way, it would make them easier to catch.

Jillian leaned against the kitchen wall and talked steadily into the phone. Aaron found himself wanting to shield, to protect. She took the coffee from him with a brief nod and continued talking. Shaking his head, he reminded himself he should know better by now. Protection wasn't something Jillian would take gracefully. He drank his own coffee, looking out of the kitchen window and wondering how a man dealt with loving a woman who had more grit than most men.

"He'll do what he can," she said as she hung up the phone with a snap. "I'm going to offer a separate reward for Baby." Jillian drank down half the coffee, hot and black. "Tomorrow I'll go see the Cattlemen's Association again. I want to put the pressure on, and put it on hard. People are going to realize this isn't going to stop at Utopia." She looked into her coffee, then grimly finished it off. "I kept telling myself it wasn't personal. Even when I saw the hides and bones in the canyon. Not this time. They got cocky, Aaron. It's always easier to catch arrogance."

There was relish in the tone of her voice, the kind of relish that made him smile as he turned to face her. "You're right."

"What're you grinning at?"

"I was thinking if the rustlers could see you now, they'd be shaking the dust of this county off their boots in a hurry."

Her lips curved. She hadn't thought it possible. "Thank you." She gestured with the cup, then set it back on the stove. "I seem to be saying that to you quite a bit these days."

"You don't have to say it at all. Hungry?"

"Hmmm." She put her hand on her stomach and thought about it. "I don't know."

"Go get yourself a bath, I'll rustle up something."

Walking to him, Jillian slipped her arms around his waist and rested her head on his chest. How was it he knew her so well? How did he understand that she needed a few moments alone to sort through her thoughts and feelings?

"Why are you so good to me?" she murmured.

With a half laugh, Aaron buried his face in her hair. "God knows. Go soak your bruises."

"Okay." But she gave in to the urge to hug him fiercely before she left the room.

She wished she knew a better way to express gratitude. As she climbed the stairs to the second floor, Jillian wished she were more clever with words. If she were, she'd be able to tell him how much it meant that he offered no more than she could comfortably take. His support today had been steady but unobtrusive. And he was giving her time alone without leaving her alone. Perhaps it had taken her quite some time to discover just how special a man he was, but she had discovered it. It wasn't something she'd forget.

As Jillian peeled off her clothes she found she was a bit more tender in places than she'd realized. Better, she decided, and turned the hot water on in the tub to let it steam. A few bruises were something solid to concentrate on. They were easier than the bruises she felt on the inside. It might have been foolish to feel as though she'd let her grandfather down, but she couldn't rid herself of the feeling. He'd given her something in trust and she hadn't protected it well enough. It would have soothed her if he'd been around to berate her for it.

Wincing a bit, she lowered herself into the water. The raw skin on her elbow objected and she ignored it. One of her own men? she thought with a grimace. It was too possible. Back up a truck to the paddock, load up the calf and go.

She'd start making a few discreet inquiries herself. Stealing the calf would've taken time. Maybe she could discover just who was away from the fair. Perhaps they'd be confident enough to throw a little extra money around if they thought they were safe and then… Then they'd see, she thought as she relaxed in the water.

Poor Baby. No one would spend the time scratching his ears or talking to him now. Sinking farther in the water, she waited until her mind went blank.

It was nearly an hour before she came downstairs again. She'd soaked the stiffness away and nearly all the depression. Nothing practical could be done with depression. She caught the aroma of something spicy that had her stomach juices churning.

Aaron's name was on the tip of her tongue as she walked into the kitchen, but the room was empty. A pot simmered on the stove with little hisses and puffs of steam. It drew her, irresistibly. Jillian lifted the lid, closed her eyes and breathed deep. Chili, thick and fragrant enough to make the mouth water. She wouldn't have to give it any thought if he asked if she was hungry now.

Picking up a spoon, she began to stir. Maybe just one little taste…

"My mother used to smack my hand for that," Aaron commented. Jillian dropped the lid with a clatter.

"Damn, Murdock! You scared me to—" Turning, she saw the clutch of wildflowers in his hand.

Some men might've looked foolish holding small colorful blooms in a hand roughened by work and weather. Other men might've seemed awkward. Aaron was neither. Something turned over in her chest when he smiled at her.

She looked stunned—not that he minded. It wasn't often you caught a woman like Jillian Baron off-balance. As he watched, she put her hands behind her back and gripped them together. He lifted a brow. If he'd known he could make her nervous with a bunch of wildflowers, he'd have dug up a field of them long before this.

"Feel better?" he asked and slowly crossed to her.

She'd backed into the counter before she'd realized she made the defensive move. "Yes, thanks."

He gave her one of his long, serious looks while his eyes laughed. "Something wrong?"

"No. The chili smells great."

"Something I picked up at one of the line camps a few years back." Bending his head, he kissed the corners of her mouth. "Don't you want the flowers, Jillian?"

"Yes, I—" She found she was gripping her fingers together until they hurt. Annoyed with herself, she loosened them and took the flowers from his hand. "They're very pretty."

"It's what your hair smells like," he murmured and saw the cautious look she threw up at him. Tilting his head, he studied her. "Hasn't anyone ever given you flowers before?"

Not in years, she realized. Not since—florist boxes, ribbons and soft words. Realizing she was making a fool of herself, she shrugged. "Roses," she said carelessly. "Red roses."

Something in her tone warned him. He kept his touch very light as he wound her hair around his finger. It was the color of flame, the texture of silk. "Too tame," he said simply. "Much too tame."

Something flickered inside her—acknowledgment, caution, need. With a sigh, she looked down at the small bold flowers in her hand. "Once—a long time ago—I thought I could be, too."

He tugged on her hair until she looked up at him. "Is that what you wanted to be?"

"Then, I—" She broke off, but something in his eyes demanded an answer. "Yes, I would've tried."

"Were you in love with him?" He wasn't certain why he was hacking away at a wound—his and hers—but he couldn't stop.

"Aaron—"

"Were you?"

She let out a long breath. Mechanically she began to fill a water glass for the flowers. "I was very young. He was a great deal like my father—steady, quiet, dedicated. My father loved me because he had to, never because he wanted to. There's a tremendous difference." The sharp, clean scent of the wildflowers drifted up to her. "Maybe somewhere along the line I thought if I pleased him, I'd please my father. I don't know, I was foolish."

"That isn't an answer." He discovered jealousy tasted bitter even after it was swallowed.

"I guess I don't have one I'm sure of." She moved her shoulders and fluffed the flowers in the glass. "Shouldn't we eat?" She went very still when his hands came to her shoulders, but she didn't resist when he turned her around.

She had a moment's fear that he would say something gentle, something sweet, and undermine her completely. She saw something of it in his eyes, just as he saw the apprehension in hers. Aaron tugged her against him and brought his mouth down hard on hers.

She could understand the turbulence and let go. She could meet the desire, the violence of needs, without fear of stumbling past her own rules. Her arms went around him to hold him close. Her lips sought his hungrily. If through the relief came a stir of feeling, she could almost convince herself it was nothing more complex than passion.

"Eat fast," Aaron told her. "I've been thinking about making love with you for hours."

"Didn't we eat already?"

With a chuckle he nuzzled her neck. "No, you don't. When I cook for a woman, she eats." He gave her a companionable smack on the bottom as he drew away. "Get the bowls."

Jillian handed him two and watched him scoop out generous portions. "Smells fabulous. Want a beer?"

"Yeah."

Unearthing two from the refrigerator, she poured them into glasses. "You know, if you ever get tired of ranching, you could have a job in the cookhouse here at Utopia."

"Always a comfort to have something to fall back on."

"We've got a woman now," Jillian went on as she took her seat. "The men call her Aunt Sally. She's got a way with biscuits—" She broke off as she took the first bite. Heat spread through her and woke up every cell in her body. Swallowing, she met Aaron's grin. "You use a free hand with the peppers."

"Separates the men from the boys." He took a generous forkful. "Too hot for you?"

Disdainfully she took a second bite. "There's nothing you can dish out I can't take, Murdock."

Laughing, he continued to eat. Jillian decided the first encounter had numbed her mouth right down to the vocal cords. She ate with as much relish as he, cooling off occasionally with sips of cold beer.

"Those people in town don't know what they're missing," she commented as she scraped down to the bottom of the bowl. "It isn't every day you get battery acid this tasty."

He glanced over as she ate the last forkful. "Want some more?"

"I want to live," she countered. "God, Aaron, a steady diet of that and you wouldn't have a stomach lining. It's fabulous."

"We had a Mexican foreman when I was a boy," Aaron told her. "Best damn cattleman I've ever known. I spent the best part of a summer with him up at the line camp. You should taste my flour tortillas."

The man was a constant surprise, Jillian decided as she rested her elbows on the table and cupped her chin in her hand. "What happened to him?"

"Saved his stake, went back to Mexico and started his own spread."

"The impossible dream," Jillian murmured.

"Too easy to lose a month's pay in a poker game."

She nodded, but her lips curved. "Do you play?"

"I've sat in on a hand or two. You?"

"Clay taught me. We'll have to arrange a game one of these days."

"Any time."

"I'm counting on a few poker skills to bring me out of this rustling business."

Aaron watched her rise to clear the table. "How?"

"People get careless when they think you're ready to fold. They made a mistake with the yearling, Aaron. I'm going to be able to find him—especially if nobody knows how hard I'm looking. I'm thinking about hiring an investigator. Whatever it costs, I'd rather pay it than have the stealing go on."

He sat for a moment, listening to her run water in the sink—a homey, everyday sound. "How hard is all this hitting your books, Jillian?"

She cast a look over her shoulder, calm and cool. "I can still raise the bet."

He knew better than to offer her financial assistance. It irked him. Rising, he paced the kitchen until he'd come full circle behind her. "The Cattlemen's Association would back you."

"They'd have to know about it to do that. The less people who know, the more effective a private investigation would be."

"I want to help you."

Touched, she turned and took him into her arms. "You have helped me. I won't forget it."

"I have to hog-tie you before you'll let me do anything."

She laughed and lifted her face to his. "I'm not that bad."

"Worse," he countered. "If I offered you some men to help patrol your land…"

"Aaron—"

"See." He kissed her before she could finish the protest. "I could work for you myself until everything was straightened out."

"I couldn't let you—" Then his mouth was hard and bruising on hers again.

"I'm the one who has to watch you worry and struggle," he told her as his hands began to roam down. "Do you know what that does to me?"

She tried to concentrate on his words, but his mouth—his mouth was demanding all her attention. The hot, spicy kiss took her breath away, but she clung to him and fought for more. Each time he touched her it was only seconds until the needs took over completely. She'd never known anything so liberating, or so imprisoning.

Jillian might have struggled against the latter if she'd known how. Instead she accepted the bars and locks even as she accepted the open sky and the wind. He was the only man who could tempt her to.

This was something he could do for her, Aaron knew. Make her forget, thrust her problems away from her, if only temporarily. Even so, he knew, if she had a choice, she would have kept some distance there, as well. She'd been hurt, and her trust wasn't completely his yet. The frustration of it made his mouth more ruthless, his hands more urgent. There was still only one way that she was his without question. He swept her up, then silenced her murmured protest.

Jillian was aware she was being carried. Some inner part of her rebelled against it. And yet... He wasn't taking her anywhere she wouldn't have gone willingly. Perhaps he needed this—romance he'd once called it. Romance frightened her, as the flowers had frightened her. It was so easy to lie in candlelight, so easy to deceive with fragrant blossoms and soft words. And she was no longer sure the defenses she'd once had were still there. Not with him.

"I want you." The words drifted from her to shimmer against his lips.

He would've taken her to bed. But it was too far. He would have given her the slow, easy loving a cherished woman deserves. But he was too hungry. With his mouth still fused to hers, he tumbled onto the couch with her and let the fire take them both.

She understood desperation. It was honest and real. There could be no doubting the frantic search of his mouth or the urgent pressure of his fingers against her skin. Desire had no shadows. She could feel it pulsing from him even as it pulsed from her. His curses as he tugged at her clothes made her laugh breathlessly. *She* made him clumsy. It was the greatest compliment she'd ever had.

He was relentless, spinning her beyond time and space the moment he could touch her flesh. She let herself go. Every touch, every frenzied caress, every deep, greedy kiss, took her further from the strict, practical world she'd formed for herself. Once she'd sought solitude and speed when she'd needed freedom. Now she needed only Aaron.

She felt his hair brush over her bare shoulder and savored even that simple contact. It brought a sweetness flowing into her while the burn of his mouth brought the fire. Only with him had she realized it was possible to have both. Only with him had she realized the great, yawning need in herself to have both. Her moan came as much from the revelation as from the passion.

Did she know how giving she was? How incredibly arousing? Aaron had to fight the need to take her quickly, ruthlessly, while they were both still half dressed. No woman had ever sapped his control the way she could. One look, one touch, and he was hers so completely— How could she not know?

Her body flowed, fluid as water, heady as wine, under his hands. Her lips had the punch of an electric current and the texture of silk. Could any woman remain unaware of such a deadly combination?

As if to catch his breath, he took his lips to her throat and burrowed there. He drew in the fragrance from her bath, some subtle woman's scent that lingered there, waiting to entice a lover. It was then he remembered the bruises. Aaron shook his head, trying to clear it.

"I'm hurting you."

"No." She drew him back, close. "No, you're not. You never do. I'm not fragile, Aaron."

"No?" He lifted his head so that he could see her face. There was the delicate line of bone she couldn't deny, the honey-touched skin that remained soft after hours in the sun. The frailty that came and went in her eyes at the right word, the right touch. "Sometimes you are," he murmured. "Let me show you."

"No—"

But even as she protested, his lips skimmed hers, so gentle, so reassuring. It did nothing to smother the fire, only banked it while he showed her what magic there could be with mouth to mouth. With his fingers he traced her face as though he might never see it with his eyes again—over the curve of cheekbone, down the slim line of jaw.

Patient, soft, murmuring, he seduced where no seduction was needed. Tender, thorough, easy, he let his lips show her what he hadn't yet spoken. The hand on his shoulder slid bonelessly down to his waist. He touched the tip of her tongue with his, then went deeper, slowly, in a soul-wrenching kiss that left them both limp. Then he began a careful worship of her body. She floated.

Was there any kind of pleasure he couldn't show her? Jillian wondered. Was this humming world just one more aspect to passion? She wanted desperately to give him something in return, yet her body was so heavy, weighed down with sensations. Sandalwood and leather—it would always bring him to her mind. The ridge of callus on his hand where the reins rubbed daily—nothing felt more perfect against her skin. He shifted so that she sank deeper into the cushions, and he with her.

She could taste him—and what she realized must be a wisp of herself on his lips. His cheek grazed hers, not quite smooth. She wanted to burrow against it. He whispered her name and generated a new layer of warmth.

Even when his hands began to roam, the excitement stayed hazy. She couldn't break through the mists, and no longer tried. Her skin was throbbing, but it went deeper, to the blood and bone. His mouth was light at her breast, his tongue clever enough to make her shudder, then settle, then shudder again.

He kept the pace easy, though she began to writhe under him. Time dripped away as he gave himself the pleasure of showing her each new delight. He knew afternoon was ending only by the way the light slanted over her face. The quiet was punctuated only with murmurs and sighs. He'd never felt more alone with her.

He took her slowly, savoring each moment, each movement, until there could be no more.

As she lay beneath him, Jillian watched the light shift toward dusk. It had been like a dream, she thought, like something you sigh over in the middle of the night when your wishes take control. Should it move her more than the fire and flash they usually brought each other? Somehow she knew what she'd just experienced had been more dangerous.

Aaron shifted, and though she made no objection to his weight, sat up, bringing her with him. "I like the way you stay soft and warm after I make love to you."

"It's never been just like that before," she murmured.

The words moved him; he couldn't stop it. "No." Tilting back her head, he kissed her again. "It will be again."

Perhaps because she wanted so badly to hold on, to stay, to depend, she drew away. "I'm never sure how to take you." Something warned her it was time to play it light. She was out of her depth—far, far out of her depth.

"In what way?"

She gave in to the urge to hold him again, just to feel the way his hand slid easily up and down her bare back. Reluctantly she slipped out of his arms and pulled on her shirt. "You're a lot of different people, Aaron Murdock. Every time I think I might get to know who you are, you're someone else."

"No, I'm not." Before she could button it, Aaron took her shirtfront and pulled her back to him. "Different moods don't make different people."

"Maybe not." She disconcerted him by kissing the back of his hand. "But I still can't get a handle on you."

"Is that what you want?"

"I'm a simple person."

He stared at her a moment as she continued to dress. "Are you joking?"

Because there was a laugh in his voice, she looked over, half serious, half embarrassed. "No, I am. I have to know where I stand, what my options are, what's expected of me. As long as I know I can do my job and take care of what's mine, I'm content."

He watched her thoughtfully as he pulled on his jeans. "Your job's what's vital in your life?"

"It's what I know," she countered. "I understand the land."

"And people?"

"I'm not really very good with people—a lot of people. Unless I understand them."

Aaron pulled his shirt on but left it open as he crossed to her. "And I'm one you don't understand?"

"Only sometimes," she murmured. "I guess I understand you best when I'm annoyed with you. Other times…" She was sinking even deeper and started to turn away.

"Other times," Aaron prompted, holding on to her arms.

"Other times I don't know. I never expected to get involved with you—this way."

He ran his thumbs over the pulses at the inside of her elbows. They weren't steady any longer. "This way, Jillian?"

"I didn't expect that we'd be lovers. I never expected—" Why was her heart pounding like this again, so soon? "To want you," she finished.

"Didn't you?" There was something about the way she looked at him—not quite sure of herself when he knew she was fighting to be—that made him reckless. "I wanted you from the first minute I saw you, riding hell for leather on that mare. There were other things I didn't expect. Finding those soft places, on you, in you."

"Aaron—"

He shook his head when she tried to stop him. "Thinking of you in the middle of the day, the middle of the night. Remembering just the way you say my name."

"Don't."

He felt her start to tremble before she tried to pull away. "Damn it, it's time you heard what I've been carrying around inside me. I love you, Jillian."

Panic came first, even when she began to build up the reserve. "No, you don't have to say that." Her voice was sharp and fast. "I don't expect to hear those kinds of things."

"What the hell are you talking about?" He shook her once in frustration, and a second time in anger. "I know what I have to say. I don't care if you expect to hear it or not, because you're going to."

She hung on to her temper because she knew it was emotion that brought on betrayal. If she hadn't had her pride, she would have told him just how much those words, that easily said empty phrase hurt her. "Aaron, I told you before I don't need the soft words. I don't even like them. Whatever's between us—"

"What is between us?" he demanded. He hadn't known he could be hurt, not like this. Not so he could all but feel the blood draining out of him where he stood. He'd just told a woman he loved her—the only woman, the first time. And she was answering him with ice. "You tell me what there is between us. Just this?" He swung a hand toward the couch, still rumpled from their bodies. "Is that it for you, Jillian?"

"I don't—" There was a tug-of-war going on inside of her, so fierce she was breathless from it. "It's all I thought you—" Frightened, she dragged both hands through her hair. Why was he doing this now, when she was just beginning to think she understood what he wanted from her, what she needed from him? "I don't know what you want. But I—I just can't give you any more than I already have. It's already more than I've ever given to anyone else."

His fingers loosened on her arms one by one, then dropped away. They were a match in many ways, and pride was one of them. Aaron watched her almost dispassionately as he buttoned his shirt. "You've let something freeze inside you, woman. If all you want's a warm body on a cold night, you shouldn't have much trouble. Personally, I like a little something more."

She watched him walk out of the door, heard the sound of his truck as it broke the silence. The sun was just slipping over the horizon.

Chapter 12

He worked until his muscles ached and he could think about little more than easing them. He probably drank too much. He rode the cattle, hours in the saddle, rounded strays and ate more dust than food. He spent the long, sweaty days of summer at the line camp, driving himself from sunup to sundown. Sometimes, only sometimes, he managed to push her out of his mind.

For three weeks Aaron was hell to be around. Or so his men mumbled whenever he was out of earshot. It was a woman, they told each other. Only a woman could drive a man to the edge, and then give him that gentle tap over. The Baron woman's name came up. Well, Murdocks and Barons had never mixed, so it was no wonder. No one'd expected much to come of that but hot tempers and bad feelings.

If Aaron heard the murmurs, he ignored them. He'd

come up to the camp to work—and he was going to do just that until she was out of his system. No woman was going to make him crawl. He'd told her he loved her, and she'd shoved his words, his emotions, right back in his face. Not interested.

Aaron dropped a new fence post into the ground as the sweat rolled freely down his back and sides. Maybe she was the first woman he'd ever loved—that didn't mean she'd be the last. He came down hard on the post with a sledgehammer, hissing with the effort.

He hadn't meant to tell her—not then, not that way. Somehow, the words had started rolling and he hadn't been able to stop them. Had she wanted them all tied up with a ribbon, neat and fancy? Cursing, he came down with the hammer again so that the post vibrated and the noise sang out. Maybe he had more finesse than he'd shown her, and maybe he could've used it. With someone else. Someone who didn't make his feelings come up and grab him by the throat.

Where in God's name had he ever come up with the idea that she had those soft parts, that sweet vulnerability under all that starch and fire? Must've been crazy, he told himself as he began running fresh wire. Jillian Baron was a cold, single-minded woman who cared more about her head count than any real emotion.

And he was almost sick with loving her.

He gripped the wire hard enough so that it bit through the leather of his glove and into his hand. He cursed again. He'd just have to get over it. He had his own land to tend.

Pausing, he looked out. It rolled, oceans of grass, high with summer, green and rippling. The sky was a merciless blue, and the sun beat down, strong and clean. It could be enough for a man—these thousands of acres. His cattle were fat and healthy, the yearlings growing strong. In a few weeks they'd round them up, drive them into Miles City. When those long days were over, the men would celebrate. It was their right to. And so would he, Aaron told himself grimly. So, by God, would he.

He'd have given half of what was his just to get her out of his mind for one day.

At dusk he washed off the day's sweat and dirt. He could smell the night's meal through the open windows of the cabin. Good red meat. Someone was playing a guitar and singing of lonely, lamented love. He found he wanted a beer more than he wanted his share of the steak. Because he knew a man couldn't work and not eat, he piled food on his plate and transferred it to his stomach. But he worked his way through one beer, then two, while the men made up their evening poker game. As they grew louder he took a six-pack and went out on the narrow wood porch.

The stars were just coming out. He heard a coyote call at the moon, then fall silent. The air was as still as it had been all day and barely cooler, but he could smell the sweet clover and wild roses. Resting his back against the porch rail, Aaron willed his mind to empty. But he thought of her…

Fully dressed and spitting mad, standing in the pond—crooning quietly to an orphaned calf—laughing up at him with her hair spread out over the earth of the corral—weeping in his arms over her butchered cattle. Soft one minute, prickly the next—no, she wasn't a temperate woman. But she was the only one he wanted. She was the only one he'd ever felt enough for to hurt over.

Aaron took a long swig from the bottle. He didn't

care much for emotional pain. The poets could have it. She didn't want him. Aaron swore and scowled into the dark. The hell she didn't—he wasn't a fool. Maybe her needs weren't the same as his, but she had them. For the first time in weeks he began to think calmly.

He hadn't played his hand well, he realized. It wasn't like him to fold so early—then again, he wasn't used to being soft-headed over a woman. Thoughtfully he tipped back his hat and looked at the stars. She was too set on having her own way, and it was time he gave her a run for her money.

No, he wasn't going back on his knees, Aaron thought with a grim smile. But he was going back. If he had to hobble and brand her, he was going to have Jillian Baron.

When the screen door opened he glanced around absently. His mood was more open to company.

"My luck's pretty poor."

Jennsen, Aaron thought, running through a quick mental outline of the man as he offered him a beer. A bit jittery, he mused. On his first season with the Double M, though he wasn't a greenhorn. He was a man who kept to himself and whose past was no more than could be seen in a worn saddle and patched boots.

Jennsen sat on the first step so that his lantern jaw was shadowed by the porch roof. Aaron thought he might be anywhere from thirty-five to fifty. There was age in his eyes—the kind that came from too many years of looking into the sun at another man's land.

"Cards aren't falling?" Aaron said conversationally while he watched Jennsen roll a cigarette. He didn't miss the fact that the fingers weren't quite steady.

"Haven't been for weeks." Jennsen gave a brief laugh as he struck a match. "Trouble is, I've never been much

good at staying away from a gamble." He shot Aaron
a sidelong look as he drank again. He'd been working
his way up to this talk for days and nearly had enough
beer in him to go through with it. "Your luck's pretty
steady at the table."

"Comes and goes," Aaron said, deciding Jennsen was
feeling his way along for an advance or a loan.

"Luck's a funny thing." Jennsen wiped his mouth
with the back of his hand. "Had some bad luck over at
the Baron place lately. Losing that cattle," he continued
when Aaron glanced over at him. "Somebody made a
pretty profit off that beef."

He caught the trace of bitterness. Casually he twisted
the top from another bottle and handed it over. "It's easy
to make a profit when you don't pay for the beef. Whoever skimmed from the Baron place did a smooth job
of it."

"Yeah." Jennsen drew in strong tobacco. He'd heard
the rumors about something going on between Aaron
Murdock and the Baron woman, but there didn't seem
to be anything to it. Most of the talk was about the bad
blood between the two families. It'd been going on for
years, and it seemed as though it would go on for years
more. At the moment he needed badly to believe it.
"Guess it doesn't much matter on this side of the fence
how much cattle slips away from the Baron spread."

Aaron stretched out his legs and crossed them at the
ankles. The lowered brim of his hat shadowed his eyes.
"People have to look out for themselves," he said lazily.

Jennsen moistened his lips and prodded a bit further.
"I've heard stories about your grandpaw helping himself to Baron beef."

Aaron's eyes narrowed to slits, but he checked his temper. "Stories," he agreed. "No proof."

Jennsen took another long swallow of beer. "I heard that somebody waltzed right onto Baron land and loaded up a prize yearling, sired by that fancy bull."

"Did a tidy job of it." Aaron kept his voice expressionless. Jennsen was testing the waters all right, but he wasn't looking for a loan. "It'd be a shame if they took it for baby beef," he added. "The yearling has the look of his sire—a real moneymaker. 'Course, in a few months he'd stand out like a sore thumb on a small spread. Hate to see a good bloodline wasted."

"Man hears things," Jennsen mumbled, accepting the fresh beer Aaron handed him. "You were interested in the Baron bull."

Aaron took a swig from his bottle, tipped back his hat, and grinned agreeably. "I'm always interested in good stock. Know where I can get my hands on some?"

Jennsen searched his face and swallowed. "Maybe."

Jillian slowed down as she passed the white frame house. Empty. Of course it was empty, she told herself. Even if he'd come back, he wouldn't be home in the middle of the morning. She shouldn't be here on Murdock land when she had her hands full of her own work. She couldn't stay away. If he didn't come back soon, she was going to make a fool of herself and go up to the line camp and...

And what? she asked herself. Half the time she didn't know what she wanted to do, how she felt, what she thought. The one thing she was certain of was that she'd never spent three more miserable weeks in her life. It was perilously close to grief.

Something had died in her when he'd left—something she hadn't acknowledged had been alive. She'd convinced herself that she wouldn't fall in love with him. It would be impossible to count the times she'd told herself it wouldn't happen—even after it already had. Why hadn't she recognized it?

Jillian supposed it wasn't always easy to recognize something you'd never experienced before. Especially when it had no explanation. A woman so accustomed to getting and going her own way had no business falling for a man who was equally obstinate and independent.

Falling in love. Jillian thought it an apt phrase. When it happened you just lost your foothold and plunged.

Maybe he'd meant it, she thought. Maybe they had been more than words to him. If he loved her back, didn't it mean she had someone to hold on to while she was falling? She let out a long breath as she pulled up in front of the ranch house. If he'd meant it, why wasn't he here? Mistake, she told herself with forced calm. It was always a mistake to depend too much. People pulled back or just went away. But if she could only see him again...

"Going to just sit there in that Jeep all morning?"

With a jerk, Jillian turned to watch Paul Murdock take a few slow, measured steps out onto the porch. She got out of the Jeep, wondering which of the excuses she'd made up before she'd set out would work the best.

"Sit," Murdock ordered before she could come to a decision. "Karen's fixing up a pitcher of tea."

"Thank you." Feeling awkward, she sat on the edge of the porch swing and searched for something to say.

"He hasn't come down from the camp yet," Murdock told her bluntly as he lowered himself into a rocker. "Don't frazzle your brain, girl," he ordered with an impatient brush of his hand. "I may be old, but I can see what's going on under my nose. What'd the two of you spat about?"

"Paul." Karen carried a tray laden with glasses and an iced pitcher. "Jillian's entitled to her privacy."

"Privacy!" he snorted while Karen arranged the tray on a table. "She's dangling after my son."

"Dangling!" Jillian was on her feet in a flash. "I don't dangle after anything or anyone. If I want something, I get it."

He laughed, rocking back and forth and wheezing with the effort as she glared down at him. "I like you, girl, damn if I don't. Got a fetching face, doesn't she, Karen?"

"Lovely." With a smile, Karen offered Jillian a glass of tea.

"Thank you." Stiffly she took her seat again. "I just stopped by to let Aaron know that the mare's doing well. The vet was by yesterday to check her out."

"That the best you could do?" Murdock demanded.

"Paul." Karen sat on the arm of the rocker and laid a hand on his arm.

"If I want manure, all I have to do is walk my own pasture," he grumbled, then pointed his cane at Jillian. "You going to tell me you don't want my boy?"

"Mr. Murdock," Jillian began with icy dignity, "Aaron and I have a business arrangement."

"When a man's dying he doesn't like to waste time," Murdock said with a scowl. "Now, you want to look me in the eye and tell me straight you've got no feelings for that son of mine, fine. We'll talk about the weather a bit."

Jillian opened her mouth, then closed it again with a helpless shake of her head. "When's he coming back?" she whispered. "It's been three weeks."

"He'll come back when he stops being as thick-headed as you are," Murdock told her curtly.

"I don't know what to do." After the words had tumbled out, she sat in amazement. She'd never in her life said that out loud to anyone.

"What do you want?" Karen asked her.

Jillian looked over and studied them—the old man and his beautiful wife. Karen's hand was over his on top of the cane. Their shoulders brushed. A few scattered times in her life she'd seen that kind of perfect intimacy that came from deep abiding love. It was easy to recognize, enviable. And a little scary. It came as a shock to discover she wanted that for herself. One man, one lifetime. But if that was ultimately what love equaled for her, she understood it had to be a shared dream.

"I'm still finding out," she murmured.

"That Jeep." Murdock nodded toward it. "You wouldn't have any trouble getting up to the line camp in a four-wheel drive."

Jillian smiled and set her glass aside. "I can't do it that way. It wouldn't work for me if I didn't meet him on equal terms."

"Stubborn young fool," Murdock grumbled.

"Yes." Jillian smiled again as she rose. "If he wants me, that's what he's going to get." The sound of an engine had her glancing over. When she recognized Gil's truck, she frowned and started down the steps.

"Ma'am." He tipped his hat to Karen but didn't even open the door of the truck. "Mr. Murdock. Got a problem," he said briefly, shifting his eyes to Jillian.

"What is it?"

"Sheriff called. Seems your yearling's been identified on a spread 'bout hundred and fifty miles south of here. Wants you to go down and take a look for yourself."

Jillian gripped the bottom of the open window. "Where?"

"Old Larraby spread. I'll take you now."

"Leave your Jeep here," Murdock told her, getting to his feet. "One of my men'll take it back to your place."

"Thanks." Quickly she dashed around to the other side of the truck. "Let's go," she ordered the moment the door shut beside her. "How, Gil?" she demanded as they drove out of the ranch yard. "Who identified him?"

Gil spit out the window and felt rather pleased with himself. "Aaron Murdock."

"Aaron—"

Gil was a bit more pleased when Jillian's mouth fell open. "Yep." When he came to the fork in the road, he headed south at a steady, mile-eating clip.

"But how? Aaron's been up at his line camp for weeks, and—"

"Maybe you'd like to settle down so I can tell you, or maybe you wouldn't."

Seething with impatience, Jillian subsided. "Tell me."

"Seems one of the Murdock men had a hand in the rustling, fellow named Jennsen. Well, he wasn't too happy with his cut and gambled away most of it anyhow. Decided if they could slice off five hundred and get away with it, he'd take one more for himself."

"Baby," Jillian muttered and crossed her arms over her chest.

"Yep. Had himself a tiger by the tail there. Knew the makings of a prize bull when he saw it and took it over to Larraby. Used to work there before Larraby fell on hard times. Anyhow, he started to get nervous once the man who headed up the rustling got wind of who took the little bull, figured he better get it off his hands. Last night he tried to sell him to Aaron Murdock."

"I see." That was one more she owed him, Jillian thought with a scowl. It was hard to meet a man toe to toe when you were piling up debts. "If it is Baby, and this Jennsen was involved, we'll get the rest of them."

"We'll see if it's Baby," Gil said, then eased a cautious look at her. "The sheriff's already rounding up the rest of them. Picked up Joe Carlson a couple hours ago."

"Joe?" Stunned, she turned completely around in her seat to stare at Gil. "Joe Carlson?"

"Seems he bought himself a little place over in Wyoming. From the sound of it, he's already got a couple hundred head of your cattle grazing there."

"Joe." Shifting, Jillian stared straight ahead. So much for trust, she thought. So much for her expert reading of character. Clay hadn't wanted to hire him—she'd insisted. One of her first major independent decisions on Utopia had been her first major mistake.

"Guess he fooled me, too," Gil muttered after a moment. "Knew his cattle front and back." He spit again and set his teeth. "Shoulda known better than to trust a man with soft hands and a clean hat."

"I hired him," Jillian muttered.

"I worked with him," Gil tossed back. "Side by side. And if you don't think that sticks in my craw, then you ain't too smart. Bamboozled me," he grumbled. *"Me!"*

It was his insulted pride that made her laugh. Jillian propped her feet up on the dash. What was done was over, she told herself. She was going to get a good chunk of her cattle back and see justice done. And at roundup time her books would shift back into the black. Maybe they'd have that new Jeep after all. "Did you get the full story from the sheriff?"

"Aaron Murdock," Gil told her. "He came by right before I set out after you."

"He came by the ranch?" she asked with a casualness that wouldn't have fooled anyone.

"Stopped by so I'd have the details."

"Did he—ah—say anything else?"

"Just that he had a lot of things to see to. Busy man."

"Oh." Jillian turned her head and stared out the window. Gil took a chance and grinned hugely.

She waited until it was nearly dark. It was impossible to bank down the hope that he'd come by or call, if only to see that everything had gone well. She worked out a dozen opening speeches and revised them. She paced. When she knew that she'd scream if she spent another minute within four walls, Jillian went out to the stables and saddled her mare.

"Men," she grumbled as she pulled the cinch. "If this is all part of the game, I'm not interested."

Ready for a run, Delilah sniffed the air the moment Jillian led her outside. When Jillian swung into the saddle, the mare danced and strained against the bit. Within moments they'd left the lights of the ranch yard behind.

The ride would clear her head, she told herself. Anyone would be a bit crazed after a day like this one. Getting Baby back had eased the sting of betrayal she'd felt after learning Joe Carlson had stolen from her. Methodically stolen, she thought, while offering advice and sympathy. He'd certainly been clever, she mused, subtly, systematically turning her attention toward the Murdocks while he was slipping her own cattle through her own fences. Until she found a new herdsman, she'd have to add his duties to her own.

It would do her good, she decided, keep her mind off things. Aaron. If he'd wanted to see her, he'd known where to find her. Apparently, she'd done them both a favor by pushing him away weeks before. If she hadn't, they'd have found themselves in a very painful situation. As it was, they were each just going their own way—exactly as she'd known they would from the beginning. Perhaps she'd had a few moments of weakness, like the one that morning on the Double M, but they wouldn't last. In the next few weeks she'd be too busy to worry about Aaron Murdock and some foolish dreams.

Jillan told herself she hadn't deliberately ridden to the pond, but had simply let Delilah go her own way. In any case, it was still a spot she'd choose for solitude, no matter what memories lingered there.

The moon was full and white, the brush silvered with it. She told herself she wasn't unhappy, just tired after a long day of traveling, dealing with the sheriff, answering questions. She couldn't be unhappy when she finally had what was hers back. When the weariness passed, she'd celebrate. She could have wept, and hated herself.

When she saw the moon reflected on the water, she slowed Delilah to an easy lope. There wasn't a sound but the steady hoofbeats of her own mount. She heard the stallion even as her mare scented him. With her own heart pounding, Jillian controlled the now skittish Delilah and brought her to a halt. Aaron stepped out of the shadow of a cottonwood and said nothing at all.

He'd known she'd come—sooner or later. He could've gone to her, or waited for her to come to him. Somehow he'd known they had to meet here on land that belonged to them both.

It was better to face it all now and be done with it, Jillian told herself, then found her hands were wet with nerves as she dismounted. Nothing could've stiffened her spine more effectively. In thrumming silence she tethered her mare. When she turned, she found Aaron had moved behind her, as silently as the wildcat she'd once compared him to. She stood very straight, kept her tone very impassive.

"So, you came back."

His eyes were lazy and amused as he scanned her face. "Did you think I wouldn't?"

Her chin came up as he'd known it would. "I didn't think about it at all."

"No?" He smiled then—it should have warned her. "Did you think about this?" He dragged her to him, one hand at her waist, one at the back of her head, and devoured the mouth he'd starved for. He expected her to struggle—perhaps he would've relished it just then—but she met the demands of his mouth with the strength and verve he remembered.

When he tore his mouth from hers, she clung, burying her face in his shoulder. He still wanted her—the thought pounded inside her head. She hadn't lost him, not yet. "Hold me," she murmured. "Please, just for a minute."

How could she do this to him? Aaron wondered. How could she shift his mood from crazed to tender in the space of seconds? Maybe he'd never figure out quite how to handle her, but he didn't intend to stop learning.

When she felt her nerves come back, she drew away. "I want to thank you for what you did. The sheriff told me that you got the evidence from Jennsen, and—"

"I don't want to talk about the cattle, Jillian."

"No." Linking her hands together, she turned away. No, it was time they put that aside and dealt with what was really important. What was vital. "I've thought about what happened—about what you said the last time we saw each other." Where were all those speeches she'd planned? They'd all been so calm, so lucid. She twisted her fingers until they hurt, then separated them. "Aaron, I meant it when I said that I don't expect to be told those things. Some women do."

"I wasn't saying them to some women."

"It's so easy to say," she told him in a vibrating whisper. "So easy."

"Not for me."

She turned slowly, warily, as if she expected him to make a move she wasn't prepared for. He looked so calm, she thought. And yet the way the moonlight hit his eyes… "It's hard," she murmured.

"What is?"

"Loving you."

He could have gone to her then, right then, and pulled her to him until there was no more talk, no more thought. But her chin was up and her eyes were swimming. "Maybe it's supposed to be. I'm not offering you an easy road."

"No one's ever loved me back the way I wanted." Swallowing, she stepped away. "No one but Clay, and he never told me. He never had to."

"I'm not Clay, or your father. And there's no one who's ever going to love you the way I do." He took a step toward her, and though she didn't back up, he thought he could see every muscle brace. "What are you afraid of?"

"I'm not afraid!"

He came closer. "Like hell."

"That you'll stop." It wrenched out of her as she gripped her hands behind her back. Once started, the words rushed out quickly and ran together. "That you'll decide you never really loved me anyway. And I'll have let myself want and start depending and needing you. I've spent most of my life working on not depending on anyone, not for anything."

"I'm not anyone," he said quietly.

Her breath came shuddering out. "Since you've been gone I haven't cared about anything except you coming back."

He ran his hands up her arms. "Now that I am?"

"I couldn't bear it if you didn't stay. And though I think I could stand the hurt, I just can't stand being afraid." She put her hands to his chest when he started to draw her to him.

"Jillian, do you think you can tell me things I've been waiting to hear and have me keep my hands off you? Don't you know there's risk on both sides? Dependence on both sides?"

"Maybe." She made herself breathe evenly until she got it all out. "But people aren't always looking for the same things."

"Such as?"

This time she moistened her lips. "Are you going to marry me?" The surprise in his eyes made her muscles stiffen again.

"You asking?"

She dragged herself out of his hold, cursing herself for being a fool and him for laughing at her. "Go to hell," she told him as she started for her horse.

He caught her around the waist, lifting her off the ground as she kicked out. "Damn, you've got a short fuse," he muttered and ended by pinning her to the ground. "I have a feeling I'm going to spend the best part of my life wrestling with you." Showing an amazing amount of patience, he waited until she'd run out of curses and had subsided, panting. "I'd planned to put the question to you a bit differently," he began. "As in, will you. But as I see it, that's a waste of time." As she stared up at him, he smiled. "God, you're beautiful. Don't argue," he warned as she opened her mouth. "I'm going to tell you that whenever I please so you might as well start swallowing it now."

"You were laughing at me," she began, but he cut her off.

"At both of us." Lowering his head, he kissed her, gently at first, then with building passion. "Now..." Cautiously he let her wrists go until he was certain she wasn't going to take a swing at him. "I'll give you a week to get things organized at your ranch."

"A week—"

"Shut up," he suggested. "A week, then we're both taking the next week off to get married."

Jillian lay very still and soaked it in. It was pure joy. "It doesn't take a week to get married."

"The way I do it does. When we get back—"

"Get back from where?"

"From any place where we can be alone," he told her. "We're going to start making some plans."

She reached for his cheek. "So far I like them. Aaron, say it again, while I'm looking at you."

"I love you, Jillian. A good bit of the time I like you, as well, though I can't say I mind fighting with you."

"I guess you really mean it." She closed her eyes a moment. When she opened them again, they were laughing. "It's hard to take a Murdock at his word, but I'm going to gamble."

"What about a Baron?"

"A Baron's word's gold," she said, angling her chin. "I love you, Aaron. I'm going to make you a frustrating wife and a hell of a partner." She grinned as his lips pressed against hers. "What about those plans?"

"You've got a ranch, I've got a ranch," he pointed out as he kissed her palm. "I don't much care whether we run them separately or together, but there's a matter of living. Your house, my house—that's not going to work for either of us. So we'll build our house, and that's where we're going to raise our children."

Our. She decided it was the most exciting word in the English language. She was going to use it a dozen times every day for the rest of her life. "Where?"

He glanced over her head, skimming the pool, the solitude. "Right on the damn boundary line."

With a laugh, Jillian circled his neck. "What boundary line?"

* * * * *

THE RIGHT PATH

Chapter 1

The sky was cloudless—the hard, perfect blue of a summer painting. A breeze whispered through the roses in the garden. Mountains were misted by distance. A scent—flowers, sea, new grass—drifted on the air. With a sigh of pure pleasure, Morgan leaned farther over the balcony rail and just looked.

Had it really only been yesterday morning that she had looked out on New York's steel and concrete? Had she run through a chill April drizzle to catch a taxi to the airport? One day. It seemed impossible to go from one world to another in only a day.

But she was here, standing on the balcony of a villa on the Isle of Lesbos. There was no gray drizzle at all, but strong Greek sunlight. There was quiet, a deep blanketing stillness that contrasted completely with the fits and starts of New York traffic. If I could paint, Morgan mused, I'd paint this view and call it *Silence*.

"Come in," she called when there was a knock on the door. After one last deep breath, she turned, reluctantly.

"So, you're up and dressed." Liz swept in, a small, golden fairy with a tray-bearing maid in her wake.

"Room service." Morgan grinned as the maid placed the tray on a glass-topped table. "I'll begin to wallow in luxury from this moment." She took an appreciative sniff of the platters the maid uncovered. "Are you joining me?"

"Just for coffee." Liz settled in a chair, smoothing the skirts of her silk and lace robe, then took a long survey of the woman who sat opposite her.

Long loose curls in shades from ash blond to honey brown fell to tease pale shoulders. Almond-shaped eyes, almost too large for the slender face, were a nearly transparent blue. There was a straight, sharp nose and prominent cheekbones, a long, narrow mouth and a subtly pointed chin. It was a face of angles and contours that many a model starved herself for. It would photograph like a dream had Morgan ever been inclined to sit long enough to be captured on film.

What you'd get, Liz mused, would be a blur of color as Morgan dashed away to see what was around the next corner.

"Oh, Morgan, you look fabulous! I'm so glad you're here at last."

"Now that I'm here," Morgan returned, shifting her eyes back to the view, "I can't understand why I put off coming for so long. *Efxaristo,*" she added as the maid poured her coffee.

"Show-off," Liz said with mock scorn. "Do you know how long it took me to master a simple Greek hello, how are you? No, never mind." She waved her hand before

Morgan could speak. The symphony of diamonds and sapphires in her wedding ring caught the flash of sunlight. "Three years married to Alex and living in Athens and Lesbos, and I still stumble over the language. Thank you, Zena," she added in English, dismissing the maid with a smile.

"You're simply determined not to learn." Morgan bit enthusiastically into a piece of toast. She wasn't hungry, she discovered. She was ravenous. "If you'd open your mind, the words would seep in."

"Listen to you." Liz wrinkled her nose. "Just because you speak a dozen languages."

"Five."

"Five is four more than a rational person requires."

"Not a rational interpreter," Morgan reminded her and dug wholeheartedly into her eggs. "And if I hadn't spoken Greek, I wouldn't have met Alex and you wouldn't be *Kryios* Elizabeth Theoharis. Fate," she announced with a full mouth, "is a strange and wonderful phenomenon."

"Philosophy at breakfast," Liz murmured into her coffee. "That's one of the things I've missed about you. Actually, I'd hate to think what might have happened if I hadn't been home on layover when Alex popped up. You wouldn't have introduced us." She commandeered a piece of toast, adding a miserly dab of plum jelly. "I'd still be serving miniature bottles of bourbon at thirty thousand feet."

"Liz, my love, when something's meant, it's meant." Morgan cut into a fat sausage. "I'd love to take credit for your marital bliss, but one brief introduction wasn't responsible for the fireworks that followed." She glanced up at the cool blond beauty and smiled. "Little did I know I'd lose my roommate in less than three weeks. I've never seen two people move so fast."

"We decided we'd get acquainted after we were married." A grin warmed Liz's face. "And we have."

"Where is Alex this morning?"

"Downstairs in his office." Liz moved her shoulders absently and left half her toast untouched. "He's building another ship or something."

Morgan laughed outright. "You say that in the same tone you'd use if he were building a model train. Don't you know you're supposed to become spoiled and disdainful when you marry a millionaire—especially a foreign millionaire?"

"Is that so? Well, I'll see what I can do." She topped off her coffee. "He'll probably be horribly busy for the next few weeks, which is one more reason I'm glad you're here."

"You need a cribbage partner."

"Hardly," Liz corrected as she struggled with a smile. "You're the worst cribbage player I know."

"Oh, I don't know," Morgan began as her brows drew together.

"Perhaps you've improved. Anyway," Liz went on, concealing with her coffee cup what was now a grin, "not to be disloyal to my adopted country, but it's just so good to have my best friend, and an honest-to-God American, around."

"*Spasibo.*"

"English at all times," Liz insisted. "And I know that wasn't even Greek. You aren't translating government hyperbole at the U.N. for the next four weeks." She leaned forward to rest her elbows on the table. "Tell me the truth, Morgan, aren't you ever terrified you'll interpret some nuance incorrectly and cause World War III?"

"Who me?" Morgan opened her eyes wide. "Not a chance. Anyway, the trick is to think in the language you're interpreting. It's that easy."

"Sure it is." Liz leaned back. "Well, you're on vacation, so you only have to think in English. Unless you want to argue with the cook."

"Absolutely not," Morgan assured her as she polished off her eggs.

"How's your father?"

"Marvelous, as always." Relaxed, content, Morgan poured more coffee. When was the last time she had taken the time for a second cup in the morning? Vacation, Liz had said. Well, she was damn well going to learn how to enjoy one. "He sends you his love and wants me to smuggle some ouzo back to New York."

"I'm not going to think about you going back." Liz rose and swirled around the balcony. The lace border at the hem of her robe swept over the tile. "I'm going to find a suitable mate for you and establish you in Greece."

"I can't tell you how much I appreciate your handling things for me," Morgan returned dryly.

"It's all right. What are friends for?" Ignoring the sarcasm, Liz leaned back on the balcony. "Dorian's a likely candidate. He's one of Alex's top men and really attractive. Blond and bronzed with a profile that belongs on a coin. You'll meet him tomorrow."

"Should I tell Dad to arrange my dowry?"

"I'm serious." Folding her arms, Liz glared at Morgan's grin. "I'm not letting you go back without a fight. I'm going to fill your days with sun and sea, and dangle hordes of gorgeous men in front of your nose. You'll forget that New York and the U.N. exist."

"They're already wiped out of my mind...for the next four weeks." Morgan tossed her hair back over her shoulders. "So, satiate and dangle. I'm at your mercy. Are you going to drag me to the beach this morning? Force me to lie on the sand and soak up rays until I have a fabulous golden tan?"

"Exactly." With a brisk nod, Liz headed for the door. "Change. I'll meet you downstairs."

Thirty minutes later, Morgan decided she was going to like Liz's brand of brainwashing. White sand, blue water. She let herself drift on the gentle waves. *Too wrapped up in your work.* Isn't that what Dad said? *You're letting the job run you instead of the other way around.* Closing her eyes, Morgan rolled to float on her back. Between job pressure and the nasty breakup with Jack, she mused, I need a peace transfusion.

Jack was part of the past. Morgan was forced to admit that he had been more a habit than a passion. They'd suited each other's requirements. She had wanted an intelligent male companion; he an attractive woman whose manners would be advantageous to his political career.

If she'd loved him, Morgan reflected, she could hardly think of him so objectively, so...well, coldly. There was no ache, no loneliness. What there was, she admitted, was relief. But with the relief had come the odd feeling of being at loose ends. A feeling Morgan was neither used to nor enjoyed.

Liz's invitation had been perfectly timed. And this, she thought, opening her eyes to study that perfect sweep of sky, was paradise. Sun, sand, rock, flowers—the whispering memory of ancient gods and goddesses.

Mysterious Turkey was close, separated only by the narrow Gulf of Edremit. She closed her eyes again and would have dozed if Liz's voice hadn't disturbed her.

"Morgan! Some of us have to eat at regular intervals."

"Always thinking of your stomach."

"And *your* skin," Liz countered from the edge of the water. "You're going to fry. You can overlook lunch, but not sunburn."

"All right, Mommy." Morgan swam in, then stood on shore and shook like a wet dog. "How come you can swim and lie in the sun and still look ready to walk into a ballroom?"

"Breeding," Liz told her and handed over the short robe. "Come on, Alex usually tears himself away from his ships for lunch."

I could get used to eating on terraces, Morgan thought after lunch was finished. They relaxed over iced coffee and fruit. She noted that Alexander Theoharis was still as fascinated with his small, golden wife as he had been three years before in New York.

Though she'd brushed off Liz's words that morning, Morgan felt a certain pride at having brought them together. A perfect match, she mused, Alex had an Old World charm—dark aquiline looks made dashing by a thin white scar above his eyebrow. He was only slightly above average height but with a leanness that was more aristocratic than rangy. It was the ideal complement for Liz's dainty blond beauty.

"I don't see how you ever drag yourself away from here," Morgan told him. "If this were all mine, nothing would induce me to leave."

Alex followed her gaze across the glimpse of sea to the mountains. "But when one returns, it's all the more magnificent. Like a woman," he continued, lifting Liz's hand to kiss, "paradise demands constant appreciation."

"It's got mine," Morgan stated.

"I'm working on her, Alex." Liz laced her fingers with his. "I'm going to make a list of all the eligible men within a hundred miles."

"You don't have a brother, do you, Alex?" Morgan asked, sending him a smile.

"Sisters only. My apologies."

"Forget it, Liz."

"If we can't entice you into matrimony, Alex will have to offer you a job in the Athens office."

"I'd steal Morgan from the U.N. in a moment," Alex reminded her with a move of his shoulders. "I couldn't lure her away three years ago. I tried."

"We have a month to wear her down this time." She shot Alex a quick glance. "Let's take her out on the yacht tomorrow."

"Of course." He agreed immediately. "We'll make a day of it. Would you like that, Morgan?"

"Oh, well, I'm constantly spending the day on a yacht on the Aegean, but"—her lake-blue eyes lit with laughter—"since Liz wants to, I'll try not to be too bored."

"She's such a good sport," Liz confided to Alex.

It was just past midnight when Morgan made her way down to the beach again. Sleep had refused to come. Morgan welcomed the insomnia, seeing it as an excuse to walk out into the warm spring night.

The light was liquid. The moon was sliced in half but held a white, gleaming brightness. Cypresses which flanked the steps down to the beach were silvered with it. The scent of blossoms, hot and pungent during the day, seemed more mysterious, more exotic, by moonlight.

From somewhere in the distance, she heard the low rumble of a motor. A late-night fisherman, she thought, and smiled. It would be quite an adventure to fish under the moon.

The beach spread in a wide half circle. Morgan dropped both her towel and wrap on a rock, then ran into the water. Against her skin it was so cool and silky that she toyed with the idea of discarding even the brief bikini. Better not, she thought with a low laugh. No use tempting the ghosts of the gods.

Though the thought of adventure appealed to her, she kept to the open bay and suppressed the urge to explore the inlets. They'd still be there in the daylight, she reminded herself. She swam lazily, giving her strokes just enough power to keep her afloat. She hadn't come for the exercise.

Even when her body began to feel the chill, she lingered. There were stars glistening on the water, and silence. Such silence. Strange, that until she had found it, she hadn't known she was looking for it.

New York seemed more than a continent away; it seemed centuries away. For the moment, she was content that it be so. Here she could indulge in the fantasies that never seemed appropriate in the rush of day-to-day living. Here she could let herself believe in ancient gods, in shining knights and bold pirates. A laugh bubbled from her as she submerged and rose again. Gods, knights, and pirates…well, she supposed she'd take the pirate if she had her pick. Gods were too bloodthirsty, knights too chivalrous, but a pirate…

Shaking her head, Morgan wondered how her

thoughts had taken that peculiar turn. It must be Liz's influence, she decided. Morgan reminded herself she didn't want a pirate or any other man. What she wanted was peace.

With a sigh, she stood knee-deep in the water, letting the drops stream down her hair and skin. She was cold now, but the cold was exhilarating. Ignoring her wrap, she sat on the rock and pulled a comb from its pocket and idly ran it through her hair. Moon, sand, water. What more could there be? She was, for one brief moment, in total harmony with her own spirit and with nature's.

Shock gripped her as a hand clamped hard over her mouth. She struggled, instinctively, but an arm was banded around her waist—rough cloth scraping her naked skin. Dragged from the rock, Morgan found herself molded against a solid, muscular chest.

Rape? It was the first clear thought before the panic. She kicked out blindly as she was pulled into the cover of trees. The shadows were deep there. Fighting wildly, she raked with her nails wherever she could reach, feeling only a brief satisfaction at the hiss of an undrawn breath near her ear.

"Don't make a sound." The order was in quick, harsh Greek. About to strike out again, Morgan felt her blood freeze. A glimmer of knife caught the moonlight just before she was thrust to the ground under the length of the man's body. "Wildcat," he muttered. "Keep still and I won't have to hurt you. Do you understand?"

Numb with terror, Morgan nodded. With her eyes glued to his knife, she lay perfectly still. I can't fight him now, she thought grimly. Not now, but somehow, somehow I'll find out who he is. He'll pay.

The first panic was gone, but her body still trembled as she waited. It seemed an eternity, but he made no move, no sound. It was so quiet, she could hear the waves lapping gently against the sand only a few feet away. Over her head, through the spaces in the leaves, stars still shone. It must be a nightmare, she told herself. It can't be real. But when she tried to shift under him, the pressure of his body on hers proved that it was very, very real.

The hand over her mouth choked her breath until vague colors began to dance before her eyes. Morgan squeezed them tight for a moment to fight the faintness. Then she heard him speak again to a companion she couldn't see.

"What do you hear?"

"Nothing yet—in a moment." The voice that answered was rough and brisk. "Who the devil is she?"

"It doesn't matter. She'll be dealt with."

The roaring in her ears made it difficult to translate the Greek. Dealt with? she thought, dizzy again from fear and the lack of air.

The second man said something low and furious about women, then spat into the dirt.

"Just keep your ears open," Morgan's captor ordered. "And leave the woman to me."

"Now."

She felt him stiffen, but her eyes never left the knife. He was gripping it tighter now, she saw the tensing of his fingers on the handle.

Footsteps. They echoed on the rock steps of the beach. Hearing them, Morgan began to struggle again with the fierce strength of panic and of hope. With a whispered oath, he put more of his weight on her. He smelt faintly of the sea. As he shifted she caught a brief glimpse of his face in a patchy stream of moonlight. She saw dark, angular features, a grim mouth, and narrowed jet eyes. They were hard and cold and ruthless. It was the face of a man prepared to kill. *Why?* She thought as her mind began to float. I don't even know him.

"Follow him," he ordered his companion. Morgan heard a slight stirring in the leaves. "I'll take care of the woman."

Morgan's eyes widened at the sharp glimmer of the blade. She tasted something—bitter, copper—in her throat, but didn't recognize it as terror. The world spun to the point of a pin, then vanished.

The sky was full of stars, silver against black. The sea whispered. Against her back, the sand was rough. Morgan rose on her elbow and tried to clear her head. Fainted? Good God, had she actually fainted? Had she simply fallen asleep and dreamed it all? Rubbing her fingers against her temple, she wondered if her fantasies about pirates had caused her to hallucinate.

A small sound brought her swiftly to her feet. No, it had been real, and he was back. Morgan hurled herself at the shadow as it approached. She'd accepted the inevitability of death once without a struggle. This time, he was going to have a hell of a fight on his hands.

The shadow grunted softly as she struck, then Morgan found herself captured again, under him with the sand scraping her back.

"*Diabolos!* Be still!" he ordered in furious Greek as she tried to rip at his face.

"The hell I will!" Morgan tossed back in equally furious English. She fought with every ounce of strength until he pinned her, spread-eagle beneath him. Breathless, fearless in her rage, she stared up at him.

Looking down, he studied her with a frown. "You're not Greek." The statement, uttered in surprised and impatient English, stopped her struggles. "Who are you?"

"None of your business." She tried, and failed, to jerk her wrists free of his hold.

"Stop squirming," he ordered roughly, as his fingers clamped down harder. He wasn't thinking of his strength or her fragility, but that she wasn't simply a native who had been in the wrong place at the wrong time. His profession had taught him to get answers and adjust for complications. "What were you doing on the beach in the middle of the night?"

"Swimming," she tossed back. "Any idiot should be able to figure that out."

He swore, then shifted as she continued to struggle beneath him. "Damn it, be still!" His brows were lowered, not in anger now but concentration. "Swimming," he repeated as his eyes narrowed again. He'd watched her walk out of the sea—perhaps it was as innocent as that. "American," he mused, ignoring Morgan's thrashing. Weren't the Theoharises expecting an American woman? Of all the ill-timed... "You're not Greek," he murmured again.

"Neither are you," Morgan said between clenched teeth.

"Half." His thoughts underwent some rapid readjustments. The Theoharises' American houseguest, out for a moonlight swim—he'd have to play this one carefully or there'd be hell to pay. Quite suddenly, he flashed her a smile. "You had me fooled. I thought you could understand me."

"I understand perfectly," she retorted. "And you won't find it an easy rape now that you don't have your knife out."

"Rape?" Apparently astonished, he stared at her. His laughter was as sudden as the smile. "I hadn't given that much thought. In any case, Aphrodite, the knife was never intended for you."

"Then what do you mean by dragging me around like that? Flashing a knife in my face and nearly suffocating me?" Fury was much more satisfying than fear, and Morgan went with it. "Let me go!" She pushed at him with her body, but couldn't nudge him.

"In a moment," he said pleasantly. The moonlight played on her skin, and he enjoyed it. A fabulous face, he mused, now that he had time to study it. She'd be a woman accustomed to male admiration. Perhaps charm would distract her from the rather unique aspect of their meeting. "I can only say that what I did was for your own protection."

"Protection!" she flung back at him and tried to wrench her arms free.

"There wasn't time for amenities, fair lady. My apologies if my...technique was unrefined." His tone seemed to take it for granted that she would understand. "Tell me, why were you out alone, sitting like Lorelei on the rock and combing your hair?"

"That's none of your business." His voice had dropped, becoming low and seductive. The dark eyes had softened and appeared depthless. She could almost believe she had imagined the ruthlessness she'd glimpsed in the shadows. But she felt the light throbbing where his fingers had gripped her flesh. "I'm going to scream if you don't let me go."

Her body was tempting now that he had time to appreciate it, but he rose with a shrug. There was still work to be done that night. "My apologies for your inconvenience."

"Oh, is that right?" Struggling to her feet, Morgan began to brush at the sand that clung to her skin. "You have your nerve, dragging me off into the bushes, smothering me, brandishing a knife in my face, then apologizing like you've just stepped on my toe." Suddenly cold, she wrapped her arms around herself. "Just who are you and what was this all about?"

"Here." Stooping, he picked up the wrap he had dropped in order to hold her off. "I was bringing this to you when you launched your attack." He grinned as she shrugged into the wrap. It was a pity to cover the lengthy, intriguing body. "Who I am at the moment isn't relevant. As for the rest"—again the smooth, easy shrug—"I can't tell you."

"Just like that?" With a quick nod, Morgan turned and stalked to the beach steps. "We'll see what the police have to say about it."

"I wouldn't if I were you."

The advice was quiet, but vibrated with command. Hesitating, Morgan turned at the base of the steps to study him. He wasn't threatening now. What she felt wasn't fear, but his authority. He was quite tall, she noticed suddenly. And the moonlight played tricks with his face, making it almost cruel one moment, charming the next. Now it held all the confidence of Lucifer regrouping after the Fall.

Looking at him, she remembered the feel of hard, wiry muscles. He was standing easily, hands thrust into the pockets of jeans. The aura of command fit him perfectly. His smile didn't disguise it, nor did his casual stance. Damn pirates, she thought, feeling a quick twinge. Only lunatics find them attractive. Because she felt vulnerable, Morgan countered with bravado.

"Wouldn't you?" She lifted her chin and walked back to him.

"No," he answered mildly. "But perhaps, unlike me, you look for complications. I'm a simple man." He took a long, searching look of her face. *This is not,* he decided instantly, *a simple woman.* Though in his mind he cursed her, he went on conversationally. "Questions, reports to fill out, hours wasted on red tape. And then, even if you had my name"—he shrugged and flashed the grin again—"no one would believe you, Aphrodite. No one."

She didn't trust that grin—or the sultry way he called her by the goddess's name. She didn't trust the sudden warmth in her blood. "I wouldn't be so sure," Morgan began, but he cut her off, closing the slight distance between them.

"And I didn't rape you." Slowly, he ran his hands down her hair until they rested on her shoulders. His fingers didn't bite into her flesh now, but skimmed lazily. She had the eyes of a witch, he thought, and the face of a goddess. His time was short, but the moment was not to be missed. "Until now, I haven't even given in to the urge to do this."

His mouth closed over hers, hot and stunningly sweet. She hadn't been prepared for it. She pushed against him, but it was strictly out of reflex and lacked strength. He was a man who knew a woman's weakness. Deliberately, he brought her close, using style rather than force.

The scent of the sea rose to surround her, and heat— such a furnace heat that seemed to come from within and without at the same time. Almost leisurely, he explored her mouth until her heart thudded wildly against the quick, steady beat of his. His hands were clever, sliding beneath the wide sleeves of her robe to tease and caress the length of her arms, the slope of her shoulders.

When her struggles ceased, he nibbled at her lips as if he would draw out more taste. Slow, easy. His tongue tempted hers then retreated, then slipped through her parted lips again to torment and savor. For a moment, Morgan feared she would faint for a second time in his arms.

"One kiss," he murmured against her lips, "is hardly a criminal offense." She was sweeter than he had imagined and, he realized as desire stirred hotly, deadlier. "I could take another with little more risk."

"No." Coming abruptly to her senses, Morgan pushed away from him. "You're mad. And you're madder still if you think I'm going to let this go. I'm going ″ She broke off as her hand lifted to her throat in a nervous gesture. The chain which always hung there was missing. Morgan glanced down, then brought her eyes back to his, furious, glowing.

"What have you done with my medal?" she demanded. "Give it back to me."

"I'm afraid I don't have it, Aphrodite."

"I want it back." Bravado wasn't a pose this time; she was livid. She stepped closer until they were toe to toe. "It's not worth anything to you. You won't be able to get more than a few drachmas for it."

His eyes narrowed. "I didn't take your medal. I'm not a thief." The temper in his voice was cold, coated with control. "If I were going to steal something from you, I would have found something more interesting than a medal."

Her eyes filled in a rush, and she swung out her hand to slap him. He caught her wrist, adding frustration to fury.

"It appears the medal is important," he said softly, but his hand was no longer gentle. "A token from a lover?"

"A gift from someone I love," Morgan countered. "I wouldn't expect a man like you to understand its value." With a jerk, she pulled her wrist from his hold. "I won't forget you," she promised, then turned and flew up the stairs.

He watched her until she was swallowed by the darkness. After a moment he turned back to the beach.

Chapter 2

The sun was a white flash of light. Its diamonds skimmed the water's surface. With the gentle movement of the yacht, Morgan found herself half-dozing.

Could the moonlit beach and the man have been a dream? she wondered hazily. Knives and rough hands and sudden draining kisses from strangers had no place in the real world. They belonged in one of those strange, half-remembered dreams she had when the rush and demands of work and the city threatened to become too much for her. She'd always considered them her personal release valve. Harmless, but absolutely secret— something she'd never considered telling Jack or any of her co-workers.

If it hadn't been for the absence of her medal, and the light trail of bruises on her arms, Morgan could have believed the entire incident had been the product of an overworked imagination.

Sighing, she shifted her back to the sun, pillowing her head on her hands. Her skin, slick with oil, glistened. Why was she keeping the whole crazy business from Liz and Alex? Grimacing, she flexed her shoulders. They'd be horrified if she told them she'd been assaulted. Morgan could all but see Alex placing her under armed guard for the rest of her stay on Lesbos. He'd make certain there was an investigation—complicated, time-consuming, and in all probability fruitless. Morgan could work up a strong hate for the dark man for being right.

And what, if she decided to pursue it, could she tell the police? She hadn't been hurt or sexually assaulted. There'd been no verbal threat she could pin down, not even the slimmest motivation for what had happened. And what had happened? she demanded of herself. A man had dragged her into the bushes, held her there for no clear reason, then had let her go without harming her.

The Greek police wouldn't see the kiss as a criminal offense. She hadn't been robbed. There was no way on earth to prove the man had taken her medal. And damn it, she added with a sigh, as much as she'd like to assign all sorts of evil attributes to him, he just didn't fit the role of a petty thief. Petty anything, she thought grudgingly. Whatever he did, she was certain he did big... and did well.

So what was she going to do about it? True, he'd frightened and infuriated her—the second was probably a direct result of the first—but what else was there?

If and when they caught him, it would be his word against hers. Somehow, Morgan thought his word would carry more weight.

So I was frightened—my pride took a lump. She shrugged and shifted her head on her hands. It's not worth upsetting Liz and Alex. Midnight madness, she mused. Another strange adventure in the life and times of Morgan James. File it and forget it.

Hearing Alex mount the steps to the sun deck, Morgan rested her chin on her hands and smiled at him. On the lounger beside her, Liz stirred and slept on.

"So, the sun has put her to sleep." Alex mounted the last of the steps, then settled into the chair beside his wife.

"I nearly dozed off myself." With a yawn, Morgan stretched luxuriously before she rolled over to adjust the lounger to a sitting position. "But I didn't want to miss anything." Gazing over the water, she studied the clump of land in the distance. The island seemed to float, as insubstantial as a mist.

"Chios," Alex told her, following her gaze. "And"— he gestured, waiting for her eyes to shift in the direction of his—"the coast of Turkey."

"So close," Morgan mused. "It seems as though I could swim to it."

"At sea, the distance can be deceiving." He flicked a lighter at the end of a black cigarette. The fragrance that rose from it was faintly sweet and exotic. "You'd have to be a hardy swimmer. Easy enough with a boat, though. There are some who find the proximity profitable." At Morgan's blank expression, Alex laughed. "Smuggling, innocence. It's still popular even though the punishment is severe."

"Smuggling," she murmured, intrigued. Then the word put her in mind of pirates again and her curious expression turned into a frown. A nasty business, she reminded herself, and not romantic at all.

"The coast," Alex made another gesture, sweeping,

with the elegant cigarette held between two long fingers. "The many bays and peninsulas, offshore islands, inlets. There's simple access from the sea to the interior."

She nodded. Yes, a nasty business—they weren't talking about French brandy or Spanish lace. "Opium?"

"Among other things."

"But, Alex." His careless acceptance caused her frown to deepen. Once she'd sorted it through, Morgan's own sense of right and wrong had little middle ground. "Doesn't it bother you?"

"Bother me?" he repeated, taking a long, slow drag on the cigarette. "Why?"

Flustered with the question, she sat up straighter. "Aren't you concerned about that sort of thing going on so close to your own home?"

"Morgan." Alex spread his hands in an acceptance of fate. The thick chunk of gold on his left pinky gleamed dully in the sunlight. "My concern would hardly stop what's been going on for centuries."

"But still, with crime practically in your own backyard…" She broke off, thinking about the streets of Manhattan. Perhaps she was the pot calling the kettle black. "I supposed I'd thought you'd be annoyed," she finished.

His eyes lit with a touch of amusement before he shrugged. "I leave the matter—and the annoyance—to the patrols and authorities. Tell me, are you enjoying your stay so far?"

Morgan started to speak again, then consciously smoothed away the frown. Alex was Old World enough not to want to discuss unpleasantries with a guest. "It's wonderful here, Alex. I can see why Liz loves it."

He flashed her a grin before he drew in strong tobacco. "You know Liz wants you to stay. She's missed you. At times, I feel very guilty because we don't get to America to see you often enough."

"You don't have to feel guilty, Alex." Morgan pushed on sunglasses and relaxed again. After all, she reflected, smuggling had nothing to do with her. "Liz is happy."

"She'd be happier with you here."

"Alex," Morgan began with a smile for his indulgence of his wife. "I can't simply move in as a companion, no matter how much both of us love Liz."

"You're still dedicated to your job at the U.N.?" His tone had altered slightly, but Morgan sensed the change. It was business now.

"I like my work. I'm good at it, and I need the challenge."

"I'm a generous employer, Morgan, particularly to one with your capabilities." He took another long, slow drag, studying her through the mist of smoke. "I asked you to come work for me three years ago. If I hadn't been"—he glanced down at Liz's sleeping figure—"distracted"—he decided with a mild smile—"I would have taken more time to convince you to accept."

"Distracted?" Liz pushed her sunglasses up to her forehead and peered at him from under them.

"Eavesdropping," Morgan said with a sniff. A uniformed steward set three iced drinks on the table. She lifted one and drank. "Your manners always were appalling."

"You have a few weeks yet to think it over, Morgan." Tenacity beneath a smooth delivery was one of Alex's most successful business tactics. "But I warn you, Liz will be more persistent with her other solution." He shrugged, reaching for his own drink. "And I must agree—a woman needs a husband and security."

"How very Greek of you," Morgan commented dryly.

His grin flashed without apology. "I'm afraid one of Liz's candidates will be delayed. Dorian won't join us until tomorrow. He's bringing my cousin Iona with him."

"Marvelous." Liz's response was drenched in sarcasm. Alex sent her a frown.

"Liz isn't fond of Iona, but she's family." The quiet look he sent his wife told Morgan the subject had been discussed before. "I have a responsibility."

Liz took the last glass with a sigh of acceptance. Briefly she touched her hand to his. "We have a responsibility," she corrected. "Iona's welcome."

Alex's frown turned into a look of love so quickly, Morgan gave a mock groan. "Don't you two ever fight? I mean, don't you realize it isn't healthy to be so well balanced?"

Liz's eyes danced over the rim of her glass. "We have our moments, I suppose. A week ago I was furious with him for at least—ah, fifteen minutes."

"That," Morgan said positively, "is disgusting."

"So," Alex mused, "you think a man and woman must fight to be…healthy?"

Shaking back her hair, Morgan laughed. "*I* have to fight to be healthy."

"Morgan, you haven't mentioned Jack at all. Is there a problem?"

"Liz." Alex's disapproval was clear in the single syllable.

"No, it's all right, Alex." Taking her glass, Morgan rose and moved to the rail. "It's not a problem," she said slowly. "At least I hope it's not." She stared into her drink, frowning, as if she wasn't quite sure what the glass contained. "I've been running on this path—this very straight, very defined path. I could run it blind-folded." With a quick laugh, Morgan leaned out on the rail to let the wind grab at her hair. "Suddenly, I discovered it wasn't a path, but a rut and it kept getting deeper. I decided to change course before it became a pit."

"You always did prefer an obstacle course," Liz murmured. But she was pleased with Jack's disposal, and took little trouble to hide it.

The sea churned in a white froth behind the boat. Morgan turned from her study of it. "I don't intend to fall at Dorian's feet, Liz—or anyone else you might have in mind—just because Jack and I are no longer involved."

"I should hope not," Liz returned with some spirit. "That would take all the fun out of it."

With a sigh of exasperated affection, Morgan turned back to the rail.

The stark mountains of Lesbos rose from the sea. Jagged, harsh, timeless. Morgan could make out the pure white lines of Alex's villa. She thought it looked like a virgin offering to the gods—cool, classic, certainly feminine. Higher still was a rambling gray structure which seemed hewn from the rock itself. It faced the sea; indeed, it loomed over it. As if challenging Poseidon to claim it, it clung to the cliff. Morgan saw it as arrogant, rough, masculine. The flowering vines which grew all around it didn't soften the appearance, but added a haunted kind of beauty.

There were other buildings—a white-washed village, snuggled cottages, one or two other houses on more sophisticated lines, but the two larger structures hovered over the rest. One was elegant; one was savage.

"Who does that belong to?" Morgan called over her shoulder. "It's incredible."

Following her gaze, Liz grinned and rose to join her. "I should have known that would appeal to you. Sometimes I'd swear it's alive. Nicholas Gregoras, olive oil, and more recently, import-export." She glanced at her friend's profile. "Maybe I'll include him for dinner tomorrow if he's free, though I don't think he's your type."

Morgan gave her a dry look. "Oh? And what is my type?"

"Someone who'll give you plenty to fight about. Who'll give you that obstacle course."

"*Hmm.* You know me too well."

"As for Nick, he's rather smooth and certainly a charmer." Liz tapped a fingernail against the rail as she considered. "Not as blatantly handsome as Dorian, but he has a rather basic sort of sex appeal. Earthier, and yet…" She trailed off, narrowing her eyes she tried to pigeonhole him. "Well, he's an odd one. I suppose he'd have to be to live in a house like that. He's in his early thirties, inherited the olive oil empire almost ten years ago. Then he branched into import-export. He seems to have a flair for it. Alex is very fond of him because they go back to short pants together."

"Liz, I only wanted to know who owned the house. I didn't ask for a biography."

"These facts are part of the service." She cupped her hands around her lighter and lit a cigarette. "I want to give you a clear picture of your options."

"Haven't you got a goatherd up your sleeve?" Morgan demanded. "I rather like the idea of a small, whitewashed cottage and baking black bread."

"I'll see what I can do."

"I don't suppose it occurs to you or Alex that I'm content to be single—the modern, capable woman on her own? I know how to use a screwdriver, how to change a flat tire…"

"'Methinks she doth protest too much,'" Liz quoted mildly.

"Liz—"

"I love you, Morgan."

On a frustrated sigh, Morgan lifted her drink again. "Damn it, Liz," she murmured.

"Come on, let me have my fun," she coaxed, giving Morgan a friendly pat on the cheek. "As you said yourself, it's all up to fate anyway."

"Hoist by my own petard. All right, bring on your Dorians and your Nicks and your Lysanders."

"Lysander?"

"It's a good name for a goatherd."

With a chuckle, Liz flicked her cigarette into the churning water. "Just wait and see if I don't find one."

"Liz…" Morgan hesitated for a moment, then asked casually, "do many people use the beach where we swam yesterday?"

"*Hmm?* Oh." She tucked a pale blond strand behind her ear. "Not really. It's used by us and the Gregoras villa for the most part. I'd have to ask Alex who owns it, I've never given it any thought. The bay's secluded and only easily accessible by the beach steps which run between the properties. Oh, yes, there's a cottage Nick owns which he rents out occasionally," she remembered. "It's occupied now by an American. Stevens…no," she corrected herself. "Stevenson. Andrew Stevenson, a poet or a painter or something. I haven't met him yet." She gave Morgan a frank stare. "Why? Did you plan for an all over tan?"

"Just curious." Morgan rearranged her thoughts. If

she was going to file it and forget it, she had to stop letting the incident play back in her mind. "I'd love to get a close look at that place." She gestured toward the gray villa. "I think the architect must have been just a little mad. It's fabulous."

"Use some charm on Nick and get yourself an invitation," Liz suggested.

"I might just do that." Morgan studied the villa consideringly. She wondered if Nick Gregoras was the man whose footsteps she had heard when she had been held in the bushes. "Yes, I might just."

That evening, Morgan left the balcony doors wide. She wanted the warmth and scents of the night. The house was quiet but for the single stroke of a clock that signaled the hour. For the second night in a row she was wide awake. Did people really sleep on vacations? she wondered. What a waste of time.

She sat at the small rosewood desk in her room, writing a letter. From somewhere between the house and the sea, an owl cried out twice. She paused to listen, hoping it would call again, but there was only silence. How could she describe how it felt to see Mount Olympus rising from the sea? Was it possible to describe the timelessness, the strength, the almost frightening beauty?

She shrugged, and did what she could to explain the sensation to her father on paper. He'd understand, she mused as she folded the stationery. Who understood better her sometimes whimsical streaks of fancy than the man she'd inherited them from? And, she thought with a lurking smile, he'd get a good chuckle at Liz's determination to marry her off and keep her in Greece.

She rose, stretched once, then turned and collided

with a hard chest. The hand that covered her mouth used more gentleness this time, and the jet eyes laughed into hers. Her heart rose, then fell like an elevator with its cable clipped.

"*Kalespera,* Aphrodite. Your word that you won't scream, and you have your freedom."

Instinctively she tried to jerk away, but he held her still without effort, only lifting an ironic brow. He was a man who knew whose word to accept and whose word to doubt.

Morgan struggled for another moment, then finding herself outmatched, reluctantly nodded. He released her immediately.

She drew in the breath to shout, then let it out in a frustrated huff. A promise was a promise, even if it was to a devil. "How did you get in here?" she demanded.

"The vines to your balcony are sturdy."

"You climbed?" Her incredulity was laced with helpless admiration. The walls were sheer, the height was dizzying. "You must be mad."

"That's a possibility," he said with a careless smile.

He seemed none the worse for wear after the climb. His hair was disheveled, but then she'd never seen it otherwise. There was a shadow of beard on his chin. His eyes held no strain or fatigue, but rather a light of adventure that drew her no matter how hard she tried to resist. In the lamplight she could see him more clearly than she had the night before. His features weren't as harsh as she had thought and his mouth wasn't grim. It was really quite beautiful, she realized with a flood of annoyance.

"What do you want?"

He smiled again, letting his gaze roam down her leisurely with an insolence she knew wasn't contrived but inherent. She wore only a brief cinnamon-colored teddy that dipped low at the breast and rose high at the thighs. Morgan noted the look, and that he stood squarely between her and the closet where she had left her robe. Rather than acknowledge the disadvantage, she tilted her chin.

"How did you know where to find me?"

"It's my business to find things out," he answered. Silently, he approved more than her form, but her courage as well. "Morgan James," he began. "Visiting friend of Elizabeth Theoharis. American, living in New York. Unmarried. Employed at the U.N. as interpreter. You speak Greek, English, French, Italian and Russian."

She tried not to let her mouth fall open at his careless rundown on her life. "That's a very tidy summary," she said tightly.

"Thank you. I try to be succinct."

"What does any of that have to do with you?"

"That's yet to be decided." He studied her, thinking again. It might be that he could employ her talents and position for his own uses. The package was good, very good. And so, more important at the moment, was the mind.

"You're enjoying your stay on Lesbos?"

Morgan stared at him, then slowly shook her head. No, he wasn't a ruffian or a rapist. That much she was sure of. If he were a thief, which she still reserved judgment on, he was no ordinary one. He spoke too well, moved too well. What he had was a certain amount of odd charm, a flair that was hard to resist, and an amazing amount of arrogance. Under different circumstances, she might even have liked him.

"You have incredible gall," she decided.

"You continue to flatter me."

"All right." Tight-lipped, Morgan strode over to the open balcony doors and gestured meaningfully. "I gave you my word I wouldn't scream, and I didn't. But I have no intention of standing here making idle conversation with a lunatic. Out!"

With his lips still curved in a smile, he sat on the edge of the bed and studied her. "I admire a woman of her word." He stretched out jean-clad legs and crossed his feet. "I find a great deal to admire about you, Morgan. Last night you showed good sense and courage—rare traits to find together."

"Forgive me if I'm not overwhelmed."

He caught the sarcasm, but more important, noted the change in her eyes. She wasn't as angry as she tried to be. "I did apologize," he reminded her and smiled.

Her breath came out in a long-suffering sigh. She could detest him for making her want to laugh when she should be furious. Just who the devil was he? He wasn't the mad rapist she had first thought—he wasn't a common thief. So just what was he? Morgan stopped herself before she asked—she was better off in ignorance.

"It didn't seem like much of an apology to me."

"If I make a more…honest attempt," he began with a bland sincerity that made her lips twitch, "would you accept?"

Firmly, she banked down on the urge to return his smile. "If I accept it, will you go away?"

"But I find your company so pleasant."

An irrepressible light of humor flickered in her eyes. "The hell you do."

"Aphrodite, you wound me."

"I'd like to draw and quarter you. Are you going to go away?"

"Soon." Smiling, he rose again. What was that scent that drifted from her? he wondered. It was not quite sweet, not quite tame. Jasmine—wild jasmine. It suited her. He moved to the dresser to toy with her hand mirror. "You'll meet Dorian Zoulas and Iona Theoharis tomorrow," he said casually. This time Morgan's mouth did drop. "There's little on the island I'm not aware of," he said mildly.

"Apparently," she agreed.

Now he noted a hint of curiosity in her tone. It was what he had hoped for. "Perhaps, another time, you'll give me your impression of them."

Morgan shook her head more from bafflement than offense. "I have no intention of there being another time, or of gossiping with you. I hardly see why—"

"Why not?" he countered.

"I don't *know* you," she said in frustration. "I don't know this Dorian or Iona either. And I don't understand how you could possibly—"

"True," he agreed with a slight nod. "How well do you know Alex?"

Morgan ran a hand through her hair. Here I am, wearing little more than my dignity, exchanging small talk with a maniac who climbed in the third-story window. "Look, I'm not discussing Alex with you. I'm not discussing anyone or anything with you. Go away."

"We'll leave that for later too, then," he said mildly as he crossed back to her. "I have something for you." He reached into his pocket, then opened his hand and dangled a small silver medal by its chain.

"Oh, you did have it!" Morgan grabbed, only to have him whip it out of her reach. His eyes hardened with fury.

"I told you once, I'm no thief." The change in his voice and face had been swift and potent. Involuntarily, she took a step away. His mouth tightened at the movement before he went on in a more controlled tone. "I went back and found it in the grove. The chain had to be repaired, I'm afraid."

With his eyes on hers, he held it out again. Taking it, Morgan began to fasten it around her neck. "You're a very considerate assailant."

"Do you think I enjoyed hurting you?"

Her hands froze at the nape of her neck. There was no teasing banter in his tone now, no insolent light of amusement in his eyes. This was the man she recognized from the shadows. Waves of temper came from him, hardening his voice, burning in his jet eyes. With her hands still lifted, Morgan stared at him.

"Do you think I enjoyed frightening you into fainting, having you think I would murder you? Do you think it gives me pleasure to see there are bruises on you and know that I put them there?" He whirled away, stalking the room. "I'm not a man who makes a habit of misusing women."

"I wouldn't know about that," she said steadily.

He stopped, and his eyes came back to hers. Damn, she was cool, he thought. And beautiful. Beautiful enough to be a distraction when he couldn't afford one.

"I don't know who you are or what you're mixed up in," she continued. Her fingers trembled a bit as she finished fastening the chain, but her voice was calm and unhurried. "Frankly, I don't care as long as you leave me alone. Under different circumstances, I'd thank you for the return of my property, but I don't feel it applies in this case. You can leave the same way you came in."

He had to bank down on an urge to throttle her. It wasn't often he was in the position of having a half-naked woman order him from her bedroom three times in one evening. He might have found it amusing if he hadn't been fighting an overwhelming flood of pure and simple desire.

The hell with fighting it, he thought. A woman who kept her chin lifted in challenge deserved to be taken up on it.

"Courage becomes you, Morgan," he said coolly. "We might do very well together." Reaching out, he fingered the medal at her throat and frowned at it. With a silent oath, he tightened his grip on the chain and brought his eyes back to hers.

There was no fear in those clear blue pools now, but a light, maddening disdain. A woman like this, he thought, could make a man mad, make him suffer and ache. And by God, a woman like this would be worth it.

"I told you to go," she said icily, ignoring the sudden quick thud of her pulse. It wasn't fear—Morgan told herself she was through with fear. But neither was it the anger she falsely named it.

"And so I will," he murmured and let the chain drop. "In the meantime, since you don't offer, I take."

Once again she found herself in his arms. It wasn't the teasing, seductive kiss of the night before. Now he devoured her. No one had kissed her like this before— as if he knew every secret she hoarded. He would know, somehow, where she needed to be touched.

The hot, insistent flow of desire that ran through her left her too stunned to struggle, too hungry to reason.

How could she want him? her mind demanded. How could she want a man like this to touch her? But her mouth was moving under his, she couldn't deny it. Her tongue met his. Her hands gripped his shoulders, but didn't push him away.

"There's honey on your lips, Morgan," he murmured. "Enough to drive a man mad for another taste."

He took his hand on a slow journey down her back, pressing silk against her skin before he came to the hem. His fingers were strong, calloused, and as clever as a musician's. Without knowing, without caring what she did, Morgan framed his face with her hands for a moment before they dove into his hair. The muttered Greek she heard from him wasn't a love word but an oath as he dragged her closer.

How well she knew that body now. Long and lean and wiry with muscle. She could smell the sea on it, almost taste it beneath that hot demand as his mouth continued to savage hers.

The kiss grew deeper, until she moaned, half in fear of the unexplored, half in delight of the exploration. She'd forgotten who she was, who he was. There was only pleasure, a dark, heavy pleasure. Through her dazed senses she felt a struggle—a storm, a fury. Then he drew her away to study her face.

He wasn't pleased that his heartbeat was unsteady. Or that the thoughts whirling in his head were clouded with passion. This was no time for complications. And this was no woman to take risks with. With an effort, he slid his hands gently down her arms. "More satisfying than a thank you," he said lightly, then glanced with a grin toward the bed. "Are you going to ask me to stay?"

Morgan pulled herself back with a jolt. He must have

hypnotized her, she decided. There was no other rational explanation. "Some other time, perhaps," she managed, as carelessly as he.

Amusement lightened his features. Capturing her hand, he kissed it formally. "I'll look forward to it, Aphrodite."

He moved to the balcony, throwing her a quick grin before he started his descent. Unable to prevent herself, Morgan ran over to watch him climb down.

He moved like a cat, confident, fearless, a shadow clinging to the stark white walls. Her heart stayed lodged in her throat as she watched him. He sprang to the ground and melted into the cover of trees without looking back. Whirling, Morgan shut the doors to the balcony. And locked them.

Chapter 3

Morgan swirled her glass of local wine but drank little. Though its light, fruity flavor was appealing, she was too preoccupied to appreciate it. The terrace overlooked the gulf with its hard blue water and scattering of tiny islands. Small dots that were boats skimmed the surface, but she took little notice of them. Most of her mind was occupied in trying to sort out the cryptic comments of her late-night visitor. The rest was involved with following the conversation around her.

Dorian Zoulas was all that Liz had said—classically handsome, bronzed, and sophisticated. In the pale cream suit, he was a twentieth-century Adonis. He had intelligence and breeding, tempered with a golden beauty that was essentially masculine. Liz's maneuvers might have caused Morgan to treat him with a polite aloofness if she hadn't seen the flashes of humor in his eyes.

Morgan had realized immediately that he not only knew the way his hostess's mind worked, but had decided to play the game. The teasing challenge in his eyes relaxed her. Now she could enjoy a harmless flirtation without embarrassment.

Iona, Alex's cousin, was to Morgan's mind less appealing. Her dark, sultry looks were both stunning and disturbing. The gloss of beauty and wealth didn't quite polish over an edge that might have come from poor temperament or nerves. There was no humor in the exotic sloe eyes or pouting mouth. Iona was, Morgan mused, like a volcano waiting to erupt. Hot, smoky, and alarming.

The adjectives brought her night visitor back to her mind. They fit him just as neatly as they fit Iona Theoharis, and yet…oddly, Morgan found she admired them in the man and found them disturbing in the woman. Double standard? she wondered, then shook her head. No, the energy in Iona seemed destructive. The energy in the man was compelling. Annoyed with herself, Morgan turned from her study of the gulf and pushed aside her disturbing thoughts.

She gave Dorian her full attention. "You must find it very peaceful here after Athens."

He turned in his chair to face her. With only a smile, he intimated that there was no woman but she on the terrace—a trick Morgan found pleasant. "The island's a marvelous place…tranquil. But I thrive on chaos. As you live in New York, I'm sure you understand."

"Yes, but at the moment, tranquility is very appealing." Leaning against the rail, she let the sun play warm on her back. "I've been nothing but lazy so far. I haven't even whipped up the energy to explore."

"There's quite a bit of local color, if that's what you have in mind." Dorian slipped a thin gold case from his pocket, and opening it, offered Morgan a cigarette. At the shake of her head, he lit one for himself, then leaned back in a manner that was both relaxed and alert. "Caves and inlets, olive groves, a few small farms and flocks," he continued. "The village is very quaint and unspoiled."

"Exactly what I want." Morgan nodded and sipped her drink. "But I'm going to take it very slow. I'll collect shells and find a farmer who'll let me milk his goat."

"Terrifying aspirations," Dorian commented with a quick smile.

"Liz will tell you, I've always been intrepid."

"I'd be happy to help you with your shells." He continued to smile as his eyes skimmed her face with an approval she couldn't have missed. "But as to the goat…"

"I'm surprised you're content with so little entertainment." Iona's husky voice broke into the exchange.

Morgan shifted her gaze to her and found it took more of an effort to smile. "The island itself is entertainment enough for me. Remember, I'm a tourist. I've always thought vacations where you rush from one activity to the next aren't vacations at all."

"Morgan's been lazy for two full days," Liz put in with a grin. "A new record."

Morgan cast her a look, thinking of her nighttime activities. "I'm shooting for two weeks of peaceful sloth," Morgan murmured. *Starting today,* she added silently.

"Lesbos is the perfect spot for idleness." Dorian blew out a slow, fragrant stream of smoke. "Rustic, quiet."

"But perhaps this bit of island isn't as quiet as it appears." Iona ran a manicured nail around the rim of her glass.

Morgan saw Dorian's brows lift as if in puzzlement while Alex's drew together in disapproval.

"We'll do our best to keep it quiet during Morgan's visit," Liz said smoothly. "She rarely stays still for long, and since she's determined to this time, we'll see that she has a nice, uneventful vacation."

Morgan made some sound of agreement and managed not to choke over her drink. Uneventful! If Liz only knew.

"More wine, Morgan?" Dorian rose, bringing the bottle to her.

Iona began to tap her fingers on the arm of her wrought iron chair. "I suppose there are people who find boredom appealing."

"Relaxation," Alex said with a slight edge in his voice, "comes in many forms."

"And of course," Liz went on, skimming her hand lightly over the back of her husband's, "Morgan's job is very demanding. All those foreign dignitaries and protocol and politics."

Dorian sent Morgan an appreciative smile as he poured more wine into her glass. "I'm sure someone with Morgan's talents would have many fascinating stories to tell."

Morgan cocked a brow. It had been a long time since she had been given a purely admiring male smile—undemanding, warm without being appraising. She could learn to enjoy it. "I might have a few," she returned.

The sun was sinking into the sea. The rosy light streamed through the open balcony doors and washed the room. Red sky at night, Morgan mused. Wasn't that supposed to mean clear sailing? She decided to take it as an omen.

Her first two days on Lesbos had been a far cry from the uneventful vacation Liz had boasted of, but that was behind her now. With luck, and a little care, she wouldn't run into that attractive lunatic again.

Morgan caught a glimpse of her own smile in the mirror and hastily rearranged her expression. Perhaps when she got back to New York, she'd see a psychiatrist. When you started to find lunatics appealing, you were fast becoming one yourself. Forget it, she ordered herself firmly as she went to the closet. There were more important things to think about—like what she was going to wear to dinner.

After a quick debate, Morgan chose a drifting white dress—thin layers of crêpe de chine, full-sleeved, full-skirted. Dorian had inspired her to flaunt her femininity a bit. Jack, she recalled, had preferred the tailored look. He had often offered a stern and unsolicited opinion on her wardrobe, finding her taste both inconsistent and flighty. There might be a multicolored gypsy-style skirt hanging next to a prim business suit. He'd never understood that both had suited who she was. Just another basic difference, Morgan mused as she hooked the line of tiny pearl buttons.

Tonight she was going to have fun. It had been a long while since she'd flirted with a man. Her thoughts swung back to a dark man with tousled hair and a shadowed chin. Hold on, Morgan, she warned herself. *That* was hardly in the same league as a flirtation. Moving over, she closed the balcony doors and gave a satisfied nod as she heard the click of the lock. And that, she decided, takes care of that.

* * *

Liz glided around the salon. It pleased her that Morgan hadn't come down yet. Now she could make an entrance. For all her blond fragility, Liz was a determined woman. Loyalty was her strongest trait; where she loved, it was unbendable. She wanted Morgan to be happy. Her own marriage had given her nothing but happiness. Morgan would have the same if Liz had any say in it.

With a satisfied smile, she glanced around the salon. The light was low and flattering. The scent of night blossoms drifting in through the open windows was the perfect touch. The wines she'd ordered for dinner would add the final prop for romance. Now, if Morgan would cooperate...

"Nick, I'm so glad you could join us." Liz went to him, holding out both hands. "It's so nice that we're all on the island at the same time for a change."

"It's always a pleasure to see you, Liz," he returned with a warm, charming smile. "And a relief to be out of the crowds in Athens for a few weeks." He gave her hands a light squeeze, then lifted one to his lips. His dark eyes skimmed her face. "I swear, you're lovelier every time I see you."

With a laugh, Liz tucked her arm through his. "We'll have to invite you to dinner more often. Did I ever thank you properly for that marvelous Indian chest you found me?" Smiling, she guided him toward the bar. "I adore it."

"Yes, you did." He gave her hand a quick pat. "I'm glad I was able to find what you had in mind."

"You never fail to find the perfect piece. I'm afraid Alex wouldn't know an Indian chest from a Hepplewhite."

Nick laughed. "We all have our talents, I suppose."

"But your work must be fascinating." Liz glanced up at him with her wide-eyed smile as she began to fix him a drink. "All those treasures and all the exotic places you travel to."

"There are times it's more exciting just to be home."

She shot him a look. "You make that hard to believe, since you're so seldom here. Where was it last month? Venice?"

"A beautiful city," he said smoothly.

"I'd love to see it. If I could drag Alex away from his ships..." Liz's eyes focused across the room. "Oh dear, it looks like Iona is annoying Alex again." On a long breath, she lifted her eyes to Nick's. Seeing the quick understanding, she gave a rueful smile. "I'm going to have to play diplomat."

"You do it charmingly, Liz. Alex is a lucky man."

"Remind him of that from time to time," she suggested. "I'd hate for him to take me for granted. Oh, here comes Morgan. She'll keep you entertained while I do my duty."

Following Liz's gaze, Nick watched as Morgan entered the room. "I'm sure she will," was his murmured reply. He liked the dress she wore, the floating white that was at once alluring and innocent. She'd left her hair loose so that it fell over her shoulders almost as if it had come off a pillow. Quite beautiful, he thought as he felt the stir. He'd always had a weakness for beauty.

"Morgan." Before Morgan could do any more than smile her hello at Liz, Liz took her arm. "You'll keep Nick happy for a moment, I have a job to do. Morgan James, Nicholas Gregoras." With the quick introduction, Liz was halfway across the room.

Morgan stared in stunned silence. Nick lifted her

limp hand to his lips. "You," she managed in a choked whisper.

"Aphrodite, you're exquisite. Even fully dressed."

With his lips lingering over her knuckles, he met her eyes. His were dark and pleased. Regaining her senses, Morgan tried to wrench her hand free. Without changing expression, Nick tightened his grip and held her still.

"Careful, Morgan," he said mildly. "Liz and her guest will wonder at your behavior. And explanations would"—he grinned, exactly as she remembered—"cause them to wonder about your mental health."

"Let go of my hand," she said quietly and smiled with her lips only. "Or I swear, I'll deck you."

"You're magnificent." Making a small bow, he released her. "Did you know your eyes literally throw darts when you're annoyed?"

"Then I've the pleasure of knowing you're riddled with tiny holes," she returned. "Let me know when one hits the heart, *Mr.* Gregoras."

"Nick, please," he said in a polished tone. "We could hardly start formalities now after all we've…been through together."

Morgan gave him a brilliant smile. "Very well, Nick, you odious swine. What a pity this isn't the proper time to go into how detestable you are."

He inclined his head. "We'll arrange for a more appropriate opportunity. Soon," he added with the faintest hint of steel. "Now, let me get you a drink."

Liz breezed up, pleased with the smiles she had seen exchanged. "You two seem to be getting along like old friends."

"I was just telling Mr. Gregoras how enchanting his

home looks from the sea." Morgan sent him a quick but lethal glance.

"Yes, Morgan was fascinated by it," Liz told him. "She's always preferred things that didn't quite fit a mold, if you know what I mean."

"Exactly." Nick let his eyes sweep over Morgan's face. A man could get lost in those eyes, he thought, if he wasn't careful. Very careful. "Miss James has agreed to a personal tour tomorrow afternoon." He smiled, watching her expression go from astonishment to fury before she controlled it.

"Marvelous!" Pleased, Liz beamed at both of them. "Nick has so many treasures from all over the world. His house is just like Aladdin's cave."

Smiling, Morgan thought of three particularly gruesome wishes, all involving her intended host. "I can't wait to see it."

Through dinner, Morgan watched, confused, then intrigued by Nick's manner. This was not the man she knew. This man was smooth, polished. Gone was the intensity, the ruthlessness, replaced by an easy warmth and charm.

Nicholas Gregoras, olive oil, import-export. Yes, she could see the touches of wealth and success—and the authority she'd understood from the first. But command sat differently on him now, with none of the undertones of violence.

He could sit at the elegant table, laughing with Liz and Alex over some island story with the gleam of cut crystal in his hand. The smoky-gray suit was perfectly tailored and fit him with the same ease as the dark sweatshirt and jeans she'd first seen him in. His arrogance had a more sophisticated tone now. All the rough edges were smoothed.

He seemed relaxed, at home—with none of that vital, dangerous energy. How could this be the same man who had flourished a knife, or climbed the sheer wall to her balcony?

Nick handed her a glass of wine and she frowned. But he was the same man, she reminded herself. And just what game was he playing? Lifting her eyes, Morgan met his. Her fingers tightened on the stem of the glass. The look was brief and quickly veiled, but she saw the inner man. The force was vital. If he was playing games, she thought, sipping her wine to calm suddenly tight nerves, it wasn't a pleasant one. And she wanted no part of it—or of him.

Turning to Dorian, Morgan left Nick to Iona. Intelligent, witty, and with no frustrating mysteries, Dorian was a more comfortable dinner companion. Morgan fell into the easy exchange and tried to relax.

"Tell me, Morgan, don't you find the words of so many languages a bit crowded in the mind?"

She toyed with her moussaka, finding her stomach too jittery to accept the rich sauce. Damn the man for interfering even with her appetite. "I do my thinking in one at a time," she countered.

"You take it too lightly," Dorian insisted. "It's an accomplishment to be proud of. Even a power."

"A power?" Her brows drew together for a moment, then cleared as she smiled. "I suppose it is, though I'd never really thought about it. It just seemed too limiting to only be able to communicate and think in one language, then once I got started, I couldn't seem to stop."

"Having the language, you'd be at home in many countries."

"Yes, I guess that's why I feel so—well, easy here."

"Alex tells me he's trying to entice you into his company." With a smile, Dorian toasted her. "I've drafted myself as promoter. Working with you would add to the company benefits."

Iona's rich laughter floated across the table. "Oh, Nicky, you say the most ridiculous things."

Nicky, Morgan thought with a sniff. I'll be ill any minute. "I think I might enjoy your campaign," Morgan told Dorian with her best smile.

"Take me out on your boat tomorrow, Nicky. I simply must have some fun."

"I'm sorry, Iona, not tomorrow. Perhaps later in the week." Nick softened the refusal with the trace of a finger down her hand.

Iona's mouth formed a pout. "I might die of boredom by later in the week."

Morgan heard Dorian give a quiet sigh. Glancing over, she noted the quick look of exasperation he sent Iona. "Iona tells me she ran into Maria Popagos in Athens last week." The look of exasperation was gone, and his voice was gentle. "She has what—four children now, Iona?"

They treat her like a child, Morgan thought with distaste. And she behaves like one—a spoiled, willful, not quite healthy child.

Through the rest of the meal, and during coffee in the salon, Morgan watched Iona's moods go from sullen to frantic. Apparently used to it, or too good mannered to notice, Dorian ignored the fluctuations. And though she hated to give him the credit for it, so did

Nick. But Morgan noted, with a flutter of sympathy, that Alex grew more distracted as the evening wore on. He spoke to his cousin in undertones as she added more brandy to her glass. Her response was a dramatic toss of her head before she swallowed the liquor and turned her back on him.

When Nick rose to leave, Iona insisted on walking with him to his car. She cast a look of triumph over her shoulder as they left the salon arm-in-arm. Now who, Morgan mused, was that aimed at? Shrugging, she turned back to Dorian and let the evening wind down naturally. There would be time enough to think things through when she was alone in her room again.

Morgan floated with the dream. The wine had brought sleep quickly. Though she had left the balcony doors securely locked, the night breeze drifted through the windows. She sighed, and shifted with its gentle caress on her skin. It was a soft stroking, like a butterfly's wing. It teased across her lips then came back to warm them. She stirred with pleasure. Her body was pliant, receptive. As the phantom kiss increased in pressure, she parted her lips. She drew the dream lover closer.

Excitement was sleepy. The tastes that seeped into her were as sweet and as potent as the wine that still misted her brain. With a sigh of lazy, languid pleasure, she floated with it. In the dream, her arms wrapped around the faceless lover—the pirate, the phantom. He whispered her name and deepened the kiss as his hands drew down the sheet that separated them. Rough fingers, familiar fingers, traced over her skin. A body, too hard, too muscular for a dream, pressed against hers. The lazy images became more tangible, and the phantom took on form. Dark hair, dark eyes, and a mouth that was grimly beautiful and oh, so clever.

Warmth became heat. With a moan, she let passion take her. The stroking along her body became more insistent at her response. Her mouth grew hungry, demanding. Then she heard the breathy whisper of a Greek endearment against her ear.

Suddenly, the filmy curtain of sleep lifted. The weight on her body was real, achingly real—and achingly familiar. Morgan began a confused struggle.

"The goddess awakes. More's the pity."

She saw him in the shaft of moonlight. Her body was alive with needs, her mind baffled with the knowledge that he had induced them. "What are you doing!" she demanded, and found her breathing was quick and ragged. His mouth had been on hers, she knew. She could still taste him. And his hands... "This is the limit! If you think for one minute I'm going to sit still for you crawling into my bed while I'm sleeping—"

"You were very agreeable a moment ago."

"Oh! What a despicable thing to do."

"You're very responsive," Nick murmured, and traced her ear with his fingertip. Beneath his hand he could feel the thunder of her heartbeat. He knew, though he fought to slow it, that his own beat as quickly. "It seemed to please you to be touched. It pleased me to touch you."

His voice had lowered again, as she knew it could—dark, seductive. The muscles in her thighs loosened. "Get off of me," she ordered in quick defense.

"Sweet Morgan." He nipped her bottom lip—felt her tremble, felt a swift rush of power. It would be so easy to persuade her...and so risky. With an effort, he gave her a friendly smile. "You only postpone the inevitable."

She kept her eyes level as she tried to steady her breathing. Something told her that if all else he had said had been lies, his last statement was all too true. "I didn't promise not to scream this time."

He lifted a brow as though the possibility intrigued him. "It might be interesting to explain this...situation to Alex and Liz. I could claim I was overcome with your beauty. It has a ring of truth. But you won't scream in any case."

"Just what makes you so sure?"

"You'd have given me away—or tried to by now—if you were going to." Nick rolled aside.

Sitting up, Morgan pushed at her hair. Did he always have to be right? she wondered grimly. "What do you want now? And how the hell did you get in this time? I locked..." Her voice trailed off as she saw the balcony doors were wide open.

"Did you think a lock would keep me out?" With a laugh, Nick ran a finger down her nose. "You have a lot to learn."

"Now, you listen to me—"

"No, save the recriminations for later. They're understood in any case." Absently, he rubbed a lock of her hair between his thumb and forefinger. "I came back to make certain you didn't develop a convenient headache that would keep you from coming to the house tomorrow. There are one or two things I want to discuss with you."

"I've got a crate full of things to discuss with you," Morgan hissed furiously. "Just what were you doing that night on the beach? And who—"

"Later, Aphrodite. I'm distracted at the moment. That scent you wear, for instance. It's very..." He lifted his eyes to hers, "alluring."

"Stop it." She didn't trust him when his voice dropped to that tone. She didn't trust him at all, she reminded herself and gave him a level look. "What's the purpose behind that ridiculous game you were playing tonight?"

"Game?" His eyes widened effectively. "Morgan, my love, I don't know what you're talking about. I was quite natural."

"Natural be damned."

"No need to swear at me," he said mildly.

"There's every need," she countered. How could he manage to be charming under such ridiculous circumstances? "You were the perfect guest this evening," Morgan went on, knocking his hand aside as he began to toy with the thin strap of her chemise. "Charming—"

"Thank you."

"And false," she added, narrowing her eyes.

"Not false," Nick disagreed. "Simply suitable, considering the occasion."

"I suppose it would have looked a bit odd if you'd pulled a knife out of your pocket."

His fingers tightened briefly, then relaxed. She wasn't going to let him forget that—and he wasn't having an easy time blanking out that moment she had gone limp with terror beneath him. "Few people have seen me other than as I was tonight," he murmured, and began to give the texture of her hair his attention. "Perhaps it's your misfortune to count yourself among them."

"I don't want to see you *any* way, from now on."

Humor touched his eyes again as they shifted to hers. "Liar. I'll pick you up tomorrow at one."

Morgan tossed out a phrase commonly heard in the less elite portions of Italy. Nick responded with a pleased laugh.

"*Agapetike,* I should warn you, in my business I've had occasion to visit some Italian gutters."

"Good, then you won't need a translation."

"Just be ready." He let his gaze sweep down her, then up again. "You might find it easier to deal with me in the daylight—and when you're more adequately attired."

"I have no intention of dealing with you at all," Morgan began in a furious undertone. "Or of continuing this ridiculous charade by going with you tomorrow."

"Oh, I think you will." Nick's smile was confident and infuriating. "You'd find yourself having a difficult time explaining to Liz why you won't come when you've already expressed an interest in my home. Tell me, what was it that appealed to you about it?"

"The insanity of the architecture."

He laughed again and took her hand. "More compliments. I adore you, Aphrodite. Come, kiss me good-night."

Morgan drew back and scowled. "I certainly will not."

"You certainly will." In a swift movement he had her pinned under him again. When she cursed him, he laughed and the insolence was back. "Witch," he murmured. "What mortal can resist one?"

His mouth came down quickly, lingering until she had stopped squirming beneath him. Gradually, the force went out of the kiss, but not the power. It seeped into her, so that she couldn't be sure if it was hers or his. Then it was only passion—clean and hot and senseless. On a moan, Morgan accepted it, and him.

Feeling the change in her, Nick relaxed a moment and simply let himself enjoy.

She had a taste that stayed with him long after he left her. Each time he touched her he knew, eventually, he would have to have it all. But not now. Now there was too much at stake. She was a risk, and he had already taken too many chances with her. But that taste...

He gave himself over to the kiss knowing the danger of letting himself become vulnerable, even for a moment, by losing himself in her. If she hadn't been on the beach that night. If he hadn't had to reveal himself to her. Would things have been different than they were now? he wondered as desire began to claw at him. Would he have been able to coax her into his arms, into his bed, with a bit of flair and a few clever words? If they had met for the first time tonight, would he have wanted her this badly, this quickly?

Her hands were in his hair. He found his mouth had roamed to her throat. Her scent seemed to concentrate there, and the taste was wild and dangerous. He lived with danger and enjoyed it—lived by his wits and won. But this woman, this feeling she stirred in him, was a risk he could calculate. Yet it was done. There was no changing the course he had to take. And no changing the fact that she was involved.

He wanted to touch her, to tear off that swatch of silk she wore and feel her skin warm under his hand. He dared not. He was a man who knew his own limitations, his own weaknesses. Nick didn't appreciate the fact that Morgan James had become a weakness at a time when he could least afford one.

Murmuring his name, Morgan slid her hands beneath the loose sweatshirt, to run them over the range of muscle. Nick felt need shoot like a spear, white-tipped, to the pit of his stomach. Using every ounce of will, he banked down on it until it was a dull ache he could control. He lifted his head and waited for those pale, clouded blue eyes to open. Something dug into his palm, and he saw that he had gripped her medal in his hand without realizing it. Nick had to quell the urge to swear, then give himself a moment until he knew he could speak lightly. "Sleep well, Aphrodite," he told her with a grin. "Until tomorrow."

"You—" She broke off, struggling for the breath and the wit to hurl abuse at him.

"Tomorrow," Nick repeated as he brought her hand to his lips.

Morgan watched him stride to the balcony, then lower himself out of sight. Lying perfectly still, she stared at the empty space and wondered what she had gotten herself into.

Chapter 4

The house was cool and quiet in the mid-morning hush. Gratefully, Morgan accepted Liz's order to enjoy the beach. She wanted to avoid Iona's company, and though she hated to admit it, she didn't think she could handle Liz's carefree chatter about the dinner party. Liz would have expected her to make some witty observations about Nick that Morgan just didn't feel up to. Relieved that Dorian had business with Alex, and wouldn't feel obliged to keep her company, she set out alone.

Morgan wanted the solitude—she did her best thinking when she was alone. In the past few days she had accumulated quite a bit to think about. Now she decided to work it through one step at a time.

What had Nicholas Gregoras been doing that night on the beach? He'd had the scent of the sea on him, so it followed that he had been out on the water. She remembered the sound of a motor. She'd assumed it belonged to a fisherman but Nick was no fisherman. He'd been desperate not to be seen by someone…desperate enough to have been carrying a knife. She could still see the look on his face as she had lain beneath him in the shadows of the cypress. He'd been prepared to use the knife.

Somehow the knowledge that this was true disturbed her more now than it had when he'd been a stranger. Kicking bad-temperedly at a stone, she started down the beach steps.

And who had been with him? Morgan fretted. Someone had followed his orders without any question. Who had used the beach steps while Nick had held her prisoner in the shadows? Alex? The man who rented Nick's cottage? Frustrated, Morgan slipped out of her shoes and began to cross the warm sand. Why would Nick be ready to kill either one of them rather than be discovered by them? By anyone, she corrected. It could have been a servant of one of the villas, a villager trespassing.

One question at a time, Morgan cautioned herself as she kicked idly at the sand. First, was it logical to assume that the footsteps she had heard were from someone who had also come from the sea? Morgan thought it was. And second, she decided that the person must have been headed to one of the villas or a nearby cottage. Why else would they have used that particular strip of beach? Logical, she concluded, walking aimlessly. So why was Nick so violently determined to go unseen?

Smuggling. It was so obvious. So logical. But she had continued to push the words aside. She didn't want to think of him involved in such a dirty business. Somewhere, beneath the anger and resentment she felt for him, Morgan had experienced a totally different sensation. There was something about him—something she couldn't really pinpoint in words. Strength, perhaps. He was the kind of man you could depend on when no one else could—or would—help. She wanted to trust him. There was no logic to it, it simply was.

But was he a smuggler? Had he thought she'd seen something incriminating? Did the footsteps she'd heard belong to a patrol? Another smuggler? A rival? If he'd believed her to be a threat, why hadn't he simply used the knife on her? If he were a cold-blooded killer...no. Morgan shook her head at the description. While she could almost accept that Nick would kill, she couldn't agree with the adjective. And that led to hundreds of other problems.

Questions and answers sped through her mind. Stubborn questions, disturbing answers. Morgan shut her eyes on them. I'm going to get some straight answers from him this afternoon, she promised herself. It was his fault she was involved. Morgan dropped to the sand and brought her knees to her chest. She had been minding her own business when he had literally dragged her into it. All she had wanted was a nice, quiet vacation.

"Men!"

"I refuse to take that personally."

Morgan spun her head around and found herself staring into a wide, friendly smile.

"Hello. You seem to be angry with my entire gender." He rose from a rock and walked to her. He was tall and very slender, with dark gold curls appealingly disarrayed around a tanned face that held both youth and strength. "But I think it's worth the risk. I'm Andrew Stevenson." Still smiling, he dropped to the sand beside her.

"Oh." Recovering, Morgan returned the smile. "The poet or the painter? Liz wasn't sure."

"Poet," he said with a grimace. "Or so I tell myself."

Glancing down, she saw the pad he held. It was dog-eared and covered with a fine, looping scribble. "I've interrupted your work, I'm sorry."

"On the contrary, you've given me a shot of inspiration. You have a remarkable face."

"I think," Morgan considered, "that's a compliment."

"Dear lady, yours is a face a poet dreams of." He let his eyes roam it for a moment. "Do you have a name, or are you going to vanish in a mist and leave me bewitched?"

"Morgan." The fussy compliment, delivered with bland sincerity made her laugh. "Morgan James, and are you a good poet, Andrew Stevenson?"

"I can't say no." Andrew continued to study her candidly. "Modesty isn't one of my virtues. You said Liz. I assume that's Mrs. Theoharis. You're staying with them?"

"Yes, for a few weeks." A new thought crossed her mind. "You're renting Nicholas Gregoras's cottage?"

"That's right. Actually, it's a free ride." Though he set down the pad, he began to trace patterns in the sand as if he couldn't keep his hands quite still. "We're cousins." Andrew noted the surprise on her face. His smile deepened. "Not the Greek side. Our mothers are related."

"Oh, so his mother's American." This at least explained his ease with the language.

"A Norling of San Francisco," he stated with a grin for the title. "She remarried after Nick's father died. She's living in France."

"So, you're visiting Lesbos and your cousin at the same time."

"Actually, Nick offered me the retreat when he learned I was working on an epic poem—a bit Homeric, you see." His eyes were blue, darker than hers, and very direct on her face. Morgan could see nothing in the open, ingenuous look to link him with Nick. "I wanted to stay on Lesbos awhile, so it worked out nicely. The home of Sappho. The poetry and legend have always fascinated me."

"Sappho," Morgan repeated, turning her thoughts from Nick. "Oh, yes, the poetess."

"The Tenth Muse. She lived here, in Mitilini." His gaze, suddenly dreamy, swept down the stretch of beach. "I like to think Nick's house is on the cliff where she hurled herself into the sea, desperate for Phaon's love."

"An interesting thought." Morgan looked up to where a portion of a gray stone wall was visible. "And I suppose her spirit floats over the house searching for her love." Somehow, she liked the idea and smiled. "Lord knows, it's the perfect house for a poetic haunting."

"Have you been inside?" Andrew asked her, his tone as dreamy as his eyes now. "It's fantastic."

"No, I'm getting a personal tour this afternoon." Morgan kept her voice light as she swore silently in several languages.

"A personal tour?" Abruptly direct again, Andrew tilted his head, with brows lifted in speculation. "You must have made quite an impression on Nick. But then," he added with a nod, "you would. He sets great store by beauty."

Morgan gave him a noncommital smile. He could hardly know that it wasn't her looks or charm that had secured the invitation. "Do you often write on the beach? I can't keep away from it myself." Morgan hesitated briefly, then plunged. "I came down here a couple of nights ago and swam by moonlight."

There was no shock or anxiety in his eyes at this information. Andrew grinned. "I'm sorry I missed that. You'll find me all over this part of the island. Here, up on the cliffs, in the olive groves. I go where the mood strikes me."

"I'm going to do some exploring myself." She thought wistfully of a carefree hour in the inlets.

"I'm available if you'd like a guide." His gaze skimmed over her face again, warm and friendly. "By now, I know this part of the island as well as a native. If you find you want company, you can usually find me wandering around or in the cottage. It isn't far."

"I'd like that." A gleam of amusement lit her eyes. "You don't happen to keep a goat, do you?"

"Ah—no."

Laughing at his expression, Morgan patted his hand. "Don't try to understand," she advised. "And now I'd better go change for my tour."

Andrew rose with her and captured her hand. "I'll see you again." It was a statement, not a question. Morgan responded to the gentle pressure.

"I'm sure you will; the island's very small."

Andrew smiled as he released her hand. "I'd rather call it kismet." He watched Morgan walk away before he settled back on his rock, facing the sea.

Nicholas Gregoras was very prompt. By five minutes past one, Morgan found herself being shoved out the door by an enthusiastic Liz. "Have fun, darling, and don't hurry back. Nick, Morgan will adore your house; all those winding passages and the terrifying view of the sea. She's very courageous, aren't you, Morgan?"

"I'm practically stalwart," she muttered while Nick grinned.

"Well, run along and have fun." Liz shooed them out the door as if they were two reluctant children being sent to school.

"You should be warned," Morgan stated as she slid into Nick's car, "Liz considers you a suitable candidate for my hand. I think she's getting desperate picturing me as her unborn child's maiden aunt."

"Aphrodite." Nick settled beside her and took her hand. "There isn't a male alive who could picture you as anyone's maiden aunt."

Refusing to be charmed, Morgan removed her hand from his, then studied the view out the side window. "I met your poet in residence this morning on the beach."

"Andrew? He's a nice boy. How did you find him?"

"Not like a boy." Turning back to Nick, Morgan frowned. "He's a very charming man."

Nick lifted a brow fractionally. "Yes, I suppose he is. Somehow, I always think of him as a boy, though there's barely five years between us." He moved his shoulders. "He does have talent. Did you charm him?"

"'Inspire' was his word," she returned, annoyed.

Nick flashed her a quick grin. "Naturally. One romantic should inspire another."

"I'm not a romantic." The conversation forced her to give him a great deal more of her attention than she had planned. "I'm very practical."

"Morgan, you're an insatiable romantic." Her annoyance apparently amused him, because a smile continued to hover on his mouth. "A woman who combs her hair on a moonlit beach, wears filmy white, and treasures a valueless memento thrives on romance."

Uncomfortable with the description, Morgan spoke coolly. "I also clip coupons and watch my cholesterol."

"Admirable."

She swallowed what might have been a chuckle. "You, Nicholas Gregoras, are a first-rate bastard."

"Yes. I hate to be second-rate at anything."

Morgan flounced back in her seat, but lost all resentment as the house came into full view. "Oh, Lord," she murmured. "It's wonderful!"

It looked stark and primitive and invulnerable. The second story lashed out over the sea like an out-stretched arm—not offering payment, but demanding it. None of the power she had felt out at sea was diminished at close range. The flowering shrubs and vines which trailed and tangled were placed to disguise the care of their planting. The result was an illusion of wild abandon. Sleeping Beauty's castle, she thought, a century after she pricked her finger.

"What a marvelous place." Morgan turned to him as he stopped the car at the entrance. "I've never seen anything like it."

"That's the first time you've smiled at me and meant it." He wasn't smiling now, but looking at her with a trace of annoyance. He hadn't realized just how much he'd wanted to see that spontaneous warmth in her eyes—directed at him. And now that he had, he wasn't certain what to do about it. With a quick mental oath, Nick slid from the car.

Ignoring him, Morgan climbed out and tried to take in the entire structure at once. "You know what it looks like," she said, half to herself. "It looks like Zeus hurled a lightning bolt into the mountain and the house exploded into existence."

"An interesting theory." Nick took her hand and started up the stone steps. "If you'd known my grand-father, you'd realize how close that is to the truth."

Morgan had primed herself to begin hurling ques-tions and demanding explanations as soon as they had arrived. When she stepped into the entrance hall, she forgot everything.

Wide and speckled in aged white, the hall was spo-radically slashed with stark colors from wall hangings and primitive paintings. On one wall, long spears were crossed—weapons for killing, certainly, but with an an-cient dignity she had to admire. The staircase leading to the upper floors arched in a half circle with a banister of dark, unvarnished wood. The result was one of earthy magnificence. It was far from elegant, but there was a sense of balance and savage charm.

"Nicholas." Turning a full circle, Morgan sighed. "It's really wonderful. I expect a cyclops to come stalking down the stairs. Are there centaurs in the courtyard?"

"I'll take you through, and we'll see what we can do." She was making it difficult for him to stick to his plan. She wasn't supposed to charm him. That wasn't in the script. Still, he kept her hand in his as he led her through the house.

Liz's comparison to Aladdin's cave was completely apt. Room after room abounded with treasures— Venetian glass, Fabergé boxes, African masks, Native American pottery, Ming vases. All were set together in a hodgepodge of cultures. What might have seemed like a museum was instead a glorious clutter of wonders. As the house twisted and turned, revealing surprise after surprise, Morgan became more fascinated. Elegant Waterford crystal was juxtaposed with a deadly looking seventeenth-century crossbow. She saw exquisite porcelain and a shrunken head from Ecuador.

Yes, the architect was mad, she decided, noting lintels with wolves' heads or grinning elves carved into them. Wonderfully mad. The house was a fairy tale—not the tame children's version, but with all the whispering shadows and hints of gremlins.

A huge curved window on the top floor gave her the sensation of standing suspended on the edge of the cliff. It jutted out, arrogantly, then fell in a sheer drop into the sea. Morgan stared down, equally exhilarated and terrified.

Nick watched her. There was a need to spin her around and seize, to possess while that look of dazzled courage was still on her face. He was a man accustomed to taking what he wanted without a second thought. She was something he wanted.

Morgan turned to him. Her eyes were still alive with the fascination of the sea and hints of excited fear. "Andrew said he hoped this was the cliff where Sappho hurled herself into the sea. I'm ready to believe it."

"Andrew's imaginative."

"So are you," she countered. "You live here."

"Your eyes are like some mythological lake," he murmured. "Translucent and ethereal. I should call you Circe rather than Aphrodite." Abruptly, he gripped her hair in his hand, tugging it until her face was lifted to his. "I swear you're more witch than goddess."

Morgan stared at him. There was no teasing in his eyes this time, no arrogance. What she saw was longing. And the longing, more than passion, seduced her. "I'm only a woman, Nicholas," she heard herself say.

His fingers tightened. His expression darkened. Then even as she watched, his mood seemed to shift. This time, he took her arm rather than her hand. "Come, we'll go down and have a drink."

As they entered the salon, Morgan reasserted her priorities. She had to get answers—she *would* get answers. She couldn't let a few soft words and a pair of dark eyes make her forget why she'd come. Before she could speak, however, a man slipped into the doorway.

He was small, with creased, leather skin. His hair was gray with age, but thick. So were his arms—thick and muscled. He made her think of a small-scaled, very efficient tank. His moustache was a masterpiece. It spread under his nose to drop free along the sides of his mouth, reaching his chin in two flowing arches. He smiled, showing several gaps in lieu of teeth.

"Good afternoon." He spoke in respectful Greek, but his eyes were dancing.

Intrigued, Morgan gave him an unsmiling stare. *"Yiasou."*

"Stephanos, Miss James. Stephanos is my, ah, caretaker."

The checkerboard grin widened at the term. "Your servant, my lady." He bowed, but there was nothing deferential in the gesture. "The matter we discussed has been seen to, Mr. Gregoras." Turning to Nick, the old man spoke with exaggerated respect. "You have messages from Athens."

"I'll tend to them later."

"As you wish." The small man melted away. Morgan frowned. There had been something in the exchange that wasn't quite what it should be. Shaking her head, she watched Nick mix drinks. It wasn't Nick's relationship with his servants that she was interested in.

Deciding that plunging head first was the most direct route, Morgan leaped. "What were you doing on the beach the other night?"

"I rather thought we'd concluded I was assaulting you." His voice was very mild.

"That was only part of the evening's entertainment." She swallowed and took another dive. "Had you been smuggling?"

To his credit, Nick hesitated only briefly. As his back was to her, Morgan didn't see his expression range from surprise to consideration. A very sharp lady, he mused. Too damn sharp.

"And how did you come by such an astonishing conclusion?" He turned to hand her a delicate glass.

"Don't start that charade with me," Morgan fumed, snatching the glass. "I've seen you stripped." She sat down and aimed a level stare.

Nick's mouth twitched. "What a fascinating way you have of putting things."

"I asked if you were a smuggler."

Nick sat across from her, taking a long study of her face as he ticked off possibilities. "First, tell me why you think I might be."

"You'd been out on the water that night. I could smell the sea on you."

Nick gazed down into the liquid in his glass, then sipped. "It's fanciful, to say the least, that my being out on the water equals smuggling."

Morgan ground her teeth at the cool sarcasm and continued. "If you'd been out on a little fishing trip, you'd hardly have dragged me into the trees waving a knife."

"One might argue," he murmured, "that fishing was precisely my occupation."

"The coast of Turkey is very convenient from this part of the island. Alex told me smuggling was a problem."

"Alex?" Nick repeated. There was a quick, almost imperceptible change in his expression. "What was Alex's attitude toward smuggling?"

Morgan hesitated. The question had broken into her well-thought-out interrogation. "He was…resigned, like one accepts the weather."

"I see." Nick swirled his drink as he leaned back. "And did you and Alex discuss the intricacies of the procedure?"

"Of course not!" she snapped, infuriated that he had cleverly turned the interrogation around on her. "Alex would hardly be intimate with such matters. But," she continued, "I think you are."

"Yes, I can see that."

"Well?"

He sent her a mildly amused smile that didn't quite reach his eyes. "Well what?"

"Are you going to deny it?" She wanted him to, Morgan realized with something like a jolt. She very, very badly wanted him to deny it.

Nick considered her for a moment. "If I deny it, you won't believe me. It's easy to see you've already made up your mind." He tilted his head, and now the amusement crept into his eyes. "What will you do if I admit it?"

"I'll turn you over to the police." Morgan took a bold sip of her drink. Nick exploded with laughter.

"Morgan what a sweet, brave child you are." He

leaned over to take her hand before she could retort. "You don't know my reputation, but I assure you, the police would think you mad."

"I could prove—"

"What?" he demanded. His eyes were steady on hers, probing. The polished veneer was slowly fading. "You can't prove what you don't know."

"I know that you're not what you pretend to be." Morgan tried to pull her hand from his, but he held it firm. "Or maybe it's more accurate to say you're something you pretend not to be."

Nick watched her in silence, torn between annoyance and admiration. "Whatever I am, whatever I'm not, has nothing to do with you."

"No one wishes more than I that that was the truth."

Battling a new emotion, he sat back and studied her over the rim of his glass. "So your conclusions that I might be involved in smuggling would prompt you to go to the police. That wouldn't be wise."

"It's a matter of what's right." Morgan swallowed, then blurted out what was torturing her mind. "The knife—would you have used it?"

"On you?" he asked, his eyes as expressionless as his voice.

"On anyone."

"A general question can't be given a specific answer."

"Nicholas, for God's sake—"

Nick set down his drink, then steepled his fingers. His expression changed, and his eyes were suddenly dangerous. "If I were everything you seem to think, you're incredibly brave or incredibly foolish to be sitting here discussing it with me."

"I think I'm safe enough," she countered and straightened her shoulders. "Everyone knows where I am."

"I could always dispose of you another time if I considered you an obstacle." Morgan's eyes flickered with momentary fear, quickly controlled. It was one more thing he could admire her for.

"I can take care of myself."

"Can you?" he murmured, then shrugged as his mood shifted again. "Well, in any case, I have no intention of wasting beauty especially when I intend to enjoy its benefits. Your talents could be useful to me."

Her chin shot up. "I have no intention of being your tool. Smuggling opium is a filthy way to make money. It's a far cry from crossing the English Channel with French silks and brandy."

"With mists curling and eye-patched buccaneers?" Nick countered with a smile. "Is that how your practical mind sees it, Morgan?"

She opened her mouth to retort, but found herself smiling. "I refuse to like you, Nicholas."

"You don't have to like me, Morgan. Like is too tame for my tastes in any case." Outwardly relaxed, he picked up his glass again. "Don't you like your drink?"

Without taking her eyes from his, Morgan set it down. "Nicholas, I only want a straight answer—I deserve one. You're perfectly right that I can't go to the police, no matter what you tell me. You really have nothing to fear from me."

Something flashed in his eyes at her final statement, then was quickly banked. He considered his options before he spoke. "I'll tell you this much, I am—concerned with smuggling. I'd be interested to know of any conversations you might hear on the subject."

Frowning, Morgan rose to wander the room. He was making it difficult for her to remember the straight and narrow path of right and wrong. The path took some confusing twists and turns when emotions were involved. Emotions! She brought herself up short. No, no emotions here. She had no feelings toward him.

"Who was with you that night?" Keep to the plan, she told herself. Questions and answers. Save the introspection for later. "You were giving someone orders."

"I thought you were too frightened to notice." Nick sipped at his drink.

"You were speaking to someone," Morgan went on doggedly. "Someone who did precisely what you told him without question. Who?"

Nick weighed the pros and cons before he answered. With her mind she'd figure it out for herself soon enough. "Stephanos."

"That little old man?" Morgan stopped in front of Nick and stared down. Stephanos was not Morgan's image of a ruthless smuggler.

"That little old man knows the sea like a gardener knows a rose bush." He smiled at her incredulous expression. "He also has the advantage of being loyal. He's been with me since I was a boy."

"How convenient all this is for you." Depressed, Morgan wandered to a window. She was getting her answers, but she discovered they weren't the ones she wanted. "A home on a convenient island, a convenient servant, a convenient business to ease distribution. Who passed by the grove that night whom you wanted to avoid?"

Frightened or not, he thought angrily, she'd been far too observant. "That needn't concern you."

Morgan whirled. "You got me into this, Nicholas. I have a right to know."

"Your rights end where I say they do." He rose as his temper threatened. "Don't push me too far, Morgan. You wouldn't like the results. I've told you all I intend to for now. Be content with it."

She backed away a step, furious with herself for being frightened. He swore at the movement, then gripped her shoulders.

"I have no intention of harming you, damn it. If I had, there's already been ample opportunity. What do you picture?" he demanded, shaking her. "Me cutting your throat or tossing you off a cliff?"

Her eyes were dry and direct, more angry now than frightened. "I don't know what I picture."

Abruptly he realized he was hurting her. Cursing himself, he eased the grip to a caress. He couldn't keep letting her get under his skin this way. He couldn't let it matter what she thought of him. "I don't expect you to trust me," he said calmly. "But use common sense. Your involvement was a matter of circumstance, not design. I don't want to see you hurt, Morgan. That much you can take as the truth."

And that much she believed. Intrigued, she studied his face. "You're a strange man, Nicholas. Somehow, I can't quite see you doing something as base as smuggling opium."

"Intuition, Morgan?" Smiling, Nick tangled his fingers in her hair. It was soft, as he remembered, and tempting. "Are you a woman who believes in her intuition, or in her reason?"

"Nicholas—"

"No. No more questions or I'll have to divert you.

I'm very"—a frown hovered, then flashed into a grin—
"very susceptible to beauty. You have a remarkable supply. Coupled with a very good mind, the combination
is hard to resist." Nick lifted the medal at her throat,
examined it, then let it fall before he moved back from
her. "Tell me, what do you think of Dorian and Iona?"

"I resent this. I resent all of this." Morgan spun away
from him. He shouldn't be allowed to affect her so
deeply, so easily, then switch off like a light. "I came to
Lesbos to get away from pressures and complications."

"What sort of pressures and complications?"

She turned back to him, eyes hot. "They're my business. I had a life before I went down to that damned
beach and ran into you."

"Yes," he murmured and picked up his drink. "I'm
sure you did."

"Now, I find myself tossed into the middle of some
grade-B thriller. I don't like it."

"It's a pity you didn't stay in bed that night, Morgan."
Nick drank deeply, then twirled his glass by the stem.
"Maybe I'm Greek enough to say the gods didn't will
it so. For the moment your fate's linked with mine and
there's nothing either of us can do about it."

She surprised him by laying a hand on his chest.
He didn't like the way his heart reacted to the touch.
Needs…he couldn't need. Wants were easily satisfied
or ignored, but needs ate at a man.

"If you feel that way, why won't you give me a straight
answer?"

"I don't choose to." His eyes locked on hers, cement-
ing her to the spot. In them she saw desire—his and a
mirror of her own. "Take me for what I am, Morgan."

She dropped her hand. Frightened not of him now, but of herself. "I don't want to take you at all."

"No?" He pulled her close, perversely enjoying her resistance. "Let's see just how quickly I can make a liar of you."

She could taste anger on his mouth, and just as clearly she could taste need. Morgan stopped resisting. The path of right and wrong took a few more confusing twists when she was in his arms. Whoever, whatever he was, she wanted to be held by him.

Her arms wound around his neck to draw him closer. She heard him murmur something against her mouth; the kiss held a savageness, a demand she was answering with equal abandon.

Had this passion always been there, sleeping inside her? It wasn't asleep any longer. The force of it had her clinging to him, had her mouth urgent and hungry against his. Something had opened inside her, letting him pour through. His hands were in her hair, then running down her back in a swift stroke of possession. She arched against him as if daring him to claim her—taunting him to try.

Somehow she knew, as her body fit truly to his, that they would come back to each other, again and again, against their will, against all reason. She might fight it from moment to moment, but there would be a time. The knowledge filled her with hunger and fear.

"Morgan." Her name wrenched from him on a sigh of need. "I want you—by the gods, I want you. Come, stay here with me tonight. Here, where we can be alone."

His mouth was roaming her face. She wanted to agree. Her body was aching to agree to anything—to everything. Yet, she found herself drawing back. "No."

Nick lifted his face. His expression was amused and confident. "Afraid?"

"Yes."

His brows rose at the unexpected honesty, then drew together in frustration. The look in her eyes made it impossible for him to press his advantage. "*Diabolos,* you're an exasperating woman." He strode away and poured more liquor into his glass. "I could toss you over my shoulder, haul you up to the bedroom, and be done with it."

Though her legs were watery, Morgan forced herself to remain standing. "Why don't you?"

He whirled back, furious. She watched as he slowly pulled out the control. "You're more accustomed to a wine and candlelight seduction, I imagine. Soft promises. Soft lies." Nick drank deep, then set down his glass with a bang. "Is that what you want from me?"

"No." Morgan met his fury steadily while her hand reached instinctively for the medal at her throat. "I don't want you to make love to me."

"Don't take me for a fool!" He took a step toward her, then stopped himself. Another step and neither of them would have a choice. "Your body betrays you every time I touch you."

"That has nothing to do with it," she said calmly. "I don't want you to make love to me."

He waited a beat until the desire and frustration could be tamed a bit. "Because you believe I'm an opium smuggler?"

"No," she said, surprising both of them. She felt her strength waver a moment, then told him the truth. "Because I don't want to be one of your amusements."

"I see." Carefully, Nick dipped his hands into his

pockets. "I'd better take you back before you discover I find nothing amusing in lovemaking."

A half-hour later, Nick slammed back into the house. His temper was foul. He stalked into the salon, poured himself another drink, and slumped into a chair. Damn the woman, he didn't have the time or patience to deal with her. The need for her was still churning inside him like a pain, sharp and insistent. He took a long swallow of liquor to dull it. Just physical, he told himself. He'd have to find another woman—any other woman—and release some of the tension.

"Ah, you're back." Stephanos entered. He noted the black temper and accepted it without comment. He'd seen it often enough in the past. "The lady is more beautiful than I remembered." Nick's lack of response left him unperturbed. He moved to the bar and poured himself a drink. "How much did you tell her?"

"Only what was necessary. She's sharp and remarkably bold." Nick eyed the liquid in his glass with a scowl. "She accused me flat out of smuggling." At Stephanos's cackle of laughter, Nick drained more liquor. "Your sense of humor eludes me at the moment, old man."

Stephanos only grinned. "Her eyes are sharp—they linger on you." Though Nick made no response, Stephanos's grin remained. "Did you speak to her of Alex?"

"Not at length."

"Is she loyal?"

"To Alex?" Nick frowned into his drink. "Yes, she would be. Where she cares, she'd be loyal." He set down the glass, refusing to give in to the urge to hurl it across the room. "Getting information out of her won't be easy."

"You'll get it nonetheless."

"I wish to hell she'd stayed in bed that night," Nick said savagely.

The gap-toothed grin appeared before Stephanos tossed back the drink in one long swallow. He let out a wheezy sigh of appreciation. "She lingers in your mind. That makes you uncomfortable." He laughed loud and long at Nick's scowl, then sighed again with the effort of it. "Athens is waiting for your call."

"Athens can fry in hell."

Chapter 5

Morgan's frame of mind was as poor as Nick's when she entered the Theoharis villa. Somewhere on the drive back from Nick's she had discovered that what she was feeling wasn't anger. It wasn't fear or even resentment. In a few days Nick had managed to do something Jack hadn't done in all the months she had known him. He'd hurt her.

It had nothing to do with the bruises that were already fading on her arms. This hurt went deeper, and had begun before she had even met him. It had begun when he had chosen the life he was leading.

Nothing to do with me. Nothing to do with me, Morgan told herself again and again. But she slammed the front door as she swept into the cool white hall. Her plans to go immediately to her room before she could snarl at anyone were tossed to the winds by a call and a wave from Dorian.

"Morgan, come join us."

Fixing on a smile, Morgan strolled out to the terrace. Iona was with him sprawled on a lounge in a hot-pink playsuit that revealed long, shapely legs but covered her arms with white lace cuffs at the wrists. She sent Morgan a languid greeting, then went back to her sulky study of the gulf. Morgan felt the tension hovering in the air and wondered if it had been there before or if she had brought it with her.

"Alex is on a transatlantic call," Dorian told her as he held out a chair. "And Liz is dealing with some domestic crisis in the kitchen."

"Without an interpreter?" Morgan asked. She smiled, telling herself Nick wasn't going to ruin her mood and make her as sulky as Alex's cousin.

"It's ridiculous." Iona gestured for Dorian to light her cigarette. "Liz should simply fire the man. Americans are habitually casual with servants."

"Are they?" Morgan felt her back go up at the slur on her friend and her nationality. "I wouldn't know."

Iona's dark eyes flicked over her briefly. "I don't imagine you've had many dealings with servants."

Before Morgan could retort, Dorian stepped in calmly. "Tell me, Morgan, what did you think of Nick's treasure trove?"

The expression in his eyes asked her to overlook Iona's bad manners, and told her something she'd begun to suspect the night before. He's in love with her, she mused, and felt a stab of pity. With an effort, Morgan relaxed her spine. "It's a wonderful place, like a museum without being regimented or stiff. It must have taken him years to collect all those things."

"Nick's quite a businessman," Dorian commented.

Another look passed between him and Morgan. This time she saw it was gratitude. "And, of course, he uses his knowledge and position to secure the best pieces for himself."

"There was a Swiss music box," she remembered. "He said it was over a hundred years old. It played *Für Elise*." Morgan sighed, at ease again. "I'd kill for it."

"Nick's a generous man—when approached in the proper manner." Iona's smile was sharp as a knife. Morgan turned her head and met it.

"I wouldn't know anything about that either," she said coolly. Deliberately, she turned back to Dorian. "I met Nick's cousin earlier this morning."

"Ah, yes, the young poet from America."

"He said he wanders all over this part of the island. I'm thinking of doing the same myself. It's such a simple, peaceful place. I suppose that's why I was so stunned when Alex said there was a problem with smuggling."

Dorian merely smiled as if amused. Iona stiffened. As Morgan watched, the color drained from her face, leaving it strained and cold and anything but beautiful. Surprised by the reaction, Morgan studied her carefully. Why, she's afraid, she realized. Now why would that be?

"A dangerous business," Dorian commented conversationally. Since his eyes were on Morgan, Iona's reaction went unnoticed by him. "But common enough—traditional in fact."

"An odd tradition," Morgan murmured.

"The network of patrols is very large, I'm told, and closely knotted. As I recall, five men were killed last year, gunned down off the Turkish coast." He lit a cigarette of his own. "The authorities confiscated quite a cache of opium."

"How terrible." Morgan noticed that Iona's pallor increased.

"Just peasants and fishermen," he explained with a shrug. "Not enough intelligence between them to have organized a large smuggling ring. It's rumored the leader is brilliant and ruthless. From the stories passed around in the village, he goes along on runs now and then, but wears a mask. Apparently, not even his cohorts know who he is. It might even be a woman." He flashed a grin at the idea. "I suppose that adds an element of romance to the whole business."

Iona rose and dashed from the terrace.

"You must forgive her." Dorian sighed as his eyes followed her. "She's a moody creature."

"She seemed upset."

"Iona's easily upset," he murmured. "Her nerves…"

"You care for her quite a lot."

His gaze came back to lock on Morgan's before he rose and strode to the railing.

"I'm sorry, Dorian," Morgan began immediately. "I didn't mean to pry."

"No, forgive me." He turned back and the sun streamed over his face, gleaming off the bronzed skin, combing through his burnished gold hair. Adonis, Morgan thought again, and for the second time since she had come to Lesbos wished she could paint. "My feelings for Iona are…difficult and, I had thought, more cleverly concealed."

"I'm sorry," Morgan said again, helplessly.

"She's spoiled, willful." With a laugh, Dorian shook his head. "What is it that makes one person lose his heart to another?"

Morgan looked away at the question. "I don't know. I wish I did."

"Now I've made you sad." Dorian sat back down beside Morgan and took her hands. "Don't pity me. Sooner or later, what's between Iona and me will be resolved. I'm a patient man." He smiled then, his eyes gleaming with confidence. "For now, we'll talk of something else. I have to confess, I'm fascinated by the smuggling legends."

"Yes. It is interesting. You said the rumor is that no one, not even the men who work for him, know who the leader is."

"That's the story. Whenever I'm on Lesbos, I keep hoping to stumble across some clue that would unmask him."

Morgan murmured something as her thoughts turned uncomfortably to Nick. "Yet you don't seem terribly concerned about the smuggling itself."

"Ah, the smuggling." Dorian moved his shoulders. "That's something for the authorities to worry about. But the thrill of the hunt, Morgan." His eyes gleamed as they moved past her. "The thrill of the hunt."

"You wouldn't believe it!" Liz bustled out and plopped into a chair. "A half-hour with a temperamental Greek cook. I'd rather face a firing squad. Give me a cigarette, Dorian." Her smile and everyday complaint made the subject of smuggling absurd. "So tell me, Morgan, how did you like Nick's house?"

Pink streaks joined sky and sea as dawn bloomed. The air was warm and moist. After a restless night, it was the best of beginnings.

Morgan strolled along the water's edge and listened

to the first serenading of birds. This was the way she had planned to spend her vacation—strolling along the beach, watching sunrises, relaxing. Isn't that what her father and Liz had drummed into her head?

Relax, Morgan. Get off the treadmill for a while. You never give yourself any slack.

She could almost laugh at the absurdity. But then, neither Liz nor her father had counted on Nicholas Gregoras.

He was an enigma, and she couldn't find the key. His involvement in smuggling was like a piece of a jigsaw puzzle that wouldn't quite fit. Morgan had never been able to tolerate half-finished puzzles. She scuffed her sandals in the sand. He was simply not a man she could categorize, and she wanted badly to shake the need to try.

On the other hand, there was Iona. Morgan saw the puzzle there as well. Alex's sulky cousin was more than a woman with an annoying personality. There was some inner agitation—something deep and firmly rooted. And *Alex knows something of it,* she mused. *Dorian, too,* unless she missed her guess. But what? And how much? Iona's reaction to talk of smuggling had been a sharp contrast to both Alex's and Dorian's. They'd been resigned—even amused. Iona had been terrified. Terrified of discovery? Morgan wondered. But that was absurd.

Shaking her head, Morgan pushed the thought aside. This morning she was going to do what she had come to Greece to do. Nothing. At least, nothing strenuous. She was going to look for shells, she decided, and after rolling up the hem of her jeans, splashed into a shallow inlet.

They were everywhere. The bank of sand and the shallow water were glistening with them. Some had been crushed underfoot or beaten smooth by the slow current. Crouching, she stuffed the pockets of her jacket with the best of them.

She noticed the stub of a black cigarette half-buried in the sand. So, Alex comes this way, she thought with a smile. Morgan could see Liz and her husband strolling hand in hand through the shallows.

As the sun grew higher, Morgan became more engrossed. If only I'd brought a tote, she thought, then shrugged and began to pile shells in a heap to retrieve later. She'd have them in a bowl on her windowsill at home. Then, whenever she was trapped indoors on a cold, rainy afternoon, she could look at them and remember Greek sunshine.

There were dozens of gulls. They flapped around her, circled, and called out. Morgan found the high, piercing sound the perfect company for a solitary morning. As the time passed, she began to find that inner peace she had experienced so briefly on the moonlit beach.

The hunt had taken her a good distance from the beach. Glancing up, she saw, with pleasure, the mouth of a cave. It wasn't large and was nearly hidden from view, but she thought it was entitled to an exploration. With a frown for her white jeans, Morgan decided to take a peek inside the entrance and come back when she was more suitably dressed. She moved to it with the water sloshing up to her calves. Bending down, she tugged another shell from its bed of sand. As her gaze swept over toward the cave, her hand froze.

The face glistened white in the clear water. Dark eyes stared back at her. Her scream froze in her throat, locked there by terror. She had never seen death before—not unpampered, staring death. Morgan stepped back jerkily, nearly slipping on a rock. As she struggled to regain her balance, her stomach heaved up behind the scream so that she could only gag. Even through the horror, she could feel the pressure of dizziness. She couldn't faint, not here, not with that only a foot away. She turned and fled.

She scrambled and spilled over rocks and sand. The only clear thought in her head was to get away. On a dead run, breath ragged, she broke from the concealment of the inlet out to the sickle of beach.

Hands gripped her. Blindly, Morgan fought against them with the primitive fear that the thing in the inlet had risen up and come after her.

"Stop it! Damn it, I'll end up hurting you again. Morgan, stop this. What's wrong with you?"

She was being shaken roughly. The voice pierced the first layer of shock. She stared and saw Nick's face. "Nicholas?" The dizziness was back and she went limp against him as waves of fear and nausea wracked her. Trembling, she couldn't stop the trembling, but knew she'd be safe now. He was there. "Nicholas," she managed again as though his name alone was enough to shield her.

Nick caught her tighter and shook her again. Her face was deathly pale, her skin clammy. He'd seen enough of horror to recognize it in her eyes. In a moment, he knew, she'd faint or be hysterical. He couldn't allow either.

"What happened?" he demanded in a voice that commanded an answer.

Morgan opened her mouth, but found she could only shake her head. She buried her face against his chest in an attempt to block out what she had seen. Her breath was still ragged, coming in dry sobs that wouldn't allow for words. She'd be safe now, she told herself as she fought the panic. He'd keep her safe.

"Pull yourself together, Morgan," Nick ordered curtly, "and tell me what happened."

"Can't…" She tried to burrow herself into him.

In one quick move he jerked her away, shaking her. "I said tell me." His voice was cold, emotionless. He knew only one way to deal with hysteria, and her breath was still rising in gasps.

Dazed by the tone of his voice, she tried again, then jolted, clinging to him when she heard the sound of footsteps.

"Hello. Am I intruding?" Andrew's cheerful voice came from behind her, but she didn't look back. The trembling wouldn't stop.

Why was he angry with her? Why wasn't he helping her? The questions whirled in her head as she tried to catch her breath. Oh, God, she needed him to help her.

"Is something wrong?" Andrew's tone mirrored both concern and curiosity as he noted Nick's black expression and Morgan's shaking form.

"I'm not sure." Nick forced himself not to curse his cousin and spoke briefly. "Morgan was running across the beach. I haven't been able to get anything out of her yet." He drew her away, his fingers digging roughly in her skin as she tried to hold firm. She saw nothing in his face but cool curiosity. "Now, Morgan"—there was an edge of steel now—"tell me."

"Over there." Her teeth began to chatter as the next stage of reaction set in. Swallowing, she clamped them together while her eyes pleaded with him. His remained hard and relentless on hers. "Near the cove." The effort of the two short sentences swam in her head. She leaned toward him again. "Nicholas, please."

"I'll have a look." He grabbed her arms, dragging them away from him, wishing he didn't see what she was asking of him—knowing he couldn't give it to her.

"Don't leave, please!" Desperate, she grabbed for him again only to be shoved roughly into Andrew's arms.

"Damn it, get her calmed down," Nick bit off, tasting his own fury. She had no right—no right to ask for things he couldn't give. He had no right—no right to want to give them to her. He swore again, low and pungent under his breath as he turned away.

"Nicholas!" Morgan struggled out of Andrew's arms, but Nick was already walking away. She pressed a hand to her mouth to stop herself from calling him again. He never looked back.

Arms encircled her. Not Nick's. She could feel the gentle comfort of Andrew as he drew her against his chest. Her fingers gripped his sweater. Not Nick. "Here now." Andrew brought a hand to her hair. "I had hoped to entice you into this position under different circumstances."

"Oh, Andrew." The soft words and tender stroking had the ice of shock breaking into tears. "Andrew, it was so horrible."

"Tell me what happened, Morgan. Say it fast. It'll be easier then." His tone was quiet and coaxing as he stroked her hair. Morgan gave a shuddering sigh.

"There's a body at the mouth of the cave."

"A body!" He drew her back to stare into her face. "Good God! Are you sure?"

"Yes, yes, I saw—I was..." She covered her face with her hands a moment until she thought she could speak.

"Easy, take it easy," he murmured. "And let it come out."

"I was collecting shells in the inlet. I saw the cave. I was going to peek inside, then I..." She shuddered once, then continued. "Then I saw the face—under the water."

"Oh, Morgan." He drew her into his arms again and held her tight. He didn't say any more, but in silence gave her everything she had needed. When the tears stopped, he kept her close.

Nick moved rapidly across the sand. His frown deepened as he saw Morgan molded in his cousin's arms. As he watched, Andrew bent down to kiss her hair. A small fire leaped inside him that he smothered quickly.

"Andrew, take Morgan up to the Theoharis villa and phone the authorities. One of the villagers has had a fatal accident."

Nodding, Andrew continued to stroke Morgan's hair. "Yes, she told me. Terrible that she had to find it." He swallowed what seemed to be his own revulsion. "Are you coming?"

Nick looked down as Morgan turned her face to his. He hated the look in her eyes as she stared at him—the blankness, the hurt. She wouldn't forgive him easily for this. "No, I'll stay and make sure no one else happens across it. Morgan..." He touched her shoulders, detesting himself. There was no response, her eyes were dry now, and empty. "You'll be all right. Andrew will take you home."

Without a word, Morgan turned her face away again.

His control slipped a bit as Nick shot Andrew a hard glance. "Take care of her."

"Of course," Andrew murmured, puzzled by the tone. "Come on, Morgan, lean on me."

Nick watched them mount the beach steps. When they were out of sight, he went back to search the body.

Seated in the salon, her horror dulled with Alex's best brandy, Morgan studied Captain Tripolos of Mitilini's police department. He was short, with his build spreading into comfortable lines that stopped just short of fat. His gray hair was carefully slicked to conceal its sparseness. His eyes were dark and sharp. Through the haze of brandy and shock, Morgan recognized a man with the tenacity of a bulldog.

"Miss James." The captain spoke in quick, staccato English. "I hope you understand, I must ask you some questions. It is routine."

"Couldn't it wait?" Andrew was stationed next to Morgan on the sofa. As he spoke he slipped an arm around her shoulders. "Miss James has had a nasty shock."

"No, Andrew, it's all right." Morgan laid her hand over his. "I'd rather be done with it. I understand, Captain." She gave him a straight look which he admired. "I'll tell you whatever I can."

"Efxaristo." He licked the end of his pencil, settled himself in his chair, and smiled with his mouth only. "Perhaps you could start by telling me exactly what happened this morning, from the time you arose."

Morgan began to recount the morning as concisely as she could. She spoke mechanically, with her hands limp and still in her lap. Though her voice trembled once or twice, Tripolos noted that her eyes stayed on his. She was a strong one, he decided, relieved that she wasn't putting him to the inconvenience of tears or jumbled hysterics.

"Then I saw him under the water." Morgan accepted Andrew's hand with gratitude. "I ran."

Tripolos nodded. "You were up very early. Is this your habit?"

"No. But I woke up and had an impulse to walk on the beach."

"Did you see anyone?"

"No." A shudder escaped, but her gaze didn't falter. She went up another notch in Tripolos's admiration. "Not until Nicholas and Andrew."

"Nicholas? Ah, Mr. Gregoras." He shifted his eyes to where Nick sprawled on a sofa across the room with Alex and Liz. "Had you ever seen the...deceased before?"

"No." Her hand tightened convulsively on Andrew's as the white face floated in front of her eyes. With a desperate effort of will, she forced the image away. "I've only been here a few days and I haven't been far from the villa yet."

"You're visiting from America?"

"Yes."

He made a quiet cluck of sympathy. "What a pity a murder had to blight your vacation."

"Murder?" Morgan repeated. The word echoed in her head as she stared into Tripolos's calm eyes. "But I thought...wasn't it an accident?"

"No." Tripolos glanced idly down at his notepad. "No, the victim was stabbed—in the back," he added with distaste. It was as if he considered murder one matter and back-stabbing another. "I hope I won't have to disturb you again." He rose and bowed over her hand. "Did you find many shells this morning, Miss James?"

"Yes I—I gathered quite a few." She felt compelled to

reach in her jacket pocket and produce some. "I thought they were…lovely."

"Yes." He smiled, then turned to the others. "I regret we will have to question everyone on their whereabouts from last evening to this morning. Of course," he continued with a shrug, "we will no doubt find the murder was a result of a village quarrel, but with the body found so close to both villas…" He trailed off as he pocketed his pad and pencil. "One of you might recall some small incident that will help settle the matter."

Settle the matter? Morgan thought on a wave of hysteria. Settle the matter. But a man's dead. I'm dreaming. I must be dreaming.

"Easy, Morgan," Andrew whispered in her ear. "Have another sip." Gently, he urged the brandy back to her lips.

"You have our complete cooperation, Captain," Alex stated, and rose. "It isn't pleasant for any of us to have such a thing happen so near our homes. It's particularly upsetting that a guest of mine should have found the man."

"I understand, of course." Tripolos nodded wearily, rubbing a hand over his square chin. "It would be less confusing if I spoke with you one at a time. Perhaps we could use your office?"

"I'll show you where it is." Alex gestured to the door. "You can speak to me first if you like."

"Thank you." Tripolos gave the room a general bow before retreating behind Alex. Morgan watched his slow, measured steps. He'd haunt a man to the grave, she thought, and shakily swallowed the rest of the brandy.

"I need a drink," Liz announced, moving toward the liquor cabinet. "A double. Anyone else?"

Nick's eyes skimmed briefly over Morgan. "Whatever you're having." He gestured with his hand, signaling Liz to refill Morgan's glass.

"I don't see why he has to question us." Iona moved to the bar, too impatient to wait for Liz to pour. "It's absurd. Alex should have refused. He has enough influence to avoid all of this." She poured something potent into a tall glass and drank half of it down.

"There's no reason for Alex to avoid anything." Liz handed Nick his drink before splashing another generous portion of brandy into Morgan's glass. "We have nothing to hide. What can I fix you, Dorian?"

"Hide? I said nothing about hiding," Iona retorted as she swirled around the room. "I don't want to answer that policeman's silly questions just because *she* was foolish enough to stumble over some villager's body," she said, gesturing toward Morgan.

"A glass of ouzo will be fine, Liz," Dorian stated before Liz could fire a retort. His gaze lit on Iona. "I hardly think we can blame Morgan, Iona. We'd have been questioned in any case. As it is, she's had to deal with finding the man as well as the questions. Thank you, Liz," he added as she placed a glass in his hand and shot him a grim smile.

"I cannot stay in this house today." Iona prowled the room, her movements as jerky as a nervous finger on a trigger. "Nicky, let's go out in your boat." She stopped and dropped to the arm of his chair.

"The timing's bad, Iona. When I'm finished here, I have paperwork to clear up at home." He sipped his drink and patted her hand. His eyes met Morgan's briefly, but long enough to recognize condemnation. Damn you, he thought furiously, you have no right to make me feel guilty for doing what I have to do.

"Oh, Nicky." Iona's hand ran up his arm. "I'll go mad if I stay here today. Please, a few hours on the sea?"

Nick sighed in capitulation while inside he fretted against a leash that was too long, and too strong, for him to break. He had reason to agree, and couldn't let Morgan's blank stare change the course he'd already taken. "All right, later this afternoon."

Iona smiled into her drink.

The endless questioning continued. Liz slipped out as Alex came back in. And the waiting went on. Conversation came in fits and starts, conducted in undertones. As Andrew left the room for his conference, Nick wandered to Morgan's new station by the window.

"I want to talk to you." His tone was quiet, with the steel under it. When he put his hand over hers, she jerked it away.

"I don't want to talk to you."

Deliberately, he slipped his hands into his pockets. She was still pale. The brandy had steadied her but hadn't brought the color back to her cheeks. "It's necessary, Morgan. At the moment, I haven't the opportunity to argue about it."

"That's your problem."

"We'll go for a drive when the captain's finished. You need to get away from here for a while."

"I'm not going anywhere with you. Don't tell me what I need now." She kept her teeth clamped and spoke without emotion. "I needed you then."

"Damn it, Morgan." His muttered oath had all the power of a shout. She kept her eyes firmly on Liz's garden. Some of the roses, she thought dispassionately, were overblown now. The hands in his pockets were fists, straining impotently. "Don't you think I know that?

Don't you think I—" He cut himself off before he lost control. "I couldn't give you what you needed—not then. Don't make this any more impossible for me than it is."

She turned to him now, meeting his fury with frost. "I have no intention of doing that." Her voice was as low as his but with none of his vibrating emotion. "The simple fact is I don't want anything from you now. I don't want anything to do with you."

"Morgan…" There was something in his eyes now that threatened to crack her resolve. Apology, regret, a plea for understanding where she'd never expected to see one. "Please, I need—"

"I don't care what you need," she said quickly, before he could weaken her again. "Just stay away from me. Stay completely away from me."

"Tonight," he began, but the cold fury in her eyes stopped him.

"Stay away," Morgan repeated.

She turned her back on him and walked across the room to join Dorian. Nick was left with black thoughts and the inability to carry them out.

Chapter 6

Morgan was surprised she'd slept. She hadn't been tired when Liz and Alex had insisted she lie down, but had obeyed simply because her last words with Nick had sapped all of her resistance. Now as she woke she saw it was past noon. She'd slept for two hours.

Groggy, heavy-eyed, Morgan walked into the bath to splash cool water on her face. The shock had passed, but the nap had brought her a lingering weariness instead of refreshment. Beneath it all was a deep shame—shame that she had run, terrified, from a dead man. Shame that she had clung helplessly to Nick and been turned away. She could feel even now that sensation of utter dependence—and utter rejection.

Never again, Morgan promised herself. She should have trusted her head instead of her heart. She should have known better than to ask or expect anything from a man like him. A man like him had nothing to give. You'd always find hell if you looked to a devil. And yet…

And yet it had been Nick she had needed, and trusted—him she had felt safe with the moment his arms had come around her. My mistake, Morgan thought grimly, and studied herself in the mirror over the basin. There were still some lingering signs of shock—the pale cheeks and too wide eyes, but she felt the strength returning.

"I don't need him," she said aloud, wanting to hear the words. "He doesn't mean anything to me."

But he's hurt you. Someone who doesn't matter can't hurt you.

I won't let him hurt me again, Morgan promised herself. Because I won't ever go to him again, I won't ever ask him again, no matter what.

She turned away from her reflection and went downstairs.

Even as she entered the main hall, Morgan heard the sound of a door closing and footsteps. Glancing behind her, she saw Dorian.

"So, you've rested." He came to her and took her hand. In the gesture was all the comfort and concern she could have asked for.

"Yes. I feel like a fool." At his lifted brow, Morgan moved her shoulders restlessly. "Andrew all but carried me back up here."

With a low laugh, he slipped an arm around her shoulders and led her into the salon. "You American women— do you always have to be strong and self-reliant?"

"I always have been." She remembered weeping in Nick's arms—clinging, pleading—and straightened her spine. "I have to depend on myself."

"I admire you for it. But then, you don't make a habit of stumbling over dead bodies." He cast a look at her pale cheeks and gentled his tone. "There, it was foolish of me to remind you. Shall I fix you another drink?"

"No— No, I've enough brandy in me as it is." Morgan managed a thin smile and moved away from him.

Why was it she was offered a supporting arm by everyone but the one who mattered? No, Nick couldn't matter, she reminded herself. She couldn't let him matter, and she didn't need a supporting arm from anyone.

"You seem restless, Morgan. Would you rather be alone?"

"No." She shook her head as she looked up. His eyes were calm. She'd never seen them otherwise. There'd be strength in him, she thought, and wished bleakly it had been Dorian she had run to that morning. Going to the piano, she ran a finger over the keys. "I'm glad the captain's gone. He made me nervous."

"Tripolos?" Dorian drew out his cigarette case. "I doubt he's anything to worry about. I doubt even the killer need worry," he added with a short laugh. "The Mitilini police force isn't known for its energy or brilliance."

"You sound as if you don't care if the person who killed that man is caught."

"Village quarrels mean nothing to me," he countered. "I'm concerned more with the people I know. I don't like to think you're worried about Tripolos."

"He doesn't worry me," she corrected, frowning as he lit a cigarette. Something was nagging at the back of her mind, struggling to get through. "He just has a way of looking at you while he sits there, comfortable and not quite tidy." She watched the column of smoke curl up from the tip of the long, black cigarette. With an effort, Morgan shook off the feeling of something important, half remembered. "Where is everyone?"

"Liz is with Alex in his office. Iona's gone on her boat ride."

"Oh, yes, with Nicholas." Morgan looked down at her hands, surprised that they had balled into fists. Deliberately, she opened them. "It must be difficult for you."

"She needed to escape. The atmosphere of death is hard on her nerves."

"You're very understanding." Disturbed and suddenly headachy, Morgan wandered to the window. "I don't think I would be—if I were in love."

"I'm patient, and I know that Nick means less than nothing to her. A means to an end." He paused for a moment, before he spoke again, thoughtfully. "Some people have no capacity for emotion—love or hate."

"How empty that would be," Morgan murmured.

"Do you think so?" He gave her an odd smile. "Somehow, I think it would be comfortable."

"Yes, comfortable perhaps but…" Morgan trailed off as she turned back. Dorian was just lifting the cigarette to his lips. As Morgan's eyes focused on it, she remembered, with perfect clarity, seeing the stub of one of those expensive brands in the sand, only a few yards from the body. A chill shot through her as she continued to stare.

"Morgan, is something wrong?" Dorian's voice broke through so that she blinked and focused on him again.

"No, I—I suppose I'm not myself yet. Maybe I'll have that drink after all."

She didn't want it, but needed a moment to pull her thoughts together. The stub of a cigarette didn't have to mean anything, she told herself as Dorian went to the bar. Anyone from the villa could have wandered through that inlet a dozen times.

But the stub had been fresh, Morgan remembered— half in, half out of the sand, unweathered. The birds hadn't picked at it. Surely if someone had been that close to the body, they would have seen. They would have seen, and they would have gone to the police. Unless...

No, that was a ridiculous thought, she told herself as she felt a quick tremor. It was absurd to think that Dorian might have had anything to do with a villager's murder. Dorian or Alex, she thought as that sweet, foreign smoke drifted over her.

They were both civilized men—civilized men didn't stab other men in the back. Both of them had such beautiful, manicured hands and careful manners. Didn't it take something evil, something cold and hard to kill? She thought of Nick and shook her head. No, she wouldn't think of him now. She'd concentrate on this one small point and work it through to the end.

It didn't make any sense to consider Dorian or Alex as killers. They were businessmen, cultured. What possible dealings could they have had with some local fisherman? It was an absurd thought, Morgan told herself, but couldn't quite shake the unease that was creeping into her. There'd be a logical explanation, she insisted. There was always a logical explanation. She was still upset, that was all. Blowing some minor detail out of proportion.

Whose footsteps were on the beach steps that first night? a small voice insisted. Who was Nick hiding from? Or waiting for? That man hadn't been killed in a village quarrel, her thoughts ran on. She hadn't believed it for a moment, any more than she'd really believed the man had died accidentally. Murder…smuggling. Morgan closed her eyes and shuddered.

Who was coming in from the sea when Nick had held her in the shadow of the cypress? Nick had ordered Stephanos to follow him. Alex? Dorian? The dead man perhaps? She jolted when Dorian offered her the snifter.

"Morgan, you're still so pale. You should sit."

"No… I guess I'm still a little jumpy, that's all." Morgan cupped the snifter in both hands but didn't drink. She would ask him, that was all. She would simply ask him if he'd been to the inlet. But when her eyes met his, so calm, so concerned, she felt an icy tremor of fear. "The inlet—" Morgan hesitated, then continued before her courage failed her. "The inlet was so beautiful. It seemed so undisturbed." But so many shells had been crushed underfoot, she remembered abruptly. Why hadn't she thought of that before? "Do you—do a lot of people go there?"

"I can't speak for the villagers," Dorian began, watching as she perched on the arm of a divan. "But I'd think most of them would be too busy with their fishing or in the olive groves to spend much time gathering shells."

"Yes." She moistened dry lips. "But still, it's a lovely spot, isn't it?"

Morgan kept her eyes on his. Was it her imagination, or had his eyes narrowed? A trick of the smoke that wafted between them? Her own nerves?

"I've never been there," Dorian said lightly. "I suppose it's a bit like a native New Yorker never going to the top of the Empire State Building." Morgan's gaze followed his fingers as he crushed out the cigarette in a cut-glass ashtray. "Is there something else, Morgan?"

"Something—no." Hastily, she looked back up to

meet his eyes. "No, nothing. I suppose like Iona, the atmosphere's getting to me, that's all."

"Small wonder." Sympathetic, he crossed to her. "You've been through too much today, Morgan. Too much talk of death. Come out in the garden," he suggested. "We'll talk of something else."

Refusal was on the tip of her tongue. She didn't know why, only that she didn't want to be with him. Not then. Not alone. Even as she cast around for a reasonable excuse, Liz joined them.

"Morgan, I'd hoped you were resting."

Grateful for the interruption, Morgan set down her untouched brandy and rose. "I rested long enough." A quick scan of Liz's face showed subtle signs of strain. "You look like you should lie down awhile."

"No, but I could use some air."

"I was just taking Morgan out to the garden." Dorian touched a hand to Liz's shoulder. "You two go out and relax. Alex and I have some business we should clear up."

"Yes." Liz lifted her hand to his. "Thank you, Dorian. I don't know what Alex or I would have done without you today."

"Nonsense." He brushed her cheek with his lips. "Go, take your mind off this business."

"I will. See if you can get Alex to do the same." The plea was light, but unmistakable before Liz hooked her arm through Morgan's.

"Dorian." Morgan felt a flush of shame. He'd been nothing but kind to her, and she'd let her imagination run wild. "Thank you."

He lifted a brow at the gratitude, then smiled and

kissed her cheek in turn. He smelt of citrus groves and sunshine. "Sit with the flowers for a while, and enjoy."

As he walked into the hall, Liz turned and headed toward the garden doors. "Should I order us some tea?"

"Not for me. And stop treating me like a guest."

"Good Lord, was I doing that?"

"Yes, ever since—"

Liz shot Morgan a quick look as she broke off, then grimaced. "This whole business really stinks," Liz stated inelegantly, and plopped down on a marble bench.

Surrounded by the colors and scents of the garden, isolated from the house and the outside world by vines, Morgan and Liz frowned at each other.

"Damn, Morgan, I'm so sorry that you had to be the one. No, don't shrug and try to look casual," she ordered as Morgan did just that. "We've known each other too long and too well. I know what it must have been like for you this morning. And I know how you must be feeling right now."

"I'm all right, Liz." She chose a small padded glider and curled her legs under her. "Though I'll admit I won't be admiring seashells for a while. Please," she continued as Liz's frown deepened. "Don't do this. I can see that you and Alex are blaming yourselves. It was just—just a horrible coincidence that I happened to take a tour of that inlet this morning. A man was killed; someone had to find him."

"It didn't have to be you."

"You and Alex aren't responsible."

Liz sighed. "My practical American side knows that, but…" She shrugged, then managed to smile. "But I think I'm becoming a bit Greek. You're staying in my house." Liz lit a cigarette resignedly as she rose to pace the tiny courtyard.

A black cigarette, Morgan noticed with a tremor of anxiety—slim and black. She'd forgotten Liz had picked up the habit of occasionally smoking one of Alex's brand.

She stared up into Liz's oval, classic face, then shut her eyes. She must be going mad if she could conceive, even for an instant, that Liz was mixed up in smuggling and back-stabbing. This was a woman she'd known for years—lived with. Certainly if there was one person she knew as well as she knew herself, it was Liz.

But how far—how far would Liz go to protect the man she loved?

"And I have to admit," Liz went on as she continued to pace, "though it sticks me in the same category as Iona, that policeman made me nervous. He was just too"—she searched for an adjective—"respectful," she decided. "Give me a good old American grilling."

"I know what you mean," Morgan murmured. She had to stop thinking, she told herself. If she could just stop thinking, everything would be all right again.

"I don't know what he expected to find out, questioning us that way." Liz took a quick, jerky puff, making her wedding ring flash with cold, dazzling light.

"It was just routine, I suppose." Morgan couldn't take her eyes from the ring—the light, the stones. Love, honor, and obey—forsaking all others.

"And creepy," Liz added. "Besides, none of us even knew this Anthony Stevos."

"The captain said he was a fisherman."

"So is every second man in the village."

Morgan allowed the silence to hang. Carefully, she reconstructed the earlier scene in the salon. What were the reactions? If she hadn't been so dimmed with brandy and shock, would she have noticed something? There was one more person she'd seen lighting one of the expensive cigarettes. "Liz," she began slowly, "don't you think Iona went a little overboard? Didn't she get a bit melodramatic about a few routine questions?"

"Iona thrives on melodrama," Liz returned with grim relish. "Did you see the way she fawned all over Nick? I don't see how he could bear it."

"He didn't seem to mind," Morgan muttered. No, not yet, she warned herself. You're not ready to deal with that yet. "She's a strange woman," Morgan continued. "But this morning…" And yesterday, she remembered. "Yesterday when I spoke of smuggling… I think she was really afraid."

"I don't think Iona has any genuine feelings," Liz said stubbornly. "I wish Alex would just cross her off as a bad bet and be done with it. He's so infuriatingly conscientious."

"Strange, Dorian said almost the same thing." Morgan plucked absently at an overblown rose. It was Iona she should concentrate on. If anyone could do something deadly and vile, it was Iona. "I don't see her that way."

"What do you mean?"

"Iona." Morgan stopped plucking at the rose and gave Liz her attention. "I see her as a woman of too many feelings rather than none at all. Not all healthy certainly, perhaps even destructive—but strong, very strong emotions."

"I can't abide her," Liz said with such unexpected venom, Morgan stared. "She upsets Alex constantly. I can't tell you how much time and trouble and money he's put into that woman. And he gets nothing back but ingratitude, rudeness."

"Alex has very strong family feelings," Morgan began. "You can't protect him from—"

"I'd protect him from anything," Liz interrupted passionately. "Anything and anyone." Whirling, she hurled her cigarette into the bushes where it lay smoldering. Morgan found herself staring at it with dread. "Damn," Liz said in a calmer tone. "I'm letting all this get to me."

"We all are." Morgan shook off the sensation of unease and rose. "It hasn't been an easy morning."

"I'm sorry, Morgan, it's just that Alex is so upset by all this. And as much as he loves me, he just isn't the kind of man to share certain areas with me. His trouble—his business. He's too damn Greek." With a quick laugh, she shook her head. "Come on, sit down. I've vented my spleen."

"Liz, if there were something wrong—I mean, something really troubling you, you'd tell me, wouldn't you?"

"Oh, don't start worrying about me now." Liz nudged Morgan back down on the glider. "It's just frustrating when you love someone to distraction and they won't let you help. Sometimes it drives me crazy that Alex insists on trying to keep the less-pleasant aspects of his life away from me."

"He loves you," Morgan murmured and found she was gripping her hands together.

"And I love him."

"Liz…" Morgan took a deep breath and plunged. "Do you and Alex walk through the inlet often?"

"Hmmm?" Obviously distracted, Liz looked back over her shoulder as she walked toward her bench. "Oh, no, actually, we usually walk on the cliffs—if I can drag

him away from his office. I can't think when's the last time I've been near there. I only wish," she added in a gentler tone, "I'd been with you this morning."

Abruptly and acutely ashamed at the direction her thoughts had taken, Morgan looked away. "I'm glad you weren't. Alex had his hands full enough with one hysterical female."

"You weren't hysterical," Liz corrected in a quiet voice. "You were almost too calm by the time Andrew brought you in."

"I never even thanked him." Morgan forced herself to push doubts and suspicions aside. They were as ugly as they were ridiculous. "What did you think of Andrew?"

"He's a very sweet man." Sensing Morgan's changing mood, Liz adjusted her own thoughts. "He appeared to put himself in the role of your champion today." She smiled, deliberately looking wise and matronly. "I'd say he was in the first stages of infatuation."

"How smug one becomes after three years of marriage."

"He'd be a nice diversion for you," Liz mused, unscathed. "But he's from the genteel-poor side of Nick's family. I rather fancy seeing you set up in style. Then again," she continued as Morgan sighed, "he'd be nice company for you…for a while."

Dead on cue, Andrew strolled into the courtyard. "Hello. I hope I'm not intruding."

"Why, no!" Liz gave him a delighted smile. "Neighboring poets are always welcome."

He grinned, a flash of boyishness. With that, he went up several notches on Liz's list. "Actually, I was worried about Morgan." Bending over, he cupped her chin and studied her. "It was such an awful morning, I wanted to see how you were doing. I hope you don't mind." His eyes were dark blue, like the water in the bay—and with the same serenity.

"I don't." She touched the back of his hand. "At all. I'm really fine. I was just telling Liz I hadn't even thanked you for everything you did."

"You're still pale."

His concern made her smile. "A New York winter has something to do with that."

"Determined to be courageous?" he asked with a tilted smile.

"Determined to do a better job of it than I did this morning."

"I kind of liked the way you held on to me." He gave her hand a light squeeze. "I want to steal her for an evening," he told Liz, shifting his gaze from Morgan's face. "Can you help me convince her a diversion is what she needs?"

"You have my full support."

"Come have dinner with me in the village." He bent down to Morgan again. "Some local color, a bottle of ouzo, and a witty companion. What more could you ask for?"

"What a marvelous idea!" Liz warmed to Andrew and the scheme. "It's just what you need, Morgan."

Amused, Morgan wondered if she should just let them pat each other on the back for a while. But it was what she needed—to get away from the house and the doubts. She smiled at Andrew. "What time should I be ready?"

His grin flashed again. "How about six? I'll give you a tour of the village. Nick gave me carte blanche with his Fiat while I'm here, so you won't have to ride on an ass."

Because her teeth were tight again, Morgan relaxed her jaw. "I'll be ready."

* * *

The sun was high over the water when Nick set his boat toward the open sea. He gave it plenty of throttle, wanting the speed and the slap of the wind.

Damn the woman! he thought on a new surge of frustration. Seething, he tossed the butt of a slender black cigarette into the churning waves. If she'd stay in bed instead of wandering on beaches at ridiculous hours, all of this could have been avoided. The memory of the plea in her voice, the horror in her eyes flashed over him. He could still feel the way she had clung to him, needing him.

He cursed her savagely and urged more speed from the motor.

Shifting his thoughts, Nick concentrated on the dead man. Anthony Stevos, he mused, scowling into the sun. He knew the fisherman well enough—what he had occasionally fished for—and the Athens phone number he had found deep inside Stevos's pants pocket.

Stevos had been a stupid, greedy man, Nick thought dispassionately. Now he was a dead one. How long would it take Tripolos to rule out the village brawl and hit on the truth? Not long enough, Nick decided. He was going to have to bring matters to a head a bit sooner than he had planned.

"Nicky, why are you looking so mean?" Iona called to him over the motor's roar. Automatically, he smoothed his features.

"I was thinking about that pile of paperwork on my desk." Nick cut the motor off and let the boat drift in its own wake. "I shouldn't have let you talk me into taking the afternoon off."

Iona moved to where he sat. Her skin glistened, oiled

slick, against a very brief bikini. Her bosom spilled over in invitation. She had a ripe body, rounded and full and arousing. Nick felt no stir as she swung her hips moving toward him.

"Agapetikos, we'll have to take your mind off business matters." She wound herself into his lap and pressed against him.

He kissed her mechanically, knowing that, after the bottle of champagne she'd drunk, she'd never know the difference. But her taste lingered unpleasantly on his lips. He thought of Morgan, and with a silent, furious oath, crushed his mouth against Iona's.

"Mmm." She preened like a stroked cat. "Your mind isn't on your paperwork now, Nicky. Tell me you want me. I need a man who wants me."

"Is there a man alive who wouldn't want a woman such as you?" He ran a hand down her back as her mouth searched greedily for his.

"A devil," she muttered with a slurred laugh. "Only a devil. Take me, Nicky." Her head fell back, revealing eyes half closed and dulled by wine. "Make love to me here, in the open, in the sun."

And he might have to, he thought with a grinding disgust in his stomach. To get what he needed. But first, he would coax what he could from her while she was vulnerable.

"Tell me, *matia mou,*" he murmured, tasting the curve of her neck while she busily undid the buttons of his shirt. "What do you know of this smuggling between Lesbos and Turkey?"

Nick felt her stiffen, but her response—and, he knew, her wits—were dulled by the champagne. In her state of mind, he thought, it wouldn't take much more to loosen her tongue. She'd been ready to snap for days. Deliberately, he traced his tongue across her skin and felt her sigh.

"Nothing," she said quickly and fumbled more desperately at his buttons. "I know nothing of such things."

"Come, Iona," he murmured seductively. She was a completely physical woman, one who ran on sensations alone. Between wine and sex and her own nerves, she'd talk to him. "You know a great deal. As a businessman"—he nipped at her earlobe—"I'm interested in greater profit. You won't deny me a few extra drachmas, will you?"

"A few million," she murmured, and put her hand on his to show him what she wanted. "Yes, there's much I know."

"And much you'll tell me?" he asked. "Come, Iona. You and the thought of millions excite me."

"I know the man that stupid woman found this morning was murdered because he was greedy."

Nick forced himself not to tense. "But greed is so difficult to resist." He went with her as she stretched full length on the bench. "Do you know who murdered him, Iona?" She was slipping away from him, losing herself to the excess of champagne. On a silent oath, Nick nipped at her skin to bring her back.

"I don't like murder, Nicky," she mumbled, "and I don't like talking to the police even more." She reached for him, but her hands fumbled. "I'm tired of being used," she said pettishly, then added, "Perhaps it's time to change allegiance. You're rich, Nicky. I like money. I need money."

"Doesn't everyone?" Nick asked dryly.

"Later, we'll talk later. I'll tell you." Her mouth was

greedy on his. Forcing everything from his mind, Nick struggled to find some passion, even the pretense of passion, in return. God, he needed a woman; his body ached for one. And he needed Iona. But as he felt her sliding toward unconsciousness, he did nothing to revive her.

Later, as Iona slept in the sun, Nick leaned over the opposite rail and lit a cigarette from the butt of another. The clinging distaste both infuriated and depressed him. He knew that he would have to use Iona, be used by her—if not this time, then eventually. He had to tap her knowledge to learn what he wanted to know. It was a matter of his own safety—and his success. The second had always been more important to him than the first.

If he had to be Iona's lover to gain his own end, then he'd be her lover. It meant nothing. Swearing, he drew deeply on the cigarette. It meant nothing, he repeated. It was business.

He found he wanted a shower, a long one, something to cleanse himself of the dirt which wouldn't wash away. Years of dirt, years of lies. Why had he never felt imprisoned by them until now?

Morgan's face slipped into his mind. Her eyes were cold. Flinging the cigarette out to sea, he went back to the wheel and started the engine.

Chapter 7

During a leisurely drink after a leisurely tour, Morgan decided the village was perfect. White-washed houses huddled close together, some with pillars, some with arches, still others with tiny wooden balconies. The tidiness, the freshness of white should have lent an air of newness. Instead, the village seemed old and timeless and permanent.

She sat with Andrew at a waterfront *kafenion,* watching the fishing boats sway at the docks, and the men who spread their nets to dry.

The fishermen ranged from young boys to old veterans. All were bronzed, all worked together. There were twelve to each net—twenty-four hands, some wrinkled and gnarled, some smooth with youth. All strong. As they worked they shouted and laughed in routine companionship.

"Must have been a good catch," Andrew commented.

He watched Morgan's absorption with the small army of men near the water's edge.

"You know, I've been thinking." She ran a finger down the side of her glass. "They all seem so fit and sturdy. Some of those men are well past what we consider retirement age in the States. I suppose they'll sail until they die. A life on the water must be a very satisfying existence." Pirates...would she ever stop thinking of pirates?

"I don't know if any of these people think much about satisfaction. It's simply what they do. They fish or work in Nick's olive groves. They've been doing one or the other for generations." Toying with his own drink, Andrew studied them too. "I do think there's a contentment here. The people know what's expected of them. If their lives are simple, perhaps it's an enviable simplicity."

"Still, there's the smuggling," Morgan murmured.

Andrew shrugged. "It's all part of the same mold, isn't it? They do what's expected of them and earn a bit of adventure and a few extra drachmas."

She shot him a look of annoyed surprise. "I didn't expect that attitude from you."

Andrew looked back at her, both brows raised. "What attitude?"

"This—this nonchalance over crime."

"Oh, come on, Morgan, it's—"

"Wrong," she interrupted. "It should be stopped." Morgan swallowed the innocently clear but potent ouzo.

"How do you stop something that's been going on for centuries in one form or another?"

"It's current form is ugly. I should think the men of influence like Alex and... Nicholas, with homes on the island, would put pressure on whoever should be pressured."

"I don't know Alex well enough to comment," Andrew mused, filling her glass again. "But I can't imagine Nick getting involved in anything that didn't concern himself or his business."

"Can't you?" Morgan murmured.

"If that sounds like criticism, it's not." He noted he had Morgan's full attention, but that her eyes were strangely veiled. "Nick's been very good to me, lending me the cottage and the money for my passage. Lord knows when I'll be able to pay him back. And it irks quite a bit to have to borrow, but poetry isn't the most financially secure career."

"I think I read somewhere that T.S. Eliot was a bank teller."

Andrew returned her understanding smile with a wry grimace. "I could work out of Nick's California office." He shrugged and drank. "His offer wasn't condescending, just absentminded. It's rough on the ego." He looked past her, toward the docks. "Maybe my ship will come in."

"I'm sure it will, Andrew. Some of us are meant to follow dreams."

His gaze came back to her. "And artists are meant to suffer a bit, rise beyond the more base needs of money and power?" His smile was brittle, his eyes cool. "Let's order." Morgan watched him shake off the mood and smile with his usual warmth. "I'm starved."

The evening sky was muted as they finished their meal. There were soft, dying colors flowing into the western sea. In the east, it was a calm, deep violet waiting for the first stars. Morgan was content with the vague glow brought on by spiced food and Greek ouzo. There was intermittent music from a mandolin. Packets of people shuffled in and out of the café, some of them breaking into song.

Their waiter cum proprietor was a wide man with a thin moustache and watery eyes. Morgan figured the eyes could be attributed to the spices and cook smoke hanging in the air. American tourists lifted his status. Because he was impressed with Morgan's easily flowing Greek, he found opportunities to question and gossip as he hovered around their table.

Morgan toyed with a bit of *psomaki* and relaxed with the atmosphere and easy company. She'd found nothing but comfort and good will in the Theoharis villa, but this was something different. There was an earthier ambience she had missed in Liz's elegant home. Here there would be lusty laughter and spilled wine. As strong as Morgan's feelings were for both Liz and Alex, she would never have been content with the lives they led. She'd have rusted inside the perpetual manners.

For the first time since that morning, Morgan felt the nagging ache at the base of her skull begin to ease.

"Oh, Andrew, look! They're dancing." Cupping her chin on her hands, Morgan watched the line of men hook arms.

As he finished up the last of a spicy sausage, Andrew glanced over. "Want to join in?"

Laughing, she shook her head. "No, I'd spoil it—but you could," she added with a grin.

"You have," Andrew began as he filled her glass again, "a wonderful laugh. It's rich and unaffected and trails off into something sensuous."

"What extraordinary things you say, Andrew." Morgan smiled at him, amused. "You're an easy man to be with. We could be friends."

Andrew lifted his brows. Morgan was surprised to find her mouth briefly captured. There was a faint taste of the island on him—spicy and foreign. "For starters." At her stunned expression, he leaned back and grinned. "That face you're wearing doesn't do great things for my ego, either." He pulled a pack of cigarettes out of his jacket pocket, then dug for a match. Morgan stopped staring at him to stare at the thin black box.

"I didn't know you smoked," she managed after a moment.

"Oh, not often." He found a match. The tiny flame flared, flickering over his face a moment, casting shadows, mysteries, suspicions. "Especially since my taste runs to these. Nick takes pity on me and leaves some at my cottage whenever he happens by. Otherwise, I suppose I'd do without altogether." When he noticed Morgan's steady stare, he gave her a puzzled smile. "Something wrong?"

"No." She lifted her glass and hoped she sounded casual. "I was just thinking—you'd said you roam all over this part of the island. You must have been in that inlet before."

"It's a beautiful little spot." He reached over for her hand. "Or it was. I guess I haven't been there in over a week. It might be quite a while before I go back now."

"A week," Morgan murmured.

"Don't dwell on it, Morgan."

She lifted her eyes to his. They were so clear, so concerned. She was being a fool. None of them—Alex, Dorian, Andrew—none of them were capable of what was burning into her thoughts. How was she to know that some maniac from the village hadn't had a taste for expensive tobacco and back-stabbing? It made more sense, a great deal more sense than her ugly suspicions.

"You're right." She smiled again and leaned toward him. "Tell me about your epic poem."

"Good evening, Miss James, Mr. Stevenson."

Morgan twisted her head and felt the sky cloud over. She looked up into Tripolos's pudgy face. "Hello, Captain."

If her greeting lacked enthusiasm, Tripolos seemed unperturbed. "I see you're enjoying a bit of village life. Do you come often?"

"This is Morgan's first trip," Andrew told him. "I convinced her to come out to dinner. She needed something after this morning's shock."

Tripolos clucked sympathetically. Morgan noted the music and laughter had stilled. The atmosphere in the café was hushed and wary.

"Very sensible," the captain decided. "A young lady must not dwell on such matters. I, unfortunately, must think of little else at the moment." He sighed and looked wistfully at the ouzo. "Enjoy your evening."

"Damn, damn, *damn!*" she muttered when he walked away. "Why does he affect me this way? Every time I see him, I feel like I've got the Hope diamond in my pocket."

"I know what you mean." Andrew watched people fall back to create a path for Tripolos. "He almost makes you wish you had something to confess."

"Thank God, it's not just me." Morgan lifted her glass again, noticed her hands were trembling, and drained it. "Andrew," she began in calm tones, "unless you have some moral objection, I'm going to get very drunk."

Sometime later, after learning Andrew's views on

drinking were flexible, Morgan floated on a numbing cloud of ouzo. The thin light of the moon had replaced the colors of sunset. As the hour grew later, the café crowd grew larger, both in size and volume. Music was all strings and bells. If the interlude held a sheen of unreality, she no longer cared. She'd had enough of reality.

The waiter materialized with yet another bottle. He set it on the table with the air of distributing a rare wine.

"Busy night," Morgan commented, giving him a wide if misty, smile.

"It is Saturday," he returned, explaining everything.

"So, I've chosen my night well." She glanced about, seeing a fuzzy crush of people. "Your customers seem happy."

He followed her survey with a smug smile, wiping a hand on his apron. "I feared when the Mitilini captain came, my business would suffer, but all is well."

"The police don't add to an atmosphere of enjoyment. I suppose," she added slowly, "he's investigating the death of that fisherman."

He gave Morgan a quick nod. "Stevos came here often, but he was a man with few companions. He was not one for dancing or games. He found other uses for his time." The waiter narrowed his eyes. "My customers do not like to answer questions." He muttered something uncomplimentary, but Morgan wasn't sure if it was directed at Stevos or Tripolos.

"He was a fisherman," she commented, struggling to concentrate on the Greek's eyes. "But it appears his comrades don't mourn him."

The waiter moved his shoulders eloquently, but she saw her answer. There were fishermen, and fishermen. "Enjoy your evening, *kyrios*. It is an honor to serve you."

"You know," Andrew stated when the waiter drifted to another table, "it's very intimidating listening to all that Greek. I couldn't pick up on it. What was he saying?"

Not wanting to dwell on the murder again, Morgan merely smiled. "Greek males are red-blooded, Andrew, but I explained that I was otherwise engaged for this evening." She locked her hands behind her head and looked up at the stars. "Oh, I'm glad I came. It's so lovely. No murders—no smuggling tonight. I feel marvelous, Andrew. When can I read some of your poetry?"

"When your brain's functioning at a normal level." Smiling, he tilted more ouzo into her glass. "I think your opinion might be important."

"You're a nice man." Morgan lifted her glass and studied him as intensely as possible. "You're not at all like Nicholas."

"What brought that on?" Andrew frowned, setting the bottle back down again.

"You're just not." She held out her glass. "To Americans," she told him. "One hundred percent pure."

After tapping her glass with his, Andrew drank and shook his head. "I have a feeling we weren't toasting the same thing."

She felt Nick begin to push into her thoughts and she thrust him away. "What does it matter? It's a beautiful night."

"So it is." His finger traced lightly over the back of her hand. "Have I told you how lovely you are?"

"Oh, Andrew, are you going to flatter me?" With a warm laugh, she leaned closer. "Go ahead, I love it."

With a wry grin, he tugged her hair. "You're spoiling my delivery."

"Oh, dear…how's this?" Morgan cupped her chin on her hands again and gave him a very serious stare.

On a laugh, Andrew shook his head. "Let's walk for a while. I might find a dark corner where I can kiss you properly."

Rising, he helped Morgan to her feet. She exchanged a formal and involved good-night with the proprietor before Andrew could navigate her away from the crowd.

Those not gathered in the *kafenion* were long since in bed. The white houses were closed and settled for the night. Now and then a dog barked, and another answered. Morgan could hear her own footsteps echo down the street.

"It's so quiet," she murmured. "All you can really hear is the water and the night itself. Ever since that first morning when I woke up on Lesbos, I've felt as if I belonged. Nothing that's happened since has spoiled that for me. Andrew." She whirled herself around in his arms and laughed. "I don't believe I'm *ever* going home again. How can I face New York and the traffic and the snow again? Rushing to work, rushing home. Maybe I'll become a fisherman, or give in to Liz and marry a goatherd."

"I don't think you should marry a goatherd," Andrew said practically, and drew her closer. Her scent was tangling his senses. Her face, in the moonlight, was an ageless mystery. "Why don't you give the fishing a try? We could set up housekeeping in Nick's cottage."

It would serve him right, her mind muttered. Lifting her mouth, Morgan waited for the kiss.

It was warm and complete. Morgan neither knew nor cared if the glow was a result of the kiss or the liquor. Andrew's lips weren't demanding, weren't urgent and possessive. They were comforting, requesting. She gave him what she could.

There was no rocketing passion—but she told herself she didn't want it. Passion clouded the mind more successfully than an ocean of ouzo. She'd had enough of hunger and passions. They brought pain with disillusionment. Andrew was kind, uncomplicated. He wouldn't turn away when she needed him. He wouldn't give her sleepless nights. He wouldn't make her doubt her own strict code of right and wrong. He was the knight—a woman was safe with a knight.

"Morgan," he murmured, then rested his cheek on her hair. "You're exquisite. Isn't there some man I should consider dueling with?"

Morgan tried to think of Jack, but could form no clear picture. There was, however, a sudden, atrociously sharp image of Nick as he dragged her close for one of his draining kisses.

"No," she said too emphatically. "There's no one. Absolutely no one."

Andrew drew her away and tilted her chin with his finger. He could see her eyes in the dim glow of moonlight. "From the strength of your denial, I'd say my competition's pretty formidable. No"—he laid a finger over her lips as she started to protest—"I don't want to have my suspicions confirmed tonight. I'm selfish." He kissed her again, lingering over it. "Damn it, Morgan, you could be habit forming. I'd better take you home while I remember I'm a gentleman and you're a very drunk lady."

The villa shimmered white under the night sky. A pale light glowed in a first-floor window for her return.

"Everyone's asleep," Morgan stated unnecessarily as

she let herself out of the car. Andrew rounded the hood. "I'll have to be very quiet." She muffled irrepressible giggles with a hand over her mouth. "Oh, I'm going to feel like an idiot tomorrow if I remember any of this."

"I don't think you'll remember too much," Andrew told her as he took her arm.

Morgan managed the stairs with the careful dignity of someone who no longer feels the ground under her feet. "It would never do to disgrace Alex by landing on my face in the foyer. He and Dorian are *so* dignified."

"And I," Andrew returned, "will have to resume my drive with the utmost caution. Nick wouldn't approve if I ran his Fiat off a cliff."

"Why, Andrew." Morgan stood back and studied him owlishly. "You're almost as sloshed as I am."

"Not quite, but close enough. However"—he let out a long breath and wished he could lie down—"I conducted myself with the utmost restraint."

"Very nicely done." She went off into a muffled peal of giggles again. "Oh, Andrew." She leaned against him so heavily that he had to shift his balance to support her. "I did have a good time—a wonderful time. I needed it more than I realized. Thank you."

"In you go." He opened the door and gave her a nudge inside. "Be careful on the stairs," he whispered. "Should I wait and listen for the sounds of an undignified tumble?"

"Just be on your way and don't take the Fiat for a swim." She stood on her toes and managed to brush his chin with her lips. "Maybe I should make you some coffee."

"You'd never find the kitchen. Don't worry, I can always park the car and walk if worse comes to worst. Go to bed, Morgan, you're weaving."

"That's you," she retorted before she closed the door.

Morgan took the stairs with painful caution. The last thing she wanted to do was wake someone up and have to carry on any sort of reasonable conversation. She stopped once and pressed her hands to her mouth to stop a fresh bout of giggles. Oh, it felt so good, so good not to be able to think. But this has to stop, she told herself firmly. No more of this, Morgan, straighten up and get upstairs before all is discovered.

She managed to pull herself to the top landing, then had to think carefully to remember in which direction her room lay. To the left, of course, she told herself with a shake of the head. But which way is left, for God's sake? She spent another moment working it out before she crept down the hall. She gripped the doorknob, then waited for the door to stop swaying before she pushed it open.

"Ah, success," she murmured, then nearly spoiled it by stumbling over the rug. Quietly, she shut the door and leaned back against it. Now, if she could just find the bed. A light switched on, as if by magic. She smiled absently at Nick.

"*Yiasou*, you seem to be a permanent fixture."

The fury in his eyes rolled off the fog as she stepped unsteadily out of her shoes.

"What the hell have you been up to?" he demanded. "It's nearly three o'clock in the morning!"

"Oh, how rude of me not to have phoned to tell you I'd be late."

"Don't get cute, damn it, I'm not in the mood." He stalked over to her and grabbed her arms. "I've been waiting for you half the night, Morgan, I…" His voice trailed off as he studied her. His expression altered from fury to consideration then reluctant amusement. "You're totally bombed."

"Completely," she agreed, and had to take a deep breath to keep from giggling again. "You're so observant, Nicholas."

Amusement faded as her hand crept up his shirt front. "How the hell am I supposed to have a rational conversation with a woman who's seeing two of everything?"

"Three," she told him with some pride. "Andrew's only up to two. I quite surpassed him." Her other hand slid up to toy with one of his buttons. "Did you know you have wonderful eyes. I've never seen eyes so dark. Andrew's are blue. He doesn't kiss anything like you do. Why don't you kiss me now?"

He tightened his grip for a moment, then carefully released her. "So, you've been out with young Andrew." He wandered the room while Morgan swayed and watched him.

"*Young* Andrew and I would have asked you to join us, but it just slipped our minds. Besides, you can be really boring when you're proper and charming." She had a great deal of trouble with the last word and yawned over it. "Do we have to talk much longer? My tongue's getting thick."

"I've had about enough of being proper and charming myself," he muttered, picking up a bottle of her scent and setting it down again. "It serves its purpose."

"You do it very well," she told him and struggled with her zipper. "In fact, you're nearly perfect at it."

"Nearly?" His attention caught, he turned in time

to see her win the battle with the zipper. "Morgan, for God's sake, don't do that now. I—"

"Yes, except you do slip up from time to time. A look in your eyes—the way you move. I suppose it's convincing all around if I'm the only one who's noticed. Then again, it might be because everyone else knows you and expects the inconsistency. Are you going to kiss me or not?" She dropped the dress to the floor and stepped out of it.

He felt his mouth go dry as she stood, clad only in a flimsy chemise, watching him mistily. Desire thudded inside him, hot, strong, and he forced himself back to what she was saying.

"Noticed what?"

Morgan made two attempts to pick up the dress. Each time she bent, the top of the chemise drifted out to show the swell of her breasts. Nick felt the thud lower to his stomach. "Noticed what?" she repeated as she left the dress where it was. "Oh, we're back to that. It's definitely the way you move."

"Move?" He struggled to keep his eyes on her face and away from her body. But her scent was already clouding his brain, and her smile—her smile challenged him to do something about it.

"It's like a panther," Morgan told him, "who knows he's being hunted and plans to turn the attack to his advantage when he's ready."

"I see." He frowned, not certain he liked her analogy. "I'll have to be more careful."

"Your problem," Morgan said cheerfully. "Well, since you don't want to kiss me, I'll say good-night, Nicholas. I'm going to bed. I'd see you down your vine, but I'm afraid I'd fall off the balcony."

"Morgan, I need to talk to you." He moved quickly and took her arm before she could sink onto the bed. That, he knew, would be too much pressure for any man. But she lost her already uncertain balance and tumbled into his arms. Warm and pliant, she leaned against him, making no objection as he molded her closer.

"Have you changed your mind?" she murmured, giving him a slow, sleepy-eyed smile. "I thought of you when Andrew kissed me tonight. It was very rude of me—or of you, I'm not sure which. Perhaps I'll think of Andrew if you kiss me now."

"The hell you will." He dragged her against him, teetering on the edge. Morgan let her head fall back.

"Try me," she invited.

"Morgan—the hell with all of it!"

Helplessly, he devoured her mouth. She was quickly and totally boneless, arousing him to desperation by simple surrender. Desire was a fire inside him, spreading dangerously.

For the first time, he let himself go. He could think of nothing, nothing but her and the way her body flowed in his hands. She was softer than anything he'd ever hoped to know. So soft, she threatened to seep into him, become a part of him before he could do anything to prevent it. The need was raging, overpowering, taking over the control he'd been master of for as long as he could remember. But now, he burned to forfeit it.

With her, everything could be different. With her, he'd be clean again. Could she turn back the clock?

He could feel the brush of the bedspread against his thigh and knew, in one movement, he could be on it with her. Then nothing would matter but that he had her—a woman. But it wasn't any woman he wanted. It had been her since the first night she had challenged him on that deserted beach. It had been her since the first time those light, clear eyes had dared him. He was afraid—and he feared little—that it would always be her.

Mixed with the desire came a quick twist of pain. With a soft oath, he pulled her away, keeping his grip firm on her arms.

"Pay attention, will you?" His voice was rough and unsteady, but she didn't seem to notice. She smiled up at him and touched his cheek with her palm.

"Wasn't I?"

He checked the urge to shake her and spoke calmly. "I need to talk to you."

"Talk?" She smiled again. "Do we have to talk?"

"There are things I need to tell you—this morning..." He fumbled with the words, no longer certain what he wanted to say, what he wanted to do. How could her scent be stronger than it had been a moment ago? He was drowning in it.

"Nicholas." Morgan sighed sleepily. "I drank an incredible amount of ouzo. If I don't sleep it off, I may very well die. I'm sure the body only tolerates a certain amount of abuse. I've stretched my luck tonight."

"Morgan." His breath was coming too quickly. His own pulse like thunder in his ears. He should let her go, he knew. He should simply let her go—for both their sakes. But his arms stayed around her. "Straighten up and listen to me," he demanded.

"I'm through listening." She gave a sleepy, sultry laugh. "Through listening. Make love with me or go."

Her eyes were only slits, but the clear, mystical blue pulled him in. No struggle, no force would drag him out again. "Damn you," he breathed as they fell onto the bed. "Damn you for a witch."

It was all hell smoke and thunder. He couldn't resist it. Her body was as fluid as wine—as sweet and as potent. Now he could touch her wherever he chose and she only sighed. As his mouth crushed possessively on hers, she yielded, but in yielding held him prisoner. Even knowing it, he was helpless. There'd be a payment—a price in pain—for succumbing to the temptation. He no longer cared for tomorrows. Now, this moment, he had her. It was enough.

He tore the filmy chemise from her, too anxious, too desperate, but she made no protest as the material ripped away. On a groan of need, he devoured her.

Tastes—she had such tastes. They lingered on his tongue, spun in his head. The crushed wild honey of her mouth, the rose-petal sweetness of her skin, drove him to search for more, and to find everything. He wasn't gentle—he was long past gentleness, but the quiet moans that came from her spoke of pleasure.

Words, low and harsh with desire, tumbled from him. He wasn't certain if he cursed her again or made her hundreds of mad promises. For the moment, it was all the same. Needs ripped through him—needs he understood, needs he'd felt before. But there was something else, something stronger, greedier. Then his flesh was against her flesh, and everything was lost. Fires and flames, a furnace of passion engulfed him, driving him beyond control, beyond reason. She was melting into him. He felt it as a tangible ache but had no will to resist.

Her hands were hot on his skin, her body molten. He could no longer be certain who led and who followed. Beneath his, her mouth was soft and willing, but he tasted her strength. Under him, her body was pliant, unresisting, but he felt her demand. Her skin would be white, barely touched by the sun. He burned to see it, but saw only the glimmer of her eyes in the darkness.

Then she pulled his mouth back to hers and he saw nothing, nothing but the blur of raging colors that were passion. The wild, sweet scent of jasmine seeped into him, arousing, never soothing, until he thought he'd never smell anything else.

With a last force of will, he struggled for sanity. He wouldn't lose himself in her—to her. He couldn't. Without self-preservation he was nothing, vulnerable. Dead.

Even as he took her in a near violent rage, he surrendered.

Chapter 8

The sunlight that poured through the windows, through the open balcony doors, throbbed and pulsed in Morgan's head. With a groan she rolled over, hoping oblivion would be quick and painless. The thudding only increased. Morgan shifted cautiously and tried for a sitting position. Warily she opened her eyes then groaned at the flash of white morning sun. She closed them again in self-preservation. Slowly, gritting her teeth for courage, she allowed her lids to open again.

The spinning and whirling which had been enjoyable the night before, now brought on moans and mutters. With queasy stomach and aching eyes, she sat in the center of the bed until she thought she had the strength to move. Trying to keep her head perfectly still, she eased herself onto the floor.

Carelessly, she stepped over her discarded dress and

found a robe in the closet. All she could think of were ice packs and coffee. Lots of coffee.

Then she remembered. Abruptly, blindingly. Morgan whirled from the closet to stare at the bed. It was empty—maybe she'd dreamed it. Imagined it. In useless defense she pressed her hands to her face. No dream. He had been there, and everything she remembered was real. And she remembered...the anger in his eyes, her own misty, taunting invitation. The way his mouth had pressed bruisingly to hers, her own unthinking, abandoned response.

The passion—it had been all she had thought it would be. Unbearable, wonderful, consuming. He'd cursed her. She could remember his words. Then he had taken her places she'd never even glimpsed before. She'd given him everything, then mindlessly challenged him to take more. She could still feel those taut, tensing muscles in his back, hear that ragged, desperate breathing at her ear.

He had taken her in fury, and it hadn't mattered to her. Then he had been silent. She had fallen asleep with her arms still around him. And now he was gone.

On a moan, Morgan dropped her hands to her sides. Of course he was gone. What else did she expect? The night had meant nothing to him—less than nothing. If she hadn't had so much to drink...

Oh, convenient excuse, Morgan thought on a wave of disgust. She still had too much pride to fall back on it. No, she wouldn't blame the ouzo. Walking to the bed, she picked up the torn remains of her chemise. She'd wanted him. God help her, she cared for him—too much. No, she wouldn't blame the ouzo. Balling the chemise in her fist, Morgan hurled it into the bottom of the closet. She had only herself to blame.

With a snap, Morgan closed the closet door. It was over, she told herself firmly. It was done. It didn't have to mean any more to her than it had to Nick. For a moment, she leaned her forehead against the smooth wooden panel and fought the urge to weep. No, she wouldn't cry over him. She'd never cry over him. Straightening, Morgan told herself it was the headache that was making her feel so weak and weepy. She was a grown woman, free to give herself, to take a man, when and where she chose. Once she'd gone down and had some coffee, she'd be able to put everything in perspective.

She swallowed the threatening tears and walked to the door.

"Good morning, *kyrios*." The tiny maid greeted Morgan with a smile she could have done without. "Would you like your breakfast in your room now?"

"No, just coffee." The scent of food didn't agree with her stomach or her disposition. "I'll go down for it."

"It's a beautiful day."

"Yes, beautiful." With her teeth clenched, Morgan moved down the hall.

The sound of crashing dishes and a high-pitched scream had Morgan gripping the wall for support. She pressed her hand to her head and moaned. Did the girl have to choose this morning to be clumsy!

But when the screaming continued, Morgan turned back. The girl knelt just inside the doorway. Scattered plates and cups lay shattered over the rug where the food had splattered.

"Stop it!" Leaning down, Morgan grabbed her shoulders and shook Zena out of self-defense. "No one's going to fire you for breaking a few dishes."

The girl shook her head as her eyes rolled. She

pointed a trembling finger toward the bed before she wrenched herself from Morgan's hold and fled.

Turning, Morgan felt the room dip and sway. A new nightmare crept in to join the old. With her hand gripping the doorknob, she stared.

A shaft of sunlight spread over Iona as she lay on her back, flung sideways across the bed. Her head hung over the edge, her hair streaming nearly to the floor. Morgan shook off the first shock and dizziness and raced forward. Though her fingers trembled, she pressed them to Iona's throat. She felt a flutter, faint, but she felt it. The breath she hadn't been aware she'd held came out in a rush of relief. Moving on instinct, she pulled Iona's unconscious form until she lay back on the bed.

It was then she saw the syringe lying on the tumbled sheets.

"Oh, my God."

It explained so much. Iona's moodiness, those tight, jerky nerves. She'd been a fool not to suspect drugs before. She's overdosed, Morgan thought in quick panic. What do I do? There must be something I'm supposed to do.

"Morgan—dear God!"

Turning her head only, Morgan looked at Dorian standing pale and stiff in the doorway. "She's not dead," Morgan said quickly. "I think she's overdosed—get a doctor—an ambulance."

"Not dead?"

She heard the flat tone of his voice, heard him start to come toward her. There was no time to pamper his feelings. "Do it quickly!" she ordered. "There's a pulse, but it's faint."

"What's Iona done now?" Alex demanded in a tone

of strained patience. "The maid's hysterical, and—oh, sweet Lord!"

"An ambulance!" Morgan demanded as she kept her fingers on Iona's pulse. Perhaps if she kept them there, it would continue to beat. "In the name of God, *hurry!*" She turned then in time to see Alex rush from the room as Dorian remained frozen. "There's a syringe," she began with studied calm. She didn't want to hurt him, but continued as his gaze shifted to her. His eyes were blank. "She must have o.d.'d. Did you know she used drugs, Dorian?"

"Heroin." And a shudder seemed to pass through him. "I thought it had stopped. Are you sure she's—"

"She's alive." Morgan gripped his hand as he came to the bed. A wave of pity washed over her—for Iona, for the man whose hand she held in her own. "She's alive, Dorian. We'll get help for her."

His hand tightened on hers for a moment so that Morgan had to choke back a protest. "Iona," he murmured. "So beautiful—so lost."

"She's not lost, not yet!" Morgan said fiercely. "If you know how to pray, pray that we found her in time."

His eyes came back to Morgan's, clear, expressionless. She thought as she looked at him she'd never seen anything so empty. "Pray," he said quietly. "Yes, there's nothing else to be done."

It seemed to take hours, but when Morgan watched the helicopter veer off to the west, the morning was still young. Iona, still unconscious, was being rushed to Athens. Dorian rode with her and the doctor while Alex and Liz began hurried preparations for their own flight.

Still barefoot and in her robe, Morgan watched the helicopter until it was out of sight. As long as she lived, she thought, she'd never forget that pale, stony look on Dorian's face—or the lifeless beauty on Iona's. With a shudder, she turned away and saw Alex just inside the doorway.

"Tripolos," he said quietly. "He's in the salon."

"Oh, not now, Alex." Overcome with pity, she held out both hands as she went to him. "How much more can you stand?"

"It's necessary." His voice was tight with control and he held her hands limply. "I apologize for putting you through all this, Morgan—"

"No." She interrupted him and squeezed his hands. "Don't treat me that way, Alex. I thought we were friends."

"*Diabolos*," he murmured. "Such friends you have. Forgive me."

"Only if you stop treating me as though I were a stranger."

On a sigh, he slipped his arm around her shoulders. "Come, we'll face the captain."

Morgan wondered if she would ever enter the salon without seeing Captain Tripolos seated in the wide, high-back chair. She sat on the sofa as before, faced him, and waited for the questions.

"This is difficult for you," Tripolos said at length. "For all of you." His gaze roamed over the occupants of the room, from Morgan to Alex to Liz. "We will be as discreet as is possible, Mr. Theoharis. I will do what I can to avoid the press, but an attempted suicide in a family as well known as yours…" He let the rest trail off.

"Suicide," Alex repeated softly. His eyes were blank, as if the words hadn't penetrated.

"It would seem, from the preliminary report, that your cousin took a self-induced overdose. Heroin. But

I hesitate to be more specific until the investigation is closed. Procedure, you understand."

"Procedure."

"You found Miss Theoharis, Miss James?"

Morgan gave a quick, nervous jolt at the sound of her name, then settled. "No, actually, the maid found her. I went in to see what was wrong. Zena had dropped the tray and was carrying on...when I went in I saw Iona."

"And you called for an ambulance?"

"No." She shook her head, annoyed. He knew Alex had called, but wanted to drag the story from her piece by piece. Resigned, Morgan decided to accommodate him. "I thought at first she was dead—then I felt a pulse. I got her back into bed."

"Back into bed?"

Tripolos's tone had sharpened, ever so faintly, but Morgan caught it. "Yes, she was half out of it, almost on the floor. I wanted to lay her down." She lifted her hands helplessly. "I honestly don't know what I wanted to do, it just seemed like the right thing."

"I see. Then you found this?" He held up the syringe, now in a clear plastic bag.

"Yes."

"Did you know your cousin was a user of heroin, Mr. Theoharis?"

Alex stiffened at the question. Morgan saw Liz reach out to take his hand. "I knew Iona had a problem—with drugs. Two years ago she went to a clinic for help. I thought she had found it. If I had believed she was still... ill," he managed. "I wouldn't have brought her into my home with my wife and my friend."

"Mrs. Theoharis, were you unaware of Miss Theoharis's problem?"

Morgan heard the breath hiss out between Alex's teeth, but Liz spoke quickly. "I was perfectly aware of it." Alex's head whipped around but she continued calmly. "That is, I was aware that my husband arranged for her to have treatment two years ago, though he tried to shield me." Without looking at him, Liz covered their joined hands with her free one.

"Would you, Mr. Theoharis, have any notion where your cousin received her supply?"

"None."

"I see. Well, since your cousin lives in Athens, perhaps it would be best if I worked with the police there, in order to contact her close friends."

"Do what you must," Alex said flatly. "I only ask that you spare my family as much as possible."

"Of course. I will leave you now. My apologies for the intrusion, yet again."

"I must phone my family," Alex said dully when the door closed behind Tripolos. As if seeking comfort, his hand went to his wife's hair. Then he rose and left without another word.

"Liz," Morgan began. "I know it's a useless phrase, but if there's anything I can do…"

Liz shook her head. She shifted her eyes from the doorway back to her friend's. "It's all so unbelievable. That she's lying there, so near death. What's worse, I never liked her. I made no secret of it, but now…" She rose and walked to the window. "She's Alex's family, and he feels that deeply. Now, in his heart, he's responsible for whatever happens to her. And all I can think of is how cold I was to her."

"Alex is going to need you." Morgan rose and walked

over to put a hand on her shoulder. "You can't help not liking her, Liz. Iona isn't an easy person to like."

"You're right, of course." With a deep breath Liz turned and managed a weak smile. "It's been a hell of a vacation so far, hasn't it? No, don't say anything." She squeezed Morgan's hand. "I'm going to see if Alex needs me. There'll be arrangements to be made."

The villa was silent as Morgan went up to change. As she buttoned her shirt, she stood by the terrace doors, staring out at the view of garden, sea, and mountain. How could it be that so much ugliness had intruded in such a short time? she wondered. Death and near death. This wasn't the place for it. But even Paradise named its price, she thought, and turned away.

The knock on her door was quiet. "Yes, come in."

"Morgan, am I disturbing you?"

"Oh, Alex." As she looked up, Morgan's heart welled with sympathy. The lines of strain and grief seemed etched into his face. "I know how horrible all this is for you, and I don't want to add to your problems. Perhaps I should go back to New York."

"Morgan." He hesitated for a moment. "I know it's a lot to ask, but I don't do it for myself. For Liz. Will you stay for Liz? Your company is all I can give her for a time." He released Morgan's hands and moved restlessly around the room. "We'll have to fly to Athens. I can't say how long—until Iona is well or—" He broke off as if he wasn't yet prepared for the word. "I'll have to stay with my family for a few days. My aunt will need me. If I could send Liz back knowing you'd be here with her, it would make it so much easier."

"Of course, Alex. You know I will."

He turned and gave her a phantom of a smile. "You're

a good friend, Morgan. We'll have to leave you for at least a day and a night. After that, I'll send Liz back. I can be sure she'll leave Athens if you're here." With a sigh, he took her hand absently. "Dorian might choose to stay in Athens as well. I believe he…has feelings for Iona I didn't realize before. I'll ask Nick to look after you while we're gone."

"No." She bit her tongue on the hurried protest. "No, really, Alex, I'll be fine. I'm hardly alone, with the servants in the house. When will you leave?"

"Within the hour."

"Alex, I'm sure it was an accident."

"I'll have to convince my aunt of that." He held out his hands, searching his own palms for a moment. "Though as to what I believe…" His look had hardened when he lifted his eyes again. "Iona courts disaster. She feeds on misery. I'll tell you now, because I won't ever be able to speak freely to anyone else. Not even Liz." His face was a grim mask now. Cold. "I detest her." He spit the words out as if they were poison. "Her death would be nothing but a blessing to everyone who loves her."

When Alex, Liz, and Dorian were gone, Morgan left the villa. She needed to walk—needed the air. This time she avoided her habit of heading for the beach. She was far from ready for that. Instead, she struck out for the cliffs, drawn to their jagged, daring beauty.

How clean the air was! Morgan wanted no floral scents now, just the crisp tang of the sea. She walked without destination. Up, only up, as if she could escape from everything if she could only get higher. If the gods had walked here, she thought, they would have come to the cliffs, to hear the water beat against rock, to breathe the thin, pure air.

She saw, to her pleasure, a scruffy, straggly goat with sharp black eyes. He stared at her a moment as he gnawed on a bit of wild grass he'd managed to find growing in between the rocks. But when she tried to get closer, he scrambled up, lightly, and disappeared over the other side of the cliff.

With a sigh, Morgan sat down on a rock perched high above the water. With some surprise, she saw tiny blue-headed flowers struggling toward the sun out of a crevice hardly wider than a thumbnail. She touched them, but couldn't bring herself to pluck any. Life's everywhere, she realized, if you only know where to look.

"Morgan."

Her hand closed over the blooms convulsively at the sound of his voice. She opened it slowly and turned her head. Nick was standing only a short distance away, his hair caught by the breeze that just stirred the air. In jeans and a T-shirt, his face unshaven, he looked more like the man she had first encountered. Undisciplined. Unprincipled. Her heart gave a quick, bounding leap before she controlled it.

Without a word, Morgan rose and started down the slope.

"Morgan." He caught her quickly, then turned her around with a gentleness she hadn't expected from him. Her eyes were cool, but beneath the frost, he saw they were troubled. "I heard about Iona."

"Yes, you once told me there was little that happened on the island you didn't know."

Her toneless voice slashed at him, but he kept his hands easy on her arms. "You found her."

She wouldn't let that uncharacteristic caring tone cut through her defenses. She could be—would be—as hard and cold as he had been. "You're well informed, Nicholas."

Her face was unyielding, and he didn't know how to begin. If she would come into his arms, he could show her. But the woman who faced him would lean on no one. "It must have been very difficult for you."

She lifted a brow, as though she were almost amused. "It was easier to find someone alive than to find someone dead."

He winced at that—a quick jerk of facial muscles, then dropped his hands. She'd asked him for comfort once, and now that he wanted to give it, needed to give it, it was too late. "Will you sit down?"

"No, it's not as peaceful here as it was."

"Stop slashing at me!" he exploded, grabbing her arms again.

"Let me go."

But the faint quaver in her voice told him something her words hadn't. She was closer to her own threshold than perhaps even she knew. "Very well, if you'll come back to the house with me."

"No."

"Yes." Keeping a hand on her arm, Nick started up the rough path. "We'll talk."

Morgan jerked her arm but his grip was firm. He propelled her up the rough path without looking at her. "What do you want, Nicholas? More details?"

His mouth thinned as he pulled her along beside him. "All right. You can tell me about Iona if you like."

"I don't like," she tossed back. They were already approaching the steps to his house. Morgan hadn't realized they were so close. What devil had prompted her to walk that way? "I don't want to go with you."

"Since when have I cared what you want?" he asked bitterly and propelled her through the front door. "Coffee," he demanded as Stephanos appeared in the hall.

"All right, I'll give you the details," Morgan raged as she whirled inside the door of the salon. "And then, by God, you'll leave me be! I found Iona unconscious, hardly alive. There was a syringe in bed with her. It seems she was an addict." She paused, unaware that her breath was starting to heave. "But you knew that, didn't you, Nicholas? You know all manner of things."

She'd lost all color, just as she had when she'd run across the beach and into his arms. He felt a twinge, an ache, and reached out for her.

"Don't touch me!" Nick's head jerked back as if she'd slapped him. Morgan pressed her hands against her mouth and turned away. "Don't touch me."

"I won't put my hands on you," Nick managed as they balled into fists. "Sit down, Morgan, before you keel over."

"Don't tell me what to do." Her voice quavered, and she detested it. Making herself turn back, she faced him again. "You have no right to tell me what to do."

Stephanos entered, silent, watchful. As he set the coffee tray down, he glanced over at Morgan. He saw, as Nick couldn't, her heart in her eyes. "You'll have coffee, miss," he said in a soft voice.

"No, I—"

"You should sit." Before Morgan could protest, Stephanos nudged her into a chair. "The coffee's strong."

Nick stood, raging at his impotence as Stephanos clucked around her like a mother hen.

"You'll have it black," he told her. "It puts color in your cheeks."

Morgan accepted the cup, then stared at it. "Thank you."

Stephanos gave Nick one long, enigmatic look, then left them.

"Well, drink it," Nick ordered, furious that the old man had been able to hack through her defenses when he felt useless. "It won't do you any good in the cup."

Because she needed to find strength somewhere, Morgan drank it down quickly. "What else do you want?"

"Damn it, Morgan, I didn't bring you here to grill you about Iona."

"No? You surprise me." Steadier, she set the cup aside and rose again. "Though why anything you do should surprise me, I don't know."

"There's nothing too vile you wouldn't attribute to me, is there?" Ignoring the coffee, Nick strode to the bar. "Perhaps you think I killed Stevos and left the body for you to find."

"No," she said calmly, because she could speak with perfect truth. "He was stabbed in the back."

"So?"

"You'd face a man when you killed him."

Nick turned away from the bar, the glass still empty in his hand. His eyes were black now, as black as she'd ever seen them. There was passion in them barely, just barely, suppressed. "Morgan, last night—"

"I won't discuss last night with you." Her voice was cold and final, cutting through him more accurately than any blade.

"All right, we'll forget it." This time he filled the glass. He'd known there would be a price to pay; somehow he hadn't thought it would be quite so high. "Would you like an apology?"

"For what?"

He gave a short laugh as his hand tightened on the glass. He tossed back the liquor. "God, woman, you've a streak of ice through you I hadn't seen."

"Don't talk to me of ice, Nicholas." Her voice rose with a passion she'd promised herself she wouldn't feel. "You sit here in your ancestral home, playing your dirty chess games with lives. I won't be one of your pawns. There's a woman barely alive in an Athens hospital. You make your money feeding her illness. Do you think you're remote from the blame because you cross the strait in the dead of night like some swashbuckling pirate?"

Very carefully, he set down the glass and turned. "I know what I am."

She stared at him until her eyes began to fill again. "So do I," she whispered. "God help me."

Turning, she fled. He didn't go after her.

Moments later, Stephanos came back into the room. "The lady's upset," he said mildly.

Nick turned his back to fill his glass again. "I know what the lady is."

"The past two days have been difficult for her." He clucked his tongue. "She came to you for comfort?"

Nick whirled but managed to bite back the words. Stephanos watched calmly. "No, she didn't come to me. She'd go to the devil himself before she came to me again." With an effort, he controlled the rage and his tone. "And it's for the best, I can't let her interfere now. As things stand, she'll be in the way."

Stephanos caressed his outrageous moustache and

whistled through his teeth. "Perhaps she'll go back to America."

"The sooner the better," Nick muttered and drained his glass. At the knock on the door, he swore. "See who the hell it is and get rid of them if you can."

"Captain Tripolos," Stephanos announced a few moments later. There was a gleam in his eye as he melted out of sight.

"Captain." Nick fought off the need to swear again. "You'll join me for coffee?"

"Thank you." Tripolos settled into a chair with a few wheezes and sighs. "Was that Miss James I just saw going down the cliff path?"

"Yes." With some effort, Nick prevented his knuckles from whitening against the handle of the pot. "She was just here."

Both men watched each other with what seemed casual interest. One was Morgan's panther—the other a crafty bear.

"Then she told you about Miss Theoharis."

"Yes." Nick offered the cream. "A nasty business, Captain. I intend to call Athens later this morning to see what news there is. Is Iona's condition why you're here?"

"Yes. It's kind of you to see me, Mr. Gregoras. I know you are a very busy man."

"It's my duty to cooperate with the police, Captain," Nick countered as he sat back with his coffee. "But I don't know how I can help you in this case."

"As you were with Miss Theoharis all of yesterday afternoon, I hoped you could shed some light on her frame of mind."

"Oh, I see." Nick sipped his coffee while his mind raced with possibilities. "Captain, I don't know if I can help you. Naturally, Iona was distressed that the man's murder was practically on her doorstep. She was edgy— but then, she often is. I can't say I saw anything different in her."

"Perhaps you could tell me what you did on your boat trip?" Tripolos suggested. "If Miss Theoharis said anything which seemed to indicate she was thinking of suicide?"

Nick lifted a brow. "We weren't overly engaged in conversation."

"Of course."

Nick wondered how long they could continue to fence. He decided to execute a few flourishes of his own. "I will say that Iona seemed a trifle nervous. That is, as I said, however, a habitual trait. You'll find that the people who know her will describe Iona as a...restive woman. I can say with complete honesty that it never entered my mind that she was contemplating suicide. Even now, to be candid, I find the idea impossible."

Tripolos settled back comfortably. "Why?"

Generalities, Nick concluded, would suffice. "Iona's too fond of herself to seek death. A beautiful woman, Captain, and one greedy for life's pleasures. It's merely an opinion, you understand. You know much more about this sort of thing." He shrugged. "My opinion is that it was an accident."

"An accident, Mr. Gregoras, is unlikely." He was fishing for a reaction, and Nick gave him another curious lift of brow. "There was too much heroin in her system for any but an amateur to take by mistake. And Miss Theoharis is no stranger to heroin. The marks of the needle tell a sad story."

"Yes, I see."

"Were you aware that Miss Theoharis was an addict?"

"I didn't know Iona very well, Captain. Socially, of course, but basically, she's a cousin of a friend—a beautiful woman who isn't always comfortable to be around."

"Yet you spent the day with her yesterday."

"A beautiful woman," Nick said again, and smiled. "I'm sorry I can't help you."

"Perhaps you'd be interested in a theory of mine."

Nick didn't trust those bland eyes but continued to smile. "Of course."

"You see, Mr. Gregoras," Tripolos went on. "If it was an accident, and if your instincts are correct, there is only one answer."

"One answer?" Nick repeated then allowed his expression to change slowly. "Do you mean you think someone attempted to...murder Iona?"

"I'm a simple policeman, Mr. Gregoras." Tripolos looked plumply humble. "It is my nature to look at such matters from a suspicious point of view. May I be frank?"

"By all means," Nick told him, admiring the captain's plodding shrewdness. Frank be damned, Nick mused, he's going to try to give me enough rope to hang myself.

"I am puzzled, and as a man who knows the Theoharis family well, I would like your opinion."

"Whatever I can do."

Tripolos nodded. "I will tell you first—and of course, you understand this cannot leave this room?"

Nick merely inclined his head and sipped his coffee.

"I will tell you Anthony Stevos was part of a smuggling ring operating on Lesbos."

"I must admit, the thought had crossed my mind."

Amused, Nick took out a box of cigarettes, offering one to Tripolos.

"It's no secret that a group has been using this island's nearness to Turkey to smuggle opium across the strait." Tripolos admired the thin wisp of elegant tobacco before he bent closer to Nick for a light.

"You think this Stevos was murdered by one of his cohorts?"

"That is my theory." Tripolos drew in the expensive smoke appreciatively. "It is the leader of this group that is my main concern. A brilliant man, I am forced to admit." Reluctant respect crossed his face. "He is very clever and has so far eluded any nets spread for his capture. It is rumored he rarely joins in the boat trips. When he does, he is masked."

"I've heard the rumors, naturally," Nick mused behind a mist of smoke. "I put a great deal of it down to village gossip and romance. A masked man, smuggling—the stuff of fiction."

"He is real, Mr. Gregoras, and there is nothing romantic about back-stabbing."

"No, you're quite right."

"Stevos was not a smart man. He was being watched in hopes he would lead us to the one we want. But…" As was his habit, Tripolos let the sentence trail off.

"I might ask, Captain, why you're telling me what must be police business."

"As an important man in our community," Tripolos said smoothly, "I feel I can take you into my confidence."

The old fox, Nick thought, and smiled. "I appreciate that. Do you think this masked smuggler is a local man?"

"I believe he is a man who knows the island." Tripolos gave a grim smile in return. "But I do not believe he is a fisherman."

"One of my olive pickers?" Nick suggested blandly, blowing out a stream of smoke. "No, I suppose not."

"I believe," Tripolos continued, "from the reports I have received on Miss Theoharis's activities in Athens, that she is aware of the identity of the man we seek."

Nick came to attention. "Iona?"

"I am of the opinion that Miss Theoharis is very involved in the smuggling operation. Too involved for her own safety. If...when," he amended, "she comes out of her coma, she'll be questioned."

"It's hard for me to believe that Alex's cousin would be a part of something like that." *He's getting entirely too close,* Nick realized, and swore silently at the lack of time. "Iona's a bit untamed," he went on, "but smuggling and murder. I can't believe it."

"I am very much afraid someone tried to murder Miss Theoharis because she knew too much. I will ask you, Mr. Gregoras, as one who is acquainted with her, how far would Miss Theoharis have gone for love—or for money?"

Nick paused as if considering carefully while his mind raced at readjustments to plans already formed. "For love, Captain, I think Iona would do little. But for money"—he looked up—"for money, Iona could justify anything."

"You are frank," Tripolos nodded. "I am grateful. Perhaps you would permit me to speak with you again on this matter. I must confess"—Tripolos's smile was sheepish, but his eyes remained direct—"it is a great help to discuss my problems with a man like yourself. It allows me to put things in order."

"Captain, I'm glad to give you any help I can, of course." Nick gave him an easy smile.

For some time after Tripolos left, Nick remained in his chair. He scowled at the Rodin sculpture across the room as he calculated his choices.

"We move tonight," he announced as Stephanos entered.

"It's too soon. Things are not yet safe."

"Tonight," Nick repeated and shifted his gaze. "Call Athens and let them know about the change in plan. See if they can't rig something up to keep this Tripolos off my back for a few hours." He laced his fingers together and frowned. "He's dangled his bait, and he's damn well expecting me to bite."

"It's too dangerous tonight," Stephanos insisted. "There's another shipment in a few days."

"In a few days, Tripolos will be that much closer. We can't afford to have things complicated with the local police now. And I have to be sure." Jet eyes narrowed, and his mouth became a grim line. "I haven't gone through all this to make a mistake at this point. I have to speed things up before Tripolos starts breathing down the wrong necks."

Chapter 9

The cove was blanketed in gloom. Rocks glistened, protecting it from winds—and from view. There was a scent—lush wet leaves, wild blossoms that flourished in the sun and hung heavy at night. But somehow it wasn't a pleasant fragrance. It smelt of secrets and half-named fears.

Lovers didn't hold trysts there. Legend said it was haunted. At times, when a man walked near enough on a dark, still night, the voices of spirits murmured behind the rocks. Most men took another route home and said nothing at all.

The moon shed a thin, hollow light over the face of the water, adding to rather than detracting from the sense of whispering stillness, of mystic darkness. The water itself sighed gently over the rocks and sand. It was a passive sound, barely stirring the air.

The men who gathered near the boat were like so many shadows—dark, faceless in the gloom. But they were men, flesh and blood and muscle. They didn't fear the spirits in the cove.

They spoke little, and only in undertones. A laugh might be heard from time to time, quick and harsh in a place of secrets, but for the most part they moved silently, competently. They knew what had to be done. The time was nearly right.

One saw the approach of a new shadow and grunted to his companion. Stealthily, he drew a knife from his belt, gripping its crude handle in a strong, work-worn hand. The blade glittered dangerously through the darkness. Work stopped; men waited.

As the shadow drew closer, he sheathed the knife and swallowed the salty taste of fear. He wouldn't have been afraid to murder, but he was afraid of this man.

The thick, sturdy fingers trembled as they released the knife. "We weren't expecting you."

"I do not like to always do the expected." The answer was in brisk Greek as a pale finger of moonlight fell over him. He wore black—all black, from lean black slacks to a sweater and leather jacket. Lean and tall, he might have been god or devil.

A hood concealed both his head and face. Only the gleam of dark eyes remained visible—and deadly.

"You join us tonight?"

"I am here," he returned. He wasn't a man who answered questions, and no more were asked. He stepped aboard as one used to the life and sway of boats.

It was a typical fishing vessel. Its lines were simple. The decks were clean but rough, the paint fresh and black. Only the expense and power of its motor separated it from its companions.

Without a word, he crossed the deck, ignoring the men who fell back to let him pass. They were hefty, muscled men with thick wrists and strong hands. They moved away from the lean man as if he could crush them to bone with one sweep of his narrow hand. Each prayed the slitted eyes would not seek him out.

He placed himself at the helm, then gazed casually over his shoulder. At the look, the lines were cast off. They would row until they were out to sea and the roar of the motor would go unnoticed.

The boat moved at an easy pace, a lone speck in a dark sea. The motor purred. There was little talk among the men. They were a silent group in any case, but when the man was with them, no one wanted to speak. To speak was to bring attention to yourself—not many dared to do so.

He stared out into the water and ignored the wary glances thrown his way. He was remote, a figure of the night. His hood rippled in the salt-sprayed wind— a carefree, almost adventurous movement. But he was still as a stone.

Time passed; the boat listed with the movement of the sea. He might have been a figurehead. Or a demon.

"We are short-handed." The man who had greeted him merged with his shadow. His voice was low and coarse. His stomach trembled. "Do you wish me to find a replacement for Stevos?"

The hooded head turned—a slow, deliberate motion. The man took an instinctive step in retreat and swallowed the copper taste that had risen to his throat.

"I will find my own replacement. You would all do

well to remember Stevos." He lifted his voice on the warning as his eyes swept the men on deck. "There is no one who cannot be…replaced." He used a faint emphasis on the final word, watching the dropping of eyes with satisfaction. He needed their fear, and he had it. He could smell it on them. Smiling beneath the hood, he turned back to the sea.

The journey continued, and no one else spoke to him—or about him. Now and then a sailor might cast his eyes toward the man at the helm. The more superstitious crossed themselves or made the ancient sign against evil. When the devil was with them, they knew the full power of fear. He ignored them, treated them as though he were alone on the boat. They thanked God for it.

Midway between Lesbos and Turkey, the motor was shut off. The sudden silence resounded like a thunderclap. No one spoke as they would have done if the figure hadn't been at the helm. There were no crude jokes or games of dice.

The boat shifted easily in its own wake. They waited, all but one swatting in the cool sea breeze. The moon winked behind a cloud, then was clear again.

The motor of an approaching boat was heard as a distant cough, but the sound grew steadier, closer. A light signaled twice, then once again before the glow was shut off. The second motor, too, gave way to silence as another fishing vessel drifted alongside the first. The two boats merged into one shadow.

The night was glorious—almost still and silvered by the moon. Men waited, watching that dark, silent figure at the helm.

"The catch is good tonight," a voice called out from

the second boat. The sound drifted, disembodied over the water.

"The fish are easily caught while sleeping."

There was a short laugh as two men leaned over the side and hauled a dripping net, pregnant with fish, onto the deck. The vessel swayed with the movement, then steadied.

The hooded man watched the exchange without word or gesture. His eyes shifted from the second vessel to the pile of fish lying scattered and lifeless on the deck. Both motors roared into life again and separated; one to the east, one to the west. The moon glimmered white. The breeze picked up. The boat was again a lone speck on a dark sea.

"Cut them open."

The men looked up sharply into the slitted eyes. "Now?" one of them dared to ask. "Don't you want them taken to the usual place?"

"Cut them open," he repeated. His voice sent a chill through the quiet night. "I take the cache with me."

Three men knelt beside the fish. Their knives worked swiftly and with skill while the scent of blood and sweat and fear prickled the air. A small pile of white packets grew as they were torn from the bellies of fish. The mutilated corpses were tossed back into the sea. No one would bring that catch to their table.

He moved quickly but without any sense of hurry, slipping packets into the pockets of his jacket. To a man they scrambled back from him, as if his touch might bring death—or worse. Satisfied, he gave them a brief survey before he resumed his position at the helm.

Their fear brought him a grim pleasure. And the cache was his for the taking. For the first time, he laughed—

a long, cold sound that had nothing to do with humor. No one spoke, in even a whisper, on the journey back.

Later, a shadow among shadows, he moved away from the cove. He was wary that the trip had gone so easily, exhilarated that it was done. There had been no one to question him, no one with the courage to follow, though he was one man and they were many. Still, as he crossed the strip of beach, he moved with caution, for he wasn't a fool. He had more than just a few frightened fishermen to consider. And he would have more to deal with before he was done.

The walk was long, and steep, but he took it at an easy pace. The hollow call of an owl caused him to pause only briefly to scan the trees and rocks through the slits in the mask. From his position, he could see the cool white lines of the Theoharis villa. He stood where he was a moment—watching, thinking. Then he spun away to continue his climb.

He moved over rocks as easily as a goat—walking with a sure, confident stride in the darkness. He'd covered that route a hundred times without a light. And he kept clear of the path—a path meant men. He stepped around the rock where Morgan had sat that morning, but he didn't see the flowers. Without pausing, he continued.

There was a light in the window. He'd left it burning himself before he had set out. Now for the first time he thought of comfort—and a drink to wash the taste of other men's fear from his throat.

Entering the house, he strode down the corridor and entered a room. Carelessly, he dumped the contents of his pockets on an elegant Louis XVI table, then removed his hood with a flourish.

"Well, Stephanos." Nick's teeth flashed in a grin. "The fishing was rich tonight."

Stephanos acknowledged the packets with a nod. "No trouble?"

"One has little trouble with men who fear the air you breathe. The trip was as smooth as a whore's kiss." Moving away, he poured two drinks and handed one to his companion. The sense of exhilaration was still on him—the power that comes from risking death and winning. He drained his drink in one swallow. "A seedy crew, Stephanos, but they do their job. They're greedy, and"—he lifted the hood, then let it fall on the cache of opium, black on white—"terrified."

"A terrified crew is a cooperative one," Stephanos commented. He poked a stubby finger at the cache of opium. "Rich fishing indeed. Enough to make a man comfortable for a long time."

"Enough to make him want more," Nick stated with a grin. "And more. *Diabolos,* the smell of fish clings to me." He wrinkled his nose in disgust. "Send our cache to Athens, and see they send a report to me of its purity. I'm going to wash off this stink and go to bed."

"There's a matter you might be interested in."

"Not tonight." Nick didn't bother to turn around. "Save your gossip for tomorrow."

"The woman, Nicholas." Stephanos saw him stiffen and pause. There was no need to tell him which woman. "I learned she doesn't go back to America. She stays here while Alex is in Athens."

"Diabolos!" Nick swore and turned back into the room. "I can't be worried about a woman."

"She stays alone until Alex sends his lady back."

"The woman is not my concern," he said between his teeth.

As was his habit, Stephanos sniffed the liquor to add to his appreciation. "Athens was interested," he said mildly. "Perhaps she could still be of use."

"No." Nick took an agitated turn around the room. Nerves that had been cold as ice began to thaw. Damn her, he thought, she'll make me careless even thinking of her. "That woman is more trouble than use. No," he repeated as Stephanos lifted his brows. "We'll keep her out of it."

"Difficult, considering—"

"We'll keep her out of it," Nick repeated in a tone that made Stephanos stroke his moustache.

"As you wish, *kyrios*."

"Go to the devil." Annoyed with the mock respectful tone, Nick picked up his glass, then set it down again. "She's no use to us," he said with more calm. "More of a stumbling block. We'll hope she keeps her elegant nose inside the villa for a few days."

"And if she pokes her elegant nose out?" Stephanos inquired, enjoying his liquor.

Nick's mouth was a grim line. "Then I'll deal with her."

"I think perhaps," he murmured as Nick strode from the room, "she has already dealt with you, old friend." He laughed and poured himself another drink. "Indeed, the lady's dealt you a killing blow."

After he had bathed, Nick couldn't settle. He told himself it was the excess energy from the night, and his success. But he found himself standing at his window, staring down at the Theoharis villa.

So she was alone, he thought, asleep in that big soft

bed. It meant nothing to him. He'd climbed that damn wall to her room for the last time. He'd gone there the night before on impulse, something he'd known better than to do. He'd gone to see her, with some mad idea of justifying his actions to her.

Fool, he called himself as his hands curled tight around the stone railing. Only a fool justifies what he does. He'd gone to her and she'd taunted him, driven him to give up something he had no business giving up. His heart. Damn her, she'd wrenched it out of him.

His grip tightened as he remembered what it had been like to have her—to taste her and fill himself with her. It had been a mistake, perhaps the most crucial one he'd ever made. It was one matter to risk your life, another to risk your soul.

He shouldn't have touched her, Nick thought on yet another wave of anger. He'd known it even as his hands had reached for her. She hadn't known what she was doing, drunk on the ouzo Andrew had bought her. Andrew—he felt a moment's rage and banked it. There'd been moments when he hated Andrew, knowing he'd kissed her. Hated Dorian because Morgan had smiled at him. And Alex because he could touch her in friendship.

And, he knew, Morgan would hate him for what had passed between them that night. Hadn't he heard it in the icy words she'd flung at him? He'd rather have handed her his own knife than to have the words of a woman slash at him that way. She would hate him for taking her when she was vulnerable—while that damn medal hung around her neck. And she would hate him for what he was.

On a rising wave of temper, Nick whirled away from the window. Why should it concern him? Morgan James would slip out of his life like a dream in only a few weeks in any case. He'd chosen his path before, long before he'd seen her. It was his way. If she hated him for what he was, then so be it. He wouldn't allow her to make him feel dirty and soiled.

If she'd touched his heart, he could deal with it. Sprawling into a chair, Nick scowled into the darkness. He would deal with it, he promised himself. After all he'd done, and all he'd faced, no blue-eyed witch would take him under.

Morgan felt completely alone. The solitude and silence she had so prized only a few days before now weighed down on her. The house was full of servants, but that brought her no comfort, no company. Alex and Liz and Dorian were gone. She wandered listlessly through the morning as she had wandered restlessly through the night. The house felt like a prison—clean and white and empty. Trapped inside it, she was too vulnerable to her own thoughts.

And because her thoughts centered too often on Nick, she found the idea of lying in the bed they had shared too painful. How could she sleep in peace in a place where she could still feel his hands on her, his lips ruthlessly pressing on hers? How could she sleep in a room that seemed to carry that faint sea-smell that so often drifted from him?

So she couldn't sleep, and her thoughts—and needs—haunted her. What could have happened to her to cause her to love such a man? And how long could she fight it? If she surrendered to it, she'd suffer for the rest of her life.

Knowing she was only adding to her own depression, Morgan changed into a bathing suit and headed for the beach.

It was ridiculous to be afraid of the beach, afraid of the house, she told herself. She was here to enjoy both for the next three weeks. Locking herself in her room wouldn't change anything that had happened.

The sand glistened, white and brilliant. Morgan found that on facing it again, the horror didn't materialize. Tossing aside her wrap, she ran into the sea. The water would ease the weariness, the tension. And maybe, just maybe, she would sleep tonight.

Why should she be keeping herself in a constant state of nerves over the death of a man she didn't even know? Why should she allow the harmless stub of a cigarette to haunt her? It was time to accept the simple explanations and keep her distance. The man had been killed as a result of a village brawl, and that was that. It had nothing to do with her, or anyone she knew. It was tragic, but it wasn't personal.

She wouldn't think about Iona, she told herself. She wouldn't think about smuggling or murders or—here she hesitated a moment and dived under a wave—Nicholas. For now, she wouldn't think at all.

Morgan escaped. In a world of water and sun, she thought only of pleasures. She drifted, letting the tension sink beneath the waves. She'd forgotten, in her own misery, just how clean and alive the water made her feel. For a few moments she would go back to that first day, to that feeling of peace she'd found without even trying.

Liz was going to need her in the next day or two. And Morgan wouldn't be any help at all if she were haggard and tense. Yes, tonight she'd sleep—she'd had enough of nightmares.

More relaxed than she had been in days, Morgan swam back toward shore. The sand shifted under her feet with the gentle current. Shells dotted the shoreline, clean and glistening. She stood and stretched as the water lapped around her knees. The sun felt glorious.

"So Helen rises from the sea."

Lifting her hand, Morgan shielded her eyes and saw Andrew. He sat on the beach by her towel, watching her.

"It's easy to understand how she set kingdoms at odds." He stood and moved to the water's verge to join her. "How are you, Morgan?"

"I'm fine." She accepted the towel he handed her and rubbed it briskly over her hair.

"Your eyes are shadowed. A blue sea surrounded by clouds." He traced her cheek with a fingertip. "Nick told me about Iona Theoharis." He took her hand and led her back to the white sand. Dropping the towel, Morgan sat beside him. "It's a bit soon for you to have to handle something like that, Morgan. I'm sorry you had to be the one to find her."

"It seems to be a talent of mine." She shook her head. "I'm much better today, really." Smiling, she touched his cheek. "Yesterday I felt…actually I don't think I felt much of anything yesterday. It was like I was watching everything through a fisheye lens. Everything was distorted and unreal. Today it's real, but I can cope with it."

"I suppose that's nature's way of cushioning the senses."

"I feel this incredible sorrow for Alex and Liz—and for Dorian." She leaned back on her elbows, wanting to feel the sun as it dried the water on her skin. "It's so hard on them, Andrew. It leaves me feeling helpless." She turned her face to his, pushing at her streaming hair. "I hope this doesn't sound hard, but I feel, after these past two days, I think I've just realized how glad I am to be alive."

"I'd say that's a very healthy, very normal reaction." He, too, leaned back on his elbows, narrowing his eyes against the sun as he studied her.

"Oh, I hope so. I've been feeling guilty about it."

"You can't be guilty about wanting to live, Morgan."

"No. Suddenly I realized how much I want to do. How much I want to see. Do you know, I'm twenty-six, and this is the first time I've been anywhere? My mother died when I was a baby and my father and I moved to New York from Philadelphia. I've never seen anything else." As drops of water trickled down her skin, she shook her damp hair back. "I can speak five languages, and this is the first time I've been in a country where English isn't needed. I want to go to Italy and France." She turned to face him more directly. Her eyes, though still shadowed, were huge with adventure. "I want to see Venice and ride in a gondola. I want to walk on the Cornish moors and on the Champs d'élysées." She laughed and it felt marvelous. "I want to climb mountains."

"And be a fisherman?" He smiled and laid a hand over hers.

"Oh, I did say that, didn't I?" She laughed again. "I'll do that, too. Jack always said my taste was rather eclectic."

"Jack?"

"He's a man I knew back home." Morgan found the ease with which she put him in the past satisfying. "He was in politics. I think he wanted to be king."

"Were you in love with him?"

"No, I was used to him." She rolled her eyes and grinned. "Isn't that a terrible thing to say?"

"I don't know—you tell me."

"No," she decided. "Because it's the truth. He was very cautious, very conventional, and, I'm sorry to say, very boring. Not at all like…" Her voice trailed off.

Andrew followed her gaze and spotted Nick at the top of the cliff. He stood, legs apart, hands thrust in his pockets, staring down at them. His expression was unreadable in the distance. He turned, without a wave or a sign of greeting, and disappeared behind the rocks.

Andrew shifted his gaze back to Morgan. Her expression was totally readable.

"You're in love with Nick."

Morgan brought herself back sharply. "Oh, no. No, of course not. I hardly know him. He's a very disagreeable man. He has a brutal temper, and he's arrogant and bossy and without any decent feelings. He shouts."

Andrew took in this impassioned description with a lifted brow. "We seem to be talking about two different people."

Morgan turned away, running sand through her fingers. "Maybe. I don't like either one of them."

Andrew let the silence hang a moment as he watched her busy fingers. "But you're in love with him."

"Andrew—"

"And you don't want to be," he finished, looking thoughtfully out to sea. "Morgan, I've been wondering, if I asked you to marry me, would it spoil our friendship?"

"What?" Astonished, she spun her head back around. "Are you joking?"

Calmly, he searched her face. "No, I'm not joking. I decided that asking you to bed would put a strain on our friendship. I wondered if marriage would. Though I didn't realize you were in love with Nick."

"Andrew," she began, uncertain how to react. "Is this a question or a proposal?"

"Let's take the question first."

Morgan took a deep breath. "An offer of marriage, especially from someone you care for, is always flattering to the ego. But egos are unstable and friendships don't require flattery." Leaning over, she brushed his mouth with hers. "I'm very glad you're my friend, Andrew."

"Somehow I thought that would be your reaction. I'm a romantic at heart." Shrugging, he gave her a rueful smile. "An island, a beautiful woman with a laugh like a night wind. I could see us setting up house in the cottage. Fires in the winter, flowers in the spring."

"You're not in love with me, Andrew."

"I could be." Taking her hand, he turned it palm up and studied it. "It isn't your destiny to fall in love with a struggling poet."

"Andrew—"

"And it isn't mine to have you." Smiling again, he kissed her hand. "Still, it's a warm thought."

"And a lovely one. Thank you for it."

He nodded before he rose. "I might decide Venice offers inspiration." Andrew studied the protruding section of the gray stone wall before turning back to her. "Maybe we'll see each other there." He smiled, the flashing boyish smile, and Morgan felt a twinge of regret. "Timing, Morgan, is such an essential factor in romance."

She watched him cross the sand and mount the steps before she turned back to the sea.

Chapter 10

The villa whispered and trembled like an old woman. Even after all her promises to herself that morning, Morgan couldn't sleep. She rolled and tossed in her bed, frantically bringing herself back from dreams each time she started to drift off. It was too easy for Nick to slip into her mind in a dream. Through sheer force of will, Morgan had blocked him out for most of the day. She wouldn't surrender to him now, for only a few hours sleep.

Yet awake and alone, she found herself remembering the inlet—the face under the water, the slim black stub of a cigarette. And Iona, pale and barely alive, with her thick mane of hair streaming nearly to the floor.

Why was it she couldn't rid herself of the thought that one had something to do with the other?

There was too much space, too much quiet in the

villa to be tolerated in solitude. Even the air seemed hot and oppressive. As fatigue began to take over, Morgan found herself caught between sleep and wakefulness, that vulnerable land where thoughts can drift and tease.

She could hear Alex's voice, cold and hard, telling her that Iona would be better off dead. There were Dorian's eyes, so calm, so cool, as he lifted a thin black cigarette to his lips. Andrew smiling grimly as he waited for his ship to come in. Liz vowing passionately that she would protect her husband from anyone and anything. And the knife blade, so sharp and deadly. She knew without seeing that Nick's hand gripped the handle.

On a half scream, Morgan sat up and willed herself awake. No, she wouldn't sleep, not alone. She didn't dare.

Before giving herself time to think, she rose and slipped on jeans and a shirt. The beach had given her peace that afternoon. Maybe it would do the same for her tonight.

Outside, she found the openness comforting. There were no walls here or empty rooms. There were stars and the scent of blossoms. She could hear the cypress leaves whisper. The feeling of dread slid from her with every step. She headed for the beach.

The moon was nearly full now, and white as bone. The breeze off the water was degrees cooler than the air had been in her room. She followed the path without hesitation, without fear. Some instinct told her nothing would harm her that night.

After rolling up her pants legs, she stood, letting the water lap over her ankles, warm and silky. Gratefully, she breathed in the moist sea air and felt it soothe her. She stretched her arms toward the stars.

"Will you never learn to stay in bed?"

Morgan spun around to find herself face-to-face with Nick. Had he already been there? she wondered. She hadn't heard him walk behind her. Straightening, she eyed him coolly. Like her, he wore jeans and no shoes. His shirt hung unbuttoned over his bare chest. What madness was it, she wondered, that made her long to go to him. Whatever madness drew her to him, she suppressed.

"That's not your concern." Morgan turned her back on him.

Nick barely prevented himself from yanking her back around. He'd been standing sleepless at his window when he'd seen her leave the house. Almost before he had known what he was doing, he was coming down the beach steps to find her. And it was ice, that same ice, she greeted him with.

"Have you forgotten what happens to women who wander night beaches alone?" The words rang with mockery as he tangled his fingers in her hair. He'd touch her if he chose, he thought furiously. No one would stop him.

"If you plan to drag me around this time, Nicholas, I warn you, I'll bite and scratch."

"That should make it interesting." His fingers tightened as she tossed her head to dislodge his grip. "I'd think you'd have had your fill of beaches today, Aphrodite. Or are you expecting Andrew again?"

She ignored the taunt and the peculiar thrill that came whenever he called her by that name. "I'm not expecting anyone. I came here to be alone. If you'd go away, I could enjoy myself."

Hurting, wanting, Nick spun her around. His fingers bruised her skin so that she made a surprised sound of pain before she could clamp it down. "Damn you, Morgan, don't push me any more. You'll find me a different breed from young Andrew."

"Take your hands off me." She managed to control her voice to a hard, cold steadiness. Her eyes glimmered with frost as they stared into his. She wouldn't cower before him again, and she wouldn't yield. "You'd do well to take lessons from Andrew"—deliberately, she tossed her head and smiled—"or Dorian on how to treat a woman."

Nick swore with quick Greek expertise. Unable to do otherwise, he gripped her tighter, but this time she made no sound. Morgan watched as the dark fury took total command of his face. He was half devil now, violent, with barely a trace of the man others knew. It gave her a perverse enjoyment to know she had driven him to it.

"So you offer yourself to Dorian as well?" He bit off the words as he fought to find some hold on his control. "How many men do you need?"

A flood of fury rose, but she stamped it down. "Isn't it strange, Nicholas," she said calmly, "how your Greek half seems to take over when you're angry? I simply can't see how you and Andrew can be related, however remotely."

"You enjoy leading him on, don't you?" The comparison stroked his fury higher. Morgan found she was gritting her teeth to prevent a whimper at the pain. She wouldn't give him the satisfaction. "Heartless bitch," he hissed at her. "How long do you intend to dangle and tease?"

"How dare you!" Morgan pushed against him. Anger, unreasonable and full, welled up in her for all the sleepless hours he'd given her, and all the pain. "How dare you criticize me for anything! You, with the filthy games you play, and the lies. You care about *no one*—no one but yourself. I detest you and everything you are!" Wrenching free, Morgan fled into the sea, blind and senseless with rage.

"Stupid woman!" Nick tore through two sentences of furious Greek before he caught her and pulled her around. The water lapped around her hips as he shook her. When her feet slipped on the bottom, he dragged her back up. He couldn't think now, couldn't reason. His voice whipped out with the violence of his thoughts. "I'll be damned if you'll make me crawl. Damned if I'll beg for your good feelings. I do what I have to do; it's a matter of necessity. Do you think I enjoy it?"

"I don't care about your necessities or your smuggling or your murders! I don't care about anything that has to do with you. I hate you!" She took a swing at his chest and nearly submerged again. "I hate everything about you. I hate myself for ever letting you touch me!"

The words cut at him, deeper than he wanted them to. He fought not to remember what it had felt like to hold her, to press his mouth against her and feel her melt against him. "That's fine. Just keep your distance and we'll get along perfectly."

"There's nothing I want more than to keep away from you." Her eyes glittered as the words brought her a slash of pain. "Nothing I want more than to never see your face again or hear your name."

He controlled himself with an effort—for there was nothing he wanted more at that moment than to crush her against him and beg, as he'd never begged anyone, for whatever she'd give him. "Then that's what you'll have, Aphrodite. Play your games with Dorian if you like, but tread carefully with Andrew. Tread carefully, or I'll break your beautiful neck."

"Don't you threaten me. I'll see Andrew just as often as I like." Morgan pushed at her dripping hair and glared at him. "I don't think he'd appreciate your protection. He asked me to marry him."

In one swift move, Nick lifted her off her feet and dragged her against his chest. Morgan kicked out, succeeding only in drenching both of them. "What did you tell him?"

"It's none of your business." She struggled, and though she was slick as an eel in the water, his hold remained firm. "Put me *down!* You can't treat me this way."

Fury was raging in him, uncontrollable, savage. No, he wouldn't stand by and watch her with another man. "Damn you, I said what did you tell him!"

"No!" she shouted, more in anger than in fear. "I told him *no.*"

Nick relaxed his grip. Morgan's feet met the sea bottom again as he formed a brittle smile. Her face was white as chalk and he cursed himself. God, would he do nothing but hurt her? Would she do nothing but hurt him? If there weren't so many walls in his way…if he could break down even one of them, he'd have her.

"That's fine." His voice was far from steady, but she had no way of knowing it was from panic rather than temper. "I won't stand by and watch you lead Andrew along. He's an innocent yet." He released her, knowing it might be the last time he'd ever touch her. "I don't suppose you chose to tell him about the lover you left behind."

"Lover?" Morgan pushed at her hair as she took a step back. "What lover?"

Nick lifted the medallion at her neck, then let it fall before he gave into the need to rip it from her. "The one who gave you the trinket you treasure so much. When a woman carries another man's brand, it's difficult to overlook it."

Morgan closed her hand over the small piece of silver. She had thought nothing could make her more angry than she already was. She was blind and trembling with it. "Another man's brand," she repeated in a whisper. "How typical of you. No one brands me, Nicholas. No one, no matter how I love."

"Your pardon, Aphrodite," he returned coolly. "An expression only."

"My father gave me this," she tossed at him. "He gave it to me when I was eight years old and broke my arm falling out of a tree. He's the kindest and most loving person I've ever known. You, Nicholas Gregoras, are a stupid man."

She turned and darted toward the beach, but he caught her again while the water was still around her ankles. Ignoring her curses and struggles, Nick turned her to face him. His eyes bored into hers. His breath was coming in gasps, but not from rage. He needed an answer, and quickly, before he exploded.

"You don't have a lover in America?"

"I said let me *go!*" She was glorious in fury—eyes glittering, skin white as the moonlight. With her head thrown back, she dared him to defy her. In that moment he thought he would have died for her.

"Do you have a lover in America?" Nick demanded again, but his voice was quiet now.

Morgan threw up her chin. "I haven't a lover *anywhere.*"

On an oath that sounded more like a prayer, Nick drew her close. The heat from his body fused through the soaked shirts as if they had been naked. Morgan's breath caught at the pressure and the sudden gleam of triumph in his eyes.

"You do now."

Capturing her mouth, he pulled her to the sand.

His lips were urgent, burning. His talk of branding raced through her head, but Morgan accepted the fire eagerly. And already he was stripping off her shirt as if he couldn't bear even the thin separation between them.

Morgan knew he would always love like this. Intensely, without thought, without reason. She gloried in it. Desire this strong took no denial. Her own fingers were busy with his shirt, ripping at the seam in her hurry to be flesh to flesh. She heard him laugh with his mouth pressed against her throat.

There was no longer any right or wrong. Needs were too great. And love. Even as passion drove her higher, Morgan knew and recognized her love. She had waited for it all of her life. With the heat building, there was no time to question how it could be Nick. She only knew it was, whatever, whoever, he was. Nothing else mattered.

When his hands found her naked breasts, he groaned and crushed his lips to hers again. She was so soft, so slender. He struggled not to bruise her, not again, but desire was wild and free in him. He'd never wanted a woman like this. Not like this. Even when he had taken her the first time, he hadn't felt this clean silver streak of power.

She was consuming him, pouring inside his mind. And the taste. Dear God, would he never get enough of the taste of her? He found her breast with his mouth and filled himself.

Morgan arched and dove her fingers into his hair. He was murmuring something, but his breathing was as ragged as hers and she couldn't understand. When his mouth was back on hers, there was no need to. She felt him tugging her jeans over her hips, but was too delirious to realize she had pulled at his first. She felt the skin stretched tight over his bones, the surprising narrowness of his body.

Then his lips and hands were racing over her—not in the angry desperation she remembered from the night before, but in unquestionable possession. There was no gentleness, but neither was there a fierceness. He took and took as though no one had a better right. Those strong lean fingers stroked down her, making her gasp out loud in pleasure, then moan in torment when they lay still.

His mouth was always busy, tongue lightly torturing, teeth taking her to the edge of control. There seemed to be no part of her, no inch he couldn't exploit for pleasure. And the speed never slacked.

Cool sand, cool water, and his hot, clever mouth—she was trapped between them. There was moonlight, rippling white, but she was a willing prisoner of the darkness. In the grove of cypresses a night bird called out—one long, haunting note. It might have been her own sigh. She tasted the sea on his skin, knew he would taste it on hers as well. Somehow, that small intimacy made her hold him tighter.

They might have been the only ones, washed ashore, destined to be lovers throughout their lives without the need for anyone else. The scent of the night wafted over her—his scent. They would always be the same to her.

Then she heard nothing, knew nothing, as he drove her beyond reason with his mouth alone.

She was grasping at him, demanding and pleading in the same breathless whispers for him to give her that final, delirious relief. But he held her off, pleasing himself, and pleasing her until she thought her body would simply implode at the pressure that was building.

With a wild, hungry kiss he silenced her while leading her closer to the edge. Though she could feel his heart racing against hers, he seemed determined to hold them there—an instant, an hour—hovering between heaven and hell.

When he drove them over, Morgan wasn't certain on which side they had fallen—only that they had fallen together.

Morgan lay quiet, cushioned against Nick's bare shoulder. The waves gently caressed her legs. In the aftermath of the demands of passion she was light and cool and stunned. She could feel the blood still pounding in his chest and knew no one, no one had ever wanted her like this. The sense of power it might have given her came as an ache. She closed her eyes on it.

She hadn't even struggled, she thought. Not even a token protest. She had given herself without thought—not in submission to his strength, but in submission to her own desires. Now, as the heat of passion ebbed, she felt the hard edge of shame.

He was a criminal—a hard, self-seeking man who trafficked in misery for profit. And she had given him her body and her heart. Perhaps she had no control over her heart, but Morgan was honest enough to know she ruled her own body. Shivering, she drew away from him.

"No, stay." Nick nuzzled in her hair as he held her against his side.

"I have to go in," she murmured. Morgan drew her body away as far as his arm would permit. "Please, let me go."

Nick shifted until his face hovered over hers. His lips were curved in amusement; his face was relaxed and satisfied. "No," he said simply. "You won't walk away from me again."

"Nicholas, please." Morgan turned her head aside. "It's late. I have to go."

He became still for a moment, then took her face firmly in his hand and turned it back to his. He saw the gleam of tears, tightly controlled, and swore. "It occurs to you suddenly that you've just given yourself to a criminal and enjoyed it."

"Don't!" Morgan shut her eyes. "Just let me go in. Whatever I've done, I've done because I wanted to."

Nick stared down at her. She was dry-eyed now, but her eyes were bleak. Swearing again, he reached for his partially dry shirt and pulled Morgan into a sitting position. Athens, he thought again, could fry in hell.

"Put this on," he ordered, swinging it over her shoulders. "We'll talk."

"I don't want to talk. There's no need to talk."

"I said we'll talk, Morgan." Nick pushed her arm into a sleeve. "I won't have you feeling guilty over what just happened." She could feel the simmering anger pulsing from him as he pulled his shirt over her breasts. "I won't have that," he muttered. "It's too much. I can't explain everything now…there are some things I won't ever explain."

"I'm not asking for explanations."

His eyes locked on hers. "You ask every time you look at me." Nick pulled a cigarette from the pocket of the shirt, then lit it. "My business in import-export has made me quite a number of contacts over the years. Some of whom, I imagine, you wouldn't approve of." He mused over this for a moment as he blew out a hazy stream of smoke.

"Nicholas, I don't—"

"Shut up, Morgan. When a man's decided to bare his soul, a woman shouldn't interrupt. God knows how dark you'll find it," he added, as he drew in smoke again. "When I was in my early, impressionable twenties, I met a man who considered me suitable for a certain type of work. I found the work itself fascinating. Danger can become addicting, like any other drug."

Yes, she thought as she stared out over the water. If nothing else, she could understand that.

"I began to—freelance." He smiled at the term, but it had little to do with humor. "For his organization. For the most part I enjoyed it. In any case, I was content with it. It's amazing that a way of life, ten years of my life should become a prison in a week's time."

Morgan had drawn her knees close to her chest while she stared out over the water. Nick laid a hand on her hair, but she still didn't look at him. He was finding it more difficult to tell her than he had imagined. Even after he'd finished, she might turn away from him. He'd be left with nothing—less than nothing. He drew hard on his cigarette, then stared at the red glow at the tip.

"Morgan, there are things I've done…" He swore

briefly under his breath. "There are things I've done I wouldn't tell you about even if I were free to. You wouldn't find them pleasant."

Now she lifted her face. "You've killed people."

He found it difficult to answer when she was looking at him with tired despair in her eyes. But his voice was cool with control. "When it was necessary."

Morgan lowered her head again. She hadn't wanted to think him a murderer. If he had denied it, she would have tried to have taken him at his word. She hadn't wanted to believe he was capable of what she considered the ultimate sin. The taking of a life.

Nick scowled at the cigarette and hurled it into the sea. I could have lied to her, he thought furiously. Why the hell didn't I just lie—I'm an expert at it. Because I can't lie to her, he realized with a tired sigh. Not anymore. "I did what I had to do, Morgan," he said flatly. "I can't erase the way I've lived for ten years. Right or wrong, it was my choice. I can't apologize for it."

"No, I'm not asking you to. I'm sorry if it seems that way." She drew herself up again and faced him. "Please, Nicholas, let's leave it at this. Your life's your own. You don't have to justify it to me."

"Morgan—" If she had hurled abuse at him, stabbed him with ice, he might have been able to keep silent. But he couldn't be silent while she struggled to understand. He would tell her, and the decision he'd been struggling with for days would be made. "For the last six months, I've been working on breaking the smuggling ring that runs between Turkey and Lesbos."

Morgan stared at him as though she'd never seen him before. "Breaking it? But I thought…you told me—"

"I've never told you much of anything," he said curtly.

"I let you assume. It was better that way. It was necessary."

For a moment she sat quietly, trying to sort out her thoughts. "Nicholas, I don't understand. Are you telling me you're a policeman?"

He laughed at the thought, and part of his anger drained. "No, Aphrodite, spare me that."

Morgan frowned. "A spy then?"

The rest of his anger vanished. He cupped her face in his hands. She was so unbearably sweet. "You will romanticize it, Morgan, I'm a man who travels and follows orders. Be content with that, it's all I can give you."

"That first night on the beach…" At last the puzzle pieces were taking a shape she could understand. "You were watching for the man who runs the smuggling ring. That was who Stephanos followed."

Nick frowned and dropped his hands. She believed him without question or hesitation. Already she'd forgotten that he'd killed—and worse. Why, when she was making it so easy for him did he find it so hard to go on? "I had to get you out of the way. I knew he'd cross that section of beach on his way to Stevos's cottage. Stevos was eliminated because he knew, as I don't yet, the man's exact position in the organization. I think he asked for a raise and got a knife in the back."

"Who is he, Nicholas?"

"No." His eyes came back to hers. His face was hard again, unreachable. "Even if I were sure, I wouldn't tell you. Don't ask me questions I can't answer, Morgan. The more I tell you, the more dangerous your position becomes." His eyes grew darker. "I was ready to use you once, and my organization is very interested in your talent with languages, but I'm a selfish man. You're not going to be involved." His tone was final and just a little furious. "I told my associate you weren't interested."

"That's a bit presumptuous," Morgan began. She frowned until he twisted his head and looked at her again. "I'm capable of making my own decisions."

"You haven't one to make," Nick countered coolly. "And once I know for certain the identity of the head of the ring, my job's finished. Athens will have to learn how to function without me."

"You're not going to do this…" She gestured vaguely, not knowing what title to give his work. "This sort of thing anymore?"

"No." Nick stared back out to sea. "I've been in it long enough."

"When did you decide to stop?"

When I first made love with you, he thought, and nearly said it. But it wasn't quite true. There was one more thing he would have to tell her. "The day I took Iona on the boat." Nick let out an angry breath and turned to her. He had his doubts that she would forgive him for what he was going to say. "Iona's in this, Morgan, deeply."

"In the smuggling? But—"

"I can only tell you that she is, and that part of my job was to get information out of her. I took her out on the boat, fully intending to make love to her to help loosen her tongue." Morgan kept her eyes steady and he continued, growing angrier. "She was cracking under pressure. I was there to help her along. That's why someone tried to kill her."

"Kill her?" Morgan tried to keep her voice level as she dealt with what he was telling her. "But Captain Tripolos said it was attempted suicide."

"Iona would no more have committed suicide than she would have tended goats."

"No," she said slowly. "No, of course you're right."

"If I could have worked on her a little longer, I would have had all that I needed."

"Poor Alex," she murmured. "He'll be crushed if it comes out that she was mixed up in this. And Dorian…" She remembered his empty eyes and his words. *Poor Iona—so beautiful—so lost.* Perhaps he already suspected. "Isn't there something you can do?" She looked up at Nick, this time with trust. "Do the police know? Captain Tripolos?"

"Tripolos knows a great deal and suspects more." Nick took her hand now. He wanted the link badly. "I don't work directly with the police, it slows things down. At the moment," he added cheerfully, "Tripolos has me pegged as the prime suspect in a murder, an attempted murder, and sees me in the role of the masked smuggler. Lord, I'd have given him a thrill last night."

"You enjoy your work, don't you?" Morgan studied him, recognizing the light of adventure in his eyes. "Why are you stopping?"

His smile faded. "I told you I was with Iona. It wasn't the first time I used that method. Sex can be a weapon or a tool, it's a fact of life." Morgan dropped her gaze to the sand. "She'd had too much champagne to be cooperative, but there would have been another time. Since that day, I haven't felt clean." He slid his hand under her chin and lifted it. "Not until tonight."

She was studying him closely, searching. In his eyes she saw something she had only seen once before—regret, and a plea for understanding. Lifting her arms, she brought his mouth down to hers. She felt more than his lips—the heady wave of his relief.

"Morgan." He pressed her back to the sand again. "If I could turn back the clock and have this past week to live over…" He hesitated, then buried his face in her hair. "I probably wouldn't do anything differently."

"You apologize beautifully, Nicholas."

He couldn't keep his hands off her. They were roaming again, arousing them both. "This thing should come to a head tomorrow night, then I'll be at loose ends. Come away somewhere with me for a few days. Anywhere."

"Tomorrow?" She struggled to keep her mind on his words while her body heated. "Why tomorrow?"

"A little complication I caused last night. Come, we're covered with sand. Let's take a swim."

"Complication?" Morgan repeated as he hauled her to her feet. "What kind of complication?"

"I don't think our man will tolerate the loss of a shipment," he murmured as he slipped his shirt from her shoulders.

"You stole it!"

He was pulling her into the water. His blood was already pounding for her as he saw the moonlight glow white over her body. "With incredible ease." When she was past her waist, he drew her against him. The water lapped around them as he began to explore her again. "Stephanos and I watched the connection from a safe distance on several runs." His mouth brushed over hers, then traced down to her throat. "We'd just come back from one the night I found you on the beach. Now, about those few days."

"What will you do tomorrow night?" Morgan drew

back enough to stop his roaming hands and mouth. A hint of fear had worked its way in. "Nicholas, what's going to happen?"

"I'm waiting for some conclusive information from Athens. When it comes, I'll know better how to move. At any rate, I'll be there when the boat docks with its cache tomorrow night."

"Not alone?" She gripped his shoulders. "He's already killed a man."

Nick rubbed his nose against hers. "Do you worry for me, Aphrodite?"

"Don't joke!"

He heard the very real panic in her voice and spoke soothingly. "By late tomorrow afternoon, Tripolos will be brought up to date. If everything goes as planned, I can brief him personally." He smiled down at the frown on her face. "He'll gain all official credit for whatever arrests are made."

"But that's unfair!" Morgan exclaimed. "After all your work, and the time, why shouldn't you—"

"Shut up, Morgan, I can't make love to a woman who's constantly complaining."

"Nicholas, I'm trying to understand."

"Understand this." Impatience shimmered in his voice as he pulled her close again. "I've wanted you from the minute I saw you sitting on that damn rock, and I haven't begun to have enough. You've driven me mad for days. Not anymore, Aphrodite. Not anymore."

He lowered his mouth, and all else was lost.

Chapter 11

Her jeans were still damp as Morgan struggled into them laughing. "You would make me so furious I'd run into the water fully dressed."

Nick fastened the snap on his own. "The feeling was mutual."

Turning her head, she looked at him as he stood, naked to the waist, shaking what sand he could from his shirt. A gleam of mischief lit her eyes. "Oh?" Taking a step closer, Morgan ran her palms up his chest—taking her time—enjoying the hard, firm feel of it before she linked them around his neck. "Did it make you furious thinking I was wearing a token from a lover waiting for me back home?"

"No," he lied with a careless smile. Gripping his shirt in both hands, Nick hooked it around her waist to draw her closer. "Why should that concern me?"

"Oh." Morgan nipped lightly at his bottom lip. "Then perhaps you'd like to hear about Jack."

"I damn well wouldn't," he muttered before his mouth crushed down on hers. Even as her lips answered his, Nick heard the low sound of her muffled laughter. "Witch." Then he took her deeper, deeper, until her laughter was only a sigh. "Maybe you prefer me when I'm angry."

"I prefer you," she said simply, and rested her head on his shoulder.

His arms tightened, strong, possessive. Yet somehow he knew strength alone would never keep her. "Dangerous woman," Nick murmured. "I knew it the first time I held you."

With a laugh, Morgan tossed back her head. "The first time you held me, you cursed me."

"And I continue to do so." But his lips sought hers again without an oath.

"I wish there was only tonight." Suddenly, she was clinging to him with her heart racing. "No tomorrows, only now. I don't want the sun to come up."

Nick buried his face in her hair as the guilt swamped him. He'd brought her fear from the first instant. Even loving her, he could bring her nothing else. He had no right to tell her now that his heart was hers for the asking. Once he told her, she might beg him to abandon his responsibility, leave his job half finished. And he would do just as she asked, he realized...and never feel like a man again.

"Don't wish your days away, Morgan," he told her lightly. "The sun comes up tomorrow, then goes down. And when it comes up again, we'll have nothing but time."

She had to trust him, had to believe that he would

be safe—that the danger he lived with would be over in little more than twenty-four hours.

"Come back with me now." Lifting her head again, Morgan gave him a smile. Her worry and fears wouldn't help him. "Come back to the villa and make love with me again."

"You tempt me, Aphrodite." Bending, he kissed both her cheeks in a gesture she found unbearably gentle and sweet. "But you're asleep on your feet. There'll be other nights. I'll take you back."

She allowed him to turn her toward the beach steps. "You might not find it as easy to leave me there alone as you think," she commented with another smile.

With a quiet laugh, he drew her closer to his side. "Not easy perhaps, but—" His head whipped up abruptly, as if he were scenting the air. Narrowed and cold, his eyes swept the darkness of the cliffs above them.

"Nicholas, what—"

But his hand clamped over her mouth as he pulled her, once again, into the shadows of the cypress. Her heart leaped to her throat as it had before, but this time Morgan didn't struggle.

"Be still and don't speak," Nick whispered. Removing his hand, he pushed her back against the trunk of a tree. "Not a sound, Morgan."

She nodded, but he wasn't looking at her. His eyes were trained on the cliffs. Standing at the edge of the covering, Nick watched and waited. Then he heard it again—the quiet scrape of boot on rock. Tensing, he strained his eyes and at last saw the shadow. So, he thought with a grim smile as he watched the black form move swiftly over the rocks, he's come for his cache. But you won't find it, Nick told the shadow silently. And I'll be like a hound on your tail.

Soundlessly, he moved back to Morgan. "Go back to the villa and stay there." All warmth had dropped away from him. His voice was as cold as his eyes.

"What did you see?" she demanded. "What are you going to do?"

"Do as I say." Taking her arm, he pulled her toward the beach steps. "Go quickly, I haven't got time to waste. I'll lose him."

Him. Morgan felt a flutter of fear. She swallowed it. "I'm going with you."

"Don't be a fool." Impatient, Nick dragged her along. "Go back to the villa, I'll speak to you in the morning."

"No." Morgan pulled out of his hold. "I said I'm going with you. You can't stop me."

She was standing straight as an arrow, eyes blazing with a combination of fear and determination. Nick swore at her, knowing every second he stayed meant his man was farther away. "I don't have time—"

"Then you'd better stop wasting it," Morgan said calmly. "I'm coming."

"Then come," he said under his breath as he turned away from her. She won't last five minutes on the cliffs without shoes, he thought. She'd limp her way back to the villa in ten. He moved quickly up the beach steps without waiting for her. Gritting her teeth, Morgan raced after him.

As he left the steps to start his scramble up the cliff, Nick paid little attention to her. He cast his eyes to the sky and wished the night were not so clear. A cloud over the moon would allow him to risk getting closer to the man he followed. He gripped a rock and hauled himself up farther—a few pebbles loosened and skidded down. When he glanced back, he was surprised to see Morgan keeping pace with him.

Damn the woman, he thought with a twinge of reluctant admiration. Without a word, he held out his hand and pulled her up beside him. "Idiot," he hissed, wanting to shake her and kiss her all at once. "Will you go back? You don't have any shoes."

"Neither do you," Morgan gritted.

"Stubborn fool."

"Yes."

Cursing silently, Nick continued the climb. He couldn't risk the open path in the moonlight, so kept to the rocks. Though it wouldn't be possible to keep his quarry in sight, Nick knew where he was going.

Morgan clamped her teeth shut as the ball of her foot scraped against a rock. With a quick hiss of breath, she kept going. She wasn't going to whimper and be snapped at. She wasn't going to let him go without her.

On a rough ledge, Nick paused briefly to consider his options. Circling around would take time. If he'd been alone—and armed, he would have taken his chances with the narrow path now. Odds were that the man he followed was far enough ahead and confident enough to continue his journey without looking over his shoulder. But he wasn't alone, he thought on a flare of annoyance. And he had no more than his hands to protect Morgan if they were spotted.

"Listen to me," he whispered, hoping to frighten her as he grabbed her by the shoulders. "The man's killed— and killed more than once, I promise you. When he finds his cache isn't where it should be, he'll know he's being hunted. Go back to the villa."

"Do you want me to call the police?" Morgan asked calmly, though he'd succeeded very well in frightening her.

"No!" The word whipped out, no louder than a breath. "I can't afford to give up the chance to see who he is." Frustrated, he glared at her. "Morgan, I don't have a weapon, if he—"

"I'm not leaving you, Nicholas. You're wasting time arguing about it."

He swore again, then slowly controlled his temper. "All right, damn you. But you'll do exactly as I say or I promise you, I'll knock you unconscious and shove you behind a rock."

She didn't doubt it. Morgan lifted her chin. "Let's go."

Agilely, Nick pulled himself over the ridge and onto the path. Before he could reach back to assist her, Morgan was kneeling on the hard ground beside him. He thought, as he looked into her eyes, that she was a woman men dreamed of. Strong, beautiful, loyal. Taking her hand, he dashed up the path, anxious to make up the time he'd wasted arguing with her. When he felt they'd been in the open long enough, he left the path for the rocks again.

"You know where he's going," Morgan whispered, breathing quickly. "Where?"

"A small cave near Stevos's cottage. He thinks to pick up last night's cache." He grinned suddenly. Morgan heard it in his voice. "He won't find it, and then, by God, he'll sweat. Keep low now—no more talk."

She could see the beauty of the night clearly in the moonlight. The sky was velvet, pierced with stars, flooded by the moon. Even the thin, scruffy bushes working their way through rock held an ethereal allure.

The sound of the sea rose from below them, soft with distance. An owl sent up a quiet hooting music of lazy contentment. Morgan thought, if she could look, she might find more blue-headed flowers. Then Nick was pulling her over the next ridge and pressing her to the ground.

"It's just up ahead. Stay here."

"No, I—"

"Don't argue," he said roughly. "I can move faster without you. Don't move and don't make a sound."

Before she could speak, he was scrambling away, silently, half on his belly, half on his knees. Morgan watched him until he was concealed by another huddle of rocks. Then, for the first time since they had begun, she started to pray.

Nick couldn't move quickly now. If he had misjudged the timing, he'd find himself face-to-face with his quarry. He needed to save that pleasure for the following night. But to know—to know who he had been hounding for six months was a bonus Nick couldn't resist.

There were more rocks and a few trees for cover, and he used them as he skirted the dead man's rough cottage. An attempt had been made to clear the ground for a vegetable garden, but the soil had never been worked. Nick wondered idly what had become of the woman who had sometimes shared Stevos's bed and washed his shirts. Then he heard the quiet scrape of boot on rock again. Less than a hundred yards away, Nick estimated. Eyes gleaming in the darkness, he crept toward the mouth of the cave.

He could hear the movements inside, quiet, confident. Slipping behind a rock, he waited, patient, listening. The furious oath that echoed inside the cave brought Nick a rich thrill of pleasure.

Taste the betrayal, he told the man inside. And choke on it.

The movements inside the cave became louder. Nick's smile spread. He'd be searching now, Nick concluded. Looking for signs to tell him if his hiding place had been looted. But no, you haven't been robbed, Nick thought. Your little white bags were lifted from right under your nose.

He saw him then, striding out of the cave—all in black, still masked. Take it off, Nick ordered him silently. Take it off and let me see your face.

The figure stood in the shadows of the mouth of the cave. Fury flowed from him in waves. His head turned from side to side as if he were searching for something... or someone.

They heard the sound at the same instant. The shifting of pebbles underfoot, the rustling of bushes. Dear God, Morgan! Nick thought and half rose from his concealment. As he tensed, he saw the black-clad figure draw a gun and melt back into the shadows.

With his heart beating in his throat, Nick gripped the rock and prepared to lunge. He could catch the man off-guard, he thought rapidly, gain enough time to shout a warning to Morgan so that she could get away. Fear licked at him—not for himself, but at the thought that she might not run fast enough.

The bush directly across the path trembled with movement. Nick sucked in his breath to lunge.

Bony, and with more greed than wit, a dusty goat stepped forward to find a more succulent branch.

Nick sunk down behind the rock, furious that he was

trembling. Though she had done nothing more than what he had told her, he cursed Morgan fiercely.

With a furious oath, the man in black stuck the gun back in his belt as he strode down the path. As he passed Nick, he whipped off his mask.

Nick saw the face, the eyes, and knew.

Morgan huddled behind the rock where Nick had shoved her, her arms wrapped around her knees. It seemed she'd already waited an eternity. She strained to hear every sound—the whisper of the wind, the sigh of leaves. Her heart hadn't stopped its painful thudding since he'd left her.

Never again, Morgan promised herself. Never again would she sit and wait. Never again would she sit helpless and trembling, on the verge of hot, useless tears. If anything happened—she clamped down on the incomplete thought. Nothing was going to happen to Nick. He'd be back any moment. But the moments dragged on.

When he dropped down beside her, she had to stifle a scream. Morgan had thought her ears were tuned to hear even the dust blow on the wind, but she hadn't heard his approach. She didn't even say his name, just went into his arms.

"He's gone," Nick told her.

The memory of that one shuddering moment of terror washed over him. He crushed his mouth to hers as though he were starving. All of her fears whipped out, one by one, until there was nothing in her but a well of love.

"Oh, Nicholas, I was so frightened for you. What happened?"

"He wasn't pleased." With a grin that was both ruthless and daring, he pulled her to her feet. "No, he wasn't pleased. He'll be on the boat tomorrow."

"But did you see who—"

"No questions." He silenced her again with his mouth, roughly, as though the adventure were only beginning. "I don't want to have to lie to you again." With a laugh, Nick drew her toward the path and the moonlight. "Now, my stubborn, courageous witch, I'll take you back. Tomorrow when your feet are too sore to stand, you'll curse me."

He wouldn't tell her any more, Morgan thought. And for now, perhaps it was best. "Share my bed tonight." She smiled as she hooked her arm around his waist. "Stay another hour with me, and I won't curse you."

Laughing, he ran a hand down her hair. "What man could resist such an ultimatum?"

Morgan awoke as a soft knock sounded at her door. The small maid peeked inside.

"Your pardon, *kyrios,* a phone call from Athens."

"Oh…thank you, Zena, I'll be right there." Rising quickly, Morgan hurried to the phone in Liz's sitting room, belting her robe as she went. "Hello?"

"Morgan, did I wake you? It's past ten."

"Liz?" Morgan tried to shake away the cobwebs. It had been dawn before she had slept.

"Do you know anyone else in Athens?"

"I'm a bit groggy." Morgan yawned, then smiled with memories. "I went for a late-night swim. It was wonderful."

"You sound very smug," Liz mused. "We'll have to discuss it later. Morgan, I feel terrible about it, but I'm going to have to stay here until tomorrow. The doctors are hopeful, but Iona's still in a coma. I can't leave Alex to cope with his family and everything else alone."

"Please, don't worry about me. I'm sorry, Liz. I know it's difficult for both of you." She thought of Iona's involvement in the smuggling and felt a fresh wave of pity. "How is Alex holding up? He seemed so devastated when he left here."

"It would be easier if the whole family didn't look to him for answers. Oh, Morgan, it's so ugly." Strain tightened her voice and Morgan heard her take a deep breath to control it. "I don't know how Iona's mother will handle it if she dies. And suicide—it just makes it harder."

Morgan swallowed the words she wanted to say. Nick had spoken to her in confidence; she couldn't betray it even for Liz. "You said the doctors are hopeful."

"Yes, her vital signs are leveling, but—"

"What about Dorian, Liz? Is he all right?"

"Barely." Morgan heard Liz sigh again. "I don't know how I could have been so blind not to see how he felt about her. He's hardly left her bedside. If Alex hadn't bullied him, I think he might have slept in the chair beside her last night instead of going home. From the way he looks this morning, I don't think he got any sleep anyway."

"Please give him my best—and Alex, too." On a long frustrated breath she sat down. "Liz, I feel so helpless." She thought of smuggling, attempted murder and shut her eyes. "I wish there were something I could do for you."

"Just be there when I get back." Though her tone lightened, Morgan recognized the effort. "Enjoy the beach for me, look for your goatherd. If you're going to take moonlight swims, you should have some company for them." When Morgan was silent Liz continued slowly. "Or did you?"

"Well, actually…" Smiling, Morgan trailed off.

"Tell me, have you settled on a goatherd or a poet?"

"Neither."

"It must be Nick then," Liz concluded. "Imagine that—all I had to do was invite him to dinner."

Morgan lifted a brow and found herself grinning. "I don't know what you're talking about." Life was everywhere, she remembered, if you only knew where to look.

"*Mmm-hmmm.* We'll talk about it tomorrow. Have fun. The number's there if you need me for anything. Oh, there's some marvelous wine in the cellar," she added, and for the first time, the smile in her voice seemed genuine. "If you feel like a cozy evening—help yourself."

"I appreciate it, Liz, but—"

"And don't worry about me or any of us. Everything's going to be fine. I just know it. Give Nick my love."

"I will," Morgan heard herself saying.

"I thought so. See you tomorrow."

Smiling, Morgan replaced the receiver.

"And so," Stephanos finished, lovingly stroking his moustache, "after several glasses of ouzo, Mikal became more expansive. The last two dates he gave me when our man joined the fishing expedition were the last week in February and the second week in March. That doesn't include the evening we encountered Morgan James, or when you took the trip in his stead."

Smiling, Nick flipped through the reports on his desk. "And from the end of February to the first week of April, he was in Rome. Even without my stroke of luck last night, that would have ruled him out. With the phone call I just got from Athens, I'd say we've eliminated him altogether from having any part in this. Now we know our man works alone. We move."

"And you move with an easy heart?" Stephanos noted. "What did Athens say?"

"The investigation on that end is complete. He's clean. His books, his records, his phone calls and correspondence. From this end, we know he hasn't been on the island to take part in any of the runs." Nick leaned back in his chair. "I have no doubt that since our man learned of the loss of his last shipment, he'll make the trip tonight. He won't want another to slip through his fingers." He tapped idly on the papers which littered his desk. "Now that I have the information I've been waiting for, we won't keep Athens waiting any longer. We'll have him tonight."

"You were out very late last night," Stephanos commented, taking out an ugly pipe and filling it.

"Keeping tabs on me, Stephanos?" Nick inquired with a lift of brow. "I haven't been twelve for a very long time."

"You are in very good humor this morning." He continued to fill his pipe, tapping the tobacco with patient care. "You haven't been so for many days."

"You should be glad my mood's broken. But then, you're used to my moods, aren't you, old man?"

Stephanos shrugged in agreement or acceptance. "The American lady is fond of walking on the beach. Perhaps you encountered her last night?"

"You're becoming entirely too wise in your old age, Stephanos." Nick struck a match and held it over the bowl of the pipe.

"Not too old to recognize the look of a man satisfied with a night of pleasure," Stephanos commented mildly and sucked to get flame. "A very beautiful lady. Very strong."

Lighting a cigarette, Nick smiled at him. "So you've mentioned before. I'd noticed myself. Tell me, Stephanos, are you also not too old to have ideas about strong, beautiful ladies?"

Stephanos cackled. "Only the dead have no ideas about strong, beautiful ladies, Nicholas. I'm a long way from dead."

Nick flashed him a grin. "Keep your distance, old man. She's mine."

"She is in love with you."

The cigarette halted on its journey to Nick's lips. His smiled faded. Stephanos stood grinning broadly as he was pierced with one of his friend's, lancing looks. "Why do you say that?"

"Because it is true, I've seen it." He puffed enjoyably on his pipe. "It is often difficult to see what is standing before your eyes. How much longer is she alone?"

Nick brought his thoughts back and scowled at the papers on his desk. "I'm not certain. Another day or so at least, depending on Iona's condition. In love with me," he murmured and looked back at Stephanos.

He knew she was attracted, that she cared—perhaps too much for her own good. But in love with him.... He'd never allowed himself to consider the possibility.

"She will be alone tonight," Stephanos continued blandly, appreciating Nick's stunned look. "It wouldn't do for her to wander from the villa." He puffed a few moments in silence. "If all does not go smoothly, you would want her safely behind locked doors."

"I've already spoken to her. She understands enough

to listen and take care." Nick shook his head. Today of all days he had to think clearly. "It's time we invited Captain Tripolos in. Call Mitilini."

Morgan enjoyed a late breakfast on the terrace and toyed with the idea of walking to the beach. He might come, she thought. I could phone and ask him to come. No, she decided, nibbling on her lip as she remembered all he had told her. If tonight is as important as he thinks, he needs to be left alone. I wish I knew more. I wish I knew what he was going to do. What if he gets hurt or… Morgan clamped down on the thought and wished it were tomorrow.

"Kyrios." At the maid's quiet summons, Morgan gasped and spun. "The captain from Mitilini is here to speak with you."

"What?" Panic rose and Morgan swallowed it. If Nick had spoken to him, Tripolos would hardly be waiting to see her, she thought frantically. Perhaps Nick wasn't ready yet. What could Tripolos possibly want with her?

"Tell him I'm out," she decided quickly. "Tell him I've gone to the beach or the village."

"Very good, *kyrios*." The maid accepted her order without question, then watched as Morgan streaked from the terrace.

For the second time, Morgan climbed the steep cliff path. This time, she knew where she was going. She could see Tripolos's official car parked at the villa's entrance as she rounded the first bend. She increased her pace, running until she was certain she herself was out of view.

Her approach had been noticed, however. The wide

doors of Nick's villa opened before she reached the top step. Nick came out to meet her.

"*Yiasou.* You must be in amazing shape to take the hill at that speed."

"Very funny," she panted as she ran into his arms.

"Is it that you couldn't keep away from me or is something wrong?" He held her close a moment, then drew her back just far enough to see her face. It was flushed with the run, but there was no fear in her eyes.

"Tripolos is at the villa." Morgan pressed her hand to her heart and tried to catch her breath. "I slipped out the back because I didn't know what I should say to him. Nicholas, I have to sit down. That's a very steep hill."

He was searching her face silently. Still struggling for her breath, Morgan tilted her head and returned the survey. She laughed and pushed the hair from her eyes. "Nicholas, why are you staring at me like that?"

"I'm trying to see what's standing in front of my eyes."

She laughed again. "Well, I am, you fool, but I'm going to collapse from exhaustion any minute."

With a sudden grin, Nick swept her off her feet and into his arms. She circled his neck as his mouth came down on hers.

"What are you doing?" she asked, when he let her breathe again.

"Taking what's mine."

His lips came back to hers and lingered. Slowly, almost lazily, he began to tease her tongue with his until he felt her breath start to shudder into his mouth. He promised himself that when everything was over, he would kiss her again, just like this—luxuriously with the heat of the sun warming her skin. When the night's work was finally over, he thought, and for a moment his lips were rough and urgent. Needs rushed through him almost painfully before he banked them.

"So…" He strolled into the house, still carrying her. "The captain came to see you. He's very tenacious."

Morgan took a deep breath to bring herself back from the power of the kiss. "You said you were going to speak with him today, but I didn't know if you were ready. If you'd gotten the information you needed. And to confess and humiliate myself, I'm a coward. I didn't want to face him again."

"Coward, Aphrodite? No, that's something you're not." He laid his cheek against hers a moment, making her wonder what was going on in his head. "I called Mitilini," he continued, "I left a message for Tripolos. After our talk, he should lose all interest in you."

"I'll be devastated." He grinned and took her lips again. "Would you put me down? I can't talk to you this way."

"I'm enjoying it." Ignoring her request, he continued into the salon. "Stephanos, I believe Morgan might like something cool. She had quite a run."

"No, nothing really. *Efxaristo.*" Faintly embarrassed, she met Stephanos's checkerboard grin. When he backed out of sight, she turned her head back to Nick. "If you know who the man is who's running the smuggling, can't you just tell Captain Tripolos and have him arrested?"

"It's not that simple. We want to catch him when the cache is in his possession. There's also the matter of cleaning up the place in the hills where he keeps his goods stored before he ships them on. That part," he added with an absent interest, "I'll leave to Tripolos."

"Nicholas, what will you do?"

"What has to be done."

"Nicholas—"

"Morgan," he interrupted. Standing her on feet, he placed his hands on her shoulders. "You don't want a step-by-step description. Let me finish this without bringing you in any more than I already have."

He lowered his mouth, taking hers with uncharacteristic gentleness. He brought her close, but softly, as if he held something precious. Morgan felt her bones turn to water.

"You have a knack for changing the subject," she murmured.

"After tonight, it's the only subject that's going to interest me. Morgan—"

"A thousand pardons." Stephanos hovered in the doorway. Nick looked up impatiently.

"Go away, old man."

"Nicholas!" Morgan drew out of his arms, sending him a look of reproof. "Has he always been rude, Stephanos?"

"Alas, my lady, since he took his thumb out of his mouth."

"Stephanos," Nick began in warning, but Morgan gave a peal of laughter and kissed him.

"Captain Tripolos requests a few moments of your time, Mr. Gregoras," Stephanos said, respectfully and grinned.

"Give me a moment, then send him in, and bring the files from the office."

"Nicholas." Morgan clung to his arm. "Let me stay with you. I won't get in the way."

"No." His refusal was short and harsh. He saw the hurt flicker in her eyes and sighed. "Morgan, I can't allow it even if I wanted to. This isn't going to touch you. I can't let it touch you. That's important to me."

"You're not going to send me away," she began heatedly.

He arched a brow and looked very cool. "I'm not under the same pressure I was last night, Morgan. And I will send you away."

"I won't go."

His eyes narrowed. "You'll do precisely what I say."

"Like hell."

Fury flickered, smoldered, then vanished in a laugh. "You're an exasperating woman, Aphrodite. If I had the time, I'd beat you." To prove his point, he drew her close and touched his lips to her. "Since I don't I'll ask you to wait upstairs."

"Since you *ask*."

"Mr. Gregoras. Ah, Miss James." Tripolos lumbered into the room. "How convenient. I was inquiring for Miss James at the Theoharis villa when your message reached me."

"Miss James is leaving," Nick told him. "I'm sure you'll agree her presence isn't necessary. Mr. Adonti from Athens has asked me to speak with you on a certain matter."

"Adonti?" Tripolos repeated. Nick watched surprise and interest move across the pudgy face before his eyes became direct. "So, you are acquainted with Mr. Adonti's organization?"

"Well acquainted," Nick returned mildly. "We've had dealings over the years."

"I see." He studied Nick with a thoughtful purse of his lips. "And Miss James?"

"Miss James chose an inopportune time to visit

friends," Nick said and took her arm. "That's all. If you'll excuse me, I'll just see her out. Perhaps you'd care for a drink while you're waiting." With a gesture toward the bar, Nick drew Morgan out into the hall.

"He looked impressed with the name you just dropped."

"Forget the name," Nick told her briefly. "You've never heard it."

"All right," she said without hesitation.

"What have I done to deserve this trust you give me?" he demanded suddenly. "I've hurt you again and again. I couldn't make up for it in a lifetime."

"Nicholas—"

"No." He cut her off with a shake of his head. In an uncharacteristic gesture of nerves or frustration, he dragged a hand through his hair. "There's no time. Stephanos will show you upstairs."

"As you wish," Stephanos agreed from behind them. Handing Nick a folder, he turned to the stairs. "This way, my lady."

Because Nick had already turned back to the salon, Morgan followed the old man without a word. She'd been given more time with him, she told herself. She couldn't ask for any more than that.

Stephanos took her into a small sitting room off the master bedroom. "You'll be comfortable here," he told her. "I'll bring you coffee."

"No. No, thank you, Stephanos." She stared at him, and for the second time he saw her heart in her eyes. "He'll be all right, won't he?"

He grinned at her so that his moustache quivered. "Can you doubt it?" he countered before he closed the door behind him.

Chapter 12

There was nothing more frustrating than waiting, Morgan decided after the first thirty minutes. Especially for someone who simply wasn't made for sitting still.

The little room was shaped like a cozy box and done in warm, earthy colors with lots of polished wood that gleamed in the early afternoon light. It was filled with small treasures. Morgan sat down and scowled at a Dresden shepherdess. At another time she might have admired the flowing grace of the lines, the fragility. Now she could only think that she was of no more practical use than that pale piece of porcelain. She had, in a matter of speaking, been put on the shelf.

It was ridiculous for Nick to constantly try to...shield her. Morgan's sigh was quick and impatient. Hadn't that been Liz's words when she had spoken of Alex's actions? After all, Morgan thought as she rose again, she was hardly some trembling, fainting scatterbrain who couldn't deal with whatever there was to face. She remembered trembling *and* fainting dead away in his arms. With a rueful smile, she paced to the window. Well, it wasn't as though she made a habit of it.

In any case, her thoughts ran on, he should know that she would, and could, face anything now that they were together. If he understood how she felt about him, then… but did he? she thought abruptly. She'd shown him, certainly she'd shown him in every possible way open to her, but she hadn't told him.

How can I? Morgan asked herself as she sunk into another chair. When a man had lived ten years of his life following his own rules, courting danger, looking for adventures, did he want to tie himself to a woman and accept the responsibilities of love?

He cared for her, Morgan reflected. Perhaps more than he was comfortable with. And he wanted her— more than any man had ever wanted her. But love…love wouldn't come easily to a man like Nicholas. No, she wouldn't pressure him with hers now. Even the unselfish offer of it would be pressure, she thought, when he had so much on his mind. She was only free to go on showing him, trusting him.

Even that seemed to throw him off-balance a bit, she mused, smiling a little. It was as if he couldn't quite accept that someone could see him as he was, know the way he had lived and still give him trust. Morgan wondered if he would have been more comfortable if she had pulled back from him a little after the things he had told her. He would have understood her condemnations more readily than her acceptance. Well, he'll just have to get used to it, she decided. He'll just have to get used to it because I'm not going to make it easy for him to back away.

Restless, she walked to the window. Here was a different view, Morgan thought, from one she so often looked out on from her bedroom window. Higher, more dangerous. More compelling, she thought with a quick thrill. The rocks seemed more jagged, the sea less tame. How it suited the man she'd given her heart to.

There was no terrace there, and suddenly wanting the air and sun, Morgan went through to his bedroom and opened his balcony doors. She could hear the sea hissing before she reached the rail. With a laugh, she leaned farther out.

Oh, she could live with the challenge of such a view every day, she thought, and never tire of it. She could watch the sea change colors with the sky, watch the gulls swoop over the water and back to the nests they'd built in the cliff walls. She could look down on the Theoharis villa and appreciate its refined elegance, but she would choose the rough gray stone and dizzying height.

Morgan tossed back her head and wished for a storm. Thunder, lightning, wild wind. Was there a better spot on earth to enjoy it? Laughing, she dared the sky to boil and spew out its worst.

"My God, how beautiful you are."

The light of challenge still in her eyes, Morgan turned. Leaning against the open balcony door, Nick stared at her. His face was very still, his gaze like a lance. The passion was on him, simmering, bubbling, just beneath the surface. It suited him, Morgan thought, suited those long, sharp bones in his face, those black eyes and the mouth that could be beautiful or cruel.

As she leaned back on the railing, the breeze caught

at the ends of her hair. Her eyes took on the color of the sky. Power swept over her, and a touch of madness. "You want me, I can see it. Come and show me."

It hurt, Nick discovered. He'd never known, until Morgan, that desire could hurt. Perhaps it was only when you loved that your needs ached in you. How many times had he loved her last night? he wondered. And each time, it had been like a tempest in him. Now, he promised himself, this time, he would show her a different way.

Slowly, he went to her. Taking both of her hands, he lifted them, then pressed his lips to the palms. When he brought his gaze to hers, Nick saw that her eyes were wide and moved, her lips parted in surprise. Something stirred in him—love, guilt, a need to give.

"Have I shown you so little tenderness, Morgan?" he murmured.

"Nicholas…" She could only whisper his name as her pulses raged and her heart melted.

"Have I given you no soft words, no sweetness?" He kissed her hands again, one finger at a time. She didn't move, only stared at him. "And you still come to me. I'm in your debt," he said quietly in Greek. "What price would you ask me?"

"No, Nicholas, I…" Morgan shook her head, unable to speak, nearly swaying with the weakness this gentle, quiet man brought her.

"You asked me to show you how I wanted you." He put his hands to her face as if she were indeed made of Dresden porcelain, then touched his lips almost reverently to hers. A sound came from her, shaky and small. "Come and I will."

He lifted her, not with a flourish as he had on the porch, but as a man lifts something he cherishes.

"Now…" He laid her down with care. "In the daylight, in my bed."

Again, he took her hand, tracing kisses over the back and palm, then to the wrist where her pulse hammered. All the while he watched her as she lay back, staring at him with something like astonished wonder.

How young she looks, Nick thought as he gently drew her finger into his mouth. And how fragile. Not a witch now, or a goddess, but only a woman. His woman. And her eyes were already clouding, her breath already trembling. He'd shown her the fire and the storm, he thought, but not once—not once had he given her spring.

Bending, he nibbled lightly at her lips, allowing his hands to touch no more than her hair.

It might have been a dream, so weak and weightless did she feel. Nick kissed her eyes closed so that Morgan saw no more than a pale red glow. Then his lips continued, over her forehead, her temples, down the line of her cheekbones—always soft, always warm. The words he whispered against her skin flowed like scented oil over her. She would have moved to bring him closer if her arms had not been too heavy to lift. Instead, she lay in the flood of his tenderness.

His mouth was at her ear, gently torturing with a trace of tongue, a murmured promise. Even as she moaned in surrender, he moved lower to taste and tease the curve of her neck. With kisses like whispers, and whispers like wine, he took her deeper. Gentleness was a drug for both of them.

Hardly touching her, he loosened the buttons of her blouse and slipped it from her. Though he felt the firm pressure of her breasts against him, he took his mouth to the slope of her shoulder instead. He could feel the strength there, the grace, and he tarried.

Morgan's eyes were closed, weighed down with gold-tipped lashes. Her breath rushed out between her lips. He knew he could watch those flickers of pleasure move over her face forever. With his hands once more buried in her hair, Nick kissed her. He felt the yielding and the hunger before he moved on.

Slowly, savoring, he took his lips down to the soft swell—circling, nibbling until he came to the tender underside of her breast. On a moan, Morgan fretted under him as if she were struggling to wake from a dream. But he kept the pace slow and soothed her with words and soft, soft kisses.

With aching gentleness he stroked his tongue over the peak, fighting a surge of desperation when he found it hot and ready. Her movements beneath him took on a rhythmic sinuousness that had the blood pounding in his brain. Her scent was there, always there on the verge of his senses even when she wasn't with him. Now he wallowed in it. As he suckled, he allowed his hands to touch her for the first time.

Morgan felt the long stroke of his hands, the quick scrape of those strong rough fingers that now seemed sensitive enough to tune violins. They caressed lightly, like a breeze. They made her ache.

Soft, slow, gentle, his mouth traveled down the center of her body, lingering here, exploring there until he paused where her slacks hugged across her stomach. When she felt him unfasten them, she trembled. She arched to help him, but Nick drew them down inch by inch, covering the newly exposed flesh with moist kisses so that she could only lie steeped in a pool of pleasure.

And when she was naked, he continued to worship her with his lips, with his suddenly gentle hands. She thought she could hear her own skin hum. The muscles in her thighs quivered as he passed over them, and her desire leaped from passive to urgent.

"Nicholas," she breathed. "Now."

"You've scratched your feet on the rocks," he murmured, pressing his lips against the ball of her foot. "It's a sin to mar such skin, my love." Watching her face, he ran his tongue over the arch. Her eyes flew open, dazed with passion. "I've longed to see you like this." His voice grew thick as his control began to slip. "With sunlight streaming over you, your hair flowing over my pillow, your body trembling for me."

As he spoke, he began the slow, aching journey back, gradually back to her lips. Needs pressed at him and demanded he hurry, but he wouldn't be rushed. He told himself he could linger over the taste and the feel of her for days.

Her arms weren't heavy now, but strong as they curled around him. Every nerve, every pore of her body seemed tuned to him. The harmony seemed impossible, yet it sung through her. His flesh was as hot and damp as hers, his breath as unsteady.

"You ask how I want you," he murmured, thrilling to her moan as he slipped into her. "Look at me and see."

His control hung by a thread. Morgan pulled his mouth to hers and snapped it.

Nick held Morgan close, gently stroking her back while her trembles eased. She clung to him, almost as much in wonder as in love. How was she to have known he had such tenderness in him? How was she to have known she would be so moved by it? Blinking back tears, she pressed her lips to his throat.

"You've made me feel beautiful," she murmured.

"You are beautiful." Tilting her head back, Nick smiled at her. "And tired," he added, tracing a thumb over the mauve smudges under her eyes. "You should sleep, Morgan, I won't have you ill."

"I won't be ill." She snuggled against him, fitting herself neatly against the curve of his body. "And there'll be time for sleeping later. We'll go away for a few days, like you said."

Twining a lock of her hair around his finger, Nick gazed up at the ceiling. A few days with her would never be enough, but he still had the night to get through. "Where would you like to go?"

Morgan thought of her dreams of Venice and Cornish moors. With a sigh, she closed her eyes and drew in Nick's scent. "Anywhere. Right here." Laughing, she propped herself on his chest. "Wherever it is, I intend to keep you in bed a good deal of the time."

"Is that so?" His mouth twitched as he tugged on her hair. "I might begin to think you have designs only on my body."

"It is a rather nice one." In a long stroke, she ran her hands down his shoulders, enjoying the feel of firm flesh and strong bone. "Lean and muscled..." She trailed off when she spotted a small scar high on his chest. A frown creased her brow as she stared at it. It seemed out of place on that smooth brown skin. "Where did you get this?"

Nick tilted his head, shifting his gaze down. "Ah, an old battle scar," he said lightly.

From a bullet, Morgan realized all at once. Horror

ripped through her and mirrored in her eyes. Seeing it, Nick cursed his loose tongue.

"Morgan—"

"No, please." She buried her face against his chest and held tight. "Don't say anything. Just give me a minute."

She'd forgotten. Somehow the gentleness and beauty of their lovemaking had driven all the ugliness out of her mind. It had been easy to pretend for a little while that there was no threat. Pretending's for children, she reminded herself. He didn't need to cope with a child now. If she could give him nothing else, she would give him what was left of her strength. Swallowing fear, she pressed her lips to his chest then rolled beside him again.

"Did everything go as you wanted with Captain Tripolos?"

A strong woman, Nick thought, linking his hand with hers. An extraordinary woman. "He's satisfied with the information I've given him. A shrewd man for all his plodding technique."

"Yes, I thought he was like a bulldog the first time I encountered him."

Chuckling, Nick drew her closer. "An apt description, Aphrodite." He shifted then, reaching to the table beside him for a cigarette. "I think he's one of the few policemen I find it agreeable to work with."

"Why do you—" She broke off as she looked up and focused on the slim black cigarette. "I'd forgotten," Morgan murmured. "How could I have forgotten?"

Nick blew out a stream of smoke. "Forgotten what?"

"The cigarette." Morgan sat up, pushing at her tumbled hair. "The stub of the cigarette near the body."

He lifted a brow, but found himself distracted by the firm white breasts easily within reach. "So?"

"It was fresh, from one of those expensive brands like you're smoking." She let out an impatient breath. "I should have told you before, but it hardly makes any difference at this point. You already know who killed Stevos—who runs the smuggling."

"I never told you I did."

"You didn't have to." Annoyed with herself, Morgan frowned and missed Nick's considering look.

"Why didn't I?"

"You'd have told me if you hadn't seen his face. When you wouldn't answer me at all, I knew you had."

He shook his head as a reluctant smile touched his lips. "*Diabolos,* it's a good thing I didn't cross you earlier in my career. I'm afraid it would have been over quickly. As it happens," he added, "I saw the cigarette myself."

"I should have known you would," she muttered.

"I can assure you Tripolos didn't miss it either."

"That damn cigarette has driven me to distraction." Morgan gave an exasperated sigh. "There were moments I suspected everyone I knew—Dorian, Alex, Iona, even Liz and Andrew. I nearly made myself sick over it."

"You don't name me." Nick studied the cigarette in his hand.

"No, I already told you why."

"Yes," he murmured, "with an odd sort of compliment I haven't forgotten. I should have eased your mind sooner, Morgan, about what I do. You might have slept better."

Leaning over, she kissed him. "Stop worrying about my sleep. I'm going to start thinking I look like a tired hag."

He slid a hand behind her neck to keep her close. "Will you rest if I tell you that you do?"

"No, but I'll hit you."

"Ah, then I'll lie and tell you you're exquisite."

She hit him anyway, a quick jab in the ribs.

"So, now you want to play rough." Crushing out his cigarette, Nick rolled her beneath him. She struggled for a moment, then eyed him narrowly.

"Do you know how many times you've pinned me down like this?" Morgan demanded.

"No, how many?"

"I'm not sure." Her smile spread slowly. "I think I'm beginning to like it."

"Perhaps I can make you like it better." He muffled her laugh with his lips.

He didn't love her gently now, but fiercely. As desperate as he, Morgan let the passion rule her. Fear that it might be the last time caused her response and demands to be urgent. She lit a fire in him.

Now, where his hands had trailed slowly, they raced. Where his mouth had whispered, it savaged. Morgan threw herself into the flames without a second thought. Her mouth was greedy, searching for his taste everywhere while her hands rushed to touch and arouse.

Her body had never felt so agile. It could melt into his one moment, then slither away to drive him to madness. She could hear his desire in the short, harsh breath, feel it in the tensing and quivering of his muscles as she roamed over them, taste it in the dampness that sheened his skin. It matched her own, and again they were in harmony.

She arched against him as his mouth rushed low—but it was more a demand than an invitation. Delirious with her own strength and power, Morgan dug her fingers into his hair and urged him to take her to that first giddy peak. Even as she cried out with it, she hungered for more. And he gave more, while he took.

But she wasn't satisfied with her own pleasure. Ruthlessly she sought to undermine whatever claim he still held to sanity. Her hands had never been so clever, or so quick. Her teeth nipped at his skin before she soothed the tiny pains with a flick of her tongue. She heard him groan and a low, sultry laugh flowed from her. His breath caught when she reached him, then came out in an oath. Morgan felt the sunlight explode into fragments as he plunged into her.

Later, much later, when he knew his time with her was nearly up, Nick kissed her with lingering tenderness.

"You're going," Morgan said, struggling not to cling to him.

"Soon. I'll have to take you back to the villa in a little while." Sitting up, he drew her with him. "You'll stay inside. Lock the doors, tell the servants to let no one in. No one."

Morgan tried to promise, and found she couldn't form the words. "When you're finished, you'll come?"

Smiling, he tucked her hair behind her ear. "I suppose I can handle your window vines again."

"I'll wait up for you and let you in the front door."

"Aphrodite." Nick pressed a kiss to her wrist. "Where's your romance?"

"Oh, God!" Morgan threw her arms around his neck and clung. "I wasn't going to say it—I promised myself I wouldn't. Be careful." Biting back tears, she pressed her face against his throat. "Please, please be careful. I'm terrified for you."

"No, don't." Feeling the dampness against his skin, he held her tighter. "Don't cry for me."

"I'm sorry." With a desperate effort, she forced back the tears. "I'm not helping you."

Nick drew her away and looked at the damp cheeks and shimmering eyes. "Don't ask me not to go, Morgan."

"No." She swallowed again. "I won't. Don't ask me not to worry."

"It's the last time," he said fiercely.

The words made her shudder, but she kept her eyes on his. "Yes, I know."

"Just wait for me." He pulled her back against him. "Wait for me."

"With a bottle of Alex's best champagne," she promised in a stronger voice.

He pressed a kiss to her temple. "We'll have some of mine now, before I take you back. A toast," he told her as he drew her away again. "To tomorrow."

"Yes." She smiled. It almost reached her eyes. "I'll drink with you to tomorrow."

"Rest a moment." With another kiss, he laid her back against the pillow. "I'll go bring some up."

Morgan waited until the door had closed behind him before she buried her face in the pillow.

Chapter 13

It was dark when she woke. Confused, disoriented, Morgan struggled to see where she was. The room was all shifting shadows and silence. There was a cover over her—something soft and light with a fringe of silk. Beneath it, she was warm and naked.

Nicholas, she thought in quick panic. She'd fallen asleep and he'd gone. On a moan, she sat up, drawing her knees to her chest. How could she have wasted those last precious moments together? How long? She thought abruptly. How long had he been gone? With trembling fingers, she reached for the lamp beside the bed.

The light eased some of her fears, but before she could climb out of bed to find a clock, she saw the note propped against the lamp. Taking it, Morgan studied the bold, strong writing. *Go back to sleep* was all it said.

How like him, she thought, and nearly laughed. Morgan kept the note in her hand, as if to keep Nick close, as she rose to look for her clothes. It didn't take her long to discover they were gone.

"The louse!" Morgan said aloud, forgetting the tender thoughts she had only moments before. So, he wasn't taking any chances making certain she stayed put. Naked, hands on her hips, she scowled around the room. Where the devil does he think I'd go? she asked herself. I have no way of knowing where he is…or what he's doing, she thought on a fresh flood of worry.

Wait. Suddenly cold, Morgan pulled the cover from the bed and wrapped herself in it. All I can do is wait.

The time dripped by, minute by endless minute. She paced, then forced herself to sit, then paced again. It would be morning in only a few more hours, she told herself. In the morning, the wait would be over. For all of them.

She couldn't bear it, she thought in despair one moment. She had to bear it, she told herself the next. Would he never get back? Would morning never come? On a sound of fury, she tossed the cover aside. She might have to wait, Morgan thought grimly as she marched to Nick's closet. But she'd be damned if she'd wait naked.

Nick shifted the muscles in his shoulders and blocked out the need for a cigarette. Even the small light would be dangerous now. The cove was bathed in milky moonlight and silence. There would be a murmur now and then from behind a rock. Not from a spirit, but from a man in uniform. The cove still held secrets. Lifting his binoculars, Nick again scanned the sea.

"Any sign?" Tripolos seemed remarkably comfortable in his squat position behind a rock. He popped a tiny mint into his mouth and crunched quietly. Nick merely shook his head and handed the glasses to Stephanos.

"Thirty minutes," Stephanos stated, chewing on the stem of his dead pipe. "The wind carries the sound of the motor."

"I hear nothing." Tripolos gave the old man a doubtful frown.

Nick chuckled as the familiar feeling of excitement rose. "Stephanos hears what others don't. Just tell your men to be ready."

"My men are ready." His gaze flicked over Nick's profile. "You enjoy your work, Mr. Gregoras."

"At times," Nick muttered, then grinned. "This time, by God."

"And soon it's over," Stephanos said from beside him.

Nick turned his head to meet the old man's eyes. He knew the statement covered more than this one job, but the whole of what had been Nick's career. He hadn't told him, but Stephanos knew. "Yes," he said simply, then turned his eyes to the sea again.

He thought of Morgan and hoped she was still asleep. She'd looked so beautiful—and so exhausted when he'd come back into the room. Her cheeks had been damp. Damn, he couldn't bear the thought of her tears. But he'd felt a wave of relief that she'd been asleep. He didn't have to see her eyes when he left her.

She's safer there than if I'd taken her back, Nick told himself. With luck, she'd still be asleep when he got back and then he'd have spared her hours of worry. Stashing her clothes had been an impulse that had eased his mind. Even Morgan wouldn't go wandering around without a stitch on her back.

His grin flashed again. If she woke and looked for

them, she'd curse him. The idea gave him a moment's pleasure. He could see her, standing in the center of his room with only the moonlight covering her as she raged.

He felt the low aching need in the pit of his stomach, and promised himself he'd keep her just that way—naked fire—until the sun went down again.

Lifting the binoculars, he scanned the dark sea. "They're coming."

The moon threw the boat into silhouette. A dozen men watched her approach from clumps of rock and shadows. She came in silence, under the power of oars.

She was secured with little conversation and a few deft movements of rope. There was a scent Nick recognized. The scent of fear. A fresh bubble of excitement rose, though his face was deadly calm. He's there, Nick thought. And we have him.

The crew left the boat to gather in the shadows of the beach. A hooded figure moved to join them. At Nick's signal, the cove was flooded with light. The rocks became men.

"In the King's name," Tripolos stated grandly, "this vessel will be searched for illegal contraband. Put up your weapons and surrender."

Shouts and the scrambling of men shattered the glass-like quiet of the cove. Men seeking to escape, and men seeking to capture tangled in the sudden chaos of sound and light. Gunfire shocked the balmy air. There were cries of pain and fury.

The smugglers would fight with fist and blade. The battle would be short, but grim. The sounds of violence bounced hollowly off the rocks and drifted out on the air.

Nick saw the hooded figure melt away from the confusion and streak from the cove. Swearing, he raced after it, thrusting his gun back in his belt. A burly form collided with him as another man sought escape. Each swore at the obstacle, knowing the only choice was to remove it.

Together, they rolled over the rocks, away from the noise and the light. Thrown into darkness, they tumbled helplessly until the ground leveled. A blade glistened, and Nick grasped the thick wrist with both hands to halt its plunge to his throat.

The crack of shots had Morgan springing up from her chair. Had she heard, or just imagined? she wondered as her heart began to thud. Could they be so close? As she stared into the darkness, she heard another shot, and the echo. Fear froze her.

He's all right, she told herself. He'll be here soon, and it'll be over. I know he's all right.

Before the sentence had finished racing through her mind, she was running down the steps and out of the villa.

Telling herself she was only being logical, Morgan headed for the beach. She was just going to meet him. He'd be coming along any minute, and she would see for herself that he wasn't hurt. Nick's jeans hung loosely at her hips as she streaked down the cliff path. Her breath was gasping now, the only sound as her feet padded on the hard dirt. Morgan thought it would almost be a relief to hear the guns again. If she heard them, she might be able to judge the direction. She could find him.

Then, from the top of the beach steps, she saw him walking across the sand. With a sob of shuddering relief, she flew down them to meet him.

He continued, too intent on his own thoughts to note her approach. Morgan started to shout his name, but the word strangled in her throat. She stopped running. Not Nicholas, she realized as she stared at the hooded figure. The moves were wrong, the walk. And he'd have no reason to wear the mask. Even as her thoughts began to race, he reached up and tore off the hood. Moonlight fell on golden hair.

Oh God, had she been a fool not to see it? Those calm, calm eyes—too calm, she thought frantically. Had she ever seen any real emotion in him? Morgan took a step in retreat, looking around desperately for some cover. But he turned. His face hardened as he saw her.

"Morgan, what are you doing out here?"

"I—I wanted to walk." She struggled to sound casual. There was no place for her to run. "It's a lovely night. Almost morning, really." As he advanced on her she moistened her lips and kept talking. "I didn't expect to see you. You surprised me. I thought—"

"You thought I was in Athens," Dorian finished with a smile. "But as you see, I'm not. And, I'm afraid, Morgan, you've seen too much." He held up the hood, dangling it a moment before he dropped it to the sand.

"Yes." There was no use dissembling. "I have."

"It's a pity." His smile vanished as though it had never been. "Still, you could be useful. An American hostage," he said thoughtfully as he scanned her face. "Yes, and a woman." Grabbing her arm, Dorian began to pull her across the sand.

She jerked and struggled against his hold. "I won't go with you."

"You have no choice"—he touched the handle of his knife—"unless you prefer to end up as Stevos did."

Morgan swallowed as she stumbled across the beach. He said it so casually. *Some people have no capacity for emotion—love, hate.* He hadn't been speaking of Iona, Morgan realized, but himself. He was as dangerous as any animal on the run.

"You tried to kill Iona too."

"She'd become a nuisance. Greedy not only for money, but to hold me. She thought to blackmail me into marriage." He gave a quick laugh. "I had only to tempt her with the heroin. I had thought the dose I gave her was enough."

Purposely, Morgan fell to her knees as though she'd tripped. "You would have finished her that morning if I hadn't found her first."

"You have a habit of being in the wrong place." Roughly, Dorian hauled her to her feet. "I had to play the worried lover for a time—dashing back and forth between Lesbos and Athens. A nuisance. Still, if I'd been allowed one moment alone with her in the hospital…" Then he shrugged, as if the life or the death of a woman meant nothing. "So, she'll live and she'll talk. It was time to move in any case."

"You lost your last shipment," Morgan blurted out, desperate to distract him from his hurried pace toward the beach steps. If he got her up there—up there in the rocks…and the dark….

Dorian froze and turned to her. "How do you know this?"

"I helped steal it," she said impulsively. "Your place in the hills, the cave—"

The words choked off as his hand gripped her throat. "So you've taken what's mine. Where is it?"

Morgan shook her head.

"Where?" Dorian demanded as his fingers tightened. A god, she thought staring into his face as the moonlight streamed over it. He had the face of a god. Why hadn't she remembered her own thought that gods were bloodthirsty? Morgan put a hand to his wrist as if in surrender. His fingers eased slightly.

"Go to hell."

Swiftly, he swept the back of his hand across her face, knocking her to the sand. His eyes were a calm empty blue as he looked down at her. "You'll tell me before I'm through with you. You'll beg to tell me. There'll be time," he continued as he walked toward her, "when we're off the island."

"I'll tell you nothing." With the blood singing in her ears, Morgan inched away from him. "The police know who you are, there isn't a hole big enough for you to hide in."

Reaching down, he grabbed her by the hair and hauled her painfully to her feet. "If you prefer to die—"

Then she was free, going down to her knees again as Dorian stumbled back and fell onto the sand.

"Nick." Dorian rubbed the blood from his mouth as his gaze traveled up. "This is a surprise." It dropped again to the revolver Nick held in his hand. "Quite a surprise."

"Nicholas!" Scrambling up, Morgan ran to him. He never looked at her. His arm was rigid as iron when she gripped it. "I thought—I was afraid you were dead."

"Get up," he told Dorian with a quick gesture of the gun. "Or I'll put a bullet in your head while you lie there."

"Were you hurt?" Morgan shook his arm, wanting some sign. She'd seen that cold hard look before. "When I heard the shots—"

"Only detained." Nick pushed her aside, his gaze fixed on Dorian. "Get rid of the gun. Toss it over there." He jerked his head and leveled his own revolver. "Two fingers. If you breathe wrong, you won't breathe again."

Dorian lifted out his gun in a slow, steady motion and tossed it aside. "I have to admit you amaze me, Nick. It's been you who's been hounding me for months."

"My pleasure."

"And I would have sworn you were a man concerned only with collecting his trinkets and making money. I've always admired your ruthlessness in business—but it seems I wasn't aware of *all* of your business." One graceful brow rose. "A policeman?"

Nick gave a thin smile. "I answer to one man only," he said quietly. "Adonti." The momentary flash of fear in Dorian's eyes gave him great pleasure. "You and I might have come to this sooner. We nearly did last night."

A shadow touched Dorian's face briefly, then was gone. "Last night?"

"Did you think it was only a goat who watched you?" Nick asked with a brittle laugh.

"No." Dorian gave a brief nod. "I smelled something more—foolish of me not to have pursued it."

"You've gotten careless, Dorian. I took your place on your last run and made your men tremble."

"You," Dorian breathed.

"A rich cache," Nick added, "according to my associates in Athens. It might have been over for you then, but I waited until I was certain Alex wasn't involved. It was worth the wait."

"Alex?" Dorian laughed with the first sign of true pleasure. "Alex wouldn't have the stomach for it. He thinks only of his wife and his ships and his honor." He gave Nick a thoughtful glance. "But it seems I misjudged you. I thought you a rich, rather singleminded fool, a bit of a nuisance with Iona this trip, but hardly worth a passing thought. My congratulations on your talent for deceit, and"—he let his gaze travel and rest on Morgan—"your taste."

"Efxaristo."

Morgan watched in confusion, then in terror, as Nick tossed his gun down to join Dorian's. They lay side by side, black and ugly, on the white sand.

"It's my duty to turn you over to Captain Tripolos and the Greek authorities." Calmly, slowly, Nick drew out a knife. "But it will be my pleasure to cut out your heart for putting your hands on my woman."

"No! Nicholas, don't!"

Nick stopped Morgan's panicked rush toward him with a terse command. "Go back to the villa and stay there."

"Please," Dorian interrupted with a smile as he got to his feet. "Morgan must stay. Such an interesting development." He pulled out his own knife with a flourish. "She'll be quite a prize for the one who lives."

"Go," Nick ordered again. His hand tensed on the knife. He was half Greek, and Greek enough to have tasted blood when he had seen Dorian strike her. Morgan saw the look in his eyes.

"Nicholas, you can't. He didn't hurt me."

"He left his mark on your face," he said softly, and turned the knife in his hand. "Stay out of the way."

Touching her hand to her cheek, she stumbled back.

They crouched and circled. As she watched, the knives caught the moonlight and held it. Glittering silver, dazzling and beautiful.

At Dorian's first thrust, Morgan covered her mouth to hold back a scream. There was none of the graceful choreography of a staged fight. This was real and deadly. There were no adventurous grins or bold laughs with the thrusts and parries. Both men had death in his eyes. Morgan could smell the sweat and the sweet scent of blood from both of them.

Starlight dappled over their faces, giving them both a ghostly pallor. All she could hear was the sound of their breathing, the sound of the sea, the sound of steel whistling through the air. Nick was leading him closer to the surf—away from Morgan. Emotion was frozen in him. Anger, such anger, but he knew too much to let it escape. Dorian fought coldly. An empty heart was its own skill.

"I'll pleasure myself with your woman before the night's over," Dorian told him as blade met blade. His lips curved as he saw the quick, naked fury in Nick's eyes.

Morgan watched with horror as a bright stain spread down Nick's sleeve where Dorian had slipped through his guard. She would have screamed, but there was no breath in her. She would have prayed, but even her thoughts were frozen.

The speed with which they came together left her stunned. One moment they were separate, and the next they were locked together as one tangled form. They rolled to the sand, a confusion of limbs and knives. She could hear the labored breathing and grunted curses. Then Dorian was on top of him. Morgan watched, numb with terror, as he plunged his knife. It struck the sand, a whisper away from Nick's face. Without thought, Morgan fell on the guns.

Once, the revolver slipped through her wet hands, back onto the sand. Gritting her teeth, she gripped it again. As she knelt, she aimed toward the entwined bodies. Coldly, willing herself to do what she had always despised, she prepared to kill.

A cry split the air, animal and primitive. Not knowing

which one of them it had been torn from, Morgan clutched the gun with both hands and kept it aimed on the now motionless heap in the sand. She could still hear breathing—but only from one. If Dorian stood up, she swore to herself, and to Nick, that she would pull the trigger.

A shadow moved. She heard the labored breathing and pressed her lips together. Against the trigger, her finger shook lightly.

"Put that damn thing down, Morgan, before you kill me."

"Nicholas." The gun slipped from her nerveless hand.

He moved to her, limping a little. Reaching down, he drew her to her feet. "What were you doing with the gun, Aphrodite?" he said softly, when he felt her tremble under his hands. "You couldn't have pulled the trigger."

"Yes." Her eyes met his. "I could."

He stared at her for a moment and saw she was speaking nothing less than the truth. With an oath, he pulled her against him. "Damn it, Morgan, why didn't you stay in the villa? I didn't want this for you."

"I couldn't stay in the house, not after I heard the shooting."

"Yes, you hear shooting, so naturally you run outside."

"What else could I do?"

Nick opened his mouth to swear, then shut it again. "You've stolen my clothes," he said mildly. He wouldn't be angry with her now, he promised himself as he stroked her hair. Not while she was shaking like a leaf. But later, by God, later...

"You took mine first." He couldn't tell if the sound she made was a laugh or a sob. "I thought..." Suddenly, she felt the warm stickiness against her palm. Looking down, she saw his blood on her hand. "Oh, God, Nicholas, you're hurt!"

"No, it's nothing, I—"

"Oh, damn you for being macho and stupid. You're *bleeding!*"

He laughed and crushed her to him again. "I'm not being macho and stupid, Aphrodite, but if it makes you happy, you can nurse all of my scratches later. Now, I need a different sort of medicine." He kissed her before she could argue.

Her fingers gripped at his shirt as she poured everything she had into that one meeting of lips. Fear drained from her, and with it, whatever force had driven her. She went limp against him as his energy poured over her.

"I'm going to need a lot of care for a very long time," he murmured against her mouth. "I might be hurt a great deal more seriously than I thought. No, don't." Nick drew her away as he felt her tears on his cheeks. "Morgan, don't cry. It's the one thing I don't think I can face tonight."

"No, I won't cry," she insisted as the tears continued to fall. "I won't cry. Just don't stop kissing me. Don't stop." She pressed her mouth to his. As she felt him, warm and real against her, the tears and trembling stopped.

"Well, Mr. Gregoras, it seems you intercepted Mr. Zoulas after all."

Nick swore quickly, but without heat. Keeping Morgan close, he looked over her head at Tripolos. "Your men have the crew?"

"Yes." Lumbering over, he examined the body briefly. He noted, without comment, that there was a broken arm as well as the knife wound. With a gesture, he signaled one of his men to take over. "Your man is seeing to their transportation," he went on.

Nick kept Morgan's back to the body and met Tripolos's speculative look calmly. "It seems you had a bit of trouble here," the captain commented. His gaze drifted to the guns lying on the sand. He drew his own conclusions. "A pity he won't stand trial."

"A pity," Nick agreed.

"You dropped your gun in the struggle to apprehend him, I see."

"It would seem so."

Tripolos stooped with a wheeze and handed it back to him. "Your job is finished?"

"Yes, my job is finished."

Tripolos made a small bow. "My gratitude, Mr. Gregoras." He smiled at the back of Morgan's head. "And my congratulations."

Nick lifted a brow in acknowledgment. "I'll take Miss James home now. You can reach me tomorrow if necessary. Good night, Captain."

"Good night," Tripolos murmured and watched them move away.

Morgan leaned her head against his shoulder as they walked toward the beach steps. Only a few moments before she had fought to keep from reaching them. Now they seemed like the path to the rest of her life.

"Oh, look, the stars are going out." She sighed. There was nothing left, no fear, no anxiety. No more doubts. "I feel as if I've waited for this sunrise all my life."

"I'm told you want to go to Venice and ride on a gondola."

Morgan glanced up in surprise, then laughed. "Andrew told you."

"He mentioned Cornwall and the Champs d'élysées as well."

"I have to learn how to bait a hook, too," she murmured. Content, she watched as day struggled with night.

"I'm not an easy man, Morgan."

"*Hmm?* No," she agreed fervently. "No, you're not."

He paused at the foot of the steps and turned her to face him. The words weren't easy for him now. He wondered why he had thought they would be. "You know the worst of me already. I'm not often gentle, and I'm demanding. I'm prone to black, unreasonable moods."

Morgan smothered a yawn and smiled at him. "I'd be the last one to disagree."

He felt foolish. And, he discovered, afraid. Would a woman accept words of love when she had seen a man kill? Did he have any right to offer them? Looking down, he saw her, slim and straight in his clothes—jeans that hung over her hips—a shirt that billowed and hid small, firm breasts and a waist he could nearly span with his hands. Right or wrong, he couldn't go on without her.

"Morgan…"

"Nicholas?" Her smile became puzzled as she fought off a wave of weariness. "What is it?"

His gaze swept back to hers, dark, intense, perhaps a little desperate.

"Your arm," she began and reached for him.

"No! *Diabolos.*" Gripping her by the shoulders, he shook her. "It's not my arm, listen to me."

"I am listening," she tossed back with a trace of heat. "What's wrong with you?"

"This." He covered her mouth with his. He needed the taste of her, the strength. When he drew her away, his hands had gentled, but his eyes gleamed.

With a sleepy laugh, she shook her head. "Nicholas, if you'll let me get you home and see to your arm—"

"My arm's a small matter, Aphrodite."

"Not to me."

"Morgan." Nick stopped her before she could turn toward the steps again. "I'll make a difficult and exasperating husband, but you won't be bored." Taking her hands, he kissed them as he had on his balcony. "I love you enough to let you climb your mountains, Morgan. Enough to climb them with you if that's what you want."

She wasn't tired now, but stunned into full alertness. Morgan opened her mouth, but found herself stupidly unable to form a word.

"Damn it, Morgan, don't just stare at me." Frustration and temper edged his voice. "Say yes, for God's sake!" Fury flared in his eyes. "I won't let you say no!"

His hands were no longer in hers, but gripping her arms again. She knew, any moment, he would start shaking her. But there was more in his eyes than anger. She saw the doubts, the fears, the fatigue. Love swept into her, overwhelmingly.

"Won't you?" she murmured.

"No." His fingers tightened. "No, I won't. You've taken my heart. You won't leave with it."

Lifting a hand, she touched his cheek, letting her finger trace over the tense jaw. "Do you think I could climb mountains without you, Nicholas?" She drew him against her and felt his shudder of relief. "Let's go home."

* * * * *